TALES
FROM
PLEXIS

The Clan Chronicles:

TALES FROM PLEXIS

Edited by Julie E. Czerneda

DAW BOOKS, INC.

DONALD A. WOLLHEIM, FOUNDER

375 Hudson Street, New York, NY 10014

ELIZABETH R. WOLLHEIM
SHEILA E. GILBERT
PUBLISHERS
www.dawbooks.com

First Printing, December 2018
1 2 3 4 5 6 7 8 9

DAW TRADEMARK REGISTERED
U.S. PAT. AND TM. OFF. AND FOREIGN COUNTRIES
—MARCA REGISTRADA
HECHO EN U.S.A.

PRINTED IN THE U.S.A.

To Ruth "Ruti" Stuart

Bard of the Grey Stone Tower,
Heart-kin to us all.
We will remember.

Acknowledgments

A Hold Full of Truffles © 2018 Julie E. Czerneda

The Stars Do Not Dream © 2018 Amanda Sun

Finding Parker © 2018 Doranna Durgin

A Traded Secret © 2018 Donald R. Montgomery

Anisoptera With a Side Order of Soft Blast © 2018 Fiona
   Patton

Jilly © 2018 Paul Baughman

Chicken © 2018 Elizabeth A. Farley-Dawson

An Elaborate Scheme © 2018 Marie Bilodeau

The Sacrifice of Pawns © 2018 Mark Ladouceur

Little Enigmatic Monster © 2018 Wayne Carey

A Thief by Any Other Name © 2018 Violette Malan

Memory © 2018 Sally McLennan

Home is a Planet Away © 2018 Ika Koeck

Will of the Neblokan Fates © 2018 Natalie Reinelt

The Rainbow Collection © 2018 Nathan Azinger

A Song of Plexis © 2018 Janet Elizabeth Chase

Cinnamon Sticks © 2018 B. Morris Allen

The Locksmith's Dilemma © 2018 Rhondi Salsitz

Contents

Welcome to Plexis!

* * *

PLEXIS, THE GIANT asteroid refinery turned shopping mall, was one of my happiest creations as a writer. I did it because an editor—not my beloved Sheila Gilbert of DAW Books—read my first book, *A Thousand Words for Stranger,* and felt there were too many planet stops.

Okay.

I took out one (Ettler's Planet, so you know, too), then had a problem. A time and space problem. Worthy of a Time Lord, in fact. I'd used Ettler's as a crucial meeting place. How was I to get Sira, Morgan, and Huido together at the same time without a planet? Well, there being only me to fix it, I envisioned their meeting point as traveling, too. It's space, after all. Everything's moving. Why not?

Plexis was born.

Bonus? Writing about a shopping mall in space was hilarious. I stuffed Plexis with everything from grand displays of the most exquisite art to fake boob-by-species salesbeings and whatever I could think of to fit between. With each new mention in the Trade Pact, Plexis grew and grew—still a great way to get around conundrums of hither and yon—but also taking on a life of its own.

As I concluded the Clan Chronicles series, the only place I

wasn't ready to leave? Plexis Supermarket. There were stories still to tell here. Backstory. New things. What about—

All at once I realized those stories didn't have to be mine. With Sheila's consent, DAW's expertise, and sage advice from those who've done shared worlds such as the amazing Ed Greenwood (Hi, Ed!), I officially opened the air locks and invited in anyone who'd care to write a tale from Plexis. Or do the cover art. (Why, yes, that fabulous cover is by the talented Roger H. Czerneda, who also named the *Silver Fox*. Now you know that, too!) Erin Czerneda, expert in all things Clan, was my first reader, sounding board, and strong right everything throughout (And, yes, Captain Usuki Erin of the *Wayfarer*. Now you know!)

Readers, fans, friends. Your response was and is a sincere compliment to the characters, the setting, and your own wonderful creativity. Thank you—all of you—from the bottom of my heart.

Parked your starship? Got your airtag?

Welcome to a Plexis you haven't seen before!

Julie E. Czerneda

How to Read This Book
by Julie E. Czerneda

T HIS ANTHOLOGY IS unusual in that its twenty-three stories compose a single, blended narrative. My novella, "A Hold Full of Truffles," weaves through and around, leading from one story to the next, drawing together the wonderful ideas, great back-stories, and new characters of my amazing fellow authors.

In other words, *Tales from Plexis* is meant to be read like a novel, from start to end. While you may be tempted to rush to your favorite author and gobble their story first, I highly encourage you to trust me, come along for the ride, and take in the whole tapestry.

"A Hold Full of Truffles" takes place between *Ties of Power* and *To Trade the Stars*. Sira and Jason have brought the *Silver Fox* to the famous supermarket with cargo for the *Claws & Jaws: Complete Interspecies Cuisine*. It should have been simple. Routine.

But this *is* Plexis.

A Hold Full of Truffles

1

* * *

by Julie E. Czerneda

"CONFIRMED, PLEXIS APPROACH. *Silver Fox*, Karolus registry, inbound on your directions." My oh-so-proper tone was an accomplishment, given our current state. Letting go of the com button, I settled back into that still-new, still-wondrous distraction of tangled limbs and warm torsos, the pilot seat of the *Fox* adjusting with a familiar aggrieved whine, my hair slipping, delirious, around my captain's neck. *Where were we—*

A slightly desperate mumble.

I snuggled in tighter, deepening my senses to include the beat of his heart, as wild as mine. *Oh, yes, here—*

Witchling, with a dose of *regret,* even as Jason Morgan lifted me up and away, setting me gently on the deck. He shoved a hand through his hair and gave me a look. Fond exasperation, that was. "We're on final to a space station, chit."

I grinned, unrepentant. It wasn't as if my Human couldn't dock with Plexis in his sleep. "It's routine." Another still-new treasure.

"Only if we don't crash." An arm around me, a quick, affectionate squeeze, then my Chosen was at the control panel, all business.

I took up my perch on the copilot's couch. If I slid back, the couch would curl to accommodate my stature, but I liked to sit where I could watch his nimble fingers working the console. Oh, the ship could—and did—fly herself.

Just not, in Morgan's estimation, into something as complex as a parking spot. Especially here, on the most famous space station of all: Plexis Supermarket. Its lurid sign—"If You Want It, It's Here"—could only be seen from space, but Raj Plexis' gamble, turning a failed asteroid refinery into a traveling shopping complex, had succeeded beyond all expectations. We'd be one of tens of hundreds of ships on the move, inbound or out, while the station remained in real space. Morgan kept a wary eye on the proximity sensors, it being too late, he'd informed me, once alarms sounded.

I put my arms back in my coveralls, shrugged the garment on, and fastened the front. My hair twitched in disagreement, presumably because Morgan's coveralls remained around his waist, the control room lights limning the muscles working under the skin of bare shoulders and back.

Routine. A home. New to me as love was to us both. We'd come a long way since our first visit to Plexis.

Something *cold* arrived with the memory. I pushed it back.

"What is it?" Morgan didn't look around, but he'd *felt* my discomfort. Chosen could, being Joined through the M'hir, that permanent link between minds and, in our case, hearts.

"Nothing." I tightened my innermost shields, enough to keep my foolishness to myself. "Are we there yet?"

A preoccupied grunt was my answer, the aging ship claiming his attention. I leaned back, hands around one knee, to wait. There'd be checks to run once the *Fox* was clamped to the station. As Hindmost, several were my responsibility, so I recited the list to myself, determined to impress—or, more honestly, not to miss anything crucial. Unlike a planetary landing, on worlds suited to our form of life where we could open ports and breathe what arrived, here we'd have to pay for any air we "shared" with Plexis. Along with anything else, so for ships like ours, hookups were the minimum permitted by station regs.

Possible before the *Fox* had sprung a few—I called them "leaks," which made my Human wince—peculiarities. We'd have to accept the full spread of links this docking, at least until our parts were delivered and installed.

A home needing parts was also routine, if an adjustment for someone of my heritage. After all, the Clan didn't work with tech, they employed—or *influenced*—Humans to do it for them. In that, I supposed I was something new myself. My kind would get used to it.

After this trip, with this cargo? I smiled to myself. We'd be able to afford the parts on Morgan's lengthy list. Enough to keep us flying.

"Say again, Plexis?" The edge to my Human's voice would have penetrated a Carasian's shell.

Not so the being on the com. "You can make payment now, Captain Morgan—*shurrrrr*—" The bland voice was nasal, not in itself indicative of nonhumanoid; the faint whistled pause was. "—or before you unload."

It—a F'Feego, according to Morgan, and "it" was appropriate, only the neuter caste dealing with aliens—had identified itself as Officer Esaliz E'Teiso, authorized representative of the Plexis Department of Consumables Duties and Tariffs, a seedy bit of bureaucracy of which I'd been blissfully unaware until we'd parked the *Silver Fox*.

They'd noticed the truffles.

We'd a hold full of the black earthy-smelling lumps, fresh from the jungles of Pocular. Merle truffles, to be exact: a rare and utterly delicious—according to others—delicacy. Morgan had helped dig these with his own hands, while I, as our custom, stayed behind in Ancoma, the Poculan shipcity, to look after ship tasks suited to being Hindmost. Our third such cargo for Huido Maarmatoo'kk— more and more species now enamored of his recipe for the things— and the first promising to turn a significant profit for us all.

I'd a sick feeling Plexis had noticed that, too.

"What payment? Our cargo's a delivery for a Plexis restaurant," Morgan retorted. *Something's not right,* he sent with a tinge of *frustration. Plexis takes its cut off the end product—portions served.* "There's some mistake, Officer E'Teiso. I'd like to speak to your superior."

"I—*shurrr*—am in charge of what is designated an import under our regulations. Truffles fall within a new category:—*shurrr*—Items Imported For Local Consumption. As such, you owe—"

At the outrageous amount, I covered my mouth with both hands to stifle words I'd learned in the not-nice part of shipcities.

"The sum includes the missed fees for the previous two cargoes—*shurrr*—no late penalty added," the F'Feego finished magnanimously. "Your ship will—*shurrr*—remain attached to Plexis pending settlement."

A threat even I, late-to-space, understood.

If we paid, now and doubtless for any future truffles, Huido's venture was over before it really started, any and all profit going to Plexis.

If we didn't, we could lose the ship, an outcome only too likely given Huido, in a fit of optimism, had sunk everything solvent into our cargo. We'd nothing of our own. As the expression went, the *Silver Fox* flew on promises. If the *Claws & Jaws* couldn't pay us, we couldn't pay for those essential new-to-us parts.

Foreclosure by Plexis. Grounded by failing engines, followed by foreclosure by Plexis. I didn't see much difference.

Morgan replied, his tone mild, "Thank you for this information, Officer. We'll be in touch." His finger found the com button and pressed. Lingered. "Interesting."

I'd other words for it, but swallowed them when he walked to a plain portion of wall. Putting fingertips together, my Human concentrated.

A hidden console flipped out: controls for equipment that should have been removed when the former patrol ship was decommissioned. Morgan worked them in silence for a moment, then stepped back, watching until the console returned to its hiding place. His eyes found mine and there was nothing mild in their expression. "I've enabled secured-in-hostile-territory mode. No one can enter the *Fox* or tamper with her exterior without—unfortunate—consequences."

From the now-frantic flash of the com light, Plexis noticed that, too. Oh, good.

More fines.

"We could just 'port the truffles to the *Claws & Jaws*," I suggested. Within my Power, certainly, and likely, with Morgan's own growing Talent, his as well. "No one would know."

A wry grin. "We're attached to the station, chit. An unusual shift in the ship's mass will set off every alarm they have." Morgan rolled his shoulders, then nodded. "First things first. We tell Huido. In person."

Because the Carasian tended to break things when upset, starting with his com unit. "I'll 'port us to his apartment."

"We walk," he ordered before I could form the locate, that memory of *place* my Clan Power could use to draw us through the M'hir. A half smile. "You told me you wanted to see more of the station."

It was a delaying tactic, I judged, to give Morgan time to plan how to break the news to our headstrong friend, but I made myself smile. "That I did."

Just not today.

I stopped where the floor gave way to air, crossing my arms on the token rail to look down. Way down. Looking up was an option also, but I'd only see the underside of the next level and advertising. The odd misplaced cloud. Escaped pets—what I hoped were pets. A Skenkran sleeping off a hangover.

Down, though, was a colorful seething carpet knit from heads, body parts, and packages unrolling as far as I could see; admittedly not far, given the night zone slicing across the promenade in the distance, but enough.

We were seriously outnumbered.

Another pair of crossed arms joined mine on the rail; a shoulder bumped companionably. "Second thoughts, Sira?"

The Human expression for doubt. However many I had, how much I longed to turn around and return to the safety of the *Silver Fox*, shouldn't matter. Memories weren't to be feared. A place—wasn't. I should be stronger than this.

Before I could say so, a small lock of my hair wound itself around his thumb, then stilled.

"That'd be yes."

Exasperated, I tugged the lock free and straightened. "And

irrelevant. We might as well take our time. Until we settle this business, we're stuck here."

Warmth. I'd pleased him, blending our fate with the ship's. "We can't leave yet," he corrected, gazing down at the crowd, his regard casual to anyone else, but those blue eyes scanned the mass below, seeking potential trouble spots, ever aware of exits. If anyone knew Plexis, it was Morgan.

If anyone knew me, it was my Human, who gave me a sideways glance. "We'll fix this."

If anyone could—first, though, we had to plunge into the maelstrom of shoppers on the next level to reach the *Claws & Jaws: Complete Interspecies Cuisine.* Which wasn't a problem, I told myself, steadying nerves this place—and situation—persisted in rattling. We were safe. Our shields were in place—they had to be. Plexis Supermarket attracted Clan shoppers as well as occasional, if now rare, renegade Human telepaths. Security might stir at our worn spacer garb, but we bore the blue airtags of authorized visitors—

Besides, I realized glumly, Officer Esaliz E'Teiso had probably put out our idents, so we wouldn't be hindered in our search for funds.

"We'll fix this," Morgan repeated firmly.

"Soon, I hope."

I'd said it with too much feeling. He turned, a brow rising. "What happened to exploring Plexis?" A small frown. "Was I wrong?"

"No. I did want—I do." Caught, I made a face then gave in. "I don't." The whole truth with him, always. "It's too much. Plexis— Them—" I gestured at the masses below. *After just us.* Days upon blissful days of the two of us—three if you counted the ship, as Morgan would—the sum the best part of my life. Especially in space. Especially after—

Cold. It filled me, memories welling up like the bellies of dead fish. Auord. Scats. Acranam. Pocular. The Drapsk. Ret 7.

Plexis, oh, I'd memories here, too, dark ones.

My cheeks burned. What was wrong with me? With an effort he wouldn't miss, I rallied. "I'll be fine, Jason. I need—I need a moment to adjust." And better memories, sure to come now that we were together.

A wave of *understanding*, the better because it came without question. Morgan nodded toward a nearby sombay stand. "That's Sedly's. Care for a cup?"

Surprised, I looked more closely at the Ordnex serving from the stand, trusting my Human's identification. I couldn't get past their lack of nose to recognize individuals. "Wasn't he a chef at the *Claws & Jaws?*"

"Cook. After Sedly almost poisoned some Humans, Huido broke down and hired a certified multi-species chef."

If memory served, our choosy friend was on his third, a Neblo-kan named Neltare. "I thought Sedly was let go because—you know." Sedly—admittedly at Huido and my cousin Barac's urging—had served Larimar di Sawnda'at to a table of delighted Thremms, the Clansman's corpse having been left in the freezer of the *Claws & Jaws* in a failed attempt to frame Morgan for murder.

While I didn't mourn Larimar, a spy from Acranam, still—my nose wrinkled in disgust. "Sure you want to drink Sedly's sombay?"

"Don't be squeamish, chit." A grin. "We have before."

We hung back to let the cluster of Turrned Missionaries collect their steaming cups with the requisite vows to pray for the Ordnex, the being's multi-jointed arms a blur as it tried to speed them along.

As the missionaries left, the nearest gazed up at us with those limpid, so-feeling eyes, and I quickly focused on a nearby plant. Excellent beings, Turrned, but their unceasing desire to care for others involved a level of soul-searching I preferred to avoid. Not to mention the time it took to shake loose of them, once engaged.

Sombay acquired, Morgan lingered to chat with Sedley. I found a seat and cautiously sipped my drink, which was made exactly how I liked it. My gaze followed the cluster of Turrneds. Their path appeared aimed to intercept whatever approaching spacer looked to need prayer, and I felt a sudden envy. "Plexis never flusters them," I informed my Human when he joined me.

"Generalizing about a species, chit?"

Something no successful trader would do. I grinned at my teacher. "You can't mean Turrneds. Look at them."

Morgan chuckled. "Every species. Not every Turrned is the same. Just ask Huido."

The Stars Do Not Dream

* * *

by Amanda Sun

SALT, HE DECIDED. It needed more salt.

L'inarx Hoch rummaged through the cupboards in the galley. It was nearly lunchtime by deck hours, but the hall was surprisingly quiet, except for the repeating announcement on the voicecom. Most of the Turrneds were on the observation deck now, swarming against the large viewing windows. It wasn't long until they would be within docking range, and except for the motley crew who were taller, multi-limbed, and better suited to navigation, it would be the first time most of them had laid eyes on it.

L'inarx slid the vials aside, reaching his short arms as far into the shadows of the cabinets as he could. It needed salt, but which kind? He found a bottle of *nyx* tears, the pearly grains spilled and half-melted into the shelf. Beyond that, some ancient seasonings, likely too far gone to use. With the servos, there was little need for cooking on this shuttle. But, small as it was, the kitchen was better equipped than anything on the homeworld, and L'inarx wasn't going to let it go to waste.

The voicecom chirped as the same message repeated. "Destination approaching. Please proceed to the observation deck for viewing." There was no one left to proceed except L'inarx—the others had eagerly rushed to glimpse the awaited port as it careened slowly through the darkness. It was finally at the extent of its trajectory, close to the Turrned homeworld.

Plexis Supermarket. Their first missionary appointment.

Not all Turrned were first deployed at Plexis, but it was a common and fairly risk-free position. When it was time, eligible missionaries applied to the various posts they hoped to attain. Some were only available to experienced evangelists—a novice was more likely to be consumed than to convert on Jhabin IV, for example. But Plexis was the safest post for those who weren't inclined to missionary success—L'inarx included.

As a Hoch, he should have been an adept missionary. But there was a key factor to the Turrned's success across the galaxies, and it was this: they were masters at being harmless, nonthreatening, and nearly invisible. While other species had evolved to use superior intellect, or aggression, or even rumored telepathic transference, the Turrned had survived by the blinking of their adorable disklike eyes, better suited to the dim conditions of their homeworld than the bright lights of Plexis. They were even *cute*, as Turrned reported from missionary assignments on humanoid worlds. The evolutionary traits that caused parents to care for their young worked to the Turrned's advantage.

Which was a problem for L'inarx Hoch. He had come into the world misshapen, his eyes half the size of the others, the color more gray than brown, one leg shorter, and his appearance more startling than cute. Other species *noticed* L'inarx. Even Turrned noticed him. He was a distraction to the uniformity of the sermons, even on his homeworld.

L'inarx blinked into the cupboard, his paw closing around a reddish vial of salt from the dried-up sea on Garastis 17. A bit smoky in flavor, but he didn't have much choice. He shook the crystals into the pot; they sank into the stew like droplets of rust.

It had been no question that L'inarx would wind up on Plexis, where abnormality was expected. He could blend in amid the chaos of biodiversity. Mostly he was glad for a post where he was the least likely to be eaten, and where he might have access to more spices and seasonings than he'd ever seen in his quadrant of the galaxy.

The voicecom went silent, the crew and passengers now gathered on the observation deck. L'inarx stirred the dense stew. The bubbles trapped under thick slices of fungi suddenly heaved toward the surface with loud, slapping pops.

A gasp of air signaled the opening of the galley door. A towering frame of sapphire-and-crimson feathers bent down and through the metal doorway. The figure clicked his tongue against his beak, folding his hands neatly behind his back.

"Smells intriguing," First Mate W'harton squawked, his message translated by the com implant buried under the rows of feathers overlapping his neck.

"Your deceitful kindness is a blessing," L'inarx purred back, lowering a lid onto the pot. The glass clouded with ruby-colored droplets.

W'harton snorted. "'Deceitful'? What do you mean?"

L'inarx blinked his gray eyes. "Tolians have a terrible sense of smell."

The first mate held a feathered fist to his beak and coughed. "Yes, well," he said. "I didn't know *you* knew that."

"As missionaries, we study all species," L'inarx said. "But your charity is recognized. Please allow me to serve and pray for you."

W'harton reclined in a crimson chair next to the small row of windows that looked out over the stars. "So, it's not true what they say."

"What do they say?" L'inarx removed the glass lid from the pot and dipped in a deep ladle.

"That you feel a warmth when the Turrned talk," W'harton said. "That they draw you in like the pull of gravity on a ship's hull." He sniffed as L'inarx hobbled over, bowl in hand. "I don't feel any such draw."

Tolians could be terse, but it didn't bother L'inarx. Turrned were trained for every manner of reaction from skepticism to enthusiasm. In truth, it mattered little what the Tolian thought of his missionary abilities. He was far more concerned with what he would think of the stew. "I'm . . . a bit different than the others."

"Hmph." The first mate reached for the bowl, tipping the thick, steaming contents into his beak. The salt from Garastis 17 clung to his feathers like tiny gleaming embers. He tilted his head to the side, his crest flaring as he considered the taste.

"I've had a great deal worse," he said finally. "Turrned aren't known for their cuisine, but . . ." He gave a tiny squawk. "Not bad at all."

A purr escaped L'inarx in response.

"So," W'harton said between sips, "why aren't you on the observation deck with the rest of them?"

L'inarx attempted a shrug, pinching his tiny shoulders together as though he were trying to squeeze through a servo vent. Every light-year closer to Plexis was a light-year closer to his mission. Most Turrneds looked forward to it, but L'inarx . . .

The Tolian's crest lifted. "I thought all Turrned were devoted missionaries."

"Every Turrned serves," L'inarx answered, looking at the pot. A thick bubble popped in response.

There was a saying on the homeworld. The stars do not dream; they shine. Turrned were born to serve, to shine the light of the Prelude on others. It was their role; no more, no less.

W'harton paused. "I think I parse your meaning. My kin had plans for me, too. But Plexis is a mix of strange and familiar." He tipped his head back, his rounded tongue licking the last droplets of stew from the bowl. "You might find a home there yet."

L'inarx took the bowl in his hands as W'harton stretched to his full height. "I'll pray for you," the Tolian said, ducking under the metal arch. The door slid shut.

It took several moments before L'inarx realized *he* was supposed to have said that.

Hesitantly, he padded toward the window, empty bowl clutched to his chest. *Not bad at all.* He peered into space, pinpricks of light swirling past as the ship hurtled toward the future.

The voicecom crackled to life once again. "All passengers proceed to their quarters. Upon arrival at Plexis Supermarket, you will be escorted to a tag point."

L'inarx pressed his nose against the cold glass, his gray eyes blinking as he looked toward the prow.

Plexis gleamed in the distance.

His new home.

L'inarx trudged along the length of the altar, igniter in hand. Every few feet he paused, lifting the digital torch to the tapers set in the niches of the wooden frame. He hesitated—these weren't the usual black candles, inset with clipwing shells that caught the light and shimmered like stars. This one was red, the last one green and orange. Farther along was a transparent candle with obnoxious neon rainbows spiraling down the sides in alien script.

A veteran Turrned slowed to blink his comforting eyes. "Not as easy to source candles here as the homeworld," he offered. "Archaic devices, shopkeeper said. Don't want to burn down Plexis."

"Archaic? Candles?" L'inarx let out a gurgling puff in his throat. You might as well call the stars archaic, the planets, the universe. Ancient, yes, but to label them *archaic*, as though their meaning were lost, irrelevant. There was nothing closer to the beginning of things than the combustion of elements. The universe ignited in a spark, and the Prelude before it collapsed into embers. When you thought about it, candles were more central to Turrned worship than feeding the hungry.

Archaic. L'inarx sniffed as he lifted his igniter to the wick. The flame crackled to life, the darkness of the converted cargo room just a little brighter.

Normally he disliked this sort of menial task, reserved for lower initiates. But after the overwhelming crowds, he didn't mind as much. This tiny, Turrned-sized room was snug and familiar after the expanse of the supermarket. Stifling, a little. Claustrophobic, yes.

But safe. Mundane.

Even the docking bay had been shocking, with its soaring ceilings and floor-to-rafters windows. A giant posting board announced arrivals, departures, crew listings, cargo sought or found or loaded, scrolling in every color and curling script. Most were in Comspeak, but despite L'inarx's vast training of other species, there were many he didn't remotely recognize.

The Turrneds had come to greet them with Prelude bells,

intended to draw interest and curiosity. The veteran leader hesitated when he saw L'inarx but, of course, didn't say anything. Turrned are nothing if not polite.

They had proceeded in rows of four, waves of warmth radiating from the tiny missionaries. It was working, L'inarx had thought. He kept his head down, his eyes away from the crowd. Perhaps he could go mostly unnoticed after all.

Now, in this stuffy cargo hold, he wasn't so sure. It was dim, but he was at the front of the altar lighting candles. Not exactly invisible. He'd volunteered immediately for cooking duty, but had been told all positions were filled.

He lit the last of the tapers as the first of the spacers arrived, guided to rows of chairs crammed tightly around long aluminum tables. It was nearly time. He tried to look pious as he waited.

"You're a Hoch, aren't you?"

L'inarx turned. The veteran missionary who had explained the candles stood beside him. "I'd heard one was among the newest arrivals."

"How did you know?"

He leaned closer. "It has to be you. It couldn't be any of the others."

L'inarx stifled the purr rolling into his throat. Hoch was a rare title, given only to the descendants of at least three generations of outstanding missionaries. The gifts were said to pass down genetically from one Hoch to the next. To outsiders, all Turrned appeared the same, but to the missionaries, it was easy to spot a Hoch. They walked with more grace; they blinked with more warmth. They gave more generously, an extra ladleful on every plate. They fit their missionary lives as smoothly as the grooves of the altar notched into each other.

It was what made L'inarx as rough as raw lumber.

"The rest of the new recruits lurch like orbiting planets," the veteran said. "You're the only one who doesn't. So you must be the Star."

I was supposed to be, L'inarx thought. But then he was born like this, with his uneven legs and his cold, gray eyes. No one said anything cruel, ever. But they didn't have to. L'inarx heard it all himself, the rush of cold water in the whispers of overwrought kindness poured upon him his entire life.

"Don't be nervous," the veteran said. "I'll pray for you."

"You're very kind," L'inarx answered.

More of the hungry entered the room. They walked, slithered, scuttled in, and the Turrneds seated them, purring gentle words, filling the room with stifling warmth.

A scent caught in L'inarx's nose. He must have made a face, for the missionary beside him whispered, "Is it the Gentek? They take getting used to, I'll admit."

"That smell," he said. "The wine." What were they called again? "*Flimberries?*"

The veteran's eyes darted to the saucer of dark red on the altar. "Ah," he said. "Impressive nose you have there, flickering Star."

"But—"

The Turrned nodded with empathy. "I know. It isn't the same. Not even close. But it's too hard to source the right ingredients so far from the homeworld."

"But doesn't Plexis have everything? If You Want It, It's Here?" The script outside the giant station had shouted as much.

"I'm sure there's a seller somewhere onboard. But the price would be beyond our means. Not much demand for our home-world goods, it seems. Our only export is the truth."

And a free lunch, thought L'inarx, but he didn't say it. It sounded possibly heretical, and certainly rude.

At least they should have fermented the flimberries with a dash of crane vinegar. That would have dampened the fishiness of it.

It didn't matter now. The Mission was in service, and the leader nodded his head for it to begin. "Good luck, Hoch," the veteran purred.

L'inarx reached for the decanter and poured wine for the spac-ers at the first table. He concentrated on exuding empathetic warmth. He could feel waves of it radiating from the others, and he knew he was the only one who struggled to produce it. But as long as there was so much kindness emanating, it didn't matter if so little was coming from him.

He poured for the Gentek, the sulfurous smell of him flooding his nose. The veteran had been right; it took getting used to. But the Gentek nodded warmly, the attractive dappling along its neck lighting with pleasant colors. L'inarx wondered if other humanoid species found *them* adorable, too.

He shuffled to the next table and poured just a sip for a small child, who tugged on her caretaker's arm and said, "Gram, why's that one have weird eyes?" She shushed her, but L'inarx didn't mind. It was truth without malice, and truth was the fabric of the universe; whether you believed in it or not, the entire structure was entangled in absolutes.

"You look weary," he said to them. "We will pray for you."

He moved to the next table. He poured for a harried-looking shopkeeper, and for a spacer complaining about his unfair contract with a trade ship. He poured for a Tolian, who reminded him of First Mate W'harton and the way he'd gobbled down the stew. *I've had a great deal worse.*

It was that rusty salt, he thought. He should've added the nyx tears. A bit sweet, yes, but the aftertaste would have combined more smoothly with the lingering rubber texture of the fungi . . .

"Hey! Watch it!"

The Tolian rose to his feet, his chair pushing back with an awful screech. The alien towered over him, red wine dripping off the quills of his emerald feathers and pooling on the floor beneath.

The whole room was looking now, the service disrupted. The Turrneds blinked in unison, staring at L'inarx.

His heart pounded. "I . . . I'm so sorry. Let me get you a towel." He turned, but as he limped away, his robe snagged on the edge of the table and sent him tumbling, paws over eyes. The rest of the decanter splashed all over the next table before shattering on the floor.

The veteran Turrned hurried over, a towel draped over his arm. "You are troubled," he said smoothly. "Let us help you."

"Of course I'm troubled!" the Tolian's com squawked. "This runt poured wine all over me! I smell like rotting *creteng*!" But his angry voice lost its edge as the veteran missionary blinked his warm eyes.

"Let us help you," he said.

The Tolian lowered slowly, conversation resuming. L'inarx

unhooked his robe from the table as his ears folded tight with embarrassment. The missionaries moved like cogs in a vintage watch, whirling around each other in perfect synchronization as they resumed service.

Only one other Turrned didn't move with them—the Mission leader, standing with a bundle of prayer vistapes clutched to his chest. He was looking at L'inarx with excessive kindness and sympathy, which only meant one thing.

L'inarx was in big trouble.

"A free lunch for the weary-hearted," L'inarx said, passing a visbrochure to a nearby spacer. "We will pray for you."

This was what it had come to. He had feared he'd be scrubbing every last inch of the altar for the next three years, scouring the sleeping quarters, and mending the scruffy robes. He'd be doing all of those, too, the leader had assured him, but he'd start by handing out the stacks of thousands of visbrochures. "A chance for one-on-one service," he'd purred. L'inarx had shuddered.

How long had he stood here? Half a station day? More? This particular corner of Plexis had quickly lost its novelty—nothing but a blur of potential converts, and L'inarx without the warmth to even charm them into taking a digital leaflet.

Perhaps if he changed locations.

He rode the ramp up to the next level, limping under the weight of the visbrochures. The bench? Not enough traffic. Beside the ramp? Too easy for his targets to get away.

A cacophony of spices and seasonings flooded the air around him.

Was that . . . clipwings? And sour *dolm* leaves? He turned the corner and saw the booth—small compared to those selling refurbished ship parts, but stocked to every corner with barrels and boxes and tubs. Spices in every color imaginable burst out of the tops of them, pyramids of azure and gold and luminescent green, each a different and intoxicating scent. L'inarx stared.

"Looking for something in particular?"

A Human sat among the spices—or some type of humanoid. Swirling patterns had been tattooed over every visible stretch of skin.

"You're one of them Turrneds, aren't you?"

L'inarx blinked his gray disks down at his robe, his hands full of prayer leaflets. "What gave you that idea?"

He shouldn't have said that. It was bordering on rude.

But the shopkeeper laughed. He hooked a thumb behind him. "I've got some flimberries in the back."

L'inarx shuddered. "Only if you have enough crane vinegar to drown a clipwing nest."

The shopkeeper looked at him carefully. "Crane vinegar, you say?"

"Gets rid of the fishy—"

"—the fishy aftertaste," the patterned Human finished for him. "Hmph. First Turrned worth your salt. Why'd they wait so long to send you?"

L'inarx ran his hand along the rim of a barrel of bright blue *seroling*. It was so fresh he could smell the citrus tones from here. "I'm a new arrival."

"'bout damn time," the shopkeeper said. "Er. Sorry. Interested in that seroling? Nice and sour. It'll curl your eye disks right inward."

He wanted to try it—and everything else. He stumbled for words. "How much?"

"Two credits a pound."

If Turrned cursed, now would be the time. His ears drooped. "Two credits?"

"Didn't the Mission give you enough?"

The shopkeeper thought he was an envoy, even with an armful of visbrochures and no shopping list. He didn't even have a grav cart. Turrneds didn't carry credits; there was no need. The Mission provided your robe, your quarters, your food. L'inarx had blurred the lines of truth a little in the past when buying ingredients for his recipes. At least cooking was a service for others, but so luxurious a dish? Time after time, it was explained away as enhanced Hoch abilities.

"Ah," the Human said. "This isn't for them, is it?"

L'inarx felt as transparent as that obnoxious altar candle. "How can you tell? Are you an empath?"

The shopkeeper laughed. "I'm a salesbeing on Plexis. I've seen it all. Here." He reached into his pocket and flicked a small crystal into the air. L'inarx nearly dropped the visbrochures as he caught it. "That's a five-credit cluster," the Human nodded. "You take the next two ramps up, hang a right, walk down the hallway until you hit the biggest sign you've ever seen. Go see how flimberries and seroling should be handled, hmm?"

L'inarx stared at the credit cluster. It caught the light, gleaming as it magnified the visbrochures underneath. "You are very kind," he said. "I will pray for you."

"Just make sure the Mission buys their flimberries here, okay?" The shopkeeper grinned. "And crane vinegar, if you can convince them. Half a credit a flask."

L'inarx knew how vast the universe was, how slowly everything had burned and cooled and drifted to become what it was. He knew how slowly the Prelude had composed and decomposed, how many billions of years stretched behind and ahead until the first gleam of the collapse would finally appear on the universe's multifaceted rim. And yet no moment had ever felt so long as passing out those visbrochures while the credits weighed heavily in the pocket of his robe.

When a spacer finally took the last one, L'inarx hobbled toward the ramp, nearly tripping over his hem. The buzz of conversation was everywhere, coms crackling and aliens manipulating all types of mandibles into the fricatives and affricates of the communal Comspeak. The Mission always necessitated hushed, reverent exchanges. How loud Plexis was in comparison. It bubbled like an overcooked stew, a bit of this and a dash of that, an intoxicating blend that filled the Hoch with newfound hope that there was more to the universe than his disappointing missionary post.

At the end of the alleyway, he found the promised sign. It hung high above a set of doors, opening constantly with the flow of customers. *Claws & Jaws: Complete Interspecies Cuisine*. The waft of delicious smells curled around L'inarx's nostrils.

Interspecies cuisine? His heart pounded. The most exotic thing he'd ever eaten was the gruel on the shuttle from the homeworld. He limped into line, ignoring the strange looks from the others. After a moment's thought he turned and bowed politely, sending as much warmth their way as he could.

Imagining the delights within, it was an easy feat to manage.

At last he made it through the doors and to the counter. The server looked to be a humanoid of some type, though pale lavender, and she smiled warmly at him. She must think him *cute*.

"Table for one?" He nodded, reaching a paw into his pocket to curl around the credit cluster.

It was strange not to be the server for once. The Fem led him to a table next to an indoor fountain and a handful of fake bushes, arranged to amuse customers into thinking they were at an outdoor plaza. Some marine species had apparently allowed their children to splash around in the fountain. They swam laps and leaped with shimmering fins, to the aggressive eye-rolling of the other patrons.

L'inarx didn't mind. He liked children, and all the activity only added to the buzz of his excitement. No one ever splashed around in a fountain at the Mission.

"Welcome to *Claws & Jaws*," a voice said, and it took L'inarx a moment to see who was talking. It was a shelled alien, about the same height as a Turrned. Only the eyes on the ends of his antennae wobbled above the edge of the table, a digital ordering device poised in his claw. He lifted it to the table and used his eyeball to push it toward L'inarx. "May I take your order?"

L'inarx clicked on his chosen script. There were a variety of ways to order—by species, by quadrant, by digestive system, by ingredient type. The world was his *prawly*—but looking at his waiter, he decided it might be rude to order shellfish. "What would you recommend?"

The alien blinked its eye antennae one at a time. "Well, to be honest, we don't get many Turrneds in here."

"Oh?"

"In fact, just you. Ever."

"Oh."

"But we do pride ourselves on the *completeness* of our interspecies cuisine. I'm sure we can find something that tastes like home."

"Oh, no," L'inarx purred. "I don't want anything that tastes like home. I want . . . anything else."

The eyes blinked again, individually. "Ah," he said. "A gourmet.

We do get lots of those. I'd recommend the Sunset Bisque from the beaches of Abalania V. Very nice flavor; seaweed a touch bitter, but with a bite you won't soon forget."

"Great," L'inarx said. "And maybe some . . . Mixed Forest Fungi Stew, Suitable for All Manner of Gastrointestinal Systems?"

"Certainly," the waiter said, looping his antenna around the device. "You'll find the Tork mushrooms are particularly smoky today."

L'inarx stared around the room as he waited. There were arguments at some tables, laughter at others. Everything was alive and vibrant. He'd always been taught to move purposefully, that the pace of the stars and the expanding galaxy was to be modeled in every way. But this burst of lifespans, eons shorter than star lives . . . his mentors had never told him what kind of energy they held, what kind of excitement he could find in all the hustle and bustle of life.

They hadn't told him how brightly dreams could *shine*.

No one was staring at his small, gray eyes in here. In his differences, he was the same as the rest. For once, L'inarx didn't wish he was one of many, orbiting. He was pleased to be his own star.

The return of his server was signaled by the clunk of a tray onto the table, antennae straining as they pushed it toward him. L'inarx said his thanks, prayed over the food, and took a bite of the soup. The blend of flavors burst on his tongue—the spice of the seaweed, evolved over millions of years on a distant planet, suddenly fizzing against his taste buds while he twirled around the universe on a repurposed asteroid refinery.

It felt like the end of his own prelude, like the melody had finally begun.

He took another taste of soup, then tried the stew, then called his server back and ordered a side of mellowroot fries. His world broke open, the possibilities for his own dishes swirling in his mind. If only that shuttle kitchen was still his to explore. He had so many new ideas, so many tastes to combine.

"Anything else?" the waiter asked, but L'inarx was so stuffed he could barely tilt his head no. He passed the credit cluster to the waiter.

"May I greet the chef?" he said. "It's rude in our culture to accept service without reciprocation."

The waiter's antennae nodded up and down like reeds in a marsh wind. "We are familiar with a few species that have such requirements. This way."

The kitchen offered even more intoxicating aromas than the restaurant. Unlike the quiet, orderly Mission, every station here whirred with action. Stew pots bubbled, pans flared with fire and oils and sautéed delicacies. Something was burning in an oven, and L'inarx fought the urge to grab a towel and pull the dish out.

"He's in there, somewhere," the waiter said. "Not sure exactly which one to thank, but . . . please, don't take long. This is our busiest night of the week."

"Of course," L'inarx said. He bowed to the waiter and began to pray, but when he looked up, the alien was already rushing out the door, his antennae wrapped tightly around four different dishes.

L'inarx observed the chaos and rhythm of the kitchen—the boiling, the braising, the cooling, the freezing. A microcosm of everything the Turrned believed, he thought. Maybe his longing never had been at odds with his missionary inheritance.

"Are you the one?" said a gruff, tentacled chef, not even looking up from his stewpot.

"Um," said L'inarx. "Yes. I'm here to offer up my vow of returned service."

"Yes, fine, just get me the mellowroot, would you?"

"The . . ." L'inarx hadn't even started his prayer of gratitude yet. But Turrneds served, first of all. "Of course." He scanned the room, noticing a large stasis unit through a flap next to the sinks. He shuffled in, eyeing all sorts of sacks and boxes and bins. Mellowroot. There were a lot of root vegetables, but he remembered the yellow tone. How many to take? He loaded up the pockets of his robe and returned to the chef.

The chef harrumphed, studied the roots sticking out of L'inarx's pockets. "These'll do."

L'inarx nodded. "I wish to offer up my gratitude. May the Prelude forever rest your—"

"Now peel them."

"P . . . peel them?"

The chef turned, his eyebrows knit over his glistening, tired face. "I haven't got all night, missionary. You stay and cook, or you get out those doors and they'll send me someone who can. Can you do it or not?"

L'inarx peeled the mellowroot.

And after they were peeled, he took a paring knife and chopped them into fries, and then he sliced ten Tork mushrooms for a stew, careful not to touch his paws to his eyes. The rest of his night passed in a flurry of ingredients, rushing back and forth to the dry pantry and the stasis unit, slicing and peeling and occasionally rescuing a burning hank of shorlam from the ovens. He knew there must have been some misunderstanding—the chef had been expecting a new recruit, he was certain—but he lost himself in the joy, in the stress and the effort and the *meaning* of it all. This was the type of service he was meant for. This was the giving of himself to the universe. The kitchen flooded with warmth, whether from stews or roasts or from L'inarx himself as he finally delighted in the genetic gifts of a Hoch.

"What's this Turrned doing in my kitchen?" boomed a voice that snapped L'inarx out of his haze. A massive alien shuffled toward L'inarx on a flurry of bulbous pads, its four arms dodging around the constantly moving chefs. Its metallic head separated in a swarm of eyes that put L'inarx's waiter to shame.

"He's the new assistant, Hom Huido," the chef informed him, never looking up from his sizzling saucepan.

"The 'new assistant' informed me he's taken a job on the *Silas Queen*," Huido bellowed. His eyes clustered like a wave to gaze at L'inarx. "Any reason you're here peeling fungi in my establishment without a contract or even an invitation?"

Turrned were trained to respond to situations of stress with grace and assurance, but both left L'inarx in his moment of need. "I . . . I came to say my prayers of gratitude for the meal. There was a misunderstanding. I meant no harm. I have never tasted anything so wonderful."

Huido chortled with delight, his eyes rattling back and forth on their stems in the cacophony. "I'd like to answer humbly, but we both know it's true." He clacked his claws together with pleasure. "We find ourselves unable to keep up with the demand, and we appreciate your mistaken help. A pleasure to have met you."

L'inarx shook Huido's claw, the rim of his universe pulling in to collapse. The glimmer of light was fading. "Oh. Yes, of course. I'm grateful to have served. I . . . I will pray for you."

The doors to the dining area burst open. "It's been sent back!" wailed L'inarx's waiter.

Huido let out a hiss of breath. "Impossible," he said. "Who made this dish? Unacceptable!"

The chefs crowded around to stare at the returned dinner. It was a cut of the shorlam L'inarx had rescued from the oven. It looked all right, a single bite carved from the side of the pale white meat.

"The hom said it was . . . off," the waiter said. "Not the flavor of Garastis 17 at all."

The Turrned leaned in to sniff the meat. He wondered. . . .

"Bah!" boomed Huido. "He lacks refined taste. Who asks for such a style of meat?"

L'inarx took the paring knife in his hand and sliced a tiny sliver off the roast. He popped the bite into his mouth.

"What are you doing?" asked the waiter.

L'inarx swallowed.

"Salt," he said.

"Salt?" Huido echoed.

"It has the wrong salt. Try the smoky red salt from the dried-up sea. Scorch Salt, they call it. And do you have any clipwings? They'd enhance the flavor."

The chefs stared at each other. They stared at Huido.

"Maybe a dash of moonberry curd, too," L'inarx added. "Infused with blue saffron." His gray disks blinked back at Huido's swarm.

"Don't just stand there," Huido boomed. "Go and get them for him!" The chefs dispersed in a flurry.

L'inarx thought carefully about his training in other species as he mixed the ingredients, about the cuisine of Garastis 17. He spread the paste onto the roast and burned it into a golden crust with a sugar torch. He watched the waiter in silence as he returned the meal to the table. Seamfish and mellowroot alike burned in their pans as the kitchen held a collective breath, peering out the sides of the doors for the sign.

The waiter waggled his antennae up and down wildly. Huido laughed, L'inarx collapsing against the counter as relief flooded through him.

"Not bad, little one," Huido said, his eyes clustering as they looked the missionary up and down. "I'd never thought the Turr-neds to have a gourmet among them. Perhaps we've found our new assistant. What do you think?"

Not bad at all, he thought, remembering First Mate W'harton on the shuttle. It felt so long ago, the empty bowl in L'inarx's paws, his nose pressed against the cold glass as Plexis hovered as bright as a star. "That . . . that would be my dream, sir."

L'inarx was a Hoch. And Hochs didn't just dream; they shone.

"Tell me," Huido said, reaching a kind claw around L'inarx's back. The pads of his feet squelched pleasantly as they walked. "Do you have any experience in service?"

... *Truffles* continues

2

* * *

SOMBAY WARM IN my stomach, alert for "different" Turr-neds, just in case, I took the downlevel ramp beside my captain.

The first step off onto the teeming concourse was—as I'd feared, or because—like plunging into cold water. I might have drowned, swept aside and under by the flow of busy, preoccupied shoppers, but Morgan's steadying hand cupped my shoulder. Through the contact, words. *Easy, Witchling.*

With a hint of *amusement.*

I stiffened as he no doubt intended. "This way." Reasoning that, as in water, going with the flow would use less energy—and result in less trampling—I stepped boldly forward on the heels of a trio of blue-clad spacers. They looked ready to find a bar, meaning the night zone ahead. The *Claws & Jaws* was on the other side. How hard could it be?

Which was when something small and brown and *intent* appeared between my legs. I jumped, it yelped, and we both went down tangled in what felt like cargo cabling.

That we weren't immediately trampled into paste surprised me almost as much as the speed with which the Human female—apparently in pursuit of the small, brown something—untangled us. "Apologies, Fem," she said rather breathlessly, holding on to a squirming, frantic ball with pleading eyes that could put a Turrned's to shame. "He's got a scent and— Oh, Fair Skies, Captain Morgan," with a relieved smile.

My Human stood nearby, doing his unhelpful best not to laugh. "Hello, Parker. No harm done. Good hunting."

Before I could comment from the floor, Parker put down the creature. Freed, it ran off through the crowd, towing her along by what appeared now to be a long ribbon. Morgan reached down and helped me to my feet.

"Who was that—and what?" I demanded.

"Friends." He gazed thoughtfully into the distance. "They find things."

An oncoming stampede of Whirtles, each clutching a whitewrapped bundle, every one shrieking, "DEBBICK!!!" made the rest a conversation for later.

Finding Parker

* * *

by Doranna Durgin

PARKER EUN SU tripped over a lower level bulkhead frame, caught herself, and stumbled onward. Excitement surged through her bio interface as Cory Dog hit the harness hard, utterly focused on the target scent and its surrounding scent pools, the puzzle of direction and air currents and—

Cory came to a stop, stymied by the utterly still air. The *stale* air. Parker emerged from her bio'face haze to take in the battered nature of the metal plating beneath their feet, the dimly lit corridors . . .

The deep levels of the former asteroid refinery called Plexis were no place for a Human Finder and her partner, no matter how enthusiastically that partner had brought them here. Especially not in a space already occupied by a Scat.

The Scat in question lounged an insouciant threat against the bulkhead, forked black tongue flicking from long snout, teeth everywhere. "Oh, my dear," he said. "Just a bit far from home, aren't we? And with such a tidy morsssssel."

Parker already had her badge palmed; she thrust it out in display. "Plexis Authority!" she said, as if her brisk delivery would make a difference. She pointed at Cory, whose wary frustration slapped hard through the bio'face. "Project property!"

The trade script on Cory's work vest lit in response to her words. Given the correct phrase, it would also alert Hospitality Chief Randall to any peril, but that was the last thing Parker wanted right now—for Randall to know. For *anyone* to know.

For she and Cory Dog were in trouble again. No matter that Cory sniffed tentatively in the Scat's direction, wagging a tremulous tail. *goodgoodgood?*

"How delightful!" said the Scat. "Is itsssss flesh sssweet?"

Parker shortened the harness line, touching beside her eye. "I'm sending your image to my chief. We'll be leaving now."

"Little Hossspitality Finder," the Scat said, "You are not important enough for that particular implant." He straightened, flicking free a thin, supple line that would as soon cut a throat as encircle it. His predatory grin made her step back, hand tightening on Cory Dog's line.

Because he was right. She hadn't sent an image. She didn't have that implant. She had only one option, and she really didn't want to take it. "Oh, come *on*. Do you really think no one's keeping track of us?"

"You will be gone before anyone comes looking," the Scat pointed out, altogether too amiable.

"Oh, *fine*," Parker snapped. "Let's just do this, then. Security, Alert: Cory Parker!" She glared as Cory's harness strobed into an alarm flasher. "Are you happy now?"

Because it was really the very, very last thing she'd wanted to do. *Again*.

"Food penalties!" Hospitality Chief Randall sputtered, waving the stasis-wrapped toy—battered, beloved, and well and truly lost—from which Parker had taken scent samples. "Find this thing's owner and move on, or we'll see if hunger motivates the little beast!"

Parker bit back a snapping reply. Chief Randall had yet to be convinced that her bio'face with Cory didn't imbue the dog with magical intelligence, but Cory was only what he'd ever been: trained, implanted, deeply connected, and so bursting with brilliance that no other handler had been able to adapt to his bio'face

interjections. Neither he nor Parker were able to conjure up the
owner of a lost item from Plexis' sometimes admittedly thin air.

Randall's strident tones were too loud; canine anxiety pushed
through the bio'face. Cory looked at her with dark eyes gone worried, ginger-brown ears hanging low: a scent dog bred to theoretical perfection, bio'face-enhanced and packed into a sturdy
twenty-pound body with a happy, whipping brush of a tail.

And, Parker told herself, *a whole lot of crazy.*

"Chief," she said, mustering all her patience, "Cory's trained to
recognize and follow scent, and that's what he's doing."

"Wasting air is what he's doing!" Randall gestured with the
stuffed toy, a thing so generically depicted as to obscure its original species—big round ears propped atop an equally round head
with a conical swoop of a muzzle and six floppy limbs. Its eyes were
beady and scratched, its whiskers broken off, and its fur loved
down to a soft fuzz. It had been found in the luxury sections not
recently dropped from some youngling's grip, but encased in a
broken stasis wrap.

Cory had loved it fiercely, instantly, even mouthing it briefly
before Parker could stop him. Such purity of scent! Such intensity!
Such uniquely persistent skin rafts! He wasn't about to abandon
that scent to lesser pursuits. And Parker wasn't about to push the
point, not after he had been so close to ruin once already.

Because really, the liaison to the Triads should have *known* not
to display Cory's recently unearthed Hoveny artifacts behind the
refreshments table where the dignitaries sat, no matter the cele-
bratory occasion. And *really*, Cory had only been doing his job. But
no one from the Project had stopped the dignitaries from turning
on them, a verbal cacophony of assault from the people Parker had
trusted, echoing through the bio'face to crush Cory's honest,
eager little heart.

So Parker had resigned from the Bio Interface Project, protecting Cory the only way she could—removing him from service simply because no other handler would have him. She hadn't expected
the offered compromise—a brand new outreach position in the
giant traveling Plexis Supermarket, returning precious lost items
to the luxury travelers who'd lost them.

From Finder of precious Hoveny artifacts to Finder of lost items and owners. From working in vast outdoor spaces and amazing landscapes to sniffing through the enclosed corridors and artificial air of Plexis.

No wonder Chief Randall thought their unique arrangement to be a demotion, and treated them accordingly.

Now Randall eyed her with an impatience that meant he'd decided the conversation was over. "Find the owner of this thing or move on, Parker." Like many, he persistently confused her first and last names. She no longer corrected him; only her friends realized her personal name was Eun Su, and so far no one on Plexis had offered that gesture of welcome. Randall, of course, was oblivious. "Find them, or else we'll see what the Project says about providing this dog with a handler who can."

It was an empty threat on all fronts. Parker's amusement, hidden from Randall, could not be hidden from Cory himself, relieving him of his worry as no empty reassurance could do. He jumped to his feet, head cocked, his *new hunt* excitement pouring through the bio'face with the intensity of a solar flare. For a moment, Parker couldn't see, couldn't hear, wasn't sure what she touched. She had no access to senses of her own.

Just proving the point. If Cory could be worked by just any handler, then he'd still be with a Triad, scenting out the Hoveny sites. But not *any handler* could manage his obsessive intensity, his nova-like bursts through the bio'face, or his ridiculously impulsive nature. Parker, a bolt of a headache coming on, could barely do it herself.

But, for Cory's sake, she was here. Here in this enclosed space, working with this close-minded supervisor.

For Cory's sake.

Out in the Hospitality Section proper, Parker accepted office manager Mellilou's sympathetic smile. She watered Cory, sprayed his hard-working nose with soothing emollient that would also help him retain scent, and chose an easy item from the found property bin. The scarf was an impossibly light silk, the painted design unmistakably that of a master. The food stain, aside from being tragic, was also still fresh. And the locator tag readily pinpointed the exact site of the find, offering Cory the perfect start to his hunt.

Besides, Parker knew where the trail would lead even before they entered the upscale convenience eatery. The luxury shuttle lounge was only two modules away, and a frequent end point. She let Cory pick up the scent and then let him drag her with undue speed to the entrance of the lounge, emoting *praise-pride* at every step, waving back at the smiles and greetings they received along the way— some familiar, some passing through.

When she entered the lounge, momentarily dizzied by Cory's reaction to this sensory-rich environment of cushions and pheromones and plush flooring, privacy curtains and quiet music and relaxed whispers, the scarf's owner stood and waited for their approach.

Cory spiked excitement and flung himself down to indicate their target—an individual of an unfamiliar species, with another of its kind; both wore highly decorative armbands.

Parker touch-released the small stasis pocket in her work vest, retrieving the ultimate reward treat—real meat. She tossed it Cory's way as she greeted the person, presenting the scarf with a respect that acknowledged its worth.

Sometimes she and Cory were greeted with true excitement; sometimes with the ennui of those who felt themselves entitled to special effort. But Parker couldn't remember seeing this person's expression before—ears slanting back, eyes narrowing, lips firm and flat. She tried to not make assumptions based on Human expressions, but she was pretty sure she knew disapproval when she saw it.

The person said, "Then you do, on occasion, manage to find lost items."

Was that disdain in those large brown eyes, heavily lashed and lined by a natural mascara that had been enhanced with cosmetics? As had the crisp white markings along the individual's lengthy nose, and the black gleam of a nose pad above a small dark mouth with firm lips. A pair of upright ears swiveled with a rapidity that struck Parker as an anxious display, flicking at every sharp sound.

foodfoodfoods

Parker tossed Cory another scrap, hiding the sting of the person's reaction and preparing for a rapid exit. "It was an honor to return this item. I hope you enjoy your stay on Plexis."

The individual's partner stood, too—a larger person with similar but coarser features and the same innate, long-limbed grace. "Address her as Fem Cervidde," he said. "And then do what you should have done these many days ago: find and return our child's *mananna* so we can leave this place."

There was no other individual of their species within sight; Parker glanced at the door to the lounge's staffed nursery and found the gentle glow of the occupancy light. Of course; the child was being watched. "Fem," she said, offering a small bow. "Hom. Perhaps your lost item has not yet been turned in to us, or it may be in the queue." She understood then that the scarf had been a test, deliberately dropped. "Our office is open for your convenience, should you want to examine the queue. We return items in the order that we receive them." Unless Cory had other ideas.

The Hom snorted through the length of his nose, a sharp sound. "You," he said. "You are Human?"

"Yes," Parker said, and interpreted the Fem's head tip as puzzlement. "Some of my features may be different from other Humans, depending on their world of origin." Hers was a colony in the Fringe, settled by a more compact group than most, closer knit than most, and still full of their own customs.

"You are small."

"Others are larger," Parker agreed.

"Are you *too* small?" the Hom asked. "Is that why you fail to find and return the mananna?"

"I am just the right size," Parker said firmly, and repeated her previous offer. "If you'd like to examine the queue, our office welcomes your inquiry. We can also bring items here for your viewing, and I hope you'll call on us if that option interests you." She offered a crisp, shallow bow that meant the end of the conversation and gathered the harness line.

foods!

Cory never reached out in actual thought-words. He didn't have to, not with the intent that spiked every emoted reaction. Parker's own stomach, fooled, rumbled at her. She told the couple, "I hope you find your other lost item, and that you enjoy your beautiful scarf."

Parker made a brisk retreat, marching Cory out of the lounge. Once the door swiped closed, she threw her arms out in a wildly gleeful gesture, emoting the high-pitched praise that sent his tail into a frenzy. No matter the heads and appendages it turned—she was long used to looking the clown on his behalf, and she'd learned to recognize the affectionate smiles various beings sent her way.

Cory burst into playful spurts of motion, swapping ends without ever hitting the limit of the harness line. His excitement burst through her thoughts in firecracker sparks until she dropped a handful of food pellets at her feet, finishing their game while he satisfied himself with a search for crumbs.

She settled her thoughts, unclipping his line from the tracking ring to the collar ring to take him off-duty and emerging from handler mode long enough to wave to the concierge stationed across the corridor, a Tolian with feathers ruffled in amusement. The Hom bent his head to a well-dressed customer who pointed at Parker and Cory, querying with a colorful flare of humor in his cheek pouches.

Parker didn't linger—she had raw steak to resupply. She waved at Fem Chirruk on her way past the delicacies vendor and called a greeting to Hom Shneeple as that worthy used all eight of his flexible upper limbs to rearrange his couture footwear. Delicate Fem Flir emerged from her vendor space of light scents and comforting oils to toss Cory a tiny treat from the box Parker had inspected and approved, skittering back inside with a giggle and susurrus of skirts and filmy veils.

Parker decided that she, too, could use a meal. Down one level and along the corridor to a well-placed but less pretentious location, and Cory's mounting excitement fluttered through her own chest as they approached his—

Very. Favorite. Spot.

Huido's *Claws & Jaws.*

Hom M'Tisri must have seen them coming. By the time Parker

reached the entrance, the Vilix, beaming such as he could, had already extracted a treat for Cory. "Earth shrimp," he said. "Very high food value for this canine."

"I trust you," Parker assured him as M'Tisri required Cory to sit and wave a paw for the treat. "Can I get my usual?"

"*Deung-galbi*," M'Tisri said. They always kept some aside for her, and Parker had never understood why some people complained about stasis-stored food. It tasted just the same to her, and always hit her tongue with a familiar and welcome tang of home. "Huido will be right—ahh, here he is."

As if anyone could miss the arrival of the Carasian, a massive being plated in gleaming black natural armor and festooned with implanted hooks and swinging cooking implements. How an individual so large could also be so quick . . .

Parker had never fathomed it. But Cory had his own opinion of Huido.

Adoration. Wild, exuberant, unadulterated adoration.

Thus it was that Parker always greeted Huido with fireworks in her head and Cory's silly grin on her face. "Sorry," she said, as Cory, unable to contain himself, erupted in a series of melodious hound barks, a bigger sound than one would ever expect from that wiry, muscled little body. "You know how he is."

Huido only boomed a laugh, one claw-hand clacking in emphasis. "This one might even have the nose for *grist!*" He held out two sealed bags—one would be her dinner, and the other undoubtedly contained the scraps he would never admit he could have otherwise used.

Parker took the bags with a grateful duck of her head. She had no idea what grist was and had long decided not to ask. "He's got a nose, all right. Doesn't know when to quit."

Huido's upper carapace tipped so she could see the gleam of several eyes. "Best you both learn, little friends." He sounded as somber as he ever could. "I heard about your encounter with the Scat."

She couldn't help an incredulous look. "Already?"

He gestured at Cory, who now stood with his front feet against Huido's lower carapace, sniffing vigorously and sending bio'face goosebumps down Parker's spine. "The Scat will not hesitate to acquire you both, if he sees your value."

"Acquire?" Parker repeated.

Huido leaned forward as if imparting a confidence, a gesture completely offset by the boom of his voice. "Recruiters." He straightened and added, in a paradoxically quieter tone, "The vest and badge will not save you. The lower levels are not for you or this Cory Dog."

Recruiters. Predators of the vulnerable, those hard up on their luck and scraping by in the shadows. Predators of whoever they thought they could nab. Here, on Plexis?

"Now!" Huido said, booming again. "Eat your dinner! I must go share beer, for the *Fox* departs in station morning!"

Parker thanked him again, but he was already leaving, a clatter of cutlery moving nimbly through the restaurant interior. She numbly bid the Vilix good-bye and took Cory back to their diminutive quarters, feeding him in accordance with the treats he'd received that day and feeding herself with somewhat less care.

Recruiters. And Cory had followed his favorite scent right to them.

Cory spent the night in a tight little ball, sleeping as hard as he did everything else and offering Parker a mental respite. She sank into meditation to clear her mind of the reactions and sensations that weren't hers, read a chapter in her book, and tried not to think about Randall's behavior.

She wasn't quite ready to reach out to the Project. Ultimately, she'd be dealing with the same people who failed to protect Cory the first time, and who had relocated him only because no other handler had been able to absorb his interface-pounding nature— no matter his quick accumulation of Hoveny finds. Brilliance with a price.

But Cory shouldn't be the one paying that price. And Parker no longer had trust. So no, not quite yet.

But she slept restlessly, with the feel of the soft worn toy in her hand and the scent of it somehow in her nose.

In the morning she fed Cory his token breakfast and loaded her vest with meal pellets and a chunk of reconstituted ox horn, enduring the heavy-handed flavor of her own basic food bar. Cory performed his morning toilet in the special enclosure off her tiny bathroom and gave a mighty shake, his tiny sparks of pleasure bouncing through her thoughts as she fastened his vest and harness. He trotted close at heel on the way to the Hospitality offices and once there, leaped upon his personal little cot with the glee of knowing he was *such a good boy!*

Parker tossed him the horn chunk and waited for the fizzy popping sparks of delight to pass, full of relief that he wasn't worried about the scolding from the day before, and that he hadn't picked up on her own mood. Too busy in his own mind for now.

She gave him a subtle mental press—*wait there until I return*—and he wagged his tail twice, already chewing hard. She walked past the Found Things bin—not at all in its usual neat state—and knocked on the wall beside Randall's open office. "Parker Eun Su," she announced, which he never acknowledged but which she'd never stopped doing.

He looked up from the display at which he'd been frowning. "Why aren't you out making deliveries?"

"Our shift starts in fifteen." Parker stepped into the office, one ear on Cory's vigorous chewing. "I came early so we could talk. No . . . that's not quite right. So you could listen."

His expression darkened. He was a coarse Human, with coarse features, and he'd never welcomed discussion. "I suppose you think you have something to say."

"I do." She kept her voice neutral and kept her mind that way, too. "Chief, Cory and I are Bio'face Project personnel contracted to work in your section." She approached his desk, going so far as to prop her hands on it. "Cory is a brilliant, talented, *sensitive* being who's astronomically improved the rate of returned items. He's doing exactly what he's trained to do, and it's not our fault—or problem—if you don't fully understand that process. Don't ever think you can take out your day's frustrations on him through me again. You took me by surprise yesterday, but it won't happen again."

Randall sat back in his chair, arms crossed over a stout chest, a clearing noise in his throat. He grunted, "You done?"

Parker straightened. "Yes. We'll start work now."

"You do that," Randall said. "And best you not get into any trouble today. Seems it's not my problem if you can't figure out how to do *what you're trained* here in my station." He flicked a dismissive hand at her.

Parker thought of Cory's worth. She thought about the likelihood that she could leave the Project and still retain her implant, or that Cory Dog could retain his. She thought about how long it would take her to pay off the costs of taking Cory if she left.

Forever.

But she couldn't trust the Project to protect him. She clearly couldn't trust Randall to care about him at all. She was all Cory had—and she was on her own.

She swallowed that reality deep where Cory wouldn't find it and went to pluck an item from the bin, reassured by the steady grind of canine teeth on horn.

Another person joined her at the bin; a familiar hand slipped in beside hers and deftly chose the next item in the queue, an appendage mitten of some sort. Office manager Mellilou whispered, "Parker, Cory let me kiss his head!" and held out the item. Then, in a normal and much more brusque tone, she added, "The toy is gone—a couple came in last night and claimed it. Cerviddes. They had grief bands—makes me wonder if there's some story there."

"Cerviddes?" Parker asked, accepting the mitten. Or whatever. "That's their species, and not their name?"

"They don't reveal their names to outsiders." Mellilou quite matter-of-factly knew more about Trade Pact species than Parker thought she'd ever learn. "They have a species-long history of being hunted; they can be quite touchy. Hom or Fem Cervidde will do for any of them."

"But—" Parker stopped her own thought. No good would come of protesting that Cory hadn't found the child's scent in the lounge. The toy was gone, and if it had gone to the wrong family, they apparently weren't any the wiser. She retrieved the horn from Cory, offered him a drink, and then gathered the harness line. The mitten had been lost outside one of the upper levels' most discreet pleasure businesses, and she thought if she was lucky she wouldn't ever quite find out what it was for.

She was halfway there, taking and returning cheerful greetings on Cory's behalf, when her thoughts exploded in joyful recognition, her vision completely obscured by internal fireworks, her fingers numbed from those same joyful fireworks fizzling along her skin.

Such purity of scent! Such intensity! Such unique persistence!

She had just enough presence of mind to duck as Cory lunged against the harness with every vibrating fiber of his being, jerking her abruptly into a tiny service run. She had no opportunity to clip the line to the harness working ring, had no idea where they were going—couldn't see, couldn't hear, found herself drowning in scent. *Slow, slow!* she flung at him, to no effect whatsoever. To no surprise, either—most of their Hoveny finds had been just this frenetic. She raised an arm to protect her face from what she couldn't quite see, slipping and stumbling and waiting for that moment when she could regain just enough of herself to ease Cory back under control. They skidded around a corner and slid down a ramp, servo traction strips tearing her tough pants and skin alike.

The sting of it fed back to Cory, giving him just enough pause so Parker could wrest back control of her vision, or most of it.

Where are we?

Dim corridor, battered bulkheads, bare scratched floors.

Where—?

Cory's distraction lasted only an instant, and then he leaped forward in a frenzied wag of tail, giving rare voice to his excitement in a flurry of melodious barks. Scent washed through Parker's awareness, so strong, so clear.

A squeak of fear. Cory's joyful baying bark. A FIND!

The bursting fireworks faded from her mind's eye, leaving behind Cory's rare but complete haze of success—gentle waves of personal endorphins that left him incoherent, if only ever after a Hoveny find until now. They made Parker prone to giggling but gave her room to think.

And allowed the visual acuity to see the child curled up against the bulkhead, shivering. A tiny thing of absurdly long limbs, huge doe eyes, and tightly flattened ears. Grimy white coloration lined her petite nose and the nostrils of her dark, dry nose pad flared in fear.

"Oh," Parker said, stunned. "Oh, hey. It's okay. I'm sorry. We won't hurt you."

"Hur me," the child echoed in a nonsensical whisper, eyeing Cory through a slow blink.

Cervidde. What were the chances?

The toy. The Cervidde couple who had claimed it. The grief bands. The lack of the toy owner's scent in the lounge . . . the presence in sly tiny spaces and battered station back alleys. *Recruiter turf*.

Parker crouched; she, too whispered. "How long have you been here?"

The child blinked again, tiny incisors appearing under a quivering upper lip of indecision. "Hep me?"

Parker had no indecision at all. "Yes," she said, offering her hand. It didn't matter whether she was right about the Cervidde couple or the slaver Scat—*help* she would. As a dry little hand slipped into hers, she shifted her attention to the corridor, glancing into its ill-lit spaces. Was that movement, there, to the left? A sound of movement? "Come, Fem Cervidde. Come quickly." She withdrew the child from her hidey space and reached out to Cory in silence, tapping him for attention without any particular response. "This is Cory Dog. He helped me find you, and he won't hurt you."

"Frien," said the Cervidde child, uncertainly.

"Definitely," Parker asserted, prodding Cory again; he rose, staggering a little. "Come quickly now."

A deliberate scrape of footwear against plated flooring, a shadow at the corner of Parker's eye.

"Too late, s-ssssweetlings." The Scat blocked the corridor in front of them. The other direction? *His* territory. "Too late for *you*, that is-ss. For me, quite delis-ssshously perfect. Ss-sshe is-ss mine, and now ss-sssso are you."

The child froze, her ears so flat in her head fuzz as to be invisible. Parker shortened Cory's line, looping it up in a deft one-handed maneuver. "She is no one's, and neither am I." The child's hand tightened on hers. "Let us pass. Or did you forget what happened last time?"

"That was-ss lasst time," the Scat observed, quite equitably. "You have come far. I think to find us-ss finissshed before your help arrives-ss." His foot moved to the side in a sudden blur; he bent to it, and straightened with a small station vermin in hand, a thing with glowing red eyes that lasted only another startled squeak longer. The Scat's long snout snapped closed, lifting as he swallowed. "Your small creature will be ssssso much more tender."

Cory interrupted the moment with a small tenor growl, finally coming out of his haze. Dark canine alarm washed through Parker's mind; she would be unable to manage clearly if he roused further. "Security, alert! *Cory Parker!*"

Cory's vest lit the corridor, strobing white and yellow. The Scat hissed displeasure, stepping forward to shake out his loop weapon—but then stopping, glancing over his shoulder . . . taking a step back toward discretion and defeat.

Cory's vest went dark.

The Scat laughed, an unpleasant coughing hiss. "Oh, but they have forssssssaken you!"

Parker felt understanding hit her stomach with the impact of a physical blow. *Randall had canceled the alarm!* Without even knowing why she'd triggered it. He'd *canceled* it!

"Don't get into any trouble today . . . it's not my problem . . ."

They were alone. *Again.*

She had no need to signal the child, or even Cory. She turned and bolted, and they ran with her.

Into the dim spaces that belonged to the Scat.

His coughing laugh followed them, and so did he.

Cory's fear splashed across Parker's mind; she stumbled. The child tugged; Parker followed—stumbled again. Ran and ran and *ran,* barely seeing, following the child's direction—aware that they'd turned left and left and left again, crawled through a smaller junction, surely headed back toward brighter spaces—*surely.* She heard Cory yelp, felt the bright spike of his fear even as the harness line jerked her up short. She spun back to see the line caught in a damaged bulkhead and hit the emergency release, the child's soft, fast panting in her ear.

The Scat's loop weapon slithered out of the darkness to fall across Cory's haunch; freed from the line, he spurted forward. Parker found herself urging him on. *Run, Cory, run! Find* home*! Be safe!*

Because the Scat was closing on them. No matter how hard they ran.

And did they run. Panting and scrabbling and tiring and terrified, and when the child tripped and nearly took Parker down, she swept the little Cervidde up and spurted awkwardly onward, the way bright and getting brighter—

Her foot yanked out from under her; the loop bit into her ankle. She would have fallen on the child had she not twisted wildly aside, all the while crying *run, Cory, run* because wouldn't it be just like Cory to come dancing back in confusion.

Knobby fingers closed around her ankle, sharp nails digging into her skin. "The Csssservidd is-ss *mine*," the Scat said, yanking her back. "*Mine.* I ssstole her long ago and I find her very, very *ussseful.* The very bes-sst thief and ssspy—you s-sshould not have tried to take her!"

"She is not *yours!*" Parker cried, kicking at him. *Run, Cory,* run*!* She could sense little of Cory through her terror, her own sensations finally overwhelming the ones he flung at her. "And Cory will never be yours—*never!*"

The child tried to scramble away and the Scat backhanded her against the corridor without taking his hard black gaze from Parker's. "Then *you* are nothing but trouble, and will die!"

minemineminemine! Cory's bay of fury echoed along the corridor— not distant as it should have been. *Closing.* Parker cried out in dismay as the Scat's head lifted sharply—eagerly. But he recoiled just as quickly, his cough one of dismay, and Parker twisted in what remained of his grip to plant her elbows on the grimy floor and lift her head.

Cory.

But not Cory alone.

Cory, attached to a plas rope and tied off to a ring in the black gleaming carapace of Huido Maarmatoo'kk, disruptor in hand.

Cory, followed by a crowd of familiar faces—vendors and security and even a few well-dressed customers.

Cory, with friends.

All of whom were talking at once as the loop disappeared from Parker's ankle and the Scat slipped hastily away. They babbled that Mellilou had seen the alert and seen Randall cancel it and so called the coordinates to Huido, who'd picked up a mishmash of posse members and then met Cory who insisted on coming back *this* way and here they were, even the two Cervidde gentles who insisted that this disappearance would not happen to someone *else's* child, not while they were here.

Huido picked her up with two careful claw-arms and set her on her feet, upon which Parker burst into tears of relief and then had to pat his carapace and let him know she was fine, that this was a Human sort of thing and it would pass.

And then the little Cervidde child stood up and bleated a heart-rending sound, and ran straight to the arms of the Cervidde couple who had thought they were, after all, rescuing someone else's child.

"I don't . . ." Parker said, looking at them all. Cory wiggled in her arms and pushed his nose against her face for a few quick licks. "I don't really—"

"You're welcome," said Mellilou, knowing Humans best. "And don't think that Randall won't bear consequences for this." A gleam came into her eye. "I believe I'm due a promotion."

"But how—" And Parker looked at them all, filling the corridor with all their sizes and shapes and mobilities. "You all came . . . so quickly . . . and you had no idea . . ." She shook her head. "No one has ever . . ."

Ever.

Mellilou put a hand on her arm as the others crowded around. "But this time, Cory found us," she said simply. "And, Eun Su, *we* found *you.*"

... *Truffles* continues
Interlude

* * *

ON THIS LEVEL, the night zone was dim, noisy, and their boots stuck to something regrettable on the floor every few steps.

Yet there were stars overhead, albeit the Plexis version, and their light rode the waves of Sira's hair, embers of molten gold flowing with her every movement as she led the way between the seemingly random tables and planters the station used to slow traffic. Never inconspicuous, his Witchling, no matter how she tried. Knowing himself hopelessly smitten, glad of it to his core, Morgan smiled, fingers curled at the thought of the warm, silken stuff.

His smile faded, fingers forming fists he deliberately relaxed. Plexis was no place to be distracted. Those who lived and worked here weren't a problem—not more than once, anyway. Morgan focused on the strangers to every side. That cheery in-their-cups band of spacers they were about to pass could turn to trouble with an instant's perceived slight. The gold airtag on the haughty Skenkran beside him had the sheen of a fake, but being out in the open made its business none of his. On Plexis, pickpockets took lifting valuables to a fine art and those convenient planters offered blind spots for more serious threats.

Sira took care to avoid them.

She battled her own demons, Morgan knew, much as she tried

to dismiss them. The First Chosen of the di Sarcs, Speaker for the Clan Council, and now his partner on the *Silver Fox*—her courage, innate Power, and single-minded determination to help her kind had earned those titles. What had happened to her along the way ached in his heart. That it had brought them together, to this, was their shared joy and yes, she was healing. The scars she bore with such courage had begun to fade.

If not those in her mind. Being back on Pocular brought her nothing but nightmares, dreams she tried to hide behind her formidable shields. They were Chosen; even before that bond, he'd experienced her dreams, and now? He'd wake in the jungle, sensing Sira's *pain*—

Sharing it. He should have refused the job. Said no to Huido after the first trip, when he'd seen what returning to that world did to Sira. But she had her pride. Argued they needed the work, the ship needed the parts, Huido needed the truffles. It helped they'd both forget, during the trips to and from, consumed by the urgent joy of discovering one another.

But her nightmares each landing grew worse, not better, and he'd decided before leaving Pocular this load of truffles would be the last. Nothing was worth those painful shadows in her mind.

Shadows within shadows here, Morgan thought, catching the glint of other eyes in the nearest. Watching eyes. He tensed his wrists to drop his force blades into waiting palms, only to still as a face moved forward from the darkness. Enough to be seen.

Enough to be known—

He gave the smallest of nods.

—Gone again.

That he'd been shown the face at all was a warning—or threat. They were, the Human thought in some exasperation, one and the same when it came to Plexis. Odds were this—this *attention* had nothing to do with them or the officious F'Feego at Duties and Tariffs. Yet.

Nonetheless, he took a longer stride to catch up to Sira.

A Traded Secret

* * *

by Donald R. Montgomery

YOU MAY CALL me Morrab the Vermincatcher.

Two other things you should know: I work on Plexis Super-market, and I am not someone you want to meet. Luckily, you're unlikely to, unless you're prone to wandering where you don't be-long. My territory lies beneath the surface—not in Plexis' inhabited levels or its veins and arteries, but the spaces between. I've no inter-est in the crowds of beings who come here to buy and sell wares that range from the cute and harmless to the utterly depraved and ille-gal. My world is dark and lonely: maintenance crawlways and tun-nels where unwelcome creatures are likely to scurry.

As for why I prefer solitude to being in the company of others, I'd say the reaction my appearance elicits from them has a lot to do with it. I don't look much like other members of my species, or any other for that matter. I am Human—genetically speaking—but my growth is stunted, my voice is a dry rasp, and my mouth splits my face in two. Taken with my protruding brow and deep-set eyes, a simple smile from me is toothy, predatory, and grim.

I owe my squashed, four-foot stature to heavy gravity—muscles and bones had to grow thick to support my weight. My warped skeleton bears witness to hundreds of fractures I suffered in in-fancy, while my blood assays reflect a long battle with mismatched drug treatments. One might say I suffered this mistreatment at the claws of an incompetent doctor. However, it was my parents who sold me to an experimental project—one designed to see if children could be made to survive harsher worlds without proper treatment. Given that Human medicine was not the Sakissishee's strong point, I'm lucky to have lived at all.

As for the rest of my scars, I'd say they're split about evenly between youthful stupidity and decades of violent work. The notch missing from my left ear, claw marks that rake across my skull, and the many puckered remnants of stabbings, burns, and ballistic wounds covering my body are only a few of the trophies I've collected guarding fools, hunting bounties, and fighting wars.

Many were near misses—more than a few should have been outright fatal. Luckily, I'm harder to kill than the average Human. One of the few good things about prolonged exposure to heavy gravity and building the strength necessary to survive it is that my tissues and organs are denser and tougher than they should be.

There are costs, of course.

I'm heavy for my size. And bald.

Worse, however, is my susceptibility to weather. Even slight atmospheric changes make me ache something awful. Five years ago I was ready to retire, but then I heard there might be work on Plexis Supermarket for a person of my skills. I'd never admit it, but the station's regulated atmosphere, low humidity, and steady temperatures were the reasons I applied. The salary helps, but it's more a means to an end.

So please remember that while you roam the shopping levels above, rubbing elbows with various alien joints, know that I plumb the depths beneath your feet, scurrying through dark crawlways and over massive tanks of growing prawlies, breathing air heady with a bouquet of rancid gases and keeping company with the ghosts of a mining complex that never was. All so you can revel in the sights and delights only money can buy without having to worry about pest infestations or toothy predators dropping out of the vents.

Because that's what Raj Plexis wants you to do.

She owns Plexis—saved herself from bankruptcy and ridicule by transforming the bulbous husk of a failed mining venture into a bustling commerce ship almost overnight. She didn't have a lot of time for the redesign, so the guts of her ship are a little more haphazard than most. She threw together all the systems needed to maintain a livable environment, not to mention process and purify the waste of dozens of species. She allocated storage space for supplies and inventory, housing complexes for residents and visitors, recyclers to process all our garbage, and servos to manufacture and deliver trinkets and souvenirs to her own stores.

In the years since her garish signs first went up, Plexis has enjoyed significant success. Between reducing her dependence on outside resources and producing most of her branded merchandise locally, she's able to keep the station operational. Which means docking fees, shop leases, tariffs, gifts, bribes, and a host of miscellaneous taxes are almost entirely profit.

Those are just some of the reasons others have chosen to emulate her. As for why no one's undermined what she's built or, worse, staged a hostile takeover—you can thank people like me. We keep the riffraff out, or at least under control. As for the persistent rumor that she's a crime lord—responsible for a variety of unexplained deaths, disappearances, and illegal operations—let's just go with no comment.

I'm part of a defensive network; that's why I spend a significant amount of my time running down pests imported onto the station, accidentally or otherwise. A significant percentage of which happen to be sentient. You might be surprised how often I have to rescue a lost child or pet, but smallish sacks of biology tend to climb into unsecured grates and fall down holes with alarming regularity. And while the dangers are many and the staff are few, I've never failed. Returning each one to the waiting appendages of its anxious breeder/owner is quite rewarding, if only because I charge a substantial fee for the service.

But that's just a sideline.

I stalk more dangerous prey for Plexis: smugglers and thieves attempting to circumvent the station's security cordon or avoid paying their fair share to do business here. I am also known to hunt pirates and murderers—targets too dangerous for normal security to handle. There are plenty of places on this station that don't appear on any schematics, but I've spent years finding them. Some were accidents no one bothered to fix during the redesign, when Raj Plexis had to turn her failed refinery into a bustling marketplace in record time. Others were intentional—she herself marked them off and filled them in. I've seen vaults down there—foreboding places where she keeps her own secrets safe.

As for today, you might think it's odd that the one who runs this roaming colony would meet with someone such as myself. However, the one thing everyone learns about Plexis sooner or later is that this place is anything but normal.

Besides, Plexis is a hands-on kind of boss.

She's dealt with enough trouble over the years to know the value of a reliable throat cutter. Hired muscle is all well and good, but I'm more of a *discreet* agent—the kind that takes care of problems without attracting attention or asking needless questions.

Our bargain is simple: no intermediaries. She briefs and pays me herself, and she pays well. I am, in return, available whenever she needs me.

Plexis' message is never more than a time and place. I recognize the address as a safe house I've visited before. I'm not the only undesirable she has to deal with, so having space prepared for discreet meetings makes sense.

It's disguised as a secure warehouse on one of the mid-sublevels, deep enough that we won't have to worry about gawking tourists. It's also easy enough to reach by tunnel, so I don't have to rub elbows with anyone along the way.

Unfortunately, my only way inside is through the front door. Plexis is smart enough to seal off all other access points, barring a personal lift for herself. Rumor is she's got a network of them throughout the station, giving her access to any point onboard within a few moments.

I wouldn't be surprised if it turned out to be true.

Now, a being in full armor, even a short one, would command some level of attention on the upper decks. Down here I am afforded a small bubble of personal space and barely a glance. Not that I'm ignored; I can feel a variety of eyeballs and stalks tracking my movements as I push the street-level maintenance hatch closed with my foot and seal the lock, but I'm more oddity than threat.

At least no one seems eager to bother me.

It's hard to see anything through the crowd, but traffic is polite enough to shift around me. I suspect that has more to do with my appearance than anything else. Providing I stay below the main concourses, I am permitted to wear protective clothing and carry my weapons openly.

Matte black plates slide over a flexible undercoat as I walk, safe-guarding my vitals without restricting movement. I have a matched tactical helmet, but I left it below. As useful as its sensor feeds and automatic sights are, I'd rather not start a panic or bring station security down on me. Not when I've got two force blades on my belt and an energy pistol strapped to my thigh.

Street traffic parts around me, creating a small eddy. A security patrol spots me and runs my identity—keeps its distance once they verify my ident. I tongue the inside of my cheek reflexively, making sure the airtag on the outside is still there. I don't like the thing, but sharing air is sharing air, and I'd like to keep my job if possible.

It's been an easy few years.

I spend several long minutes out in the open, trudging my way toward the warehouse entrance. I'm not good with even semi-packed streets—too much stimulation. Hawkers yell from their stalls, selling anything and everything at steep discounts. Most of their inventory seems used or damaged—tired and old. Junk cast off from the upper levels.

Discount shoppers mill about, desperate for a deal.

The bazaar thins out toward my destination.

Which is when I sense a disconcerting change in the atmosphere around me.

I can't say it's a smell in the traditional sense—I've become ac-customed to the stench of methane and sulfur and various other waste gases produced by the many species down here—but it's no less real. Tension has a distinct taste. Violence, too.

These little whiffs have kept me alive many, many times. I've side-stepped ambushes, dodged snipers, and laid my own traps for both.

Here my options are limited, so I start cataloging escape routes in my head.

As unlikely as it is, Plexis might be dissatisfied with me, or worse, have figured out—*no*. I consciously shut down that thought before it can bloom. Maintaining control is essential when there could be mindcrawlers about; otherwise I might as well broadcast my secrets over a loudspeaker.

Better to keep my doubts quiet, my betrayals buried.

Even if this turns into a worst-case scenario, she isn't likely to act publicly. Such displays are bad for business. Even down here she'll carefully weigh consequences, potentials, and risks.

This foreboding is coming from somewhere else.

Experience is what saves me. Between my nose and my eyes, I'm able to isolate the source of my misgivings. I show no outward sign, but once I recognize what I'm dealing with, my body relaxes.

There are five studiously unremarkable beings among the regular foot traffic, all doing their best to blend in with the locals. Cheaply dressed and watchful, but not overly so. There are a handful of tells that give them away—tense body language, uniform height, and chiseled physiques; even their bleached, perfect teeth. A shave and a shower would make them all parade ready. Add in how each one has at least one hand buried in a pocket or tucked under a loose-fitting jacket, clutching hidden weapons, and my hunch turns into fact.

Plexis' personal bodyguards.

More than usual, but they're not here to bother me. They're here to make sure no one bothers her. I do her team the courtesy of feigning ignorance while I stride purposefully up to the door and input my code.

The lights come up after I pass over the threshold, flickering awake. The smell of chemical cleaners burns my nostrils. It's always bothered me that the walls and floor are so gray and featureless, coated with nonporous paint. Where there should be tools and machines, long shelves of neatly organized inventory, there's just empty space and periodic drains.

That unnerving monotony is broken only by two features: a wide metal table in the center of the room and a pair of slippers placed neatly on top.

This is a dance I've done before, so I approach the table, unclip my weapons and arrange them carefully. Next come my holsters, armor plates, and spare ammunition—even my gloves and boots. Anything I could theoretically use as a weapon.

I take the slippers, wondering for the hundredth time why Plexis' security thinks my bare hands wouldn't be enough. My size and strength are deceptive given I'm the size of a child, if an extremely wide one, but I wouldn't be here if I didn't know how to use them. *Ha.*

I'll be shot dead if I so much as blink at her wrong. We might meet alone, but that doesn't mean she isn't protected by personal shielding and a twitchy trigger finger or three.

There's a door against the back wall. It clicks open once I've met the conditions for entry. I'd strip naked if I had to, but I'm glad to retain a semblance of dignity. Beyond the door is a short hallway, a scanning chamber loaded with sensors and samplers that check for less visible threats.

It makes sense. Raj's wealth tends to grow at an exponential rate, as do her precautionary measures. Money can buy just about anything, but it comes with its own set of problems. Enemies, grifters and . . . relatives.

The office at the other end is empty, as always. The furnishings are basic—an executive desk flanked by several comfortable chairs and a sitting area off to the side. Couches and low table for less formal engagements. Several amenity stations are set into the wall, offering an assortment of drinks and simple foods. As for what's hidden behind them, I have no idea. At a guess, I'd say it was something between nothing and a full-on administrative installation.

My thoughts on the subject are irrelevant, given my lack of information.

Call them symptoms of impatience—Plexis knows I hate waiting. And she doesn't care.

A little over half an hour passes before she appears.

I know because I count the seconds. I'm at 1,922 when a section of wall slides open and she steps through. The air shimmers around her, a privacy field obscuring any secrets I might see in the space behind it. I've chosen to stand in the corner to the left of the door. I'm not used to bright lights and open spaces, so I prefer to keep my back against something solid. That way I can keep an eye on all possible approaches.

She doesn't seem surprised.

"Morrab." Raj dispenses with pointless formalities and motions me over to the desk. "Delayed." She shrugs. "Merchants." Those clipped words are as close as I'll get to an apology.

"I understand." My voice is a rattle of broken glass. My vocal cords have never liked standard gravity, part of the reason I prefer not to speak whenever possible.

Plexis is not young, but I wouldn't call her old. She's certainly dealing with her years more gracefully than me. Her black hair is speckled with gray and tied back in a bun. There are hints of crow's feet at the corners of her eyes. As for her suit, she's chosen a conservative pale blue today—its one concession to color being a kaleidoscope of red, green, and yellow on its lapels.

She's attractive. Not waif-thin or bony. She has pleasant curves with some meat on her bones.

I sit across from her. My feet dangle off the floor.

Plexis remains standing, her manicured hands resting on the back of her chair. Small hands, with delicate fingers and perfect nails. Word is they were once scarred and callused. She's no stranger to physical work, but the decades she's spent behind a desk have softened them up.

Wealth tends to do that.

"We have a problem." She's opened this way before, but this time my nose itches. Whatever she's about to say isn't good. "You've been digging where you don't belong, selling information you shouldn't have."

My insides twist, flush with adrenaline, but I show no outward sign of it. I've spent years learning how to suppress my reactions. Plexis will have scanners pointed at me, measuring every meaningful physiological variable and weighing them against the profile created during my previous visits. Or she should have. It's what I would do.

I expected this day to come if not nearly so soon.

I don't deny the accusation. Instead, I nod slowly, buying precious seconds.

Behind that calm exterior, my mind races, the question of how to play this rampaging through my synapses. I can lie; I'm good at it. I might even fool her readouts. Even a telepath or two. Except I don't know what evidence she has against me—how wide the gulf is between what she suspects and what she already knows.

Considering the work I've done for her, this conversation is not to be taken lightly.

I clear my throat and I meet her gaze. "I wondered when you'd find out." My admission is straightforward.

Truthful.

She breaks that contact first. "Have I been unfair to you?" When she looks at me again, her face is calm. It's her eyes that have hardened. "I pay you well."

"You do." A dozen plans flicker through my head. Attack or run. Bargain or beg. I toy with different combinations, but each one leads me to the same result.

Failure.

Death or disappearance.

I wouldn't be the first to survive her anger and never be seen again. Dying is a relatively quick punishment compared to a lifetime of suffering. And who would miss me, if I never emerge from this room? Each time I ask myself that question, my answer is the same. And equally depressing.

"Have I ever cheated you?" she asks.

"No, Fem."

"Is this a revenge thing?" I suspect she's been stung before.

"No." She's never hurt me personally, and I don't care enough about anyone else to carry a grudge.

"Then why do this?" She finally takes her seat, dropping heavily into the padded leather. Not a smart thing to do unless she is extremely confident I can't hurt her. "Well?" Her voice rises when I don't answer her immediately. She's getting frustrated.

Might as well go for broke.

"How much do you know?" My question catches her off guard.

"You're asking me— Do you even understand the position you're in right now?" she fires back.

"I do." I've done plenty of dirty work for her. "However, I have contractual obligations to consider." I might not have the resources to invest in gathering a full psychological profile of her, but I've studied her as much as she's studied me during our sporadic conversations. I didn't just dig up and package her past. I've cataloged her tells, the cracks in her façade, and sold them as well. What matters now is whether she knows who I've sold them to.

Because trade and its inherent risks are as much about what you know as what you have. What an opponent has done or is doing is far less valuable than what they're *going* to do. Markets—physical and metaphorical—are largely the same. Success depends on correctly judging the ebb and flow of supply versus demand. Which means having an edge on your competitors, no matter how slight, can be the difference between profit and ruin.

Plexis knows this better than anyone. She'd be ten times the information broker I am if she wanted to be. But she's smart enough to recognize the size of the target on her back already.

Which is probably why we're still talking—she'll want to know who's aiming at her.

"You work on my ship, Morrab. For me. I *own* everything you do." Whatever she really thinks and feels, she's got a good enough poker face to hide most of it. "You aren't allowed to have other contracts."

"I'm afraid that's not entirely true. I was hired as an occasional contractor, a classification that frees you from traditional employer obligations. Taxes, benefits, and the like. It also permits you to charge me for the space I occupy, the food I eat, and the air I breathe." I slowly raise my hand and brush my airtag. "There are certain advantages on my side, such as retaining my independence. Basically, whenever I work for you—from the moment I accept a task to the instant you pay me for it—I am everything you want me to be: loyal, discreet, thorough. At all other times, I owe you nothing."

"*Clareid?*" Plexis asks the ceiling. "Tell him he's wrong."

We sit in momentary silence while her employment specialist digests my statement.

"I am unable to do so." Clareid, I assume, answers. "He negotiated terms—significant cost savings in return for greater freedom. Further discussions should take place over private channel."

"Who signed off on his contract?" Plexis' tone has changed. Now she's clearly angry—and dangerous.

"Your nephew."

"Fire him." Whatever her staff was about to say is lost under that command. "All right, Morrab, I knew you were clever when I hired you. Fair enough." She swipes the space over the desk and taps a series of commands into the holographic pad that materializes there. "Why don't we change the game."

No armored thugs burst in.

No gas assaults my lungs and no needle injects venom.

Instead, several wall panels retract, revealing automated turrets. High energy emitters–the kind that vaporize flesh. She's got at least three of them pointed at me. I don't dare turn around to see if there are more at my back.

"We're alone now," she continues. "No cameras, no security. Just the two of us."

"And the weapons."

"I've seen you work. I know what you're capable of."

"Likewise."

"Then let's cut to the chase, shall we?" She doesn't state the obvious: that she could kill me here and now, and no one would ever find my body. "You had my trust yesterday." Plexis says plainly. "I thought I had your loyalty. Now what's left? An old witch and a crusty goblin. You and I, we've seen enough problems to know how to deal with them. We should be able to figure this out." She's changed tack; the threat is still there, but she's moved on to bartering. Hopefully, that's a positive sign. "Good help is hard to find, and frankly you've been useful these past five years. Nevertheless, you know I can't have an unknown element on my team. So, start talking."

"You have more enemies than allies." I shift uneasily in my seat, careful to keep my movements at a minimum. There's no comfortable position with weapons pointed at you.

"I'm aware." Plexis is an important person. She regularly receives trade envoys and diplomats from the various worlds and stations, each one hoping for a stop along her route, and each one as devious as they come. But those aren't her only problems. Pirates and smugglers, tax cheats and rowdy passengers—her supermarket may be a bastion of commerce, but she's assailed on all sides. Hells, my job is to deal with the least savory types—chasing off those who repeatedly break the rules and outright killing the ones who decide to use weapons instead of learning from their mistakes.

"You also know some are more powerful than others." Has she felt that ebb and flow, the webs that touch and bind her business? "Some of those, nobody fights."

"So you're being blackmailed?"

"Hah." My laugh is empty. "They don't blackmail. They instruct. They command. And because I know what they are, I obey."

"You're not making any sense."

She doesn't know. I'm almost giddy with that realization.

"Good." I mean it. "We should leave it at that. You can ban me from the station, and I'll book passage on the next outward ship." I know she won't. That's why I make the offer.

"You dangle a secret like that and expect me not to bite?" She laughs. "I could kill you now."

"Fem Plexis, if I tell you what I know, there's no going back. And you'll need help. Mine, specifically. You'll have to keep me around." Time to make my play. Hopefully, it works.

"I doubt that."

"Don't say I didn't warn you." While this might save my life, I'm still in dangerous territory.

There are stories about a cabal manipulating events from the shadows, but few would admit to believing them. I am one of those few. But I know they're real. I've had the misfortune of meeting one, of seeing and speaking with a God. What else can I call a being who materialized out of thin air? Who damned near killed me for the transgression?

Only he didn't. He—Yihtor di Caraat—let me live because I made myself useful. That's how I learned they're not omnipotent. Powerful enough to be feared, but not everywhere all the time.

Not Gods, but Plexis doesn't need to know that.

"Fine." I rasp. "Let me tell you about the Clan."

...*Truffles* continues

3

* * *

I TOOK AN easier breath when Morgan stepped close. I'd no specific concern this instant, other than to avoid having my foot stepped on and likely crushed by a passing, preoccupied Norsenturtle—but this wasn't my home.

It was his. Plexis was the closest thing to a base the *Fox* had, Huido her captain's only family. Morgan was known here, had connections throughout the station, most especially on levels like this where most tags were blue and spacers outnumbered customers. Little wonder he'd chatted with the sombay seller. There were many who acknowledged our—his—passing: be it a scowl from security or a cheery wave of a staffer's tentacle. Morgan responded to each with a casual familiarity I envied.

While I'd lived in deliberate isolation in the Cloisters, even from most of my kind, this solitary Human had accumulated a staggering array of friends—and their opposite. How could he not? My Chosen, I thought with a very unClan-like pride, wasn't a person to overlook another's need or ignore what harmed others.

As for the predators here? And there were, of course. They knew better than to show him their faces. Except, I thought grimly, for a certain official, and took a moment to imagine its likely reaction had we 'ported right into the Duties & Tariffs office, except I'd no idea where or what that was—

So serious. Fingers slipped between mine and gave a gentle tug. "Forget E'Teiso. Let's go dancing."

I stared at him. "Pardon?"

Morgan spun around to walk facing me, deftly leading us around the Norsenturtle who, fortunately, appeared paralyzed by such behavior in a Human. I empathized. "Dance, Witchling." He took possession of my other hand.

Music thumped, thudded, and wailed from all sides, luring— or driving—patrons from the assorted clubs, bars, and other establishments lining the night zone. None of it appealed, but when Morgan smiled at me, I couldn't help smiling back. Playful wasn't his public face—until now, apparently. "Huido will know we've docked," I pointed out in a last effort to be sensible. "He'll expect us."

"And we'll get there when we're ready." His smile widened as he looked over my shoulder. "Perfect. There's Daniel, one of Rose's. He'll run a message for us." Morgan swung us around. "Dance with me, Witchling."

I planted my feet to forestall another spin, feeling a sudden *chill*. The last—and first—time I'd danced had been in the Poculan jungle, admittedly with more vigor and sweat than grace.

Until the night shattered into tragedy. *Jason, I can't—*

His face altered, and I knew that mix of impatience and compassion: I'd missed some essential truth. *We treasure our friends for how they lived, Witchling.*

He was my teacher in more than trader life. I nodded, swallowing grief, doing my best to remember laughter and the beat of drums. I managed a tremulous smile. "Dancing it is."

"Good. Daniel!"

A tall Human seemed to materialize out of the surrounding crowd, though it hardly seemed possible I'd missed him earlier. A brilliantly colored lock of hair drooped over his forehead and the spacer coveralls he wore made mine look new. His age eluded me. Younger than my Human, but with the same too-controlled expression. Until he grinned. "Hey, Morgan. Whaz happening?"

"Excuse us." Taking Daniel aside, Morgan spoke to him quickly, then returned to me. "We're set."

I glanced back to find our messenger had melted back into the crowd.

Anisoptera With a Side Order of Soft Blast

* * *

by Fiona Patton

SUBLEVEL 84 SPINWARD ⅓ of Plexis Supermarket was crowded, noisy, dingy, and smelled of . . . fourteen-year-old Daniel Kekoa considered and discarded several profane descriptions before settling on . . . feet; alien feet. The fluorescent blue trim on his shaggy black hair flopping into his eyes, he glared at the Tolian spice merchant across from him, then slapped a plas sheet down on the counter beside a pile of packages, the holographic tattoo of a spaceship flying from a sun going supernova on the golden skin of his forearm winking in and out of the red-and-orange solar flares.

"Where's the twenty percent merchant discount, Faz?" he demanded between gritted teeth.

One four-fingered hand waved dismissively at him. "No discount!" the Tolian retorted haughtily through his throat com. "You're no merchant."

Daniel kept a rein on his temper. "They're for Rose. They're always for Rose," He leaned forward, his heavy boots giving him height on the other being. "They've always been for Rose every thruster-burned month for the last thruster-burned year. You. Know. That."

"I don't know that!" Faz shot back, his iridescent red-and

-blue–feathered crest snapping back and forth. "You're probably selling them! You probably don't even know Rose! You take them at full price, or I'll sell them elsewhere!"

"Space that! I take them with the twenty percent discount, or I take Rose's business—all of her business—to Gerloff one level up! He doesn't try and cheat other Plexis merchants which, trust me, everyone you and Rose deal with is gonna hear about!"

Faz opened his beak to give another stinging retort, before one large emerald eye turned to focus on a figure slouching in through the shop door.

"No, no, no, no! You not being coming in here!" he shrieked, his sudden outrage garbling his usually flawless Comspeak. "There being no living creatures in here! I'm being telling you before, I being selling no living creatures! Only spices! You go! Go now!"

Daniel glanced over his shoulder. The figure that had generated such anger was a kid about his own age, skin almost luminescently pale, green hair standing up in wild spikes save for a single lock that dropped down in front of a pair of narrowed blue eyes. He wore secondhand, cutoff spacer trousers two sizes two big for him, a retro gray T-shirt with the words "Eat the Rich" emblazoned across the front in lurid orange letters, and red plas wrist guards. He held a small device in his hand, which he waved menacingly at the shopkeeper.

Faz nearly choked on his fury. "No weapons in here! I being calling security!"

The young Human gave him a chilly smile, the line of temporary mood gem decals on his upper teeth flashing a dangerous yellow. "Coma-down, back-beak, it's not a weapon," he sneered. "it's a scanner. Just making sure you're complying with all the Plexis and Trade Pact regulations governing the trafficking of living creatures."

"Not being your business, not being your business!" Faz screeched back. "I being calling security!"

The shouting was starting to attract a crowd, and Daniel shook his head in disgust. "Faz. Faz!" He banged his palm on the counter. "Rose's discount!"

The Tolian snapped one eye around while keeping the other trained on the Human in the doorway as he sauntered a few steps into the shop, waving the scanner in the direction of the back room.

"Fine, fine!" Faz snarled, snatching up the plas sheet. "You being getting discount and going! You being telling Rose, I being having no more her hatchlings in here; no more!" He changed the amount and threw it back at him, panting in agitation.

The transaction complete, Daniel scooped up the parcels, depositing them into a bag on his shoulder before dropping a small cloth bundle on the counter. "From Rose. She heard your brood sibs were visiting and thought you might want something for your nerves."

The Tolian snorted loudly, but the fluttering of his vestigial neck feathers noticeably calmed. "Sure, sure, nerves, frustration, temper, whatever," he muttered. "They've gone home now." But he scooped the bundle up anyway, breathing in the scent of bertwee oil with obvious pleasure. "Tell Rose there's a big shipment coming in next week from Letis III. Good stuff. Many savings."

"I'll tell her. See you then." Daniel left without bothering to acknowledge the person who was still waving his scanner about with an air of mock authority.

He merged effortlessly into the crowded concourse, avoiding half a dozen grav carts and as many bundle-laden servos weaving their way through the multitude of peoples before reaching a plain, gray pillar covered in plas flyers. As he leaned against it with a calculated air of bored indifference, the other joined him, the untied laces of his boots slapping against the floor announcing his approach before he appeared. He nodded amiably to a group of Turrned Missionaries handing out small plas tracts before vaulting over a line of scraggy bushes.

Daniel glanced over at him.

"Hey, Jack,"

"Hey, Dazer. S'all right?"

"S'all right as starlight."

"You get it?"

"Oh, yeah. He was so novaed up by your little toy there that he totally miswrote it just like you figured." He showed the plas sheet to his companion. "Twenty-five percent off. Rose'll be happy."

"Sonic." Jack's gaze suddenly focused on the concert imprint on Daniel's T-shirt. His eyes widened.

"Thought you hated Soft Blast music?"

"Got four at seventy-five percent off at *The Be There Shop*. The band's playing a one-day gig here next week, and the shop misprinted about fifty shirts."

"I'll say. They spelled After-BRNR wrong, and the Neblokan in the band doesn't even play the keffleflute."

"And the color's putrid, too, but they were cheap, so . . ." Daniel shrugged. "What's your excuse?" he asked, jerking his chin toward Jack's shirt. "Thought you were a vegan?"

"Yeah, well. For them, I'd make an exception."

"Any one in particular?"

"A few in particular, but I'll let Wark explain it to you. He's waiting for us back at Rose's."

Daniel glanced at the grim set of Jack's jaw.

"Something's happened."

"Not happened and won't happen."

"Do we need to pick up supplies?"

"Later. Wark'll have most of his shopping list ready by now, but like I said, I'll let him explain it to you. I'll just blow my jets again if I tried."

"Fair enough."

Daniel headed back into the crowded concourse, Jack falling into step beside him. Jack's temper was legendary, especially if it involved what he'd called "the trafficking of living creatures," but Daniel had seen the mood gems sparkling the pale blue of extreme distress and wondered if Jack knew how much they actually revealed about him. Probably not, and he probably wouldn't care even if Daniel told him. Other people's opinions about him meant nothing to Jack.

They ducked through a service door a few moments later; after ensuring that they were alone and that no vermin were lurking in dark corners, their glittering, red-eyed stare promising a nasty bite to anyone stupid enough to approach them, they followed a series of labyrinthine corridors swarming with servo transports, messengers, and tankers. Daniel paused now and then to check his tiny, hand-painted symbols on the walls and to ensure the security vids in the areas they were traveling were still in need of repairs before they swarmed up a ladder for three levels. Another maze of corridors, another ladder, and they emerged into an entirely new section. From there, they caught a ramp.

It took nearly half an hour to reach their destination; Upper Retail Level 104, spinward ¾. The concourse here was wider, the floors shinier, with delicate fountains and tall decorative shrubbery in heavy, silver-colored planters, and warm golden lighting creating areas of quiet privacy for shoppers who were, to Daniel's eyes, also wider and shinier. The shops themselves were big and bright with invitingly open doors and neatly arranged racks of goods displayed on either side of genuine glass display windows.

Station security was also more pronounced here, but they purposely ignored them. Despite their appearance, Jack and Daniel traversed this level under the auspices of one of the richest merchants on Plexis, and security knew it. Weaving through the plants, they made for a large shop situated between an expensive wine seller and a high end art gallery. Above the opaque crimson glass doors, a beautifully hand-painted sign spelled out *Rose Red's Tree of Life Emporium*.

Quiet music and the delicate odor of warmed spices wrapped about them as they reached the door. It opened soundlessly at their approach, causing an involuntary relaxation of Daniel's muscles. He glanced over to see the perpetual scowl on Jack's face smooth to one approximating relative peace. They were safe here. They were, as much as either of them could admit to it, home.

A trio of tiny bells sounded as they crossed the threshold, causing the soft portlights to brighten just enough for them to see inside. The front showroom was wide, taking up twice the floor space of most shops even on this level. Crystals, wind chimes, and small handwoven tapestries depicting trees and arcane symbols hung from the ceiling, while racks of caftans, scarves, wraparounds, and voluminous silk trousers took up the center. One wall held shelves of actual books and vids, while the other contained glass cases filled with all manner of candles, incense, incense burners, spices in colorful cloth bags, and ceramic bowls of potpourri. Tables scattered about displayed packs of cards, polished stones of various sizes and colors, and small animal statuary. Toward the back, several easi-rests were filled with customers of one species or another, all reading books and drinking steaming beverages from tiny porcelain cups. On the back wall, an alcove to the right contained various musical objects: flutes, finger chimes, shakers, and reed pipes on the upper shelves, with music stands, cases, and stacks of sheet music on the lower. The alcove to the left held old-fashioned art supplies ranging from real wooden brushes and pots of paint to hand-carved pens and tiny bottles of ink. Two central doorways covered in beaded curtains led to various back rooms, some open, some closed. Daniel glimpsed movement in the nearest and knew Terval's *Tee-Can-Do* class was still in session. Near the front door, beside a basket of cloth bags decorated with the store's tree symbol, stood a polished wooden counter; a state-of-the-art retail reader on one side, and a rack of candy sticks on the other. The Human female behind the counter, her thick, curly white hair liberally streaked with neon pink, wore a garish orange sweater covered in holographic sequins and a multi-colored pleated silk skirt. She was short and plump; her deep, honey-golden skin, some four shades darker than Daniel's, was lined with fine wrinkles and dappled with flower tattoos. Her dark eyes, sparkling with the memory of a mischievous and joyful childhood, lit up still further when she spied the pair.

They ambled over, Daniel slipping behind the counter to deposit the packages underneath along with the two Emporium business airtags he and Jack had been using.

"Hey, Rose."

"Hey, yourself, sweet-pie. And how's my darling Jotherion today?"

Jack rolled his eyes, both at the endearment and at his given name, but smiled despite himself. "All right as portlights, Rose. You?"

"Sunny and centered as always, dear one." She paused to accept payment for a small carved pipe and a packet of herbs from a Vilix customer, wrapping it carefully in one of the Emporium tote bags for him before returning her attention to them. "Everything go smoothly with Faziquan?"

Daniel nodded. "He squawked a bit, but it's all starlight."

"Good. I hope the bertwee oil helps. He's always so unsettled when his brood sibs visit."

"He's over it. He mentioned the shipment coming in from Letis III. Looks like we'll have first pick."

"That's very kind of him. Are you two hungry?"

In the process of tearing open a ration tube with his teeth, Jack grinned widely, his mood gems flashing a greedy, bright green. "Always."

"The *Leaf Basket Cafe* held a workshop last night and there's plenty of veggie pies left, unless Warren's finished them all . . ."

Rose chuckled as Jack headed for the back immediately, but held out one beringed hand to forestall Daniel from following just yet.

"Warren's got my storeroom covered with plas sheets and blueprints," she said quietly. "Will I be having security knocking at my door today?"

Daniel frowned, remembering Jack's grim expression. "Probably not, but . . ."

"Say no more for now, just keep me informed, okay?"

"Will do."

Rose turned as a waft of nostril-burning . . . the closest comparison Daniel had ever managed was rotten potatoes dipped in Retian pond scum . . . drifted over to them. "Berle, put that down please. I've told you three times, it's a *Barsium* egg; it's *not* for eating."

She brushed past Daniel, making for a Lemmick customer holding the object in question in one delicate hand.

Checking to be sure the air filters were on—Rose was notorious for forgetting to activate them when she opened the shop—Daniel followed Jack, careful to keep upwind of Berle.

Unlike the front, the Emporium's storeroom was modern and well protected by a heavy door that was pass-code and palm-lock protected. Daniel didn't manage to catch up to Jack before it snicked closed behind him. By the time he got in and reached the table at the far side of the room, Jack had piled most of the veggie pies onto a plate and was pouring cold sombay into a self-warming cup. Daniel grabbed the last two pies and turned.

"Hey, Wark."

The last of their group, Human, same age but larger, was seated at a table covered in plas sheets. He waved distractedly at him. Tall and muscular, he was dressed in cutoff spacer trousers similar to the others, but rather than Jack's retro T-shirt and Daniel's cast-off concert misprint, he wore a plain sleeveless purple tank top that Jack had once accused him of wearing just to show off the muscles of his arms and shoulders. Warren hadn't bothered to deny it. His hair was much shorter than theirs at the sides, with a stiff strip of bone-white bristles stretching from forehead to the nape of his neck and ending in a thick long braid, that threw his dark brown skin and glittering black eyes into sharp relief.

"Did you tell him?"

His mouth filled with food, Jack shook his head.

"Right." Warren caught up a remote, pointed it at the viswall behind the food table, then frowned.

"Pull that plas ad down, will you, Dazer?"

Once Daniel had tossed the offending flyer for Plexis' latest anonymous clinic, Jack called down the portlights, and Warren pressed the start button.

"YOUR LOVED ONES ARE IMPORTANT TO YOU, ESPE-CIALLY IN DEATH. SEND THEM OFF WITH A MEMORABLE TRIBUTE, TAILORED TO YOUR INDIVIDUAL NEEDS, BY THE CARING PROFESSIONS AT CARDALE, MORLON, AND PIX FUNERARY SERVICES!"

The ad-vid continued in slightly less strident tones, showing scenes of weeping peoples comforted by three somberly clad be-ings amid a variety of sites from grassy hills and small lakes to factory-style crematoriums and vast banquet halls.

"AND NOW, OUR NEWEST SITE LOCATED IN A PRIME UPPER LEVEL OF THE LEGENDARY PLEXIS SUPERMARKET, IS ABLE TO OFFER AN EXCLUSIVE SYMBOLIC EVENT GUAR-ANTEED TO BRING SOLACE TO EVEN THE MOST BEREAVED FAMILY MEMBER!"

The viswall filled with the image of a luxury yacht with a group of apparently grieving beings huddled together before a wide view-port. While appropriately serious music tinged with a note of anticipation played in the background, a dozen searchlights suddenly illuminated the blackness of space, an air lock opened, and the group of beings gasped as a vast swarm of iridescent insects shot out to cover the viewport in a shimmering curtain of living color, then, one by one, burst apart in a spray of brilliant crimson, emerald and sapphire. The group gasped again, and one of them, a Human female with dark makeup about her eyes *realistically* smudged from tears, threw her arms wide in an outpouring of emotion.

"IT'S SO BEAUTIFUL!"

"CARDALE, MORLON, AND PIX; FULFILLING THE FUNERARY NEEDS OF THE GALAXY ELITE. CONTACT US TODAY!"

The vid froze on the faces of the three soberly clad beings, then shut off. The glow-in-the-dark tattoos on Warren's face sparkled for an instant before he called up the portlights again.

"They're Anisoptera," Jack said, the flatness of his tone belied by the pale blue of his mood gems. "They're native to every continent on Ladin V where they're known as Rainbow-cloaks."

"The funeral company called them *Parvus-flies* in their ad-vids," Warren added quietly. "It means . . ."

"It means cheap, ignorable, unimportant!" Jack snarled. "The Ladin V Anisoptera can grow up to the length of my arm, with double wing pairs three times that length. They can live up to eighteen planetary years, camouflage their flight paths, migrate across entire oceans, and fly faster than an aircar with a nine G acceleration on sharp turns. They have incredibly complex life stages. They can eat half their weight in insects every day. They're not unimportant! During mating flights, the clusters are so big they almost blot out the sun, covering the entire landscape in rainbows. They're not ignorable either!"

He threw himself into a chair, panting with rage.

"And they're being exploited and killed in the vacuum of space by three greedy waste-holes trying to suck as many creds as possible out of a bunch of elitist waste-holes," Warren added.

Daniel glanced from one to the other.

"So when is this *newest site* opening, Wark?"

"In four station days."

"Where?"

Warren caught up a plas sheet.

"Upper Level 231, spinward ¾," he read. "They have four docks, one for deliveries, one for themselves, and two that link up to private corridors—one that brings clients to their facilities and one that takes them to that viewing yacht we saw in the ad-vid. It's already here." He tossed another plas sheet; a schematic of the level in question, across the table.

Daniel studied it. "Yeah, I know the site. It used to be an exotic catering company."

"Chewy something."

"*Chew-able Luxuries.* The CEO embezzled it into bankruptcy and flew off to some non-Trade Pact planet."

Jack made a rude noise.

"Have they got a first . . . *event* booked?" Daniel asked.

"In six station days."

"Who's the client?"

Warren shuffled through the plas sheets. "*Lithe-Lime Athletic Wear.* You know them?" he asked when Daniel whistled.

"Yeah. They have three retail stores here on Plexis plus their own delivery dock, a satellite office, a restaurant, and a host of expensive hotel suites."

"They the ones with that stupid ad slogan?" Jack asked suddenly.

"Yeah. '*Lithe-Lime,* Your Life-line to a Better Life,' " Daniel sneered. "Seems to me I heard that some vice president of theirs kicked it. So, what's the plan?"

"Stop *Cardale, Morlon, and Pix* from operating on Plexis," Warren answered.

Jack nodded his agreement. "Stop 'em, crush 'em, and drive 'em out. Plus punch *Lithe-Lime* in the nose for being a bunch of elitist waste-holes."

"That's a pretty tall order. How?"

"We break it down, one job at a time as always. First, recon." Warren pointed at Daniel. "I need to know when the Anisoptera are coming in, how they're being transported—it'll probably be in a tripbox, but I need to know its dimensions and where—" He made a face at the thought of repeating the long list of names, "—where C. M. P. are storing it. I also need the itinerary of both companies around the event and any other programming; how many staff, how long their shifts are and where, and if they're operating on a daytime/nighttime schedule. I have an idea how to get the Anisoptera back to Ladin V, but I'm gonna have to do some more thinking about that."

He pointed at Jack. "I need security personnel schedules and security tech. That's part one."

As if on cue, the room's com buzzed. Jack reached up and hit the receive button.

"Are you decent, sweeties? Can I interrupt?"

"Sure, Rose."

She bustled in, catching up a bright green shawl from a hook by the viswall before waving at them. "I'm off. Can you lads look after the shop? Myrtle, Paige, and I are having a Business Co-op meeting at the *Exalted Goddess Tea Room,* and then we're going clubbing. If you get hungry, there's a pot of veggie stew in the back kitchen. The one on the right, not the one on the left. That's patchouli oil for the candles. Share it with any customers hanging around at meal time. The stew, not the oil. Try not to stay open too late, but if you do, please don't play any of Atomic Planet's newer songs, okay? It sets off the crystals. Try their earlier, more conceptual work." She gave them what amounted to a shrewd look for Rose, but it mostly came across as slightly worried. "If you use the comp for anything other than business, take the usual precautions, use the secondary password, that sort of thing. No one's staying upstairs, so feel free to sleep there. I wish you lads would decide to live in. There's plenty of room, and I'd feel better knowing you were all safe, but make up your own minds, of course." She kissed each of them on the cheek. "Warren's in charge. Terrah, lovies."

She bustled out again.

"Add a bit of Rose to your day for health and happiness," Jack murmured, his mood gems flashing a warm purple.

"Sonic." Warren headed for the door. "I'll take the counter; like

I said, I've got some thinking to do. You two get busy with the recon. I'll need it by tonight."

Daniel and Jack nodded.

"There's gonna be about forty of them, all mid-level execs, arriving the day after tomorrow," Daniel reported. "They've booked a whole luxury package with the station: spas, shopping, banquets, workouts, and seminars, ending with the event. It's all there." He handed Warren a plas sheet. "A freighter called the *Trident* out of Ormagal Prime is bringing the Anisoptera by tripbox, like you figured; stasis to keep 'em dormant. Here's the dimensions. They're due to dock beside the yacht two days after *Lithe-Lime* comes in."

"Regs, Jack?"

Daniel and Warren hushed expectantly as the other pulled an old, much battered book from his pocket. Jack's father, a notoriously intractable Port Authority Inspector, had disappeared six years before while fighting the trafficking of sapients by Recruiters. His manual of Trade Pact regulations was all that Jack had of him, and the son knew each and every one of the father's *tenets of behavior,* how they were enforced, and how their loopholes were exploited. And the best way to get a punch in the head was to even look like you were going to call his father a Port Jelly. Now he straightened, cupping the book in his hands the way a Turrned Missionary might clasp a theological relic.

"There's no reg for the symbolic murder of a whole group of innocent creatures," he said with some heat. "And the Anisoptera don't fall under any endangered or destructive reg. Because a group on Ladin V still uses 'em in their Adult Initiation feasts, C. M. P.'s legal lackies classed them under the Interspecies Food Transport regs on their Plexis Entry Request docs rather than the Live Product or Live Promotional regs 'cause they're a lot less strict. The specs on the tripbox they're using fall within range. We can't use regs. Even the latest updates won't help."

He put the book away and, as if released from a religious rite, Daniel shook himself.

"The tripbox'll be unloaded first and transported to C. M. P.'s facility. The layout's here." He passed over another plas sheet. "It's a retrofit from *Chew-able Luxuries*. They have four coolers and two freezers behind the showroom to the left of the offices and viewing rooms. C. M. P. are using the freezers for bodies and the coolers for food and things like keeping the Anisoptera dormant."

"Security tech?"

"Nothing we can't bypass with the right pass-cards," Jack sniffed dismissively. "And they're easy enough to get."

Daniel passed over another plas sheet. "C. M. P.'s staff and itinerary. They're having an open house and then a private party after the opening catered by *Claws & Jaws*. All in all, about twenty-four beings. They're on a shifting day/night schedule; station norm for now, but that changes to suit their clientele. *Lithe-Lime* works on the Camos timeline since that's where their headquarters are."

He broke off to head into the back kitchen, reappearing with a huge plate of pastries. "There's no more stew," he announced mournfully. "I knew we shouldn't have let the Random Rocks rep have seconds."

"Security schedules." Once Daniel'd taken a seat, Jack dumped an entire pile of plas sheets on the table. Warren glared at him, and he snickered. "Don't have colon collapse, okay. They're in order: docking, C. M. P.'s level, and any other security schedules that might be useful for the next week, especially on this level."

Warren nodded. "Okay," he said, catching up a pastry. "I'll need to digest all this, but we can move on to the Supplies stage for now. First, since we can't hijack the tripbox . . . What?" he asked when the other boys gave him an incredulous look. "How'd you figure we'd get away with that, never mind hide it and then get it on a transport outta here?"

"So how're we gonna get the Anisoptera away?" Daniel asked.

"I told you; I have an idea about that. It's not thrashed out fully yet, but trust me, it'll work. But we need a way to get into the tripbox. Getting the pass-codes would be good, but a way to make it look like the security and temperature controls failed would be best, 'cause we're probably gonna have to revive them first. If not, we'll have to go in with a simple smash-grab-and-stash and wait till they wake. For that, we'll need a specialty tool."

"Like a biodisruptor, only for metal?" Jack asked, stuffing a pastry into his mouth and spewing crumbs across the table.

Warren brushed them off his plas sheets. "Yeah, like that."

"Easy-peasy translight-squeezy. Let me know when you need it."

Warren frowned at him. "Try for the codes first, then the big weapon, okay?" He sat back. "The next thing we need is an alibi, something public. We're jumping the blast cube on this a bit 'cause I haven't figured out the best time to liberate the Anisoptera yet, but I'm open to alibi ideas that'll keep security off our backs, especially after."

Jack grinned widely, the mood gems flashing a deep, mischievous orange. "I've got the perfect one."

Daniel stared down at the three retro-style rectangular concert plas tickets in horror.

"No, no, no, NO!"

"You sound like Faz," Jack snickered.

"Now I know how he feels. No!"

"It's a great idea."

"I hate AfterBRNR! You know I hate AfterBRNR!"

"The whole station knows you hate AfterBRNR," Warren observed dryly.

"You already have the T-shirts," Jack continued. "We each wear one. We go in the front, Kibibi sneaks us out the back—she'll do it; she likes me."

"You wish," Warren snorted. "Kibibi likes Fems."

"Not likes me like that, likes me like she likes me, like she thinks I'm a nice guy."

"Can't imagine why," Daniel muttered.

"Because I am a nice guy, that's why. Quit interrupting. We do the job, Kibibi sneaks us back in the back, and we waltz out the front when the concert's over. And what's even better . . ." He paused for dramatic emphasis. "Constable Hutton's working the front door; before and after the concert. We make sure she sees us, and we've got the best witness we could ask for. Everyone on Plexis knows she can't be bought. If she says she saw us going in and coming out, no one'll question it. You could even complain about how much you hate AfterBRNR as we go past her to make sure she notices us. After that, we'll have an entire theater's worth of witnesses to draw on."

"Why, are you planning to force us to rush the stage?"

"If that's what it takes!"

"Forget it!"

"Stop being such a whiny baby!"

"You stop being such a sphincter!"

"Enough!" Warren's shout spun them both around. "It's perfect, we're doing it, get over it."

Daniel glared at him, then dropped into a chair with a disgusted expression. "I hate Soft Blast music," he muttered. "It gives me ear hives."

"So now we have the date for the job," Warren said, pointedly ignoring him. "We still need to crack the tripbox, though." He stood. "But tomorrow. It's late. I'm gonna catch some zees." He headed for the back door. "You two sleeping here?"

Daniel nodded, but Jack shook his head. "I got things to do."

"Okay. Don't forget to reset the pass-code for whatever door you go through, and try not to get arrested if you get into a fight. We don't want your security contacts ticked off at you this week."

"Yes, Rose. No, Rose. I'm a big boy, Rose, I know how to keep outta trouble, Rose."

Warren rolled his eyes. "Dazer's right," he noted. "You are a sphincter."

Jack just blew him a loud kiss before heading out the front.

The next day, Daniel was working the counter while Rose explained the use of essential oils to counteract deep space fur-frizz to a group of Turrneds, when Jack slouched in.

"Any luck on the codes?"

"Not yet."

The afternoon was the same. Warren tidied all his plans away and took the counter while Jack assisted Rose with her ceramics class in the storeroom and Daniel manned the comp. When the shop closed, Warren took over the system, while Rose directed

Daniel through a dizzying amount of inventory and Jack stocked shelves.

The second day went no better. Jack spent most of the day running errands for his security contacts and spying on the *Lithe-Lime* execs swarming the station like a crowd of tall, fit, Turrned Missionaries preaching the benefits of regular exercise. Daniel had to meet with three of Rose's suppliers, leaving Warren to move between customers, counter, comp, and Rose. When they finally met in the backroom over flatbread and *sarlas* paste, Warren pushed back from the table with a weary sigh.

"Okay, that's a crash landing. We go to Plan B."

Jack grinned, mouth awash with orange and gleeful red flashes. "We bust in?"

"So that it looks like the controls failed," Warren cautioned. "It can't *look* like a bust in. And it'll have to be done right under C. M. P.'s noses 'cause the tripbox'll be in the cooler by the night of the concert. So we'll need you to sign the fastest, safest, and farthest from the repair schedule route between the two sites, Dazer."

"On it."

"Do we need to bust into the cooler, too?" Jack's mood gems flashed even brighter, if possible.

Daniel shook his head. "We've got those codes. They never changed 'em from when they were *Chew-able Luxuries*."

"Okay. We'll need something to break into the tripbox while messing up its locking and temperature controls so that it looks like that's why it popped. I know just the guy to ask." Jack texted furiously into his wrist com, then nodded in satisfaction at the reply before bounding for the door. "You coming, Dazer?"

Daniel blinked at him for a moment, then nodded his understanding. "We're not meeting at the restaurant."

It wasn't a question, but Jack shook his head anyway.

"At a table on the concourse."

"Yeah, I'm coming. He'll bring food."

"Wark?"

"No. I've got a few more details to work out, and I've gotta talk to Rose. Bring me some back."

"No promises," Jack warned.

Warren gave him a baleful look. "You'd better promise, little Hom, or you'll find yourself bounced out an air lock."

Jack just laughed.

The main doors of the *Claws & Jaws: Complete Interspecies Cuisine* could be seen from the cluster of tables in the main concourse. Jack dropped bonelessly into a chair where he could watch for its proprietor while Daniel pressed his back against a nearby pillar. Swiping irritably at an ad that hovered just out of reach, its tinny voice replaying its message of the upcoming AfterBRNR concert over and over, he tried to keep his chest from tightening. Huido Maarmatoo'kk was big, even for a Carasian, but he was not the biggest Daniel'd ever seen.

His mother had died of a ysa-smoke overdose when he'd been nine. His father, a ysa-smoke addict himself, had somehow managed to stumble into a restricted docking area and pick a grief-induced fight with the first being he'd met. It turned out to be one of Huido's newly arrived nonsentient wives, hungry and out-of-sorts from her journey. Sent to find him by the med unit, Daniel'd arrived just in time to see the towering Carasian female take his father's head in one massive claw, squeeze, then start to eat.

He had no memory of running forward, of being snatched into the air by Constable Hutton in the nick of time, of being carried away, screaming and struggling, and of being sedated in the same med room where his mother's body still lay. He had no idea if there'd been an investigation or even a funeral. His parents had been station dregs, barely able to pay their air tax. When he'd finally come to, it was as if they'd never existed. It was years before he learned that Huido had paid Plexis his med bills.

The Carasian himself had always been very kind to him, taking an interest in his welfare, finding him work among the restaurant owners and merchants of his acquaintance and ensuring he had food and shelter when needed. He'd introduced him to Jack who'd introduced him to Rose. He'd never made a threatening gesture in his direction, or even raised his voice, but the sight of his huge carapace and great, snapping claws still made Daniel's breathing come in short, rasping gasps.

Now, he rejoined Jack as the crowds instinctively parted before the large, armor-plated Carasian striding through their midst, his ever-present Human servant, Ansel, carrying a large takeaway box, following behind.

The other rose at their approach, his expression and his posture formal. Jack both liked and respected Huido, but had never, and would never, set foot in the *Claws & Jaws,* even though Huido had explained to him, with a rare display of patience, that all species had to eat to survive, and many had to eat live food; it was nature's way. Jack accepted this but remained adamant, and Huido, in another rare display of patience, had agreed to rendezvous outside his establishment whenever the two needed to meet.

Settling his great bulk so that his lower claws hit the floor with an audible click, Huido gestured at Ansel with one upper claw, a full third of his eyes watching with obvious amusement as Jack tried to ignore the box placed in front of him. Another third watched Daniel, while the remainder kept an eye on the concourse, the nearby rival restaurants, and his own front doors.

"Russell, Kekoa," he said, his voice reverberating through the two plates that held his eyes and mouth. "I hope you're both keeping out of trouble and this sudden gathering is not because you need my protection against the Hard Core Iglies."

Jack raised his upper lip in a dignified sneer.

"That vermin knows better than to even look our way," he replied. "Ever since we put their last leader in a med unit."

"Glad to hear it. And where is Mwangi today?"

"Covering for Rose. She's teaching a Meditation during Translight class."

"Has he heard from his parents recently?"

"Yeah, they'll be on that paleobotany assignment on Ettler's Planet for another year."

"Is his uncle still working on his dissertation?"

Jack shrugged. "Dunno. He hasn't seen him for two years. They have a tactful agreement."

Ansel frowned. "What's that supposed to mean?"

"It means they hate each other, but they both love his folks, so they tactfully pretend he's still living with him. That for us?" Unable to wait any longer, Jack jerked his chin at the box.

Huido chuckled; a deep rumble that caused the tabletop to vibrate under his upper claws. "A little something my new chef Pearleau is working on: inner nekis bark garnished with elosia flowers. I thought you might give me an opinion."

Daniel smiled despite his nervousness. Huido had been asking for Jack's opinion since his mother, a waitress at *Claws & Jaws*, had run off to the Bonanza Belt with a Kimmcle mine foreman the year before his father had disappeared. It was Huido's way of ensuring they all had enough to eat without actually offering them charity.

"Pearleau says it comes in a pya reduction," Huido continued as Jack threw the lid open. "So you won't need to add any *Feenstra's Patented Hot Sauce*. And since Pearleau is probably watching us as we speak, and since she has a tendency to throw things when her cooking is insulted, I suggest you resist the urge to add it just to annoy her."

Jack laughed, then dug in with gusto, gesturing for Daniel to do the same. The two boys gave the food the attention it deserved until, with obvious reluctance, Jack closed the lid again.

"Tell her it was nebular," he said.

Three of Huido's eyestalks stretched toward him in a parody of adult confusion. "I'm not sure she'll have any idea if that's a good review or a poor one," he rumbled.

"A good one, a great one."

"Well, then, she'll be pleased. So now that we've finished with the culinary portion of your visit—I assume you've left enough for Mwangi to partake of later—what is it that you need from me?"

Daniel leaned back, keeping an eye out for approaching Jellies or shoppers who might stray too close to them, while Jack explained their request.

The largest music venue on Plexis, the *Downie Grand,* had seen its share of bands from the galaxy-renowned Pink Riders whose logo was a huge cocktail, to the experimental Fly-the-Pies, a sixteen-strong troupe of Whirtle musician-acrobats. As a Soft Blast band, AfterBRNR generally drew its fan base from a somewhat older crowd, but there were still plenty of youths milling about so that Daniel, Jack, and Warren did not look out of place in the crowd that surged toward the main doors on concert night.

"This thing's way too tight," Warren groused, pulling at the neck of his borrowed T-shirt. He'd already cut the sleeves off, but it still stretched alarmingly across the chest. "Did you have to buy it in size scrawny?"

Daniel scowled at him. "Don't worry. They're heading for the waste stream first thing tomorrow."

"I'm keeping mine, and heads up," Jack warned, "Constable Hutton's in view."

As they came abreast of the security officer, her expression one of professional courtesy, her eyes sweeping the crowd, alert for signs of scalpers, pickpockets, or drunks, he punched Daniel in the arm.

Daniel glared at him in genuine annoyance. "Cut it out, jerk!"

"Think we should ask Tal Miccandrian to sign your ticket?"

"She's gonna sign your cast in a minute."

"Ooooo, I think I just discovered your little secret. Daniel Kekoa, AfterBRNR fan."

"Jotherion Russell, corpse."

"Keep it level, Homs."

Constable Hutton's even tone drew their heads around. Jack flashed his mood gems at her, Warren allowed himself a single nod, but Daniel just shoved his hands in his pockets and stalked past.

Jack's tickets were for Standing Left, a section of the wide, roped-off semicircle in front of the stage, just below AfterBRNR's vid crew who were busily recording the crowd for the official tour tape. It was already more than half-filled with beings when they arrived and, waving his rolled-up plas program at a few acquaintances, Warren leaned down. "Mingle, get noticed," he whispered. "When the lights drop, we meet at the back door."

Jack gave him a clear flying sign, slid between two laughing

Norsenturtles in tent-sized concert T-shirts, and vanished into the crowds. After a moment, Daniel did the same.

He wandered about the lower lobby, checking out merchandise and saying hello to the stall and booth workers, most of whom he knew. He made a show of deciding between a self-warming cup with Tal Miccandrian's face on it, or a chrono pendant that played the band's latest song, then chose a simple black plas wrist guard on clearance for thirty percent off. As the lights dimmed and the loudspeaker announced the opening act, one of Rose's favorites, another Soft Blast group named Constellation, rumored to be patronized by the infamous Grays of Deneb, he headed for the back door.

The other two boys were already there, chatting quietly with a blue-haired fem, her skin as dark as Warren's and her eyes as green as Daniel's, wearing a *Downie Grand* staff T-shirt. She winked at him, then swiped her pass-card at the lock. The door clicked open and, one by one, they slipped out into the service corridor beyond.

"Thanks, Kibibi. We'll be back before the encores," Warren told her.

"I'll be here."

She blew Jack a sarcastic kiss, then shut the door behind them.

Warren immediately pulled a bag from behind a waste digester, and all three donned old maintenance coveralls and caps to cover their somewhat unique hair styles. Then, after slinging the bag over his shoulder, Warren checked the first of Daniel's signs before heading for a ladder.

They climbed for two levels, caught a service ramp up for another, wove through a series of increasingly tight service corridors, then up another ladder, and another two ramps before reaching a door marked: Upper Level 231, spinward ¾.

Warren opened it a crack, peered out, then gestured the other two through.

They came out in a dimly lit, faux marble hallway, with heavy, real wooden doors inset in their own soberly carved alcoves in the far wall, each one with a small bronze plate beside it, and each one closed. They passed three doors—an accounting firm, an insurance firm, and a mass market media conglomerate—before finally fetching up against the door to *Cardale, Morlon, and Pix Funerary Services.*

Warren plucked a card from his pocket and swiped it in front of the pass-lock. There was a faint click, a tiny light flashed green, and the door opened with a soft shushhh. They slipped inside, and Warren used another card to bypass the security alarm.

"The cleaning staff are gone," Daniel whispered as they made their way through the darkened showrooms. "This way."

The cooler door proved no more difficult than the front door had; a moment later, they stood before a medium-sized tripbox.

Warren vaulted to the top, reached up, and jerked the cover from a small vent in the cooler ceiling, then jumped down again before turning to Jack. "Okay. Get it open, then set to revive."

The other's mood gems flashed a savage yellow. "With pleasure."

Five minutes later, they stood staring down at five hundred dormant Anisoptera.

"They'll be awake soon," Jack said quietly. "You sure this'll work?"

Warren nodded.

"And they won't get hurt?"

"Not if everything goes to plan, and everything should."

With a proud smile, he opened his bag and withdrew an elongated drone, built to resemble a green-and-gold Anisoptera. He set it gently on the open lid of the tripbox, then activated a recessed button behind its wide compound eyes. Its pale yellow translucent wings flexed, then began to vibrate rapidly, carrying the drone straight up to alight on the edge of the vent.

"The Ladin V females have developed a unique pheromone system," he explained. "With a sexual receptivity signal for the males, and a food discovery signal for other females. Once I set her in motion . . . well, you'll see; it's gonna be super sonic real soon." He tapped a few buttons on his wrist chrono, then turned. "Okay, let's get back."

AfterBRNR was just finishing its first encore when they returned to the standing area. Jack immediately took up an impromptu dance with the two Norsenturtles, coming very close to getting stepped on several times. Warren hummed tunelessly along with the second, third, and fourth encores; by the time the lights came up and the crowds began to make their way to the exits, Daniel's opinion of Soft Blast music was, if possible, even lower. They strode past Constable Hutton at the front doors, jostling each other so that she had to give them another admonishment, then headed for the nearest ramp.

An hour later they stood with Kibibi and the rest of the *Downie Grand* backstage staff in the Upper Retail Level 104 spinward ¾'s main assembly hall where Rose and her Business Co-op were hosting an after-concert reception catered by *Claws & Jaws*. Rose herself was standing with the lead singers of both bands, wearing a thirty-year-old Constellation tour T-shirt in a soft dove gray, one plump arm about each musician while the vid crew recorded their conversation. Huido was drinking beer with the two Norsenturtles who turned out to be ambassadors, while keeping three or four eyes on Ansel commanding an army of wait staff handing out wine, canapes, and sweetmeats. As honored guests, the *Lithe-Lime* visitors could be seen striking artfully crafted athletic poses under the most flattering portlights surrounded by even more flattering Upper Level merchants. A disproportionately large contingent of Turrned Missionaries wove their way through the room, quietly preaching their mandate of respect and understanding, while station security ringed the walls and ramp entrances, maintaining a silent but effective mandate of their own.

Daniel nudged Warren in the ribs. "Looks like C. M. P.'s accepted Rose's invitation," he said, jerking his chin at the three funeral directors standing with two others, obviously lawyers.

Warren nodded. "Good, 'cause it's gonna be any second now."

He pressed a button on the side of his wrist chrono and, as a vent cover high above slid quietly open, carefully slipped the device into his pocket.

Jack was the first to hear the sound of two thousand and four pairs of wings in the upper ductwork. Seconds later, five hundred and one Anisoptera spewed through the vent.

The sheer size of the cluster nearly blotted out the portlights, causing a shimmering array of reds and greens and blues to cascade over the gathered who gasped in delight, believing this to be part of the festivities. One half of the creatures began a complex aerial battle, swooping, gliding, and diving at each other, while the other half spread out and landed, not on the delicacy-laden tables, but on every bit of plas in the room, most of which was on the gathered. The sound of several hundred *labra* shooting forward to catch hold of plas jewelry, chronos, hair-extensions, clothing-fasteners, coms, and—in some cases—entire wardrobes, then several hundred toothed jaws biting down, was satisfyingly loud. A few of the guests, like Rose, who'd donned a pair of bright orange plas hair ribbons for the occasion, welcomed the attention with rapt smiles. Most, however, greeted the assault on their personal property with hysterics, but found themselves unable to even swat at the creatures as each guest and each security constable was suddenly surrounded by Turrneds.

"Apparently, the Ladin V females have also developed a unique response to dwindling habitat," Warren noted. "Using chewed-up bits of plas foraged from nearby sapient settlements to create viable substrate on which to lay their eggs. Who'da thought it."

"And who'da thought a few missionaries could keep an entire room from hurting them," Jack added happily.

"Rose."

"I love our Rose."

Two of the *Lithe-Lime* underexecutives hiding beneath the main banquet table, however, refused to be pacified, squawking in panic and screaming for security. When they caught sight of Inspector Wallace, the epaulettes on his dress uniform already minus their plas fringes, they swarmed out at him.

"Do something!" one of them shrieked, grabbing him by the arm and causing the two Anisoptera on his collar buttons to rise up and go for her earrings.

"Do what," he demanded, trying without success to extricate himself from her grip.

"Kill them! Kill them before they strip us all naked!"

Inspector Wallace struggled to reach his sidearm, only to have Tal Miccandrian's hand land heavily on his shoulder.

"Do you really want to open fire on a room full of the galaxy elite?" the Neblokan asked sweetly.

"Because you might miss them and hit one of these charming flying creatures," the lead singer for Constellation added, the multicolored tattoos on his cheeks crinkling as he gave an evil chuckle.

"Then what do you expect me to do about them?" the inspector demanded.

"Well, you could begin by asking *Cardale, Morlon, and Pix* in what manner they were acquired before they were transported here, Gregor Christopher." Rose gestured at the three funeral directors who were trying to hide behind their lawyers. "And then reacquire them, unharmed, so that they might be returned to their homeworld. I think that should just about do it."

Clearly relieved to have an official course of action, Inspector Wallace headed C. M. P.'s way, his expression thunderous.

"I see Aleksander's here. I'll speak with him," Tal Miccandrian told Rose, her amber eyes beneath sequined brow ridges sparkling with merriment. "The *Gamer's Gold* is certainly big enough to carry the tripbox. And I'm sure we can find room on our vistape for a short piece about a valiant and environmentally conscientious captain. Our viewers will want a happy ending to this story."

Across the room, Jack was dancing with glee, two crimson Anisoptera happily nibbling at each wrist plas, their long, delicate legs wrapped about his forearms.

"IT'S SO BEAUTIFUL!" he shouted in sarcastic triumph.

"Many regs for the transport of a destructive species, are there?" Daniel asked, as a large emerald Anisoptera pulled his own wrist plas free and carried it off.

"Oh, yeah! And the reg for the *importation* of a destructive species onto a *public space facility* are sonically strict, and the fines are super sonically harsh! C. M. P.'ll be lucky to get away with their underwear!"

"Once this lot's finished with their lists of damages and grievances, they won't even have those."

"Yup," Warren agreed. "There's your stop 'em, crush 'em, and drive 'em off." He glanced across the hall where the vid crew were still happily recording. "C. M. P. brought lawyers, but AfterBRNR brought *media*. And the P.R. folk at *Lithe-Lime* know it." He gestured at a Human in a business-style track suit now whispering urgently in the ears of several executive types whose faces were already registering alarm. "I'm guessing they're about to put so much distance between themselves and C. M. P. there'll be a backdraft."

"Won't help 'em," Jack retorted. "Their name's all over the contract, and I'll bet C. M. P.'ll make sure everyone knows it. That's my punch in the nose. Hang on; Rose wants us."

They made their way through the gathered, trailed by half a dozen Anisoptera each.

"I think it may be time to usher our guests into the ballroom," Rose said when they reached her side. "Paige, Myrtle, if you would begin. Daniel and Jotherion will help you, won't you, boys? Have Ansel send the waiters ahead with the food and the wine; that should get everyone moving in the right direction. And I'm sure that if Warren were to station himself at the other end of the assembly hall, the Anisoptera will allow us to take our leave. Hmm?"

Warren nodded. "On it."

Jack tucked his arms into those of the two Norsenturtles who seemed to have taken a liking to him, and headed for the large double doors at the back of the room. "Still hate AfterBRNR, Dazer?" he asked with a laugh.

Twisting his neck around to see Tal Miccandrian, one hand absently stroking a green-and-gold Anisoptera, deep in conversation with Captain Aleksander, Daniel shrugged.

"I guess they're okay," he allowed. "As people. I still don't like their music."

"Close enough."

Gently removing a small sapphire creature from his ear, Jack held her briefly on the tip of his finger until she finished removing the plas from the metal stud of his earring, then buzzed off to join the rest of the cluster swirling about the green-and-gold creature perched on Warren's head.

"What a stellar night," he breathed, his mood gems flashing a deep, contented purple.

... *Truffles* continues
Interlude

* * *

"SO THIS HUMAN owns a high-level store, with top-end products, catering to grandies," Sira puzzled through what he'd told her. Her shapely brows knit. "All to take in strays?"

Close enough. "I daresay making a living comes into it, but that's the sum." Morgan chuckled. Sira wasn't the only one on Plexis confounded by Rose and her ever-changing cadre of young Humans. *Rose Red's Tree of Life Emporium*'s non-Human clientele persisted in a belief Rose somehow budded half-grown offspring, to the extent that naïve Whirtles, new to the station, refused to enter the store in case such fertility was contagious. "She's been on the other side," he finished soberly.

Of hope. Of the chasm between those who had and those who didn't. Plexis had them all. The station preferred the wealthy but—as any self-contained community—found use for its poor. Unless the poor found use for it first. Depended on perspective.

His had blossomed to include another's. Sira's smaller hand remained in his; her thoughts, close and warm, were barely distinct from his own. Morgan would have distrusted feeling so ridiculously content except that the emotion *flowed* between them, as real as breath. As essential.

"There's kindness here," she said aloud, glancing at him as if in question.

He couldn't blame her for being skeptical. Sira'd seen scant evidence of it so far—something he hoped to change. What he'd set in motion, starting with the sombay seller, now Rose, might help. "Plexis is more than storefronts. It's regular people, doing their best—"

"SCEEEK! MY BAG!! THIEVES!!!" While the Skenkran continued to screech loudly, three scruffy youngsters—humanoid, perhaps Human—darted through the crowd, laughing and shouting taunts at their victim. As they passed, Morgan neatly freed the beaded sack from the shoulder of one. A set of yellowed non-Human teeth bared at him, then the would-be thieves vanished into the oblivious sea of beings around them.

He returned the bag, waved away the gratitude of the Skenkran and her companion, then came back to Sira. "Where were we?"

"You were telling me about regular people and their kindness. What about those?" with clear doubt.

"You'd be surprised," he told her, remembering an old friend. The next time they were on Auord, he'd intro—

Morgan stopped himself, hoping she hadn't caught the thought. Pocular was bad enough. Auord had been the start of Sira's trial by fire.

He couldn't take her back.

Jilly

* * *

by Paul Baughman

THE PACK MOVED with the crowd. Drifting, accelerating, weaving in and out. Embedded in the tapestry of a hundred species browsing the first, and still most famous, mobile shopping center—Plexis Supermarket. Embedded, but not part of it.

We were almost as high up as we could go without attracting the wrong attention. The overhead simulated open skies, and puffs of crisp or scented breezes teased our hair. No matter that they all originated in some ventilator outlet or other, the effect was strikingly like walking the surface of a kind and smiling planet.

Freed was running the net. The Pack kept in contact using hand talk and the occasional soft word spoken in passing. We were sweeping for information this time, so we were under orders of no lifting. Someone had paid high to find their target.

I was link today, with Jilly as my cover and back. I liked working with Jilly. She was neat and precise and deadly—most of the time and against most people.

A year ago she was full of herself. We all were, but it turned out she was really overconfident in her combat skills. Back then, we were working a pair strolling up from the docks. We rarely worked spacers and never worked the old-timers, but these two didn't look dangerous. The spacer was youngish and his friend was an inner system fop. They didn't look like anything to worry about. We were just going to lift some creds.

The setup was perfect, and Jilly was taking point. We were anticipating an easy take. Jilly drifted across their path and spun in to threaten with her knife. The next thing we knew she flew into a wall, and the spacer was pocketing her blade. None of us even saw what happened.

Then they had stepped onto a slide ramp and were gone. I don't even think they had broken off their conversation. Jilly had spent the last year obsessing over that one spacer and honing her combat skills from anyone who would teach her.

Seemed fate we had gotten this assignment. The target we were looking for now was the spacer from a year ago, Leland Nota.

"Remember, Jilly," I whispered at one of our near passes, "locate and report. No contact."

"I know," she whispered, glee breaking through.

I shook my head and headed for a public com. It was time to check in.

Jilly leaned casually against the wall while I made the call. I was halfway through the check-in procedure when she straightened up suddenly. I caught the motion out of the corner of my eye and turned my head to look at her.

We'd had too many years of practice for her expression to change, but I could tell that something was up. She walked past me and whispered. "Go ghost."

I stiffened and turned back to the screen.

"Got to go, Casper. See you later."

I cut the connection while my contact was still reacting to the code word.

By the time I had turned from the com screen, the net was already unraveling as the Pack drifted into side corridors, sped up, or slowed down, dropping out of the fragile communication web. Jilly had called the "ghost"; the Pack's automatic response was to go to ground.

I tried to spot Jilly in the crowd, but with the shifting mass of multi-species singles and groups, it should have been impossible. I hesitated. The proper response to a ghost call is to vanish and make your way back to a rendezvous far from here. Then I spotted her; she was tailing a pair of Trade Pact Enforcers headed back the way we had come.

I cursed and hurried in her wake, trying to catch up without attracting attention. Most of the shoppers on this level strolled, occasionally stopping to check out a display or enter a shop. No one was rushing anywhere, and that made me stand out. I slowed a little and tried to keep Jilly in sight.

Why the hell was she tailing *enforcers,* for Deity's sake!

I tailed Jilly while she tailed two enforcers. Slowly, I managed to gain on her without drawing attention to myself. As the minutes stretched, my tension grew. I was standing out in the casually strolling crowd. Like a flashing light hovered above my head, proclaiming to all that I didn't belong.

Then the enforcers turned off into a side concourse. I was preparing to trot forward to catch up to Jilly before she turned the corner to follow them, when she dodged the opposite way and fell in behind a group of Tolians.

I stopped in shock, then skipped ahead to match the crowd's pace again.

Frat! She hadn't been tailing the enforcers, she'd been using them as cover.

Starting to angle in Jilly's direction, I kept my pace unchanged, all the while studying the crowd ahead. Eliminating the Tolians—she wouldn't be hiding behind the people she was tailing—it could be anyone. There was an amazing amount and variety of sapients in the concourse ahead, in almost equal parts of shoppers, spacers, local workers, and some that were hard to classify.

I don't know why, but I concentrated on the spacers. There were singletons and pairs in a half dozen species: a trio of Scats; a sea of feathery antennas marked a bunch of Drapsk; a pair of humanoids in sealed spacesuits clumped along in a straight line.

I glanced back over to Jilly to see if I could spot who she was watching, but she was gone!

I stumbled to a halt and looked back to see if she had turned down a side corridor or stepped into a shop. Someone bumped into me from behind and muttered what had to be curses in a language I didn't know, then pushed past me.

I twisted back and forth, stretched on tiptoe trying to spot her in a moving crowd of sapients, most of whom were taller than both of us.

Abruptly worried, I started to run, weaving in and out of shoppers. I was drawing attention from everyone, but I didn't care.

Then I saw her. She was angling in toward the three Scats, in her hunter's stalk. Her gait didn't look unusual among this crowd, but to anyone who had seen her work before, it was unmistakable. Even then, there was something different about her attitude, something almost desperate.

I don't know what Jilly had been planning, but bad luck tripped her up—literally. A drunken Human staggered out of a bar and bumped into her. She tripped and rolled, then bumped against the leg of the middle Scat she had been stalking.

The creature whipped around with unbelievable speed and pinned her to the ground with a clawed foot on her wrist. Jilly winced.

"What have we here?" the creature hissed. "Has-ss fate delivered my next meal right to my claws-sss?"

"Frat," I muttered. I changed course and joined the crowd that had started to gather.

"Leave me alone, you murderer!" Jilly shouted.

The crowd started to whisper comments, but I ignored them and pushed as close as I could to the action. Jilly was darting glances around those ringing her in. Her face showed fear. From our long association I could tell most of it was feigned. Most, but not all. In addition, was there satisfaction?

I was not in the inner ring of spectators, but I could see most of the action between the shoulders of the two in front of me. When Jilly's eyes swept my way, I stuck my hand between and gave her one of the Pack's hand signs.

She didn't react. Had she seen my signal, or was the crowd too chaotic for her to pick it out?

The Scat reached down and pulled Jilly up by the front of her tunic until her feet dangled a full foot off the ground. The other two stood back. "You s-sssmellll deliciousssss, s-ssoftflesssh." A thin tongue flicked out between his fangs.

I stiffened. Everyone knew Scats were fond of warm-blooded prey; still living, if they could get it. I racked my brain for any way to get Jilly free of those claws. I felt sure she could escape in this crowd if it would let go of her for just an instant.

I made a swift inventory of my possessions, but I wasn't hopeful. I had only a small folding knife, unsuitable for a weapon, a few coins, and a folded wad of credits, plus a tiny alarm screamer. We had headed out on a search and locate mission, so I'd left any significant gear behind. Maybe I could distract it somehow.

"What's going on here?" a gruff but polite voice interrupted my desperate attempts to come up with a plan.

A Human in station security uniform pushed her way through the inner ring of observers and planted herself in front of the three Scats and their helplessly struggling captive. Great, it was Hutton.

"Ahhh, cons-sstable," Jilly's captor said, "this Human as-ssaulted me while I was about my lawful business. I claim it in reparation."

"I didn't attack him," Jilly blurted out. "I tripped, and he stepped on me!"

"Did you step on her?" Hutton asked, eyes keen. Most Plexis Jellies we could work around; not this one.

"Ahh, only to keep it from essscaping after its-ss unwarranted attack," the Scat said, jaws gaping open in what could be a smile or threat or both. It was hard to be sure.

Jilly stopped struggling. "He's a murderer!"

I groaned to myself. What was she doing now?

"Murder?" Hutton echoed. "What's this about?"

"The creature is-ss mad," the Scat said.

"He killed my mother!" Jilly shouted. "He *ate* her in front of me. He said she was tough and stringy!"

One of the other Scats broke in. "Does-sss it object to the eating or to the 'ss-sssstringy?'" All three broke into their chittering laugh, foam oozing between their fangs.

"When and where was this?" Hutton demanded, frowning at the Scats.

"Five years ago," Jilly said, "on Lorelei."

Ah? I thought, *That was before she was recruited into the Pack.*

"If it didn't happen onstation," the constable dismissed with a wave, "it's none of our business. Take it up with the enforcers." She switched her gaze to the Scat holding Jilly. "Sounds like what happened here was an accident. Let her go."

"What about my reparations-sss?"

"Show me the damage, and I'll consider it." Hutton crossed her arms and stared the Scat in the eyes.

He lowered Jilly slowly to her feet and reluctantly pulled his claws from her tunic.

"You," the constable said to Jilly, "what's your name?" Her hand was poised over a noteplas.

I flicked my screamer and tossed it over the heads of the crowd. The ear-piercing wail started when it hit the floor. Everyone turned to see the cause of the new disruption in the day's shopping. Hutton pushed out of the crowd at a run.

I was keeping an eye on Jilly, ready to run interference for her escape. I was shocked to see her punch the Scat in the middle of his chest.

The creature's blazing reflex trapped her hand in place and he leaned in close to her with dripping jaws.

"A pitiful attack like that wouldn't even hurt a hatchling."

Then I heard it. The tooth-twisting whine of a force blade powering up.

The Scat froze in shock and I spotted the small butt in Jilly's hand.

Jilly always carried a force blade she had found somewhere. It was old, almost obsolete. It worked, but took a significant second or two to form the blade, and while the field was stabilizing, anything in a six-inch cone in front of it was subjected to the spinning, twisting force. And the weapon was trapped against the Scat's chest by his own strength.

"Die!" Jilly shouted into the creature's pain-shocked face as its internal organs were shredded.

The crowd was fracturing in a screaming mass, those in front pushing back to escape the mad teenager with the deadly weapon.

The other Scats reached for Jilly, but she slashed the now fully-formed blade out of their dying companion and through the arm and chest of the one on her right, then she was dashing in a crouching, dodging run through the crowd.

The uninjured Scat dashed off in pursuit, bulling his way through the crowd where Jilly slipped nimbly between obstacles.

I was about to start my own pursuit when a heavy hand grabbed my shoulder and held me in place.

I twisted my head to find Constable Hutton glaring at me while speaking into a handcom. "Two injured sapients, Level thirty-five, sector blue, concourse seven. Major injuries, med-techs required."

She clicked off and turned me around with irresistible strength. "What happened here?" She gave my shoulder a light shake for emphasis.

"I–I'm not sure." I made certain to stammer. "I think they were arguing over who got to eat her and someone pulled a 'blade. She got free in the fight and ran. The third one chased her."

"Which way?" Hutton shook me again, a little harder. I could see anger simmering in her eyes, but against who I had no idea.

"Th–that way, constable." I pointed in the direction Jilly had fled, confident that she wouldn't be found in that direction by now.

"Stay here and make a statement to the med team." She dropped her hold and pounded off in the same direction as the Scat and Jilly.

Slumping a little in case anyone was watching, I eased back through the ring of sapients watching with morbid curiosity. I took another step back and left. Then I waited a long moment, turned, and walked toward the shops across the concourse.

My saunter turned into a purposeful stride as I heard the sirens on the aircar, modified for station use, dashing toward the site of the fight. Med-techs were the only allowed air transport onstation, and they hugged the ceiling whenever they were dispatched.

I turned into a side concourse and increased my pace. I had to find Jilly and get her off the station. Plexis wouldn't let a murder or two go unavenged. It was bad for business. If the shoppers felt unsafe, they'd stop coming.

The Pack were all encouraged to find their own hidey-holes for emergencies. In general, they were kept secret, just on principle, but you might share one for a close friend. One, but never all. Jilly's one hideaway I knew, two levels down, but would she go there or to one of her other places? Or would she go to my place?

I increased my pace and headed to my closest hidey. Jilly knew it, and it was closer than hers anyway.

After a half hour walk, I reached my hidey and approached it carefully. This was a real, official residence, unlike Jilly's. It took a significant part of my income to pay rent on this place, small as it was. I had a couple more places I could go to ground, but this was the most comfortable.

I slid inside and gave the room a quick scan. I spotted Jilly immediately. She was crouched in the corner behind the bed.

"Jilly!" I rushed around the bed and stopped a step away.

She was rocking with eyes closed and tears running down her face.

"Jilly?" I asked gently. "What's wrong?"

She lunged up, wrapped her arms around me, and started sobbing.

I put my arms around her and held her until her sobs slowed and stopped.

She didn't step back, but she started talking in a muffled voice. "He's dead. He's finally dead. I never thought I'd ever see him again. And now he's dead—and I killed him."

"You've never talked about your past before you arrived onstation," I said hesitantly.

"We were homesteading on Lorelei," she said without moving out of my hold. "We lived in the back of beyond, but we had a nice piece of property. We were in town stocking up on supplies when the pirates hit. My dad was killed, along with anyone who tried to pick up a weapon. The survivors were herded into an empty hall while they stripped the town. I can't imagine there was all that much of value; it wasn't a large town, but they stripped it anyway."

Her arms tightened.

"Mother was shielding my sister and me. Others were the same, huddled in small groups. I guess after their work was done, they wanted a snack."

I rubbed her back as she shuddered, the only comfort I could offer.

"Maybe a dozen of them came in and started dragging people out of their groups. That one took our mother. Bren screamed and twisted out of my hold to attack him. He killed her instantly. Someone grabbed my collar which was the only thing that kept me from following her example."

She stepped back and shifted her hold to my arms. She looked at me through haunted memories.

"After they left, one of the surviving families wanted to take me in, but I couldn't stand the thought of staying there. I sold our homestead and bought passage aboard the first ship, ending up here.

"I never thought I'd see him again. I didn't *want* to see him again, but when I saw him passing by, I couldn't help myself."

"Sit down," I said. I gently pushed her toward the bed and turned to the little closet. I started shoving clothes into a small jump bag I kept here.

"What are you doing?" Jilly said.

"We have to get you offstation. Hutton won't let a murder pass. They'll be looking for you already."

"I don't have money to buy passage."

"So what were you planning?"

"I don't know," she mumbled. "I was panicked. All I could think of was getting to you."

I finished packing the clothes, shoved a few toiletries on top, and closed the bag.

Pulling her to her feet, I said, "Come on. We're leaving."

"Where are we going?"

"Your hidey. You need some clothes if you're going to run. Or is there a better place to pick up necessities?"

"No, that place will do."

"All right, let's go."

Jilly's hidey was a tiny room off a dingy service corridor sandwiched between the back entrances of two shops. I suspect it had once been nothing but an alcove, but in the past someone had walled it off and installed a hidden door. Whether it was Jilly herself or someone else, she never said.

I checked for watchers, released the catch, and pulled Jilly inside.

The room was big enough for a pallet and a single cupboard. I knew that she kept a few changes of clothes and some c-cubes for emergencies.

"Hurry up and pack," I said.

Jilly rushed to the cupboard. She pulled out a shoulder bag and started shoving clothes and a few other items into it. Then she moved to the bed, whipped out a knife, and made a couple of slashes across it. She reached in and transferred an item or two I couldn't make out to her bag.

"Ready," she said.

I looked around. The place looked like a Brexk had run through it.

"Whoever takes this place over from you will have a job to put it in order first," I said.

We exchanged grins.

"Where to now?" Jilly said.

"The posting boards."

She dragged back on my hand. "No one's going to hire us," she said. "We've no experience."

"How do you think new spacers are made?" I said. "Everyone starts at the bottom."

"But—"

"No buts," I interrupted. "This is your best chance, but we have to go now."

She followed as I took the most secluded concourses and slide ramps I knew.

I led the way into a café across the concourse and bought us some drinks. I picked a bench where we could watch the open space in front of the massive board. Data crawled over it. Postings for crew on outbound ships as well as cargo. Hiring tables were set up in front.

"What are we waiting for?" Jilly whispered.

"Just give me a minute. I want to make sure no one's watching the place."

"Oh. Makes sense. Guess I'm still not thinking straight."

"Shock. You'll be fine in a bit."

We finished our drinks and headed across.

I'd been in here several times just from curiosity, so I had an idea of how to proceed. I pulled Jilly to the side and studied the board.

"There, that one," I said after a few minutes. "The *Wanderer*."

"Why that one?"

"It's a trader, big enough they might need a couple of new hands, small enough to keep to no fixed schedule. Their next stop is Auord."

I led the way to the listed table at the far end of the room.

A middle-aged Human in faded blue coveralls looked up when we stopped across from him.

"Fair skies," I said. "We're looking for working passage."

The spacer looked us up and down and shrugged. "Either of you hold any ratings?"

"No, sir," I said, "But we've both worked station hydroponics. We know what not to touch without explanation."

"That's something anyway." He ticked something off on a note-plas. "Good enough. I'm the cargomaster of the *Wanderer*. We need someone to handle cargo stowage and general cleaning. You'll also learn basic maintenance. I've only got one berth free. Your pick."

Jilly looked startled and a little uneasy.

I spoke up before she could say anything. "She'll take it."

"But—"

I pulled her aside and whispered. "You have to get off the station, now. I'll follow later. We'll meet up on Auord. Get a job and wait for me."

"All right. But you'd better come, or I'll track you down."

"Don't worry about it," I said. "I'd never want you hunting me."

She smiled weakly.

Jilly started to turn back to the cargomaster, but I grabbed her arm. "Use a different name," I said. "No telling what those Scats will do to track you down."

She nodded and thought for a moment. "I'll get a job at the shipcity on Auord. Ask for Thel Masim."

"'Thel Masim,'" I repeated. "Got it. I'll get there as soon as I can."

Jilly—no, Thel—turned back to the cargomaster and put her hand on the accept scanner.

He nodded, then pushed back from the table. "Time to go." He turned to the door leading to the ships beyond.

Jilly shifted back and forth, then grabbed my face, and gave me a long, hard kiss before she grabbed up her bag and followed him.

I stood frozen and watched her leave. She turned back once at the portal and waved, then she was gone.

I stood a long moment more before I faded into the crowd. Plexis—the Pack—was my home. I'd have to stay low for a while; Hutton had a long memory.

And it was time Thel left hers behind.

...*Truffles* continues

4

* * *

MORGAN GREW QUIET, not that we could have spoken aloud over the growing din of what I no longer could call music, but then I didn't have the auditory nerves of a Blazod. Fortunately, our path wasn't into the *Blazoduncelin Thud Hut*. I let my Chosen lead us farther into the night zone.

The beings around us ranged from those intoxicated—or seeking to be, in whatever form suited their biology—to those bewildered by their surroundings, to those seemingly lost but determined to be anywhere but here. And tourists. A servo-towed bubble cart passed by, purple eyes peering out with interest through a cloud of yellow: a non-oxy breather taking a stroll on the wild side.

None would've noticed an explosion, let alone the two of us disappearing; however, I'd no trouble resisting the urge to 'port us to Huido's apartment, filled with a new curiosity.

Dancing. The Human sort.

Clan didn't dance, but I'd watched vids of Humans with Rael, my sister being fond of ballet, an artistic form claimed to predate the species leaving their homeworld. It required both practice and costume, neither of which either of us had. Safe from ballet, then.

Hopefully, it'd be hopping to a beat. Morgan, however, had that worrisome grace. Doubtless, dancing would be something he did as well as everything else, and he'd expect me to learn some complicated series of steps; I just knew it. The sweeper was hard enough. This was hardly fair—

Sira, I don't know how to dance, his mindvoice oddly uncertain. *I haven't wanted to before.*

It didn't matter if I'd leaked my insecurity on the issue or if, as usual, Morgan perceived what I'd rather hide. Relieved, I eased close and slipped my arm around his waist. My hair happily curled around his shoulder to caress his smooth cheek, and all was right with the universe. *We'll hop together,* I sent smugly. *Unless you'd prefer to practice back on the ship?* With an undercurrent of *heat.*

Unfair, Witchling, with flattering *HEAT* of his own, and I was ready to forget the truffles and concentrate on our cabin on the *Fox* in that instant—

Except a bundle of shapes exploded through a doorway just ahead, followed by a chanting mob. I couldn't tell what they were chanting, other than some exhorted one set of combatants against another.

Or rather a set against one, which might have brought up the notion of fairness except the one appeared to be winning.

Morgan muttered something rude under his breath. Louder, in my ear, "We have to help."

Bodies flew in all directions then regrouped as the struggle tumbled back into what the sign proclaimed, unlikely as it seemed, to be *McWhirtle's Iconic Pub,* onlookers pressing eagerly behind. "Why?" I asked sensibly, taking hold of his arm with both hands in case. I'd owned a tavern on Pocular. In my experience, such fights were short-lived and ultimately expensive for those involved—and outsiders were not welcome to participate.

Before he could answer, I spotted a uniformed figure pushing through the spectators toward the pub and relaxed. "There. Let Plexis Security—" my voice trailed away. The uniform wasn't gray.

It was the red and black of a Trade Pact Enforcer, on a being we knew. Constable P'tr wit 'Whix, on the staff of Assistant Sector Chief Lydis Bowman. Making the individual in the fight most likely to be his Human partner—

"Terk," Morgan grumbled, finishing my thought. "Brexk for brains." He lifted his arm and waved.

The Tolian spotted us and hurried over. "Captain Morgan. Fem Morgan. Greetings. Have you seen—" He winced, crest feathers fluttering, at a crash from within *McWhirtle's*. "Oh, dear."

Not for the first time, I wondered how these two ever came to be partners.

Chicken

* * *

by Elizabeth A. Farley-Dawson

P'TR WIT 'WHIX entered the lounge and clacked his hooked bill in relief as the din of the Plexis concourse dropped away. All species shared air on Plexis Supermarket, but no species was completely comfortable here. Except maybe Humans. Invasive species that they were, Humans seemed comfortable in any oxy environment. Over the years, enterprising souls of most other commonly spacefaring species had created species-specific establishments on the traveling station. This place had a name that few had the anatomy to properly pronounce. Those limited to Comspeak simply called it "The Tolian Sanctuary."

'Whix's clawed feet clicked on the cold plating of the short hall until they were muffled by thick-piled carpeting in the common area as he walked toward his private room. Overhead, holoscreens mimicked clouds passing through a deep blue-purple sky. 'Whix relaxed a bit more as some of his claustrophobia abated, and he gave himself a good shake to fluff his feathers. Which got stuck awkwardly under the stiff collar of his new uniform tunic. He felt a rachis break. Blasted clothing! Why did everyone have to conform to what the Humans considered appropriate professional wear?

'Whix glanced over at the concierge desk, envying the male attendant's glittering metal chain-and-gemstone jewelry and diaphanous scarf tied to hide the Comspeak implant at his throat. The young male had adopted the recent fad of using ultraviolet pigment to paint "tattoos" of geometric patterns across his feathers, visible only in lighting such as this, which simulated that of their homeworld. 'Whix thought the paint an unnecessarily flamboyant touch. The desk attendant beckoned.

"Message for you, Hom. Looks important," the attendant said, handing over a sealed, official-looking envelope. He craned his long neck, trying to see over 'Whix's shoulder as 'Whix turned away, slipping a finger-claw under the plas flap. 'Whix closed the flap, stood taller, and glared down his bill. The ill-considered swirls of paint around the large golden eyes, flecked with remnants of juvenile brown, emphasized the younger male's startled crest-raising at 'Whix's response. 'Whix said nothing, walking toward his room as the other male retracted his head, slicking down all his feathers. *Immatures*, he thought, *are never subtle*, suddenly feeling absurdly smug about his bright emerald irises that until recently sported gold specks. *Looks like my first assignment has come in*, 'Whix thought, skimming the page. *At least I'll have some time to . . .*

A blast of crowd noise and the clump of heavy, definitely non-Tolian boots in the vestibule startled an undignified squawk from the concierge. 'Whix's head twisted backward over his shoulder before he finished his thought.

A Human male stood in the common room, the red-and-black Trade Pact uniform showing the insignia of an enforcer, those shoulders barely contained by the fabric. He glared around under heavy brows at the few curious Tolians relaxing in the common room. "Which one of you is . . ." he consulted a piece of paper, "Pit—teer . . . Peet–tir . . . *grr* . . . Whicks?"

"P'tr wit 'Whix, Biochemist, Trade Pact Science Division, at your service," 'Whix carefully enunciated his name, which wasn't . . . quite . . . faithfully translated into Comspeak by his own throat implant. He stepped to turn his body around to align with his head, and strode forward. He lifted his crest slightly as he stood taller and spread his arms in formal greeting, though he knew the full effect of flashing his truly exquisite iridescent throat and crest feathers would be lost on the Human's sadly inadequate vision.

"Constable Russell Terk. I need you to come with me."

"That is illogical. I have just been granted leave before my first assignment,"'Whix replied, displaying the opened envelope he still clutched in his slim, four-fingered hand.

"This inquiry takes precedence. We can't speak here," Terk said brusquely.

'Whix whistled in dismay, inwardly bemoaning the heated sandbox and bertwee oil rub that he'd ordered waiting for him. Tugging the stiff collar of his own much plainer black-with-red uniform again, he strode toward the door. *Grooming,* he decided, *would have to wait.*

With his arms crossed, Constable Russell Terk stood next to the Tolian and looked down at the corpse. *Nicely browned,* the thought popped into his head before he could suppress it. He glanced sideways at the tall alien standing beside him but couldn't read the horny-billed, feathered face. At least the giant, domed green eyes had stopped roving unnervingly in separate directions.

Terk cleared his throat. "So?"

"This is clearly a Tolian. I fail to understand why you needed me here to tell you that," came the flat, robotic response of the translator that confusingly overlapped the whistles, chirps, trills, and clicks actually produced from the creature's throat. The closest eye rotated to focus on the Human's face while the other continued viewing the corpse.

"There are no others of your species currently onstation with the clearance to be involved in this investigation. We need this kept quiet to avoid tipping off whoever might be involved," Terk explained. He continued, "Why do you think anyone would do . . . *this* . . . then go through all the trouble to bring the body to Plexis?"

"That also seems clear. To eat, of course." Said with a cock of the head and lift of the crest, as he gestured toward his dead fellow. "My interspecies' studies suggest this is a traditional preparation for one of your Human livestock animals. A chicken. Am I wrong?"

Cold-blooded featherhead, Terk thought, then cleared his throat again. "Yes, well . . . or um, no, you're right, there is a superficial resemblance. . . ." He trailed off, shifting his shoulders uncomfortably, sure he felt some stitches start to give way. "A newly off-planet Human looking for familiar meats tipped off Plexis Security when she noticed *this*," he flapped a large square hand at the body, "was much larger than what's possible for the advertised species."

Terk continued brusquely, "Could a Tolian have committed this crime? If so, then we'll part ways and your authorities can resolve the matter." He faced 'Whix directly.

Though he saw the constable well enough already, 'Whix aimed his bill politely at Terk to indicate the direction of his attention. Then he eyed the corpse again, trying to ignore the scent rising from the plucked and tastefully garnished body. "Not possible," he replied. *We prefer it raw; we only eat cooked food around you.* He clamped his bill and throat tight on those words he dared not utter to an alien. "My people would never do such a thing," he offered instead.

"Of course not. It had to be too much to hope for a vacation," muttered the pale-haired Human, running a hand through his limp hair in frustration and making it stick up wildly. "If a Tolian didn't do it, then who did?" he challenged, taking a deep breath that puffed up his very broad chest.

'Whix forced himself to recall his training and not respond instinctually; this wasn't another Tolian male. Instead, he shifted from foot to foot, thinking, looking around at the other precooked meats on offer in *Bob's Fine Provender.* "Surely the proprietor has tracked this shipment? Isn't 'Bob' a common Human male name?"

"Bob is Dibran, but it thinks Bob sounds friendlier than its own name." Terk snorted rudely. "It did track the shipment, but the Dibran idea of record keeping involves licking everything in sight. There's plenty of sticky slobber to go around."

'Whix replied dryly, "I am aware the species keeps details of that sense to themselves, citing exemptions for reproductive processes. The Science Division is actively researching how Dibrans detect the relative strength of molecular signatures."

"Anyway, we haven't been able to crack its code, so that doesn't help us," Terk shrugged.

"'Crack its code'? Was the Dibran encrypting information? That suggests criminal intent—"

"It was a figure of speech," Terk interrupted.

"How can speech, being verbal, become a figure, which is visual?"

Terk opened his mouth, then closed it. "Never mind," he muttered. More loudly, he said, "No transfers of ownership occurred since the cargo was stamped upon arrival onstation and then sold to this Dibran. We don't think Bob had any idea *this* was anything other than what the crate labels indicate. Plexis Security assured us of that—before happily handing over this little problem."

'Whix trilled to himself as his eyes roamed the shop, continually shifting his weight, claws ticking softly on the unmodified metal station decking. He wished he could pace, but the small space was too crowded with refrigerated cases, displays of self-heating platters, foodstuffs, and the bulky Human. A tiny corner of noteplas peeking from under a shelving rack caught his eye as he twisted his head on his long neck. 'Whix stalked over and pulled it out along with a cloud of dust that set Terk to sneezing.

'Whix handed Terk the plas, largely clean except for one curled edge coated thickly with dust on one side. A sticky backing had dried out, causing the shipping label to fall off its crate and slip under the shelving, though only after the dust adhered to the edge.

'Whix squeezed past Terk to the storeroom, where the floor was also liberally dusty. He considered the haphazardly stacked boxes. "Constable, I require your assistance," he called.

They started shifting crates made heavier by the tech necessary for keeping their contents preserved. A couple of hours later, Terk's face was coated in a fine layer of dust cut through by drips of the salty water Humans produced so profusely and 'Whix was gaping and fluttering his throat to thermoregulate. Finally, the Tolian spied a crate with a shipping tag that sported a halo of darker color where another label had once covered it and prevented it from fading—matching the size of the label in Terk's hand. 'Whix gave a *kaw* of triumph.

"Plexis was sloppy to have overlooked this. Or they were paid to," Terk judged. He bent close to read off the original label.

"'Meragrik Transports.' Gotcha, you *crasnig*," he growled. He showed his teeth in a wide primate grin, looking up at the Tolian.

'Whix didn't think it indicated pleasure.

'Whix walked alongside Constable Terk, long legs easily keeping up with the Human's determined stride as they wove their way through the crowded concourse. "Constable, cannot you find someone else to assist you? Surely others on your ship are more able."

"No," Terk responded brusquely, adroitly sidestepping a Lemmick towing an anti-grav sled towering with party supplies. "None of them are Tolian, and my plan requires a Tolian. Luckily, all members of your division must pass the same background and ethical checks as enforcers. That means you."

"You have a plan?" 'Whix asked with a surprised squawk he couldn't quite suppress, though his implant rendered it flat and unemotional. "You cannot even be certain that this Sakissishee Roraqk is involved!"

"Roraqk is involved—directly or indirectly—in half of the illegal activity on this station. He's not known to own a share of this company, but it is registered to a Scat. Roraqk likely has his clawed, scaly hands dug into it somehow."

"None of the records we examined indicate such a connection, and we must be methodical," 'Whix protested.

Terk barked a laugh, "'Methodical' might be fine for you scientists, but—out here—sometimes you have to follow a hunch."

'Whix stopped walking. "But potentially innocent lives rely on—"

"Yes, they do," Terk didn't stop, but threw over his shoulder, "And if, by rare chance, the Scats are innocent, then we'll just have to be sure not to kill them."

'Whix scrambled to catch up, panting in distress. If he couldn't avoid being part of the Human's hasty plan, perhaps he could prevent it from becoming a disaster.

'Whix gave himself a good shake to settle his freshly-groomed feathers properly, this time without the restriction of his uniform tunic. He whistled with pleasure, turning to Russell Terk, who fiddled with a small recording device disguised as a jeweled pendant in his hands.

Terk fastened the device to the end of a fine golden chain suspended from other chains draping 'Whix's body. "There," he said with satisfaction. "I can keep tabs on what is being said. If they have a bug-detecting scanner, we might be in trouble, but they should have no reason to suspect you. I'm counting on these Scats to be arrogant and lazy."

'Whix looked critically in the mirror and decided the device was indeed unremarkable. "I still think this is too flashy. I never wear this much. Not all at once."

"That's the point," Terk explained patiently. "You need to grab their attention. You'll look like you're so new to travel that you stupidly wear expensive accessories while exploring the more—colorful—sections of Plexis. Sure I can't convince you to wear some of that paint that I've been told is so popular?"

"Absolutely not, Constable," 'Whix said firmly. "Besides, you cannot be certain I am not wearing any now."

"True enough. Okay, then, just try to behave like a tourist. Gape-mouthed amazement, that sort of thing. I'll be following close behind you, so don't worry. You'll be safe."

'Whix leisurely strolled along the concourse. As leisurely as the deep crowds allowed, anyway. He entered a night zone full of revelers of all sorts: vacationers, spacers spending their hard-earned wages, and the ever-present grifters and outright thieves looking to profit from separating said beings from their credits.

The Tolian found it difficult to be both aware of the surroundings and press of beings while keeping up the pretense of being a neophyte station sightseer. *Oh, right, gape-mouthed amazement.* He stopped in the middle of the concourse, dropped his lower jaw slightly, and stared unblinkingly around at the flashing lights screaming the names of a multitude of eateries and entertainment clubs. Floor-thumping music of a dozen styles clashed in an unsettling dissonance. It wasn't so hard to pretend amazement, now that he had stopped tuning everything out. It really was an overwhelming sensory overload.

Just as he started walking again, a robed being stepped from the shadows between two venues, thrust a pamphlet into his face, and proclaimed, "You look troubled. Come visit the Mission." 'Whix crossed his eyes trying to see the flyer, but it was shoved so close to his beak, it was in his blind spot. He reared his head back and tried to take a step back to get a better look at the paper and the alien who wore the hooded robe, only to find his elbow clenched in a vise-like grip.

How had someone snuck up on him? Tolians having a nearly complete, panoramic field of view, 'Whix only had to turn his head the slightest bit and roll his left eye backward to see the creature who stood directly behind him. A pair of slit-pupiled eyes in a reptilian snout met his gaze. A Sakissishee, more commonly called a "Scat." His other eye noted the hooded figure scampering off, likely in fear of the predatory being.

"Ssss . . . you look like a diss-scerning being. Can I interes-sst you in a vacation deal s-sso good you might believe it imposs-sible? Lodging, food, and entertainment! All for one low pric-ssse!" A long, forked tongue flicked out to collect acidic spittle off its many sharp teeth.

Are some beings so gullible as to fall for this obvious ploy? 'Whix thought. *I did agree to act the innocent chick.* He fluffed his crest in feigned interest and said uncertainly, "I have limited funds . . ."

"Then thisss isss your lucky day!" The Scat's paired cranial crests pulsed colors slowly in satisfaction.

'Whix rolled his eyes around, trying and failing to spot Constable Terk as the hard hand around his arm pulled him inexorably through the dark doorway of a nearby nightclub. While the Tolian had little confidence in this plan of Terk's, he hoped the Human's promise of remaining close was reliable.

Constable Russell Terk watched P'tr wit 'Whix being towed into the club. He loitered outside for a few minutes. Without his uniform, even his unusual Human breadth was unremarkable among the press of beings milling about in fickle eddies. The occasional oblivious being would stop abruptly, becoming a rock in the river of foot traffic, to a chorus of curses and ripple of glares in assorted languages and facial features. Some species never did get the hang of crowd etiquette, he thought.

The tiny speaker in Terk's ear transmitted more static than expected, but he caught a tinny word here and there. ". . . *offer a fantas-sstic deal . . .*"

Eeling across the concourse, he eventually made his way into the dim bar. He paused a moment to let his eyes adjust before stepping to one side of the door and scanning the crowd. No feathers bobbed above the heads of the shorter beings, and few tall aliens stood in the establishment, perhaps owing to the unusually low ceiling.

". . . *wait here . . .*" came through the speaker.

Terk wormed around the edges of the throng, but still saw no sign of the Tolian. His eyes kept drifting back to the ceiling. Not one to ignore his subconscious in such circumstances, he focused more purposefully on the ceiling. Too low.

And now the speaker only transmitted a faint hiss. Time to move.

He hurried toward the back where the service corridors and storerooms would be. Ah-ha! A stairwell. Clearly not part of the original station structure and built by someone who was slightly construction-challenged.

A door stood at the top of the rickety stairs. Terk tried the handle. Locked. No surprise there. Pulling a stunner from the back waistband of his pants, he kicked at the handle. The cheap, poorly-installed door gave way, and he burst into the room, weapon drawn.

P'tr wit 'Whix sat at a table holding a scatter of bright pamphlets, his crest raised in startlement, but otherwise apparently unharmed. "Get Away!" screamed one brochure in lurid colors, above the image of an improbably colored beach. A poster on the wall behind the Tolian boasted "Luxurious!" and featured a Plexis hotel that Terk well knew didn't have any rooms that looked like that. Their most luxurious feature was the sheer number of pests. Of course, for some species, maybe the promise of free meals was a bonus.

"What . . ." Terk began, only to be interrupted by another

well-concealed—but very well-built—door opening opposite his own entry point. 'Whix jumped to his feet. A large, unshaven Human entered, leaving the door ajar behind him. His tunic looked suspiciously lumpy.

Terk brought his weapon up and slowly advanced on the other Human. "Stop right there!"

A scuff behind Terk made him spin around to see the Scat from the concourse standing in the gap of the broken door. He stepped backward, swinging the stunner between the Scat and Human, unsure which was the greater threat. The Scat held a drink in both scaly hands and a wad of colorful plas wedged beneath his arm. "What—?" *I seem to be saying that a lot,* he thought.

In that split-second of distraction, the Human lunged. Terk shot his stunner as he dodged the grasping arms, but the shot went wide and grazed the other Human's leg. It was enough to fell him, and Terk turned the weapon on the Scat.

The Scat raised his arms in a Human gesture of surrender, the drinks smashing and splashing on the floor and brochures fluttering like blown leaves. *Well, that's unusual,* Terk thought. *Scats never give up so easy.* "Here, point this at him," he said, nodding in the Scat's direction and handing the stunner to 'Whix, who blinked in confusion and hadn't yet moved.

The nearly-immobilized Human was clutching his leg in pain, and Terk swiftly bent to secure the thick, hairy wrists behind his back. Lifting his tunic, he found the lumps he had observed earlier. Not a blaster, as he'd thought, but a small syringe and carry-sack containing an empty vial of a strong, fast-acting sedative typically used to induce medical comas or for preparing livestock animals for shipment in stasis boxes.

'Whix, clearly uncomfortable with the blaster, handed it back to Terk, never moving the weapon's muzzle off the Scat. The To-lian took a couple of steps to the side. Smart to give himself a better view of the entire room.

"How long has Roraqk been involved in smuggling Tolians for food?" Terk demanded of the Scat.

The Scat hissed. "Roraqk? I don't know Roraqk, exss-scept by reputation. I s-sstay away from him."

"Then what about the Tolian cooking?"

"I know nothing of that, either." The Scat's eyes darted nervously about, and spittle flecked his jaws. "We do not cook."

"So is this salesman business your only part in this illegal operation? Are you merely the distraction or do you participate in the butchery, too?"

"It'ss-s not illegal to s-ssell time-s-ssharessss!"

"Time-shares? I doubt that. What drug is in those drinks? Was it a backup if he failed?" Terk jerked his head in the direction of the handcuffed Human.

The Scat protested, "No drugsss! Nic-nic margaritas-ss! To s-sset the mood!"

Terk snorted rudely. "Tell me another one."

"Drop the weapon, Constable," came a soft, purring voice from the sturdier doorway just behind 'Whix. "Stop harassing this embarrassment of a Scat. He really does just sell vacation packages. If this had gone right, he would've thought your friend here just changed his mind and left."

'Whix whirled to face the short, hooded figure holding a lethal biodisruptor pointed at Terk. He leaped straight up and lashed a clawed foot out in a powerful kick faster than the figure could respond. His foot hit the being squarely in its midsection, forcing air out of its lungs in a surprised *whoosh* as it flew backward. As it hit the wall behind it, gasping for air, its hood fell to its shoulders. A small, furred being stared back with huge, limpid, brown eyes.

"A Turrned?!" exploded Terk. "A *Turrned* is behind all this?"

Everyone turned shocked eyes at the Turrned, which said in a gasping voice, "We must fund the Mission."

"Commander Lydis Bowman," the stocky female enforcer introduced herself to 'Whix as he stood next to Constable Terk in an appropriated Plexis Security conference room. Her uniform was almost as new as his own, though she'd managed to work enough stiffness out of the fabric to shove the sleeves to her elbows.

'Whix gave the formal upward-leaning bow of greeting, flashing his crest and throat feathers politely, "P'tr wit 'Whix, Trade Pact Biochemist, at your service."

"Constable Terk says that you provided him with invaluable as-sistance," she said consideringly, cocking her head to the side and fixing him more with one eye than the other in an almost Tolian posture. "He doesn't say that about very many people. Of course, very many people can't stand to work with him. Which is how he ended up here with me."

Not knowing what to say to that, 'Whix remained silent, though he rotated one eye to better see the large Human leaning casually against the wall with his arms crossed. Terk shrugged at him.

Bowman continued, "It's against regulations for me to tell you this, but in light of the role you played yesterday, I want to tell you the outcome of our investigation. The Scat you encoun-tered was a dupe of the smuggling ring." She chuckled, "He really does sell time-shares for a living."

Terk muttered, "Badly. He couldn't afford higher rent, and who would believe a Scat was innocent of smuggling and running a le-gitimate vacation business?" He shook his head in disbelief. "It's ridiculous! He never noticed that most of the clients that walked out of his rented office space were Tolians. We located a few more missing persons, fortunately before their stasis became perma-nent."

Bowman went on, "The Scat shipping business was also, while not innocent, not truly involved, either. They simply don't care enough about what they ship to find out if their clients lie on man-ifests, so long as they can collect the credits."

"The Turrned thought multiple Scats between him and the law was foolproof. Because who would suspect it? A Turrned!?" Terk concluded with a shout.

'Whix asked, "But why kill Tolians for food? There are so many nonsapients. . . ."

Bowman explained, "In some circlcs, dishes made from sapient beings pull in a high price. There's a cachet for wealthy connois-seurs because of the risk involved in obtaining and consuming them, the more difficult to obtain the better. The Turrned was a member of a splinter sect. It planned to do this only once or twice to bring in the money it needed for its Mission. Which did go un-detected."

Terk finished, "But it got greedy. And this particular shipment got mislabeled and sent to the wrong location."

"I've recently been promoted and given my own ship," Bowman indicated the insignia on her open collar. "I have an—irregular—assignment, with broad leeway to recruit anyone who may be valuable to my team. You have expertise I could use, and you didn't run off squawking in a stressful situation you hadn't planned to be in. You need some formal combat training of course, but I think you'd be wasted in a lab. Tell me, P'tr wit 'Whix. Have you ever thought about becoming an enforcer?"

... *Truffles* continues

5

* * *

'WHIX TENDED TO tilt his head so one emerald eye could regard me. I'd no idea if that eye produced a clearer image, or if the sidelong gaze was more comfortable for him, but it made paying attention to what he said difficult, especially when I could see myself reflected back. "Pardon?" I asked politely, sure I'd missed his meaning.

The feathers over his neck implant were so soft, they stirred when he spoke as if moved by breath. Which wasn't the case; another curiosity I couldn't satisfy. "Partner Terk considers this activity—" we both turned at a new roar from inside the pub, "—to be recreational in nature."

"You don't."

He shook violently, feathers falling back in their immaculate order. "I do not, Fem Morgan."

"You said you're both off duty," I said gently. I liked this being, with his earnest desire to be correct. "Sira, please."

"Sira. I do not engage in risk-filled pursuits outside of our work."

"And you wish Terk didn't."

His head swiveled to bring the alternate eye in line, disproving one hypothesis. "A preference I have stated in strong terms many times. There have been memos." A sorrowful chirp. "I do not believe our commander shares my concern. She advised me to let Partner Terk 'get it out of his system.' This is, however, the third such establishment in succession. Even Plexis Port Authority must take note soon."

I'd my doubts on that. True, Plexis had its Port Authority, as would any world with a shipcity. Here, though, it was a private security force, one the station blatantly promoted as official, even naming members constables—overseen by a chief inspector—all with the right to catch and deal with felons. As they'd no court system and the laws here were what Raj Plexis deemed necessary for effective commerce, Plexis levied fines for misbehavior or seized property, once more making profit wherever possible.

According to Morgan, the truly wicked—or inconvenient—tended to vanish, space being conveniently close.

Still, 'Whix had a point. I found myself wondering why we hadn't seen a single security guard. The night zone rated more than most.

A sequence of crashes—there went furniture—followed by a ROAR. "Morgan will get him out," I said, resisting the impulse to check on my Chosen. All I sensed from him was *focus*. No, there was an undertone of *fierce glee*. Terk wasn't the only one enjoying himself.

"I hope in one piece." The Tolian began to pant, his beak agape; a sign, I'd learned, of unresolved distress.

A distress he shouldn't have to bear. "Can't you ask Bowman for a different partner?" I asked bluntly.

Another uproar from the bar flattened the Tolian's crest. "I admit comprehending his behavior can be a challenge, but I would not," he replied firmly, crest rising anew. "Partner Terk and I work well together, Sira. Our skills sets are complementary, something I learned in our first official case. It involved a most elaborate scheme."

An Elaborate Scheme

***

by Marie Bilodeau

RUSSELL TERK NUDGED the pack of wires with his boot, his partner sucking in breath behind him, the sound resonating through the secured access corridor.

"Must you do that?" she hissed through her thick Astromian accent.

Terk nudged it again, partly in annoyance at his less than junior partner, and partly out of curiosity. He crouched down for a closer look. To the untrained eye, this would look like a bomb, with multiple wired access points, either to ignite multiple offsite loads or to make the signal impossible to cut without triggering an explosion. Like the most redundant bomb ever created.

But to trained eyes, which Enforcer Terk's certainly were, it was just a messy bundle of wires bundled together like some demented floral arrangement. Of course it had taken him five hours to determine that, but now he was sure.

Sure enough, anyway.

He pulled free his knife, an unorthodox but practical gift from his father on his graduation day, and stripped a few of the wires with deft movements.

"You will get us killed!" Pamplona hissed again.

"We'd be dead by now, if that was the case," Terk mumbled,

turning a bit to see her. But he could only see her retreating back as she ran out of the room, her tail low and between her legs.

"If you're going to run," he called, "let's play it safe. Get them to evacuate the Jar." On the other side of the wall behind him were the offices of Plexis Security, most particularly the Decision-Pending Wait Room, where those under a cloud—or late with taxes—awaited judgment. The Jar.

Pamplona held up her arm, indicating she'd heard, before vanishing around the corner. He shook his head, glad she would be the one to tell the guards that. Not going to endear the Port Jellies. Not that he cared.

A bomb this close to his commander, that he cared about. He focused on the wires. Copper, some titanium, a few synthetic filaments he didn't recognize . . . this was messy work.

Messy, Terk grabbed a few wire samples and put away his knife, *but still impressive work. Maybe someone preparing a colorful bomb arrangement for his beloved?*

Terk chuckled as he stood up. He heard raised voices, and his mood quickly soured.

Evacuating the Jar would land him lots of paperwork. And he still wasn't convinced this was the only device on or near the premises.

Or that all of them were as harmless.

"They took the third Vani'sh'la painting! One of the only known originals in the entire Trade Pact, and beyond, I assure you!" the Gentek Trade Commissioner's aide, a short humanoid with a florid complexion that did nothing for his dappled skin, waved his arms at the wall.

P'tr wit 'Whix nodded sympathetically. "And you say no one was spotted on the premises?"

Even after all these years, his own voice, relayed through his implanted com, sounded foreign to him.

"The alarm system, composed of multiple layers, including motion detectors, electrical fences, oxygen traps, and laser—" The aide lowered his arms and cleared his throat at the look 'Whix gave him. Those were not all exactly legal. "Yes, well," he continued, "let's just say it would prove impossible to get away without being detected."

'Whix nodded. "Could it be an inside job?"

The aide's skin turned a rather sickly peach. "No. Only myself and the commissioner's family." 'Whix raised his beak slightly to look down suspiciously at the being, this the closest he could come to Commander Bowman's ominous raised eyebrow, then focused both eyes on the aide, though he always felt more comfortable keeping a closer eye (or two) on his surroundings.

The aide's eyes grew even larger, the pupils widening with worry. "I would, I would never . . ." he stumbled.

"I imagine you would be wise enough not to," 'Whix said. "Nevertheless, we must pursue all avenues of investigation. If the painting was not stolen from without, it leads me to conclude that it was appropriated from within."

The aide stood very still. In the silence, 'Whix could hear his current partner, his voice a continuous drone. Like an insect. Not for the first time, he wondered how Clonsen managed to lead any successful interviews. The Ordnex never seemed to stop talking long enough to breathe, much less listen to an answer.

"We'll bring you all to the station," 'Whix ordered. "It's for your own safety, as well," he added more kindly. He doubted the aide did have anything to do with this, by his agitation and long service. "For all we know, the thief is still hiding somewhere in this residence."

The aide's face grew even peachier, and he quickly left to find the commissioner and her family. 'Whix looked at the blank wall, where the painting had, for all accounts, vanished into thin air.

He opened his beak slightly in pleasure.

This mystery was exactly what he needed to remove some of his growing doldrums. He'd returned to Plexis, a fully fledged enforcer, fourteen standard days ago. He hadn't become an enforcer just to patrol the supermarket.

His analytical mind needed the stretch more than his legs.

Terk wished he could have left Pamplona at the office, but she had a nose on her that made her hard to shake. Regulations, which he mostly tried to follow, also stated he shouldn't try to abandon her. Safety in numbers, and all that.

But still, her fight-or-flight instincts weren't exactly tuned to his liking. They hadn't been in any danger. The bomb had been a dud, after all.

Unless, of course, the would-be bomber had actually just set up a distraction, and something worse is waiting for us.

He wasn't sure. A sophisticated criminal could plant false leads easily. And distractions. Smokes and shadows. And he didn't know yet if he was dealing with a sophisticated mind. All that he was sure of was that the security offices buzzed with activity, and he needed to think.

He thought better while walking.

"Some of these wires are weird," Terk offered, trying to engage his partner.

"Oh?" she said, not looking his way. Her species was more aloof; the commander had warned him. He tried not to take it personally.

They stepped outside into the lively air of Plexis, and he took a deep breath. This place was rarely dull, which he loved. As long as it didn't get him blown up.

"Some of the wires had a dual copper plate on the end caps with synthetic reinforcements. That's not exactly standard. And it's illegal because of dangerous signal degradation and fire hazard, so there would be limited supplies on Plexis." He offered her one of the stripped green wires. She looked at it with feigned interest— but not quite feigned enough.

"Why don't we go see if someone could tell us where they come from? You know, as a clue," he added in frustration.

"Sure," she said, noncommittal. "But we should report in, first."

He sighed. Plexis was interesting enough, yes, but his partner certainly managed to wash all color from it.

"Theinterestingthingaboutthe*surrson*snailsisthattheyactuallyeat selectedmaterialsandthenregurgitatetheminordertobuildtheirownshell.They'lldoitwithanymaterialandsomecombinationsareunexpectedlybeautiful."

'Whix again marveled at his partner's apparent lack of regard for breath. "And how does this relate to this painting?" the Tolian asked as he entered the aide's chambers and began looking for clues. The aide was certainly kept in opulence. It made him an even less likely suspect.

"Well,earlyVani'sh'laworksaresaidtobeinspiredfromsomeofthe-surrsonpatternsAndwe'retryingtofindoneofhispaintings . . ." Clonsen paused meaningfully.

'Whix sighed. "Fascinating," he offered. His partner inhaled, and 'Whix cut him off before he could leap into another lecture. "Why don't you take the rooms to the left, and I'll take the ones on the right."

Clonsen nodded and headed off. 'Whix slipped into the first room, finding very little to investigate.

The self-styled embassy—strictly speaking a trade mission with semipermanent staff—was a good size for Plexis, which meant expensive. The Gentek were determined to increase their visibility, a challenge for a species most couldn't tell from Human.

The Tolian went from room to room, looking each over carefully.

He entered another room, a large one, which he took to be the room of the commissioner's son. His taste was as lavish as his parents. Then again, with a name like Alo'cys Remmbraman the 27th, 'Whix could only imagine that the son was no stranger to lavishness.

Everything was perfectly set, from the dark shimmering canopy of the large bed to the intricate art on the walls. 'Whix hesitated, glancing around, trying to grasp every detail. Something was off, but he couldn't quite tell what.

He did another scan of the room, then another, slower, one.

His eyes were drawn to the top of a desk seemingly made of some sort of large animal pelvic bone. His eyes narrowed. The painting over the desk cast a shadow and seemed slightly askew on one corner, as though something had pushed it forward and it was no longer flush against the wall. That's what had seemed off, in such a well-kept and perfectly maintained room.

"What do we have here?" 'Whix muttered as he reached up to pull the painting down.

Behind it, nestled in a hastily-crafted crevasse in the faux stone wall, not quite deep enough to completely hide the artifact, cozied up another painting.

Smaller than he'd anticipated, the colors were striking and the wild brush strokes probably unmistakable to the trained eye.

"Clonsen," the Tolian summoned, as he continued to admire what he could only assume to be the missing Vani'sh'la painting. His theory was soon backed by the many enthusiastic facts offered by his partner.

'Whix only half listened.

Why would the commissioner's son steal his own painting?

"We should return to the security offices," 'Whix concluded. Something about this whole affair reeked. And he needed to figure out what, sooner rather than later.

Commander of the Trade Pact Enforcers for this sector, Lydis Bowman, paced back and forth in her office. The space was a grudging loan from Plexis Security, swept for eavesdropping devices and featuring shiny new enforcer-quality locks on the doors. Neither Inspector Wallace, head of that security, nor Plexis were happy to have her cruiser, the mighty *Conciliator*, parked near incoming customers.

Not that Bowman cared. "I have the Board Members breathing down my neck and a potential bomber on top of the Intergalactic Lichen Conference. Which starts today. We're about to be swamped with delegates from three hundred systems. It's our job to ensure their safety *and* to make sure they don't feel our presence. Without upsetting the local Jellies." She glared at Terk, all of her annoyance temporarily focused on him.

Terk, who was much taller, broader and, by all accounts, carried more firepower than his commander, nonetheless had to stop himself from shifting uncomfortably.

She relented and sighed, sitting down.

"I have to focus on the conference safety. That has to be my priority. Too many high-level scientists and fancy politicians coming to schmooze."

Terk was starting to relax again but stiffened back up as she focused back on him, narrowing her eyes.

"I need someone on this bomb. And a few other cases Plexis can't handle." Bowman tapped her eyebrow, activating her com. "Send him in."

Terk turned around to see a familiar face above a very new Trade Pact Enforcer uniform.

"Constable Terk," P'tr wit 'Whix greeted, one eye on him and the other tracking Bowman. Terk found himself wishing he could do the same.

"Welcome back," Terk said. The Tolian had been gone for six months for special enforcer training, something Terk had done earlier in his career, as well. The Tolian didn't look too scathed for it, which Terk respected.

"As I was saying," Bowman continued, as though the three had been having a casual conversation. "I need someone to handle distractions while my attention is on conference security." She added under her breath, "My undivided attention has been requested."

"So, we need to make sure station security is maintained?" Terk offered, crossing his arms.

Bowman waved his words away as though they offended her. "No no, any of their half-brained asleep constables can handle the day-to-day, even with Wallace in charge." She scowled. "I want eyes on the cases with Trade Pact implications. And no slipups."

She stood again, and 'Whix snapped to attention. Terk's arms were still crossed, though he hated the stretch of the uniform seams against his shoulders. A din of voices came through the walls, grating on his nerves. Plexis Security—and the Jar—were still under lockdown while techs cleared any other possible bomb threats.

And they weren't necessarily the loudest out there, either. Everyone apparently needed to be here today.

"You two are already working such cases. I want you to keep following those leads together. No supervision from me. I expect by-the-book work and nothing that'll hit any—and I mean *any*—of the various newsvids here. If anything *not* lichen-related hits the news over the next few days, or Wallace's desk, I'm coming straight to you."

She straightened her uniform, then stared them both down. Terk uncrossed his arms and stood almost fully at attention. Bowman wasn't one to trifle with, and he knew that. Fair but tough was the kindest way to describe the efficient commander of the enforcers.

"You're teamed up until further notice. I'm moving your partners to conference security. Consider it a test. I need personal staff. You might do." She narrowed her eyes some more. "Don't disappoint me."

And she was gone, shouting orders as she headed toward the five linked conference centers near the heart of one of Plexis' cleaner districts.

Terk turned to 'Whix and grinned.

"I've got a bomb. What do you have?"

After some debate, they'd decided to first ensure no one would actually get blown up.

That would definitely make Bowman unhappy.

Plexis didn't suffer from a lack of scrap dealers, but black market components were a bit rarer, unless you were going full-out latest tech. This wire was functional but more dangerous than practical. As for how it arrived in the secured corridor? On a hunch, Terk led 'Whix to a dealer of his acquaintance. The Festor's offerings were mostly junk, for cheap, along with a slew of other less than legal items.

Items that conveniently found their way into the offices of Plexis Security, as it happened. For the guards, and some for the detainees of the Jar. Good odds the owner would remember their last encounter. Just for fun, he'd done his best to shut the place down.

Two enforcers anywhere in Plexis weren't exactly a welcome sight. Eyes followed them. Some sellers vanished into the shadows.

Terk stopped at the booth where the merchant had his ooze-streaked back to him, and coughed. The Festor turned around, fear flip-flopping on his face for a fraction of a second before offering them a wan smile, hands fumbling at the bib beneath its ample chins. "What can I do for two of the sector's finest?"

He avoided meeting Terk's eyes, probably hoping the enforcer didn't remember him. As if Terk would forget. Still, no point in completely terrifying the being. Not yet, anyway.

"You can tell me where this comes from," Terk showed him the wire, "and how it got into the security section."

The Festor made a good show of examining the wire. "I don't believe I recognize this item, Hom Enforcer." A betraying green oozed from every pore.

Terk leaned in. The seller's neck bulged as he swallowed. The Human could see green beading around his pointed ears. "You remember nothing?"

"Well," the Festor said with a thin laugh, "we get a lot of business here. But I remember, ah, I remember that I had some wires with me one day, while doing a delivery in the facilities. There was this one young Hom—waiting for a resolution to some dispute or other. He'd very striking purple hair. Just loved wires. And I thought: it's just old junk. We laughed about it, joking he would build some sort of squidlike . . ." he stopped, seeing the look on Terk's face. "Well, you get the idea."

"You remember this young Hom's face and name, perhaps?" 'Whix offered, in a much gentler tone. Terk bit back a grin.

Good cop, bad cop, it is.

"Looked Human to me, but I don't quite recall his features. His hair will give him away," the seller said, looking hopeful at Terk, who could almost hear the unspoken words: *Did I say enough to get him off my back?*

Terk turned to 'Whix with a raised eyebrow.

The Tolian kept one eye on the scrap merchant, either to make sure he wouldn't run or to unnerve him. Terk wasn't sure, but he certainly appreciated the gesture.

"I think we have enough to keep pushing this investigation forward," the Tolian suggested. The merchant seemed pleased that he was no longer the enforcer's main focus.

Before Terk could answer, 'Whix turned his head toward the merchant, keeping his body facing his partner, which was a slightly disturbing move from the Human's point of view.

"But if we need more details," the Tolian said, his own voice a harsh series of clicks. "We'll expect to find you here."

The merchant blanched. 'Whix didn't wait for an answer before turning and walking back. Terk followed him, grinning.

He was already having more fun. Now, if they could stop anything from blowing up, they'd be golden in Bowman's books.

By the time 'Whix and Terk reached the Jar to look for a purple-haired Human, it had gone from a buzzing to frantic activity.

"What's going on?" the Tolian asked.

"The commissioner's son is missing," a Whirtle constable told them, its three eyes wide. "Gone, just like that, from the J—from Pending."

His case. 'Whix rolled the information quickly in his mind. Alo'cys Remmbraman the 27th didn't know that they'd discovered the hidden painting in his room. "I've an idea where he's headed," the Tolian said. "He'll return to the embassy. I have to stop him."

Terk raised an eyebrow but didn't question him. "I have to find Purple-head before he blows something else up." He glowered at the crowd.

"We'll meet back here, Partner Terk," 'Whix said. "This should be fast and easy," he added at Terk's brief look of concern. Or so he thought he'd read on the Human's face.

But he had his own leads to pursue. Besides, Terk had made it clear to him upon their first meeting that the Human preferred to work alone and believed most other enforcers were incompetent. Bowman had probably brought them together because she felt they could each handle their own cases. To cover more ground.

'Whix ran quick scenarios in his mind. Plexis Security had locked the embassy before leaving, using the security systems already in place. Systems which could easily be disabled by the son.

"I'll be back," he said before Terk could weigh in.

Time was of the essence. He intended to get the son before he vanished again.

Terk watched the Tolian practically race away. The being was a biochemist and liked to analyze stuff. Not stupid. If he felt he needed backup, he'd have let Terk know.

The Human enforcer focused back on the occupants squeezed

into the waiting rooms that made up the Jar. Just his luck they were
unusually full—some local nonsense about importing endangered
species for funerals. Being Plexis, there'd be no separation of
hardened criminals from the merely unfortunate. The innocent
rubbed appendages with the despicable, and most would pay up—
the rest be sent offstation.

Terk went through all of the areas. While he spotted plenty of
Humans, including some familiar faces, and a cluster of Genteks,
none had striking purple hair.

Of course, getting rid of that hair wouldn't be hard. And their
suspect might not even be Human.

He spotted someone who could help, one of the station's oldest
constables, a Human named Hutton. She was tough, smart, and
didn't miss a beat around her. Shame she'd stayed a Jelly.

"Hutton."

"Terk." A sharp look. "Thought you'd be with your boss."

"Still looking into the bomb threat. Did you see a male
Human—humanoid—with purple hair here before the alert?"
Terk asked.

Hutton nodded. "Left right after. Shifty-looking fellow. Had
something to hide, I'd bet." She gave a raw laugh. "But then,
don't most?"

Terk looked at her in surprise. "You watched a prisoner walk out?"

Hutton gave him an equally incredulous look. "Frat, no! He
was a guard—private security. Not one I know, mind, but they
switch out faster than a Scat spits. Likely here for one of the law
firms."

A guard . . . Terk wanted to hit himself. No, hit his informant,
which he might do, later. He'd assumed the would-be bomber was
a prisoner, but how would a prisoner have so easily gained access
to the secure access corridor?

He definitely wanted to hit himself.

"Odd thing," Hutton offered. "Saw him looking at the Gentek
Commissioner's lad when the family came in—that look people
get when they want something real bad, you know?"

Terk frowned. "Why are the commissioner and his family even
here?"

"Some thieves broke into the embassy. Or something like that. That'd be your turf, enforcer."

Broke into the embassy . . . a theory tackled Terk. "Where's the son?"

Her smile wasn't pleasant. "We'd all like to know. After your partner ordered the evacuation, he went missing along with a few others. Quite the mess, Terk."

He grunted an apology, busy thinking. Purple-head had created the bomb as a diversion after his robbery attempt had failed. A diversion that scrambled the Jar where the commissioner's family would more than likely also be.

Target the family. Get the son, and get him to give him access to an abandoned embassy.

Terk mulled it over a bit. It didn't quite fit. Too elaborate. Too many variables. Why wouldn't the guard have just walked in? Of course, without the confusion of all the extra bodies here, his activities might not have gone unnoticed.

'Whix. The Tolian might be heading into more than he'd bargained for.

"Thanks, Hutton," he said. He double-checked that his sidearm was still comfortably strapped to his side, then headed out into the station, alone.

'Whix stepped gingerly into the deserted embassy. As he'd imagined, the alarm system was disarmed. His feathers bristled slightly in anticipation.

He walked toward the son's room, hearing some noise from within. He pulled out his as yet unused enforcer-issue stunner, took a deep breath. For a moment, he regretted that Terk wasn't with him. But, knowing he needed to focus all of his attention on the here and now, he quickly shoved that thought aside.

He turned into the room.

"Hands in the air," he ordered.

And then fell forward as he was struck from behind.

Terk arrived just as two shadows scrambled down the elaborate staircase, long legs carrying them down two stairs at a time.

"Halt!" he ordered, holding up his stunner. The two hesitated, then turned around to climb back up. 'Whix stepped out at the top of the stairs. He seemed a bit wobbly on his feet, but his grim expression left Terk no doubt that he intended to block their escape. The young men seemed to reach the same conclusion, and they hesitated, standing near each other.

"Lights," the Tolian said, giving Terk fair warning to lower his eyes. The light streamed in, soft enough not to completely blind them.

The two figures stood still on the stairs. The well-groomed, dapple-skinned male must be the commissioner's son, and the purple hair on the other could indeed be deemed legendary.

Purple-head moved closer to the commissioner's son. "I swear I'll shoot him!" he shouted.

"You don't have a weapon," the Tolian said dryly from the top of the stairs.

"We do," Terk offered, stepping to the bottom of the stairs. The boys had nowhere to go. Terk exchanged a glance with the other enforcer, who nodded slightly.

"Come with us quietly, and you won't be harmed," Terk continued.

"No!" the commissioner's son said, surprising Terk. 'Whix looked just as surprised. "We won't go with you!"

Well, then; so much for the kidnapping scenario.

"Where will you go?" the Tolian asked. Terk fought against a grin at the exasperation in the Tolian's voice.

"I don't know, but we'll go far!" the son said. "I mean, this painting will get us passage lots of places. And you can't stop me for stealing it—it's my family's!" he added triumphantly.

"It's your father's and, yes, we can arrest you," 'Whix offered, more dryly than before.

"Why fake a bomb?" Terk demanded, the whole thing confusing him. "You needed to be at the security office to—what? To kidnap someone who's obviously not kidnapped? Look, I just need to know what all this running is about. I'm pretty tired from chasing you, so you can at least give me this much."

"If I tell you," Purple-head offered, "will you let Alocs and I go?"

"No," the Tolian said. "But we may ask for leniency on your be-half." He gave Terk an *I don't think so* look, but kept his peace. Terk carefully didn't crack a smile.

"We figured we'd meet at the Jar, sneak back here, and steal the painting in the confusion," he said. "Then we could escape. Just . . . leave. Be free." There was such longing in his voice as he looked at Alo'cys, who shared all of the same hopes in one long breath.

"Ah. Star-crossed lovers. Wonderful. Always popular, those," Terk said. "Wait. Why didn't you just walk out with the painting? Seems elaborate."

"My father never leaves, and he keeps an eye out. And he would never approve of my union with someone from another species," Alo'cys placed his hand on his lover's shoulder, squeezing in gentle comfort. "I needed him gone." He suddenly looked really proud. "And we needed to keep as many enforcers busy as possible. I fig-ured a bomb threat, at the same time as the start of the big con-ference, would do the trick."

"Your bomb looked too crappy for that," Terk said. "But nice try."

Purple-head looked dejected. He held out his hand and took his lover's in it.

"Will you let us go? For the sake of love?" he implored.

Terk looked up at the Tolian. The two locked gazes for a few seconds, and then nodded.

They had reached an understanding.

'Whix practically hopped along the corridor of Plexis Security beside the large Human. They both laughed.

"For the sake of love?" he said. "What kind of excuse is that?!"

Terk nearly doubled over. "And the elaborate scheme! I mean, just pull a fire alarm or something! They've watched too many trashy romance-vids."

"I imagine so,"'Whix said. Nearing their destination, the two calmed down a bit. "Still," the Tolian added. "It was kind of you to

ask that they be detained in the same waiting room, and they be
only charged with disturbing the peace."

Terk shrugged, looking embarrassed. "Made sense. We were all
young and foolish and in love at once." He looked at the Tolian
and thought, *maybe.* "Good of you not to mention the whole hitting from behind thing. And to ask that they be released at the
same time."

It was 'Whix's turn to shrug. "If that comes to anything, it'll be
nice if they do get a chance to get a fresh start, although it would
be without the painting."

"They'd find a way," Terk said.

"An elaborate one, I imagine,"'Whix added.

They both chuckled again. Terk lowered his head in thanks.
"Well, P'tr wit 'Whix, it was a pleasure working once more
with you."

'Whix mimicked the gesture. "Same here, Russell Terk. And it
was lovely not to be used as bait, for once."

Terk grinned. "You sort of naturally fall into step with that role,
though."

'Whix's reply was cut short by Bowman's arrival. She passed
them, walking briskly, looking generally annoyed.

Then spoke. "Well done on the solved cases, you two," she said.

Terk and 'Whix shared a surprised look before turning to look
at her.

"Now, get to the others on my desk. I've got a few more days of
this, this . . ." the look on her face dripped into her voice, "moss
conference."

"You want us to just—take—your cases, Commander Bowman?"

She scowled. "Of course. Categorize, prioritize, and solve. Together. Terk can stand you, and you can stand him, and you get
results."

She paused, looked at each of them carefully. "I'm a good judge
of character, which is why I am where I am. I need better than
competent staff, and I think you two are among them. Do this
right, show me I can trust you, and we'll talk about your careers
when this fratling conference is over."

Bowman held their gazes for a split-second longer, as though weighing them still, then spun around and left, constables scurrying out of her way.

'Whix and Terk shared a quick glance, straightened their uniforms, held their shoulders—and crests—with a bit more pride, and turned around to head back in, together.

. . . *Truffles* continues
Interlude

* * *

"D IN'T NEED HELP. Had th'Brill right where I wanted."
Morgan eyed his tablemate. Hard to tell if Terk was joking at the best of times, and this wasn't one of them. Most of the other Human's craggy face smeared with blood—not all red. The Brill in question had been dragged off by others of his kind, having met the business end of the bartender's stunrod.

It being simple prudence to know where such things were kept.

In silence, Morgan handed over a tooth.

The enforcer took it in his thick fingers. Held it up and squinted, then tossed it over a shoulder. "Not mine." He moved his tongue around thoughtfully. "Maybe."

"Your partner was concerned." As was Sira, but he'd reassured her.

"Featherhead," Terk said fondly and spat red before wrapping his big hand around a mug of beer. He lifted it to toast the bartender. "Nice place."

"It was." Shea McWhirtle, owner, barkeep, and Human despite her name, tossed the remnants of a stool on the growing stack of broken furniture, paused to give Morgan a meaningful nod, then went back to work.

Found his message then. Relieved, he clapped Terk on a big shoulder. "Looks like you're stuck with the tab."

A bizarre wink from an eye almost swollen shut. "Nah. Bowman's taken an interest." The enforcer produced a credit stick from a pocket. "I've expenses."

First the face in the shadow. Now Bowman, setting Terk loose in spacer bars. Morgan didn't need the *taste* of change to tell him something was stirring, but what? The sector chief didn't enter Plexis without good reason. She'd history here—let alone the traditional animosity between Port Jellies, even hired ones, and enforcers.

He kept his expression set to amused; inwardly, he tensed. Believing their troubles were over? Didn't mean—in any sense—they were. *Bowman's sniffing around, my Lady Witch. Are there Clan on Plexis?*

A pause, a flash of Power as Sira sent the question into the M'hir, then: *Cenebar di Teerac is here, in his quarters.* The Clan healer a friend, no doubt of that. A trickle of shared *amusement. With an unChosen who managed to impale his brother while the pair tried swords at a dealer's on the gold level. No others at the moment.*

No others willing to reveal themselves.

She'd know who he meant. Acranam's Clan were embroiled in a bitter struggle between those willing to resume their lives in the wider universe and those loyal to Wys di Caraat.

Wys and her followers detested Sira's rise to lead the Clan Council and how she'd brought them into the Trade Pact—almost as much as they loathed him, her Human Chosen.

Do you blame them? Sira countered. Then, sadly, *They expect me to act as they do. To abuse my Power.*

When all she sought was to help them. Morgan let her feel his *pride. They'll learn better, Witchling.*

Some will, she conceded. He sensed her mind pull away, her focus turning inward. *The rest have too much practice being cruel.*

The Sacrifice of Pawns

* * *

by Mark Ladouceur

KURR BRACED HIMSELF for the strong wave of disappointment that washed over him through the M'hir. *I don't have a choice, Dorsen. I have a mission from the Council. They want us to investigate along the Acranam Corridor. I will be with you as soon as I complete it. I'm sorry.* Home for Kurr was on Tinex 14, but currently he was on Camos, visiting his younger brother and mother after a months-long archeological dig.

I know, Kurr's Chosen sent back along the connection between them. *But I see that's not all, my Chosen.* He sensed *amusement. This is a puzzle, like your digging. You're not hiding your excitement at the chance to solve it. At least you're not hiding it from me.*

Kurr smiled. Though she couldn't see it through the M'hir, she would sense the emotion behind it. *How lucky I am to have a Chosen who's not just a match to my power, but who's so alike in thought.* He sent this along their shared link and sensed the nascent presence that grew within Dorsen: their child. The feel of that link, bonding him to Dorsen and through her to their unborn child, stirred a longing for her presence. That same feeling echoed back to him from her.

Alike in thought, but not so much in patience, she replied, and playfully sent a flick of Power through him. *You must hurry home. But first, tell me about this mission that intrigues you. Why do you need to go wherever this Acranam System is?*

Council has credible evidence that there is a M'hiray presence there. And that it might be linked to survivors of the Destarian.

Her reaction was immediate. *My sister, her Chosen—*

—Might be alive. He completed her thought with her. *Yes. And others too. So you see now?*

I do. You must go, but be careful.

I will, he replied. *Barac will be with me. He'll be careful for both of us.* He sent *reassurance* along the link between them.

A sud keep a di safe?

He felt the doubt in her reply. *Barac is First Scout. He has far more experience in this regard than I do. I'm only a historian and a philosopher. I trust him.*

Very well, you may go, she teased.

Thank you, my Chosen. He sent a rush of *affection* that she promptly returned. Barac appeared that moment, 'porting into the main room of the apartment.

"Did I interrupt?" Kurr's younger brother asked, sensing the intimate mental connection between Kurr and Dorsen.

Kurr clamped down his shields, keeping the brunt of his *annoyance* from Barac. But enough slipped through to put a smile on Barac's face.

"Where have you been?" Kurr asked.

"I was summoned by Council," Barac said. "I won't be traveling with you."

"Oh," Kurr said and let Barac sense his *disappointment.*

"It seems I'm very much in demand. Harc was sent by Jarad di Sarc to give me a new mission." Barac lifted one of the old artifacts Kurr had brought back from his latest dig on Stonerim III, a wooden bowl, and turned it over. "I'm to escort a Chooser to Auord." Barac put the bowl back down.

"Really? Who is this Chooser that they need our First Scout?"

"Sira di Sarc."

Kurr realized after a moment that he was standing with his mouth agape in surprise. "She's leaving the Cloisters? As long as I can remember, she's lived there. Does this mean they've found an unChosen strong enough for her?"

"I can't say," Barac responded and held his fingers to his lips in the Human gesture of silence.

"An even more secret mission than our—my secret mission," Kurr said. "Fitting for our First Scout."

"Is that condescension or mocking, dear brother?" Barac asked.

"Sincerity," Kurr opened his shields enough to let his brother see the truth of it.

"I don't know why she's leaving now after all these years. Council sends me wherever their whims dictate. How could a mere sud guess the grand strategy behind it all?" Barac raised his eyebrow in what Kurr sensed was a mix of bemusement and frustration.

"Before you go . . ." Kurr looked around at the half-packed boxes spread around the room. He'd begun leaving his findings with Barac; Dorsen barely tolerated the clutter of artifacts he'd returned with from his latest expedition. Kurr dug through three boxes before he found the object of his search: a bracelet. Its dull surface was etched with designs that still caught the light of the room.

"Here." He held it out to Barac. "Take it."

Barac looked at him, but didn't move. "What's this for?"

"A gift, heart-kin."

"Mhmm," Barac acknowledged and stepped forward to pluck a foam packing chunk from Kurr's hair.

"It's very old; pre-Stratification, in fact. An excellent example of our people's work. We don't make anything like this anymore. There's so much we've lost—"

"Are you about to start a history lesson?" Barac asked and rolled his eyes.

"Fine. No *lesson*."

"Are you sure you wish to part with it?" Barac asked.

"I am. Take it."

Barac nodded and slipped it on. "A generous gift. Thank you. I should go. Jarad isn't patient. He wants me to depart soon, and I must prepare."

"Of course. Safe travels, my brother," Kurr said. "Be careful. A Chooser like Sira—there haven't been any like her before."

"Don't worry. She'll be under stasis to protect your unChosen brother, and I've had enough experience dealing with my betters. I can be sufficiently deferential to her. Safe travels, Kurr. I hope Acranam proves more interesting than shepherding Jarad's daughter to some backwater rock." And with that, Barac 'ported away.

Yes, Kurr thought, *it should be interesting.* He brought up the manifest Jarad had given him in person and began planning. Twenty of their people were presumed lost when the liner *Destarian* had exploded. Now he had a chance to find them and solve a mystery that had haunted his people, but especially his Chosen. All he had to do was reach Acranam.

Acranam was far from Camos, and no Clan had a locate to port to it. Instead, Kurr ported himself to Plexis Supermarket in the usual way, materializing in an area the Clan paid to go unwatched. He'd have to wait a station day, but a ship would arrive to take him to the planet. His passage had been booked.

Kurr wished Barac were with him. Barac could have contacted his pet Human, Jason Morgan, to transport them on the *Silver Fox*.

Kurr proceeded to the tag point.

"Your airtag, Hom di Sarc."

"Of course." He leaned forward to allow the Human male to apply the gold tag.

"Do you accept responsibility for the air you share on Plexis?"

"Yes."

The male tapped his cheek to place the tag and let his finger linger on Kurr's cheek before tracing a quick line down along his jaw and winking.

"Thank you," Kurr said and moved on.

Not until he passed beyond the tag point to the luggage claim did Kurr realize what the Human male had meant by the action.

"How curious," Kurr said to himself. It was the first encounter of that nature he'd had with a Human male. He would have liked to have skimmed his thoughts to confirm what he guessed, but it was too late now. Kurr realized he should pay more attention to the beings around him and thought Barac was much better with other species than he was. In truth, he had only ever learned a bit of scouting craft from Barac. Far more often Kurr had been lost in thought and had relied completely on Barac to navigate the myriad species and cultures in places like this.

He hoped Council hadn't made a mistake in choosing him.

From the tag point Kurr caught a servo cart to his hotel, *The Orilla*. Kurr walked through its doors to the opulent lobby. The desk clerk nodded to him as Kurr stepped up to the front desk.

"Greetings, Hom di Sarc. Your room is ready and your luggage has arrived. It's in your room."

Kurr took the old-fashioned key card—no Clan used idents or palm locks—and thanked the Human. He crossed the lobby and took the lift to his room. Opening off the entranceway was a square area furnished with lush alien plants in full flower, two large couches, and a large holo-display playing a loop that advertised the hotel's amenities over slow-tempo, relaxing music. A door on the left wall led to the bedroom and one on the right to the fresher. His luggage was neatly stacked for him in the bedroom. He opened the curtains in that room and looked out onto the concourse many floors below. The mid-range concourse was as crowded as always— a sea of movement with so many aliens moving on their individual errands.

He walked back out to the central room and addressed the holo-display. "Room 4306, I'd like a table for one at the *Claws & Jaws*."

There was a slight pause. On the holo-display, the room's virtual assistant, programmed to match an occupant's species, appeared as a Human female. "I'm sorry, Hom di Sarc," it reported. "There are no spaces available for the next two station days at the *Claws & Jaws*. What would you like to do?"

He thought a moment. "Make a reservation at *Le Gros Canard*."

"For how many?"

"Still just one."

"I have booked a table for one at *Le Gros Canard*."

Kurr used the fresher and changed clothing, then headed out to the café. He kept his shields tight as he drifted along with the crowd and their different thought patterns, some ordered and some chaotic. Most disconcerting were the Humans who appeared superficially like his own people but were missing that vital connection to the M'hir and through it to each other.

"Greetings, Hom. What may I bring you?" asked his server.

"Sombay, please." Kurr had grown fond of the drink Jason Morgan had introduced him to on one of their trips together.

"Will you be eating as well?"

"Yes, please."

He'd spent three full days at Barac's before coming here, planning and researching Acranam and the passengers of the *Destarian*. It left him needing a reprieve from too much thinking. "What would you recommend?"

"Tonight's special is an excellent choice; a creamy vegetable soup with grilled *entalon*."

"I'll try it."

The waiter bowed and left.

Sitting on the cafe's patio, Kurr could watch the steady flow of beings past its railings. He relaxed and let his mind drift outward. After a short time, he sensed the barest whisper in his mind against his shields, like a question. Raising his head, Kurr's met the intense stare of a stranger's face through a gap in the crowd for just a moment before it was hidden from view.

How odd.

Reaching out through the M'hir to try and sense that other mind again revealed nothing. Its *feel* had been M'hiray, but not a sense of familiar power. Nor was the face one he knew. Who, then? If he'd been weaker, he might not have sensed it. Now it was gone or shielded. Or, more likely, he'd just imagined it after three days of too little rest. What Human had Power to concern him? As he ate, he continued observing the beings around him, but there was no sense again of the earlier presence. He put it out of his mind.

Feeling relaxed and full after his meal, Kurr left the restaurant to shop for additional supplies for his mission to Acranam. Barac had recommended several shops and alternates for him on Plexis. Since neither Barac nor Kurr could know what Kurr would need when he reached Acranam, the list was comprehensive. So much so that Kurr wondered how he'd transport all the gear once he bought it. There were medical supplies for infections and viruses, portable forcefields for use while camping, all-weather clothing and boots, and the usual unappealing, dried nutritional rations Kurr took on his own archeological expeditions.

For the shoppers, spacers, merchants, and others, the time didn't seem to matter. The many shops, restaurants, and other forms of entertainment on Plexis were busy, and the crowds bustling between them formed a steady current. Kurr followed along through the flashing lights and booming music of the entertainment hubs, the tempting aromas and noxious odors of the restaurants and cafés, and the blaring advertisements and vid displays of the merchant districts.

About to leave a shop, Kurr spotted the same stranger he'd seen earlier. This time he wasn't looking at Kurr. In that instant, the stranger had been distracted by an Ordnex merchant. When Kurr opened the shop door, the stranger looked up with an expression of surprise.

Kurr reached out a tendril of thought, a polite test of power and a *greeting*, only to be rebuffed by a powerful slap through the M'hir and a sense of *hostility*. The stranger was strong, but not as strong as Kurr. There was a sense of displacement about the Power, as though . . . This was no Clansman, it was a Human face, but behind the eyes one of his own kind looked back at him. One of his kind was controlling this Human like a puppet!

The puppet turned and ran, disappearing around a corner into a crowd. Kurr set out across the broad hall, dodging beings and using a flick of Power to *push* the slow ones out of his way. When he reached the other side and got out of the crowd, Kurr picked up his pace to the service corridor where he'd seen the other disappear. It appeared empty except for a few servos moving about on errands and a group of drunken spacers, weaving along. He searched nearby through the M'hir, but found nothing of the other's presence.

He was being followed. But why? Could it have something to do with his mission?

It must, he decided. And to risk exposure of the Clan by controlling a vulnerable Human telepath like that disturbed him.

Kurr decided he could buy the last few items he needed through the room's assistant. Kurr focused on his room and concentrated . . .

. . . as he reappeared in his room, Kurr froze. His stomach tightened. Cushions from the couches had been tossed and the plants knocked over. In his bedroom, his luggage had been opened and his clothes and belongings strewn across the floor.

It had to have been the stranger, but what had he been looking for: Kurr, or something that belonged to Kurr? He took the lift down to the front desk.

"Who came to see me?" he asked the clerk.

"No one, Hom di Sarc."

Kurr hesitated. By Council decree, no one except a Scout could reach into a non-Clan mind. Barac wasn't with him, but Jarad had stressed the importance of the mission.

He probed the clerk's mind. The clerk, a low-level Human telepath, was sensitive enough to be vulnerable, the reason Kurr and his fellow Clan used this hotel.

The being had told the truth, but there was a blurry image of someone asking for a spare key to Kurr's room. Kurr delved deeper into the Human's memories, but the "someone" had interfered with them.

"Is there a problem, Hom di Sarc?"

"No." Kurr turned from the desk and walked back across the lobby.

In his room, he picked up and sorted his belongings. Nothing appeared to be missing, but a few small items were broken.

A warm flush of blood flashed through him, along with doubt. A secret mission from the Council, and he'd treated it like a vacation. Barac would laugh. As for his superior power, so far he'd displayed only superior ignorance. Barac should be on this mission, not him, while he would have been better off doing something simple like escorting Sira to Auord. Why had he thought he could do this?

Kurr knew he should contact Jarad, but what should he say: that he was being followed? That the mission was compromised? That he was in over his head and should come home? Kurr hesitated. What did he want?

To go home, but more so to solve this deepening mystery. The *Destarian* had exploded, but there were rumors of survivors. And with someone following Kurr, it could mean that someone didn't want him getting to Acranam. But why keep him away? What would be so important? M'hiray as prisoners, or worse? Who could hold M'hiray against their will? He didn't know any kind other than his own that could keep M'hiray prisoners. Renegade M'hiray? The prospect sent a shock through him. His evidence was nonexistent; he had just his own theory. The only way to find out was to get to Acranam.

He felt the pull of the mystery on Acranam, stronger now than any of the times he'd had leads on pre-Stratification artifacts. What were artifacts to the lives that could be at stake? Against that, however, was the danger to Dorsen and their unborn child should anything happen to him. Could he justify risking all their lives for this?

What is upsetting you? Dorsen's touch in his mind was instantly soothing, as though she were right beside him. Distance meant little to M'hiray of their strength.

Someone's following me. He sent the image of the Human puppet and shared his memories from his encounters and of the hotel room in its current state.

But no one knows of your mission, she replied, shocked.

Only us, Barac, and the Council, he responded.

Barac—

—Is heart-kin and would never betray me! No more than you could. I have trusted him with my life many times before. I still trust him.

But you're in danger. He could have been forced to give up the information. He's only a sud.

Kurr hated the idea, but had to admit it was a possibility. Barac might not even know if he'd been forced to tell. Kurr *reached* out and found Barac's mind intact and shielded. From this distance he couldn't detect any damage or mental traps without alerting his brother and so withdrew.

No, he told Dorsen. *It must be someone on the Council or linked to the Council. Jarad has rivals. It could be Faitlen di Parth. Barac is right, we're just pawns in a game to them. One I refuse to play.*

He sensed *disappointment* along their link and asked, *What's this, my Chosen?*

I thought of my sister. I wished to know her fate. And I know you want to solve this, to have your answers.

I do, but my thoughts are for your safety. If anything were to happen . . .

I know, but you're a Second Level Adept—

Closer to a First. Kurr replied.

Yes.

And I survived Joining with the formidable Dorsen di Kessa'at, didn't I?

You did.

Then I will face this challenge.

You have my faith, my Chosen. Pride radiated from Dorsen before their connection faded into the background.

Kurr stood, surveyed the mess in his room, and decided he'd need a new room under a different name if he was to feel safe. In the lobby a short time later, he dipped into the clerk's mind, obscuring his appearance and making him compliant, much like the Other had done earlier. He requested a room under a different name. A short time later, Kurr moved his hastily repacked luggage into his new room by himself. He locked the door and erected the forcefield projector Barac had insisted on for camping in the jungle. With that done, Kurr slept.

As he approached the dockyard the next morning, Kurr felt *something* at the edge of his senses and stopped before realizing that would be conspicuous. He forced himself to keep walking, alert to everything around him. Ahead was the board showing arrivals and departures. Kurr walked until he was in front of it. His ship was leaving soon, but he still had to go through the tag point.

Kurr looked around as inconspicuously as he could. He didn't see the Human puppet anywhere. And *reaching* out through the M'hir, he did not feel the Other's presence.

Hidden still, he decided. If the Other wanted to keep him from reaching Acranam, he'd have to make a move soon.

Kurr stepped away from the board. Beyond the tag point there was a lounge to one side and a series of multi-species' accommodations along the other side. Above were catwalks and promenades to the docking areas of the station. Just ahead, a short line waited at each tag point. Kurr risked another look around, trying to appear casual, just a tourist taking in the sights. He saw no sign of the puppet, but he dared not risk a longer look. Taking his place in line, Kurr waited.

Then he felt it. The presence was there, strong and steady, its *malevolence* focused on him. Lost in thought, Kurr felt a tap on his shoulder and jumped.

"You're next, Hom," the Human behind him said.

"Oh. Of course." Kurr stepped forward and the tag operator tapped a metallic rod to Kurr's gold airtag. It dropped from his cheek to the operator's hand and then humped into the reader.

"One full station day charged to the account of Kurr di Sarc," the operator said. His goldtag guaranteed a rounding up. "We hope you enjoyed your stay, Hom."

"Yes," he said. "Thanks." Kurr stepped forward, adrenaline and anticipation building for the certainty of the confrontation. Turning his head as he walked away from the tag point, he saw the puppet in line. Clan eyes stared straight at him from a Human face. Kurr changed course, walking toward the series of accommodations. He found one appropriate for humanoids and opened the door. As soon as it closed behind him and he saw he was alone, he *pushed* . . .

. . . reappearing a short distance away, high up on a catwalk. Kurr maximized his shields, keeping his presence small and hidden. For a moment Kurr recalled the game of childhood: 'port and seek, which he'd played with Barac, Osbar di Parth, and others as children. But this was no game. From here he could see the stranger move through the tag point and cross the space to the door Kurr had just passed through moments before.

Once the puppet opened the door and went through, Kurr took a deep breath and *pushed* again. He appeared behind his target just as the other slid open the cubicle door to check inside. Kurr rushed forward and grabbed him by the back of his jacket. The Human jerked from his grip, turned, and raised a weapon. Instinctively, Kurr *flung* him across the room with a surge of Power. The weapon fell to the floor, and Kurr scooped it up: a compact pistol. The puppet groaned and shook his head. His hand clutched and scrabbled around the floor, searching for his weapon before he looked up and saw Kurr pointing it at him.

Kurr looked at this Human, enslaved to a M'hiray like Kurr, but one unknown to him. It was to whoever controlled this Human that Kurr spoke.

"Who are you? Why do you want to keep me from Acranam? What connection do you have to the *Destarian*?"

The Human's face twisted into a grinning rictus. "Council lackey, you shouldn't interfere in matters beyond you."

Kurr *reached* for the Human's mind and braced himself for the contest, mustering his Power against the puppet's master. Then came the attack against Kurr's shield. Tendrils of Power *lashed* at him, searching for weak points. His foe was strong, no doubt of that. He hammered aside the attack. Kurr sent a flare of power against the Other's shields. They cracked. He found a weak point and sent Power pouring into it. The Clansman tried to counter, but Kurr ripped his shields apart. He grasped the presence then, and a name: Larimar di Sawnda'at.

Shock thrilled through him. One of the *Destarian*'s passengers. Larimar was behind this?

What happened to the others from the Destarian*? Tell me what happened to Quel di Bowart and her Chosen.*

No.

Then I will find out when I reach Acranam.

You'll never reach Acranam. Scorn ran through Larimar's response.

Kurr sent a scream of *triumph* through the Power coursing between himself and Larimar. Before he could exploit this victory, though, the other presence retreated and disappeared. Kurr found himself alone in the Human's mind, and it was empty. There was nothing left. No answers for him. He severed the link and was aware he stood over a mindless husk. Blood ran from its nose and drool from its mouth.

Kurr bent down and searched the Human's pockets for anything to identify him, but wasn't surprised when he found nothing. He couldn't afford to have the body found here like this.

"Just another pawn," Kurr said and pushed the husk into the M'hir.

Kurr realized he was still holding the Human's weapon and pushed that into the M'hir as well. Exiting the accommodation, he walked along the hall to the air lock for his ship. His questions were unanswered, but he knew where the answers must be: Acranam.

Kurr boarded the liner through the connection tube. The ship's steward greeted him and directed him to the humanoid deck where his cabin would be. He was alive, and so Dorsen's faith in him had been proven. But Kurr still felt awhirl from his confrontation. Questions distracted him, but he had one answer, a name. What was Larimar's game? Were the others from the *Destarian* still alive and held hostage or dead? He would get his answers. He was stronger than Larimar. This they both knew. And he'd force them from the Clansman in person, not through some Human puppet.

The cabin on the liner was old and shabby, but there were few ships that passed through the Acranam System, and it was only for a few shipdays. In the cabin was a bunk, a workstation, a chair, a large screen, and a number of stains both fresh and faded in the carpet. At least it had a private fresher stall.

He locked the door behind him, then sat on the chair in front of the foldout table and activated the ship's network. No virtual assistant greeted him, only a menu. The external cams showed the inside of the ship's docking bay. Internal cameras in the liner's public spaces showed its limited amenities. Nothing that would tempt him from his cabin.

Around him, he could not detect any other M'hiray. Larimar, through his puppet, had been alone. Soon the ship departed Plexis, leaving the station behind and going to translight on its way to Acranam.

Kurr contacted Jarad through the M'hir and relayed what had happened so far.

Interesting, was Jarad's reply, though Kurr could detect no actual sense of interest from the head of the Council. *There is nothing to suggest Larimar has accomplices within the Clan. Nevertheless, I will question Degal on the possibility his son has contacted him. You should know,*

Kurr, that your brother has experienced no incidents. He and Sira will arrive on Auord in two standard days.

Kurr would happily leave it to Jarad to follow up on investigating a Council member, an entanglement any Clan preferred to avoid. At least Barac was having an easier time with his assignment.

Over the next day Kurr had little else to do but plan the details of his time on Acranam—how and where he would search. The ship's captain insisted there was no shipcity and that all it could do was send him down in a shuttle. Once done, he'd 'port home with answers to the mystery and, hopefully, survivors.

Space travel is boring, he complained to Dorsen on the last night of his voyage. *I'll be glad to get off this ship and onto Acranam.*

My poor dear. Cooped up in your cabin.

His contact with her over the voyage had mostly kept his sense of confinement at bay, but being almost at his destination the cabin felt especially small.

How long until you arrive?

Soon. This shipmorning.

You should rest.

Yes, my dear.

Get your answers for both of us and come home for the birth. Little Elia grows impatient to arrive.

A name they'd chosen together. Kurr reveled in the feel of their connection, letting it relax him into sleep. *Good night, my Chosen.*

Be safe.

I will be.

Danger woke him; felt on an instinctive level: a threat nearby. A presence here on the ship. Clan.

"Lights," Kurr ordered as he sat up.

A tall, lean stranger stood in his cabin, casually, as though he had every right to be there. Bright gray-green eyes stared at him from beneath a high, broad forehead and thick blond hair. In that moment Kurr knew who it was.

"Yihtor di Caraat."

With the recognition came fear. He could feel Yihtor's Power through the M'hir and knew it to be much greater than his own.

"So you're the fly who's buzzing around my business."

"You're dead."

"Am I?" Yihtor mocked.

"What do you have to do with the *Destarian* and Larimar? What game are you playing?"

"One that only the most powerful can play—" Almost casually, force *ripped* through Kurr's mind, searching, FINDING . . . *You should know, Kurr, that your brother has experienced no incidents. He and Sira will arrive on Auord in two standard days . . .*

"—and your part in it is done."

Light-years away on the planet Tinex 14, Dorsen sat alone in her family's library when Kurr's fear shocked through their connection. His pain followed hard after. Fighting for his life, but not alone. Clan Chosen were never alone. She fought for her life as part of him. Instinct drove her to lend her strength as his faded, to bolster his shields for both their sake and for the sake of the presence in her womb.

Too little. Too late.

She felt his *cry* to her along their link, and then he was dead, slipping away, dissipating into the roiling dark of the M'hir and pulling her and Elia inexorably, inevitably down with him. So strong was the bond between Chosen that they shared not just life, but death. With a scream of rage at their sacrifice she was gone then, too.

... *Truffles* continues
Interlude

* * *

"**I**T'S NOT THE Clan."

"Huh." Terk had a gift for expressive monosyllables. That grunt, coupled with a snort? Implied a target more to the constable's liking.

They'd come a long way from the days when Terk had made himself a thorough nuisance, ordering searches of the *Silver Fox* whenever the whim or opportunity struck, for some reason convinced the ship and her captain were smugglers.

Might have been, Morgan admitted to himself, a few cargoes he'd prefer not be examined by authorities, but avoiding exorbitant local fines were expected of a free trader and hardly the business of a Trade Pact Enforcer. Terk'd had a mole fly in his ear, that was all, and the game had its entertainment.

Until Sira. These days Bowman backed his Chosen and her approach with the Clan, and so long as they hunted someone else? Well, there was a quadrant's worth of miscreants to pursue, none of them his concern or Sira's.

Unless—a target Terk preferred? On Plexis? Deneb's syndicates operated here, but he knew Bowman considered them a local nuisance. The sector chief's mandate was to ensure the interactions between Trade Pact signatory species remained peaceful. Criminal activity rarely crossed her desk.

Smuggling banned goods between species did. Alarmed, Morgan lowered his voice to a whisper. "Tell me it's not the Facilitator." The name referred to the mysterious smuggler king, identity—even species—unknown, behind a growing proportion of that trade. Mostly in Human space, so far. What wasn't a secret? A chilling ruthlessness.

"Not." Terk gave an exaggerated wink, disturbing flakes of drying blood. "Happy?"

He'd be happy not to be involved. Morgan stood. "I'd say stay out of trouble, but you'd ignore me."

"S'truth." Terk lifted his mug suggestively. "What's y'hurry?"

He grinned. "We're going dancing." To meet with the next on his inner list. To ease the *melancholy* he sensed around Sira's thoughts.

And with Bowman on the hunt?

The safest place to be was out of her way.

Little Enigmatic Monster

* * *

by Wayne Carey

LYDIS BOWMAN STUDIED the body lying on the morgue's steel slab. She breathed in the cold sterile air and the chemical stench that would take weeks to remove from her uniform. The corpse was of a male Human in the latter part of his fifth standard decade, once tall, slender, and distinguished, now a hollow shell. Covered in a thin sheet from the neck down, he bore no status that the clothes, folded on a shelf, would have provided. The suit he had worn at his death was expensive, the product of one of the most exclusive shops on Plexis. It had marked him not only as a wealthy person, but also one of importance. Bowman barely recognized the sunken face as belonging to Jak Chesterton, Trade Commissioner for Imesh, but his position in the hierarchy of the Trade Pact and signatory species made this dead Human very much her business.

"Okay," she said to Inspector Gregor Wallace, head of Plexis Security, "you have a dead body with no signs of violence, no trace of foreign substances to indicate poisoning, no previous health issues such as heart disease. Nothing to actually indicate a cause of death." She wished she could see into the dead being's inert brain, to sift through any possible damage, search for evidence of someone or something that had ripped his mind away.

"Cardiac failure," Wallace announced in a bored tone. "I've told you—"

"Which merely means his heart stopped beating. Your scans have indicated no previous heart condition, weakened cardiac muscles, or anything else that would support such failure. So what caused his heart to stop?"

Wallace took a deep breath, his mouth forming a thin line. "You're suggesting an assassin. A mindcrawler assassin. It didn't happen. Chesterton had a meal at the *Claws & Jaws* and collapsed in the service corridor at the rear of the establishment. He dined with his aide, Rykard Kessler, who left the restaurant first to deal with reports or some other business. Chesterton was alone while he finished his meal and when he left."

"And how did he end up in the service corridor?" Bowman asked.

Wallace shrugged. "Visual recordings show that he exited through the rear of the restaurant rather than through the front. He was important. Might have worried about being left alone, without his typical escort, and wanted to avoid any media reporters. He was a Trade Pact Commissioner, as you keep reminding me. The vismedia are always hounding them in public for statements. It isn't unusual to use a rear entrance and take the service corridor to a less crowded section of the station, it's just rarely done."

"So he dies in the service corridor, apparently of natural causes," Bowman said, skeptical. "Who found the body?"

"A member of the restaurant staff, Hom Ansel."

"I'll want to speak with him," Bowman said.

Wallace tightened his jaw. "That will not be necessary."

Bowman glared at him. "Why?"

"We have his statement. The case is closed, Commander Bowman."

"Not until I have reviewed all of the facts, Inspector. In case you've forgotten, as a commissioner, qualified to sign interspecies trade agreements, Chesterton—and his death, natural or not—falls under Trade Pact jurisdiction, not Plexis. I will need complete access to all your files concerning this case."

"You're wasting your time, Commander."

"It's mine to waste, Inspector."

Wallace exhaled another heavy breath. "Very well. I'll provide the usual office space—"

"No need. I've taken quarters here on Plexis. Have everything transferred to the terminal there. I've made certain it is secure. Access to myself and to my staff, Constable P'tr wit 'Whix. And I assume you have holo reproductions of the scene of the death."

A glare. "I'll have copies transferred to your terminal, Commander. Anything else?"

"That's all for now. But I'd also want other scans made on the body."

Trade Pact Enforcers had no permanent presence on Plexis. This trip, Bowman did not want to remain shipbound and ordered rooms for her and one staff, 'Whix. The Tolian's Human partner, Russell Terk, was off chasing the *Silver Fox*—again. The Tolian was quartered next to her, and she set up her living space as an office, linked to the *Conciliator*.

Her room's terminal was fine for receiving data from station security, but she knew better than to depend upon it for investigative work. Wallace and his minions would be monitoring every keystroke. They'd try, anyway. True to his word, though, he had uploaded all their files to her terminal. She transferred the data to her secure devices, then pocketed a holo projector and headed toward the restaurant district with the Tolian constable hurrying at her heels.

As the sign outside proclaimed, the *Claws & Jaws* was a restaurant of complete interspecies cuisine. The owner, the Carasian named Huido Maarmatoo'kk, was known to Bowman even beyond his capacity as restaurateur. He had many colorful associates, including Terk's nemesis Jason Morgan, some of which could be suspected of assassination. Could one of them kill without leaving any determining trace? Perhaps. There were many exotic poisons from a thousand planets.

If Wallace's scans revealed no damage from foreign substances, and Bowman felt natural causes unlikely, what she was left with was the nagging suspicion of mental invasion. She expected more elaborate scans of the body, particularly the brain, would provide the evidence she needed. In the meantime, she wished to examine every aspect of the last moments of Chesterton's life.

The Queeb hostess of the *Claws & Jaws* noticed the enforcer uniforms and gave a hint of anxiety in a telltale twitch from two of her left eyes and the curl of one tentacle. Otherwise, she was remarkably calm.

"Table for two?" she asked.

"Is Hom Maarmatoo'kk available?" Bowman said. "I'd like to speak with him."

The hostess' six eyes were blinking randomly. "I regret that will not be possible. Hom Maarmatoo'kk is presently offstation. Is there any other way I can be of help?"

"How decidedly inconvenient of him," Bowman said, wondering when the Carasian had planned this latest trip off Plexis. "Then I'll speak with Hom Ansel."

"Of course, Commander," the hostess said. She was uncharacteristically polite for a Queeb. "He is in his office. I will inform him you are here."

"Just take me to his office," she said.

The hostess waved a tentacle beyond the dining area. "This way, Commander."

They passed from the elegance and subdued murmurs of the dining room to the rattle and organized confusion of the kitchen. The variety of odors assaulted Bowman, causing her stomach to growl, which was thankfully overridden by the ambient noise. She recognized some appetizing smells, but there were some exotic aromas that defied identification, even after she passed the sizzling or boiling pans and pots. There were some, too, that brought a more negative reaction, such as something with still-writhing appendages that made several attempts at escape before a lid was slammed over the squirming mess. That particular entrée's aroma reminded her of fish that had been dead for weeks.

As various as the dinners being prepared, so were the species of the cooks and chefs making the preparations. It could easily be a gathering of Trade Pact Board Members, were it not for the frenzied activities. And the lack of arguing.

The hostess hurried them to the rear of the kitchen toward a door that stood ajar. She pushed it open and motioned Bowman and 'Whix inside without so much as an announcement of their presence. Then she quickly vanished to return to her job.

Ansel's small figure hunched over a data pad, poking an index finger at the screen, sliding the digit to move icons and files. The ancient Human's wrinkled face pursed with frustration, and his tapping became more agitated.

"Our fruit vendor is charging way too much," he said without looking up, making Bowman wonder if he was speaking to her or just complaining to himself. "Outrageous fees for transporting fruit that is probably grown in the hydroponics right here on station. I shall have to investigate further and deal with the vendor accordingly."

He slid the pad aside and looked at her. "But that isn't why you came here, is it . . . Commander?"

"No," she said, "it isn't. Commander Bowman and Constable P'tr wit 'Whix. We're investigating the death of Jak Chesterton. I understand that you discovered the body."

Ansel's eyes twitched. "Yes. I did. Dreadful business, that. I was under the impression that there was no foul play, that he died of heart trouble or some such thing."

"Plexis Security hasn't made an official ruling," Bowman said, omitting the fact that any such ruling would be hers. "What makes you believe that?"

His lips made a quick smile. "One hears things. One cannot help it here, at the *Claws & Jaws*. Rumors and gossip travel faster than light speed on Plexis. So, Commander, why are the enforcers investigating?"

"Hom Chesterton was a commissioner." She gave him a disarming smile. "Purely standard procedure on someone of such high profile. You understand."

The corner of his mouth quivered. "Of course. But how can I help you? I did nothing more than stumble over his body. Plexis Security has my statement. I doubt I could add anything more to it."

"Show us where you found the body."

He pushed himself up from his chair, moving his thin body

in a slow and deliberate manner. "If that will help, of course. This way."

He led them out of the small office, squeezing between her and 'Whix to reach the door. Then down the hall, past other doors on either side until reaching the heavy metal door leading to the maintenance corridor. He undid the lock, pushed down the latch, and shoved, causing the door to slide into the wall. Outside, the buzz of machinery echoed along the long course of the service corridor. In either direction, the curve of the station caused the disconcerting upsweep of the corridor, less noticeable in more populated areas. Even on the concourses of each level, objects interrupted the view of the distant curve so that visitors had more of an illusion of being somewhere other than inside a metal can spinning through space.

Servos whizzed by. Maintenance robots rolled from one job to another, checking wiring and plumbing, monitoring for problems that might seem insignificant but could prove disastrous or deadly. Some servos cleaned, keeping away dust or corrosion. They maintained the delicate balance that kept life on Plexis continuing to exist. Servofreighters made deliveries to the various businesses along the corridor, while others digested trash, burping methane to be collected.

"Where did you discover the remains?" Bowman asked.

Ansel flared out his hands. "Right here."

Bowman handed 'Whix the small holo projector. He set it on the deck where Ansel had indicated and activated it.

The aged Human turned his head away as the body of Chesterton flashed into existence at his feet.

"Did you know Commissioner Chesterton?" she asked.

"No."

"Surely you recognized him."

"No. I don't usually pay much attention to our customers. I haven't the time or the luxury. If I watched the news media for every important person who happened to visit Plexis, I'd never get anything done."

Bowman paced around the image of the body, which lay upon its back. Certainly a different appearance than the corpse that lay in the morgue. There was a trace of agony on the frozen features, which had vanished with the relaxation of death. He had felt pain in this death. It could have been slight, as an upset stomach, or intense, as if his mind was being ripped away. She couldn't tell. Not yet.

"What brought you out here?" she asked.

Ansel stood against the bulkhead near the door, as far from the image as possible. He looked at it with something other than a passing curiosity. More like dread.

He looked up, suddenly realizing she had asked him a question. "Pardon?"

"Why did you come into the access corridor? It doesn't seem to be something you would normally do."

Ansel pointed to a device to his right. "Our trash digester had been acting up. I came out to check if it had been repaired or not. It hadn't been, as you can see. It leaked. Completely intolerable. The fees we pay, and this is the service we get."

Below the access panel to the digester, a puddle had formed. It was a dark mess of indescribable composition that congealed on the deck.

"'Whix," she said to the constable, "turn off the holo emitter for a moment."

The Tolian bent down and thumbed the control, causing the corpse to vanish.

Ansel gave a small sigh of relief.

Bowman looked for the puddle from the leaking digester. It was no longer there, but had been part of the projection.

"So your digester is fixed?" she asked.

"Apparently so," Ansel said.

She waved to the constable. "Please activate it again, 'Whix."

"Really, Commander," Ansel protested, "do I need to be here for your investigation? This is quite . . . disturbing. Bad enough the first time, but to endure it again and again . . . I do have work to do."

"Indulge me a little while longer, Hom," she said, bending down to examine the image of the stain. "Curious."

"Commander?" Ansel said.

She pointed to a mark on the deck as long as her thumb. "Don't you see it, Hom Ansel? Something had inadvertently stepped in that puddle of muck from the digester and left a print. It appears to be a paw mark."

Ansel squinted at where she pointed.

"Really? I can't see anything."

Bowman straightened and placed her fists on her hips. "Definitely a paw mark. There was another being here, a small being with bare paws or feet. Almost looks like a hand."

Ansel made a dismissive gesture. "There are vermin in these service corridors, especially around food storage bins and digesters. The servos do what they can to get rid of them, but no system is perfect. Vermin. Annoying creatures, but harmless. That's what it was. Is that everything, Commander?"

He slid open the door. "When you are done, you may come through this way. I'll leave it unlocked for now."

When Bowman did not object, Ansel quickly disappeared inside and slid the door shut, leaving her and 'Whix with the holographic corpse. Bowman ignored the image of the body but concentrated on the print on the metal deck plating. She had seen more than her share of Plexis' version of "vermin." Some could reach a formidable size, but most were no larger than the length of her hand. Their paws were narrow with claws. And they did not have opposable digits.

"The Human . . . Hom Ansel,"'Whix said through the tinny voice of his translator, his crest feathers ruffling, "was very nervous."

"Yes, he was."

"Perhaps he does not deal well with death."

"Perhaps," Bowman echoed. "But there's another reason for his anxiety. He just lied to us."

"Really? How were you able to determine that, Commander?"

"He'd know what vermin tracks look like. That print isn't from anything local. Furthermore, Chesterton did not simply walk through the kitchen and out the back door. You saw Ansel unlock the door. Someone had to escort Chesterton out."

"You suspect Hom Ansel?"

"I suspect he knows more than he has said. He lied to us. How much, we will find out. Of course he knew Chesterton, or at least recognized him. But only an idiot would kill someone and then claim to discover the body. Scan the print and transfer it to station security."

Bowman activated her com link and contacted Wallace.

"Constable 'Whix is sending you an image of an animal print," she said. "I want to know what species left it?"

"Got it, Commander." She didn't like Wallace's condescending laugh. "So now the enforcers are chasing LEMS?"

"'Lems?'"

"Little Enigmatic Monsters. We've been trying to get rid of them for years. Personally, I think they came off of Retian ships, but we don't really know. They're quick, can squeeze into tight places, and like to hide. They pop out, scare customers, then disappear. They steal things, even electronics, which we'll later find dismantled, as though they were examining them. Mostly, they steal shiny things and food. There's probably only a half dozen on the entire station, but they're annoying. The good thing about them is that they eat vermin, and don't ask how we found that out. It's gratifying to witness enforcers at work."

She disconnected the link in the middle of his laughter.

That was disappointing. She had hoped for some exotic species— at least one that she had never encountered, to be a clue—which now was unlikely. This so-called LEM would have nothing to do with this case.

Still, Ansel would know it wasn't vermin that left that print. Why had he been so insistent to suggest it was?

Bowman headed spinward to the more exclusive levels of Plexis. Here, in the famous Hidleberg Hotel, beings of a certain class resided when onstation. The rich and powerful. The owners of corporations and systems. The movers of systems. The hotel's lobby was large enough to dock a spaceship. The two enforcers were ignored by the clientele. At the concierge desk, Bowman had Rykard Kessler paged. An escort was arranged to take her and 'Whix to Kessler's suite.

At the apartment door, Kessler smiled and motioned her and the constable inside.

"Forgive the intrusion, Hom Kessler," Bowman said without so much as a glance at the plush surroundings of the suite. "We are investigating the death of Commissioner Chesterton."

Kessler pursed his lips. "But I thought the investigation was complete. Poor Chesterton died of cardiac failure. What more is there?"

"Routine questions," she said with a small smile. "Just some loose odds and ends. You were his assistant, correct?"

"Associate. Chesterton was the trade commissioner but also head of the Imesh Conglomerate. I am the associate administrator."

"Then you take control now that he is deceased."

"It's a little more complicated than that, Commander. The board of directors controls the conglomerate. Chesterton was appointed administrator because he was a major shareholder."

"And who gains those shares now that he is dead?"

Kessler's eyebrows rose. "I'm sure that is all in his will. As he no longer has any living family, I am certain it will be dispersed appropriately. I certainly do not stand to inherit anything, if that's what you're implying, nor do I gain any advantage over his death. If you need such information, I'll pass on your request to his law firm."

No need. She'd put 'Whix on it. "How was he when you last saw him?" Bowman asked.

"He complained of chest pains, but disregarded it as indigestion. He assured me he was fine, or I would not have left him alone."

"Why would he have used the rear exit to the restaurant?"

Kessler looked up at the Tolian. "I'm sure I don't know."

"Know of anyone who might want to see him dead? Were there any threats?" Bowman asked.

Kessler shifted uneasily. "No. We haven't had any incident like that since his cousin, Denyl Constantine, died several years ago. He was the previous administrator. Anarchists, from a revolution on one of the colony worlds. There had been all kinds of threats back then. Constantine and his family were murdered."

"How curious," Bowman murmured. Two deaths of corporate administrators? It added a more planetary flavor to the case, not that she'd give it to Imesh Port Authority. "Then would these same individuals be a danger to Commissioner Chesterton?"

"I don't see how. We haven't had any problem since then."

Bowman turned toward the door. "I won't keep you, Hom. I'm sure you want to return to your homeworld as soon as possible. Tell me," she said, pausing, "what brought you to Plexis in the first place?"

"Meetings," he said with a tired sigh. "The Conglomerate is seeking to expand. That means investing time at the Imesh Trade Mission on Plexis. We must meet with other businesses and planetary leaders to arrange or modify agreements. We need something, they need something. It's all a matter of ironing out the details. Chesterton hosted."

"And you're certain no one that either of you have met with would want to see the commissioner dead."

Kessler shook his head. "There would be no advantage in that, I assure you."

Bowman stood in the service corridor outside the *Claws & Jaws*, pondering the upsweeping horizon. Farther down, someone was working on a servo, clattering tools. Jak Chesterton came out here for a reason. It wasn't to escape media reporters or prying eyes. Something drew him here, and he died. Could he have been lured from the restaurant?

The door to the restaurant clanked open and out came the elderly Human, Ansel, escorted by 'Whix.

"Thank you for joining me, Hom Ansel," she said.

"I wasn't aware I had much choice, Commander Bowman," Ansel replied. "Although I want to cooperate as much as I can, I do hope this won't take long."

She clasped her hands behind her back and stepped closer to him. "The sooner we come to the truth, the sooner you may return to your duties."

Ansel eased back, colliding with the Tolian. The constable's feathered crest rose slowly as he stared down at the Human.

"What—what do you mean?" Ansel asked.

"Commissioner Chesterton did not simply wander through the kitchen and exit through this door. He was escorted. You brought him out here."

"How—" Ansel's eyes widened in surprise, then he composed

himself. "What could possibly make you believe I would have taken him through?"

"Your reaction just now," Bowman said, inching closer, glaring at him. "You have not been entirely honest with us, Hom Ansel. I hope that is about to change. Now, you escorted Chesterton through that door."

Ansel gave a small nod.

"Good," Bowman said with a nod of her own. She turned away and looked around the corridor. A servofreighter whizzed by to deliver merchandise to another establishment. "Now, why would Chesterton be interested in seeing your service corridor. If you were going to talk to him in private, you would have used your office. So, it was to meet someone else."

She gave him a casual glance and studied the flash of panic in his eyes, indicating that her guess had been correct.

"Who are you protecting?" she demanded.

"No one!"

"A Trade Pact Commissioner was murdered," she said, although she had no proof to indicate that. Ansel needn't know about her lack of evidence. "There are two options. Either you killed him yourself, which I doubt, or you brought him to his murderer."

"No, she wouldn't—"

Ansel clamped his mouth shut. His eyes darted to the corridor behind her.

"You know the killer," Bowman said. "Things will go easier on you if you tell me. Plexis Security won't be as understanding."

He shook his head and lowered his eyes. "It was me. I did it. I killed Chesterton."

Behind him, 'Whix ruffled the feathers crowning his head. His mouth turned up at the confession.

Bowman sighed. "Very well. I don't believe you, but if you insist on protecting an assassin and confessing to the murder yourself, I have to accept it. 'Whix, take Hom Ansel into custody and escort him to the *Conciliator*'s brig."

She heard the footsteps from behind before she saw Ansel wince and squeeze his eyes tight.

"He didn't do it," a voice said from behind her.

Bowman turned to see a young female Human. Tall and thin, just past her second decade. She wore a pair of stained and wrinkled service coveralls with the station logo on the breast, a thick belt around her thin waist carrying pouches of tools. Her narrow face was smudged and her short yellow hair tousled. Her eyes glared with determination at Bowman as she pushed back the sleeves of her coveralls, revealing slender, tightly muscled forearms.

"I know," Bowman said. "Who are you?"

"I'm Ylsa, and this is Gemma." She motioned down, without taking her intense blue eyes from the enforcer. Bowman looked down to see the animal for the first time. It slipped from behind the young Human in sleek, stealthy movements. A long shadowy shape with short black fur that glistened. Its tail lashed back and forth, twitching. The tufted, triangular ears on top of its head rotated, as though searching for sounds. It had been on all fours, but stood now on hind legs, coming as high as Ylsa's knees. Its hand-like forepaws, tipped with claws, gripped the fabric of the coveralls. Suddenly, it squirmed up Ylsa's back to perch on her shoulder, tail curled around her neck, large eyes made for nocturnal hunting fixed on Bowman.

The LEM—for it could be nothing else—made an odd throaty sound that resembled a small motor.

"You have a device," Ylsa said with a frown. "In your head. It makes it like you aren't there. The same with the bird person."

"Tolian," Bowman said. "I'm Commander Lydis Bowman and this is Constable P'tr wit 'Whix. We're Trade Pact Enforcers."

She nodded. "Yeah, got that."

"You're a telepath," Bowman said.

"No. Doesn't take a telepath to tell what you are. The uniforms are a dead giveaway."

"But you can tell we have dampeners, which means you're trying to read our thoughts. You can't, you know. We're protected."

"I don't know about protection," Ylsa said, "but it makes you unreal. Like a hologram. Or a ghost."

She had to be a telepath. Was she also an assassin? Bowman wasn't convinced. Something in those eyes, so deep and intelligent, yet hurt and lonely.

"Are you Clan, then?" she asked. The Clan lived separate from each other, spread over countless worlds, hidden among Humans, appearing like Humans, but being far more.

Confusion lined Ylsa's brow. "'Clan?'" She glanced at Ansel, as though searching his face for an answer. "I don't know what that is." She looked at the LEM on her shoulder. "Do you, Gemma?"

The animal gave a throaty warble.

"No, Gemma doesn't either."

"Okay, but you are a telepath," Bowman said, ignoring her talking to the animal.

The Human sighed and rolled her eyes. "I already told you I'm not. Gemma is, though."

Game, belief, or trick? Regardless, Bowman chose to dismiss the assertion. There were empathic plants and more than a few predators who could lure their prey close. None were sentient or true telepaths. What she needed was information. If this Ylsa was not the killer, she was still tied to the death in some way.

"What do you do, Ylsa?" she asked. "Are you Plexis maintenance?"

The corner of the her mouth twisted into a smirk. "What gave it away?"

"Does the LEM always accompany you?"

Ylsa scowled. "That's a derogatory term. I don't like it, calling them monsters. They're not, you know."

Bowman nodded toward the animal. "What is it, then?"

"She's Gemma. I don't know what you'd call her kind. I work ship maintenance sometimes. Whatever breaks down, I can fix it. Engines, air conditioners, garbage digesters. I met Gemma a long time ago, in one of the landing bays. She's my guardian. She lets me know who to stay away from and who is safe. With you, she can't tell, but she's very curious."

"Please, Commander Bowman," Ansel said. "Ylsa has nothing to do with Commissioner Chesterton's death. I'll confess. Take me into custody, just leave Ylsa alone."

Bowman looked at Ylsa. "Should I do that, Ylsa? Should I arrest Hom Ansel?"

"For murder?" Ylsa gave a short laugh. "He's innocent. That's obvious to anyone, and I'm pretty sure you're intelligent enough to know that. About the only thing he's guilty of is taking in strays."

"What about you? Did you kill Chesterton?"

"No. He fell over before I even met him."

"So you were here," Bowman said.

"You already know I was. Gemma can tell that from Ansel, even if she can't see into your mind. You saw her footprint on the deck from the time Chesteron died, before I repaired the digester and cleaned up the mess."

"Do you know who killed him?" Bowman asked.

"No one. He just fell over."

She raised an eyebrow. "He came out of the *Claws & Jaws* and fell over dead."

"No. Gemma and I came, and he was waiting. He turned to greet us, then made a face and fell over."

"As if having heart failure?"

"I'm no med-tech." Ylsa paused, then said, "He reached both hands to his throat, like he couldn't breathe, looked like he was in pain, and collapsed. He was dead before we got to him. Ansel told me to leave, then he called the meds."

"Commissioner Chesterton was an important figure in the Trade Pact. A busy one. No offense, Fem Ylsa, but why were you going to meet him?"

"Ansel wanted him to meet me," Ylsa said.

Bowman turned to the Human, who seemed to shrink under her gaze. "Well?"

Ansel looked around anxiously. "Do you mind returning to my office, Commander? This is rather . . . sensitive."

Once everyone squeezed into the small office, Ansel paced the few feet behind his desk.

Bowman waited patiently while 'Whix moved nervously from one foot to another. The LEM sat on its haunches on the desk, its tail lashing back and forth, its eyes studying the Tolian.

"I knew Commissioner Chesterton," Ansel finally said, stopping to rest his hands on the back of his chair and looking sheepishly at Bowman. "I'm from Imesh 27. We had never met before, but our families knew each other. He was aware I was on Plexis. You see, his cousin Denyl Constantine died on Plexis."

"The previous administrator," Bowman prompted.

"Yes. He and his wife were visiting Plexis and were killed by thieves. Their ten-year-old daughter was never found, but presumed dead or sold to Recruiters. Jak Chesterton was convinced she was still alive. He reached out to me, but I already had my suspicions." He glanced at the figure in the grimy coveralls, arms folded, leaning against the wall.

"Ylsa?"

Ansel nodded.

Blue eyes narrowed in annoyance. "I've told Ansel I don't remember my parents. All I remember is growing up on the station. Plexis fed me, raised me, taught me. I'm pretty good at taking things apart and putting them back together, so they trained me for maintenance. If they didn't have a use for me, they would have had me shipped to some dirt world. After I met Gemma, she urged me to find Ansel because we talk the same. He thinks I'm this Ylsa Constantine." A shrug. "We have the same first name. So what?"

"And your last name?"'Whix asked.

"I couldn't remember. Someone called me Peregrine and I liked it."

Bowman nodded to herself. "You can't remember where you came from? Was there trauma? An injury?"

Ylsa shrugged. "That was a long time ago. I don't remember and no one ever explained it to me. Look, I just do my job and don't get involved. No family ever came looking for me, so I figured they abandoned me. No big deal."

"When did you suspect she could be Denyl Constantine's daughter?" Bowman asked Ansel.

"Not at first. I had no idea. She just sounded like someone from my homeworld when she came to me with that animal."

"Gemma isn't an animal," Ylsa insisted in a weary tone as if this was an old argument. "Commander Bowman, Ansel and Hom Huido are nice enough to give me food now and then. I could never afford a meal at the *Claws & Jaws* on my salary. He's been nice and just wanted to help. We've been sort of friends." A frown. "Until he wanted me to meet this Chesterton."

"Who had access to the planetary database. Jak would have been able to prove if she actually was his cousin's daughter," Ansel said, then sighed. "But he died before he could."

"I can," Bowman said. A simple test, using Chesterton's genetic makeup as a baseline for family relationship if Constantine's wasn't on record on Plexis. As for Imesh records? She'd get access.

"If this relationship is the case," 'Whix said, "Fem Peregrine stands to inherit a sizable estate."

Motive was one thing. It left the question of how Chesterton died. Perhaps he had suffered heart failure after all, brought on by the stress of meeting his only living relative, one presumed dead. Ylsa might be a liar, shifting her telepathic talents conveniently to her pet, but Bowman did not see her as a murderer.

Leaving 'Whix to escort Ylsa to her home quarters to freshen and change, Bowman headed to the security office for a quick chat with Wallace concerning tests for Ylsa's heritage. When she entered the office, Inspector Wallace gave her a suspicious look.

"How did you hear so quickly?" he demanded. "I just got the results myself. Did your people plug into our com system?"

"What are you talking about?"

He handed her a reader with the results of the second set of scans on Chesterton's corpse. The cranial scans showed nothing unusual. No damage, so he had not been killed by a telepath.

"Go to the bottom," Wallace snapped, twirling his finger to urge her to scroll faster.

She refrained from comment, methodically reading chemical analyses and toxicology screens to the concluding paragraph, then looked up at Wallace. "Poison?"

He nodded grudgingly. "You were . . . right. It was murder."

If not the type of murder she'd originally thought. "How did your people miss this the first time?" Bowman demanded.

"They didn't," he said. He was irritated, but not with her. Well, at least not entirely with her. "The results had been deleted."

"Who had access—"

The room's doors slid open and in staggered a ruffled Tolian cradling a limp bundle of black fur. 'Whix caught himself with one hand on the desk before he toppled over, making Wallace leap back.

His eyes tried to focus. Gingerly, he laid the inert form of the LEM on the desk, then sank into a chair in front of it. He made a series of chirps that weren't translated, then, "Two Humans," he began. "A Plexis Security team, claimed they were sent to take Ylsa into custody. Of course, I refused. The animal immediately had a fit and tried to attack them. They stunned it, then stunned me. When I became coherent, Ylsa was gone."

Bowman glared at Wallace, but before she could make demands or accusations, he shook his head.

"I didn't send anyone, Commander. I know we don't see eye to eye on most issues, but this was not my doing. The same with the deleted data. Constable 'Whix, did they identify themselves?"

'Whix began preening his feathers back into shape. "I caught a name. Reyes."

Wallace nodded grimly. He tapped some keys on his terminal and watched the results appear on the monitor. "Reyes and Foard. Either of them had access to the autopsy results and could have deleted or doctored them. They're both logged off duty."

"And who are they working for," Bowman asked coldly, "if not for you?"

"It's hard to keep track anymore," Wallace said with a shrug.

"Commissioner Chesterton was poisoned," she said, looking quickly at the report again. "He had to ingest the toxin within a half hour of dying."

"That is when he was dining with his associate, Hom Kessler," 'Whix supplied.

"I think we need to talk again to the Hom, and quickly."

Wallace tapped on his keypad again. "You're too late. Kessler has already checked out of his hotel room and boarded his yacht. It's left—"

'Whix had already been using the com. "Commander, the *Conciliator* is prepping the pursuit craft."

Because moving the great cruiser would take time they didn't have. Bowman snatched up the sleeping animal—evidence—and headed for the door. "Tell them we're on the way. 'Whix!"

Despite their differences, Inspector Wallace had Plexis Control clear the lanes in time for Bowman's launch.

Rykard Kessler had filed a flight plan upon leaving. The *Conciliator*'s pursuit craft was smaller, with a more powerful drive. They should have no difficulty overtaking the yacht.

In the cramped control room, Bowman strapped into the copilot seat, cradling the groggy LEM on her lap. She found herself idly stroking the sleek black fur while it made that throaty motor sound. 'Whix, an able pilot, ran through the preflight checklist, then sent the craft streaking from Plexis. "I've input Kessler's course, Commander."

Gemma was immediately awake and a ball of angry, hissing fur.

Bowman grabbed for the LEM, too late. The creature launched herself at the controls 'Whix was attempting to set. The Tolian's hands flew back to avoid being raked by claws.

"I believe the animal wants to eat me." He drew away from the console as Gemma squatted on the slope of the controls and hissed at him.

"Nonsense," Bowman said. "She's startled. Probably frightened Ylsa isn't here. I'll put her in a locker." When she reached for the animal, Gemma turned and glared at her, baring her sharp teeth.

"Perhaps,"'Whix said, "we should explain to the beast that we are attempting a rescue of her Human."

Bowman rolled her eyes. "It's nonsentient. It can't understand—"

At which the creature sat and tilted her head at Bowman, one side of her muzzle curling up, whiskers tilted.

"Perhaps it does,"'Whix suggested.

"Ridiculous."

Gemma scooted back and lay down on the console. Between her paws were the very controls 'Whix had been attempting to set. One digit tapped a claw on the display. She looked from Bowman to 'Whix.

"Gemma does not want us to set that particular course, Commander," 'Whix said.

"Don't you start, Constable. Bad enough Ylsa has delusions about this animal, I don't need you doing it, too."

The animal stopped tapping the display and sat up, looking at 'Whix.

"Commander?"

"We're following Ylsa. She's on that yacht," Bowman told the LEM, then shook her head and scowled at 'Whix. "If the animal's intelligent enough to understand that, and I don't for an instant believe it is, why doesn't she want us to set the course?"

"Because . . . that isn't the course Kessler took?"

Gemma looked up at 'Whix and gave a short warble.

Bowman pinched the top of her nose, regarding the Tolian ominously over her fingers. It was that, or draw a weapon. "We're wasting time, Constable."

'Whix waved his hands in excitement. "Ylsa said the creature was telepathic. If the two are linked mentally, perhaps the animal can sense which direction she was taken."

"And I suppose it can read nav settings and tell what our destination is?"

Gemma turned on Bowman and gave a sharp "*Arrh!*"

"Fine!" Bowman snapped at the animal. "You set the course!"

"With all due respect, Commander," 'Whix said, "I don't believe she can. However, she might be of assistance. If I may, Gemma?" he said to the animal.

The LEM eased to the side, allowing the Tolian to access the controls. "How about . . ."

A growl.

"Okay, then . . ."

"They're getting away," Bowman pointed out.

"Ah!" 'Whix said. "The nearest system. A collection of uninhabited planetoids and asteroids. Perhaps . . . ?"

The LEM jumped off the console and onto the deck while 'Whix reset their course.

Gambling on a LEM. Bowman allowed it, having no better

option. And there was the nagging sensation she had when looking into the animal's large green eyes.

Soon, the animal stretched up with its forepaws gripping the edge of the console between the two seats, her head tilting to one side, as though waiting for something to happen.

"There's a ship ahead," 'Whix announced, giving the animal a curious glance.

Even if they were following the correct course, they couldn't possibly have overtaken the yacht so soon.

"Ident?" Bowman asked.

"Not receiving, but the configuration matches Kessler's yacht." Without waiting for orders, 'Whix dropped their craft out of subspace. "Scanning."

"Well?"

'Whix brought up a magnified image. "It's drifting. The engines appear to be offline."

"Life support?" Bowman asked, her heart pounding. There were no external lights, nothing to indicate that the ship had any power at all. From what little she could make out, there appeared to be no damage or sign of attack.

"Still functioning," 'Whix said. "Emergency power."

The pursuit craft had certain design features of use now, including a clamping mechanism with one purpose. Bowman smiled grimly. "Dock against her air lock."

"Should we radio our intention?"

Protocol was for fools. "Let's not."

Gemma followed Bowman and 'Whix to the air lock and stood on hind legs in front of the hatch while the pursuit craft's capture ring pressurized, the tip of her tail twitching back and forth. Bowman considered leaving the creature behind, but the LEM was small enough that she should not get in the way, and she might even prove useful in their search for Ylsa, provided she didn't get trampled in the chaos about to take place.

They crossed the short ring and overrode the controls to the yacht's air lock. When they cycled open the inner door, both enforcers had their weapons out and ready. Gemma dashed through as soon as the opening was wide enough. *Good*, Bowman thought. The animal could act as a distraction for anyone waiting on the other side.

Bowman did not expect to hear screaming.

They burst into the yacht's prep room to find a Human male in a shredded Plexis Security uniform cowering against the bulkhead and bleeding from dozens of long, deep scratches over his face and hands. A blaster lay a few feet away from him, but he made no attempt to grab it. Gemma sat next to the weapon.

The LEM looked up at Bowman, tilting her head to one side, tufted ears bent forward. Her tail lashed back and forth.

Bowman frowned and motioned to 'Whix. "Cuff him."

The Tolian holstered his weapon and pulled out a pair of restraining cuffs. The Human was so terrified he pushed himself up the wall and gratefully held out his hands, his huge eyes never leaving the LEM.

"Where's Ylsa?" Bowman demanded.

"Don't know who you're talking about," he said. He straightened his back and lifted his chin, trying to put on an indignant attitude. It came across as pathetic, with the swelling scratches bleeding down his face.

Gemma sauntered toward him on hind legs and he lost all pretext, fear returning to his eyes. "Keep that thing away from me!" He tried to back up, but pushed into 'Whix instead.

"Ylsa?" Bowman asked again, fighting the small smile that tugged at the corner of her mouth. "Or I put you in a room with that thing."

"Kessler has her. She did something to the engines. Kessler and Foard are trying to figure out what happened. They're in the engine room. Aft. Look, I was just paid for kidnapping. Okay, first deleting some of the autopsy reports. But anything else, that's on Kessler. He didn't want to kill her on Plexis. Planned to dump her out the air lock where she'd never be found. Said something about not wanting any DNA tests run on her."

"Constable," Bowman said, "lock him up."

'Whix shoved Reyes toward the air lock, taking him back into their ship to secure him.

Without waiting for the Tolian to return, Bowman opened the door to the yacht's single corridor. Gemma dashed out, running on all fours toward the aft of the ship. With her blaster held in both hands, Bowman followed.

The hatch to engineering was open at the end of the short corridor. Bowman had a clear view of another Human male, in a Plexis uniform, crouched behind a console. As soon as Foard saw that it wasn't his partner coming to join them, he began shooting. Bowman pushed herself against the bulkhead, only narrowly escaping the bolts of energy that sizzled past.

The shots ended with a terrified scream.

Foard leaped up from behind the console, his hands going to a raging ball of fur that clung to his head, a tail wrapped around his throat. One hand grabbed the animal raking claws over his face. The other fired his blaster into the ceiling, shattering tiles and lighting tubes. Claws sank deeper.

Bowman hurried to the doorway and fired once.

A neat hole burned through Foard's chest. He dropped backward, his frantic screams ending.

Kessler stood with his back to the reactor, Ylsa held in front of him, a small but deadly needler pressed to her temple.

Ylsa Peregrine stood perfectly still, but there was no sign of fear in her eyes. She was relaxed, a small smile curving her lips as she saw the animal with its ruffled fur.

"Keep that thing back!" Kessler shouted at Bowman.

"As if I control it," Bowman said, aiming her weapon. "Surrender, Kessler. All you'll be charged with now is kidnapping."

"What about Chesterton?" he demanded.

Too easy. She frowned. "Is that a confession?"

"Doesn't matter. I'd sooner see us all dead than go back now. If you leave now, Bowman, and forget all about this little incident, I'll see that you are well compensated. You'd be set for the rest of your life. Otherwise, all of us will have to die."

"Then you don't gain anything," Bowman said.

"You see," Kessler said, waving the weapon slightly, but never taking it from his hostage's head, "there are powerful people who did not want her found. People who control most of Imesh. Chesterton kept them satisfied, but if he located the Constantine heir, then they could lose their controlling power. Chesterton had grown tired of their manipulations. I was told to make certain he never found her. And if he happened to meet his own end, so much the better. If I allow Ylsa to return, then my life will be over. Better to end it here and now, on my own terms."

"Okay, then," Bowman agreed. "Go ahead, because I am not leaving without Ylsa."

"He can't do anything," Ylsa said. "I locked him out of his own ship. Told you I was good at fixing things."

Gemma lowered herself, tail bristling, and growled.

"I said, keep that thing away!" Kessler said.

"Gemma is *not* a thing!" Ylsa snapped.

She swung her elbow back, smacking it into Kessler's face, crushing his nose. He cried out in pain, staggering back against the reactor casing, his needler firing blindly.

Bowman shot him through the forehead.

They left a beacon on Kessler's yacht so Plexis Security could send a tug and bring it and the two bodies back. Security also took custody of Reyes, after Bowman had recorded his confession. Plexis, in the form of Inspector Wallace, would deal with him.

It wasn't a clean solution. Bowman regretted losing the opportunity to interrogate Kessler and learn the identities of those who paid him. She'd have to go about it another way.

As she packed her belongings in her quarters on Plexis, the com chimed. Fingers near a now-concealed weapon, Bowman ordered the door open.

Ansel and Ylsa stood in the hall, with Gemma at Ylsa's feet. She'd abandoned her grimy coveralls for a more fashionable dress and looked more than a little self-conscious.

"So the results are in?" Bowman asked, waving them in. "Do I call you Ylsa Peregrine or Constantine?"

"Constantine," Ylsa said. "Ansel has made arrangements. I'm on my way back home, even though I don't remember it. Although, I think I am beginning to remember some things about my parents, as though in a dream. Suppressed all these years."

"I've already sent a report to the Trade Pact," Bowman said. "A full investigation is underway. We will get to the bottom of this and find out who was behind Kessler."

"I've been going over some corporate records my uncle had," Ylsa said. "I have some of my own suspicions. They aren't very good at hiding their activities. Besides, Gemma will help ferret them out."

The LEM looked up and tilted her head, tufted ears turning outward.

"I really don't think—" Bowman started to say. She watched those green eyes. Was it actually sentient *and* telepathic? She knew some strange species in her capacity as an enforcer and in her previous career as a Port Jelly.

In the end, did it matter? "Okay," she said, not wanting to get into that argument. Let the sociologists and anthropologists worry about it.

"Even with that thing in your head that makes you like a ghost," Ylsa said, "Gemma was still able to tell that you weren't as mean as you pretend. She told me that when you threatened to arrest Ansel. She was right."

"Don't be so sure of that," Bowman said, scowling.

Gemma looked up at her and closed one eye, quickly opening it in an unmistakable wink.

... *Truffles* continues

6

＊＊＊

IN HUMAN TERMS, I'd opened the door, my *reach* to contact any nearby Clan having the unfortunate consequence of inviting contact I didn't want.

The Clan Council.

Speaker, we need you here. Sawnda'at's mindvoice was as querulous as his real one, and impossible to ignore. *On Camos.*

I touched a fingertip to my forehead, then waved apologetically at 'Whix, the Tolian well-accustomed to what it meant when my attention went elsewhere. *I'm busy. There's a problem with our truffles.*

The Councilor's *astonishment* was, I thought wryly, sincere. He knew better than to express it, knew to expend his own strength maintaining our link through the M'hir rather than ask it of mine, knew—so little, I felt a moment's pity. Until he sent, *You must! We cannot conduct a meeting of Council without your presence.*

They could—they simply had a problem if votes were tied. As I usually heard about that, and quickly, this was about something else and I'd no problem guessing. *What's Acranam done now?*

There has been Choice offered. Unsanctioned and against your direct command.

The Tolian's emerald eyes were distracting. I closed my own. *And the Candidate?*

A confused pause. Any unChosen Candidate offered to a Chooser was, to put it in Clan terms, expendable. All Sawnda'at and the Council cared about was the flaunting of rules.

I put force behind it. *What HAPPENED to the Candidate?*

He survived, Speaker, with more appropriate—and wary—*respect. The Watchers conveyed Choice was successful, and the pair have Joined. Which isn't the point—*

It was, in every way that mattered. Without such pairings, our kind would soon become extinct. A successful one? Where the Candidate hadn't been pulled into the M'hir by a more potent Chooser and left to die there? Rare. We couldn't afford any more losses. Couldn't—and this was the point I consistently failed to get across to my kind—treat unChosen males as fodder, to be risked at whim.

It was why Bowman was now our ally. Why the Trade Pact had accepted the Clan and our problem. Why I'd forbidden any more offerings of Choice until a solution was found.

Does Acranam have any more Choosers? I asked, cold and calm.

We don't know. They resist our requests for such data, Speaker.

Of course they did, having hidden their very existence all these years. Pretending to be dead. Part of me was willing to let them stay that way.

The better part knew we couldn't afford their loss. *Send congratulations and the usual gifts,* I sent. *They were lucky,* at Sawnda'at's stunned silence. *There's nothing gained by reminding them of it.* Morgan's influence, not that I'd tell the Clansman, my Human convinced the best negotiating tactic was to have others think they'd won.

Who knows, I thought. Perhaps a modicum of goodwill might result. Though, with Acranam, probably not.

As you command, Speaker, Sawnda'at replied, prudently holding back his own opinion.

I opened my eyes and smiled at 'Whix. *Next time, Councilor?* Sent with a *surge* of Power that burned his from the M'hir and likely would produce a significant headache. *Unless it's an emergency?*

Use a com.

"He's all yours," Morgan told 'Whix when he arrived at our table. He aimed a thumb over his shoulder at the now-peaceful bar. "If you can pry him loose, that is."

"A thankless task, but necessary." The Tolian rose to his feet, dipping his beak to me, then my Human. "My gratitude to you both." He left, stepping with elaborate care around the glistening puddles surrounding us.

"Ready to dance?"

I eyed Morgan and didn't budge. He appeared remarkably unscathed, considering. "What about Officer E'Teiso?" I demanded.

"I could be wrong—" his eyes sparkled with mischief, "—but I don't believe F'Feego dance."

He was up to something. I recognized the signs with an inner thrill. *Care to explain yourself?*

The corner of his lips quirked. *That obvious?*

"Only to me," I said aloud. *You've a plan, don't you? Something devious.*

"Not at all." Morgan bent to give me a firm kiss, straightening before my hair could entice him to linger. "If we needed devious, I'd call on another friend altogether."

A Thief By Any Other Name

* * *

by Violette Malan

I KEPT MY eyes on the cup of sombay I was turning around with the fingers of my right hand. I kept my left in plain sight on the table. Scats like to see both hands. When I thought enough time had passed to make it look like I'd given his proposition a decent amount of thought, I looked up.

"I'm a grifter, not a thief," I pointed out as politely as I could. I carry a small force blade, but I'm not fast enough to beat a Scat. I hear that lizards and other reptiles, get slow in the cold. Maybe Scats weren't as reptilian as they look, or maybe it's not cold enough onstation.

"You are Human. A Human has the best chance of getting near our target." Petreck must have had surgery; he didn't hiss like every other Scat I'd met. Good for blending on Plexis, but I doubted it scored points with his kind.

"I see." I nodded, as if I thought this made sense. "No disrespect intended, but wouldn't it be easier to boost this item while in transit? I know a good scheme to switch grav sleds—with a couple of friends to—"

"No. It must be done by one person only. By you."

"Again, no disrespect meant, but why me, exactly? I'm sure you have plenty of skilled Human employees, so why come to me?"

"You are, as you say, a grifter. You persuade people that you are what you are not. This is your great skill. No other Human can persuade the owners of the establishment that they can wait upon tables. For you, it would be of the simplest."

"You want me to pass myself off as a waiter? A *Human* waiter? Only the *Claws & Jaws* uses Human waiters." Well, they use *live* waiters, but that does include Humans. "And I'm not sure how good an idea it is to run a scam on a Carasian."

"Fear not. The *Galaxy Room* is vying for custom with the *Claws & Jaws*. They have begun to hire your kind."

"I see." I gave my best, gosh-I'm-sorry smile. Petreck and his crew weren't the kind of beings you worked with if there was any way out of it. That's why we were meeting in this nice, public café. "I'm afraid I'm just now in the middle of something very delicate, very time sensitive. I won't be able to help you." I'd have recommended someone else, but I didn't dislike anyone that much.

"You have a father, Fem Graine. He is much in debt to the *Spacer's Haven* on Pocular. We have purchased this debt. He has, as you may know, no realistic expectations of paying this debt. If you perform this favor for us, this debt will cease to be."

"I see." This was exactly the reason Mum had left Dad in the first place—gamblers and grifters don't make the most stable couples. But it was the first time a streak of bad luck for him had ever bounced back on any of us. "I don't suppose you have any proof of what you're saying?"

"Yes." The Scat at the next table brought out a portable reader with a vistape up and ready to view. I managed to take it from him without coming into contact with his scaly hands.. The person in the tape was definitely my father. He was laying out four hands of Stars and Comets, studying each hand in turn before gathering up the cards again. Another Scat, like the one who gave me the reader, only bigger and uglier, stood in one corner holding something I didn't recognize, but was clearly a weapon. Dad looked unworried, but that's Dad. Hom Optimism.

"I see." I seemed to be saying that a lot lately. "Looks like I don't have much choice."

"We believe not. The reputation of your family will suffer greatly if you leave your parent to die."

Mum wouldn't be all that happy, either. She couldn't *live* with him, but that didn't mean she didn't love him.

"So. What is it you want me to steal?"

"It is a package, this size by that size." He moved his clawed hands apart, indicating something about the size of a box of blank vistapes. "Its contents are no concern of yours."

"Is it alive? Can I turn the package upside down? Expose it to vacuum? Freeze it? Drop it? Submerge it in liquid—?"

The claw on the finger he held up looked almost too long to be real. "We understand. It is foodstuffs. The *Galaxy Room* seeks to prepare a new and unique dish. My client wishes that the main ingredient become unavailable."

Which certainly implied that the "client" was none other than Huido Maarmatoo'kk, proprietor of the *Claws & Jaws*. The idea wasn't totally incredible, but from what I know of the Carasian, he was more likely to shoot a rival than rob him.

"And when do you need this package?"

"We will alert you when it arrives. Take this time to establish yourself as an employee."

I didn't need Petreck to tell me my job. I know better than to turn up the day before an item went missing and disappear the next day.

Great, I thought. *I'm going to be a waiter.*

Customers don't usually think about it, but there are plenty of people like me who live on Plexis Supermarket full time. Well, maybe not exactly like me. There's every kind of sapient you can think of—and some you can't.

That includes my new "employer." Scats are more commonly spacefaring pirates, but a few of the smarter ones do set up planet-based crime rings. Petreck has the only one onstation, and everyone not strictly on the up and up pays his agents a percentage to run their businesses in his territory. I'd never met the boss before, and I wasn't happy to meet him now.

Theoretically, his little job was easier than what I normally do for a living. All I had to do was find a way into the storage room of the restaurant, locate a package, and find some way to walk out with it. Considering the chaos of a place still in its opening days, it shouldn't be much of a problem. It's way more complicated to con someone out of their hard-earned credits, though I have to admit that working in a place as big as Plexis Supermarket, with its continuously changing throngs of customers, makes it easier than most.

As huge as it is, Plexis isn't big enough for many of the long cons— I mean it's thirty-plus levels and more if you believe some people. But while that's huge for a supermarket, it's small for a planet, and short cons, directed at transient shoppers, are much safer than the risk of running into your marks a month after you've cleaned them out of all their disposable credits—and sometimes their indisposable ones. Some of the classic short cons, like the velvet slipper, the pigeon drop, or the lingering odor, work best on Humans. Since aliens don't always react to the same stimuli, you'd think they'd be harder to con, but greed seems to be a universal failing, and another sapient's greed is the basis of any good grift, long or short.

All right, sure, we're stealing. But, as you may or may not know, that's not technically illegal on Plexis. Not many things are. Marks and victims can complain, but local Jellies tend to look the other way for long-time residents, especially those of us who make regular donations to the, ahem, "Constables' Social Club." We'd be left alone, so long as we weren't stealing enough to discourage future shoppers. And with the best scams, the mark usually doesn't know he's been stung.

Trade Pact Enforcers are a different bowl of creteng, but how could an artist like me get involved with Trade Pact violations?

I haven't gone to many job interviews—make that none—but even I could tell I was hired quickly, and without much vetting. They didn't even ask to see my ident card, which was a shame, because it was a work of art. The manager of the *Galaxy Room* replaced my renewable blue airtag (fake) with a permanent one (real, I hoped), charged against the restaurant's account. At first I was worried that I'd get recognized, but I soon found that no one really looks at their waitbeing, not even living ones. I filed away that knowledge for future use. You never know what might become useful in a profession like mine.

On the other hand, it didn't take me long to figure out this wasn't *just* a restaurant.

The kitchen staff called the storage room the "freezer," though the space contained more stasis boxes than actual frozen stuff. On the other hand, it was surprisingly chilly in there. So much so, that some of the more temperature-sensitive among the staff were quite happy to let me fetch things for them, and soon it became part of my regular duties when I wasn't needed front of house. That's how I figured out that the *Galaxy Room* was a front for smugglers—which might seem odd considering that Plexis Authority didn't care what you brought in as long as you paid them their "duty," but that didn't mean people didn't try to avoid doing just that.

From what I could make out, most of the goods were legitimate, but interspersed among them were boxes, crates, and vacuum containers I was never asked to fetch out. That, and the fact that I never saw these items either arriving or leaving supported my theory. Which meant the whole rival restaurant nonsense was just that, and that Petreck was trying to run a scam on *me*.

I reminded myself to be professionally insulted as soon as it was safe.

At the end of my seventh nightshift in a row, I got off the ramp on level five as usual, and headed toward my crib, slowing as I came to my corridor. I was considering and discarding various ideas on what I had really been "hired" to "steal," so I wasn't paying as much attention to my surroundings as I should have. The hiss made me jump, and I didn't appreciate what I assumed was chuckling. I recognized him immediately, of course, from the nick on his left head frill. He was the Scat who'd handed me the reader.

"It's arrived, then?" I asked, once I knew my voice wouldn't give me away.

"Yess-ss. But I am giving you new inss-structions-ss." Whoever he was in the organization, he didn't have access to the same tech as his boss.

Which didn't make what he'd said any more palatable. I had the sting going, and changing the play midstream is never a good idea. "Your boss decide he doesn't want the item, after all? That's great! Good to meet with you."

If I could read his expression—and I could, that stiffening in the snout is a dead give away—he wasn't impressed by my attempt at humor. "You are to make delivery to me. I will overs-ssee transs-sport to the boss-ss."

Suddenly, I wasn't finding anything funny, either. "Hom Petreck was quite clear. I'm to let him know when the item becomes available and deliver it to him myself."

"No. You will bring it to me, and the credit will be mine."

Sure. Only Petreck would be expecting me to follow orders. Which made it far more likely this guy was going to pocket the item himself, put the blame on me, and the credits in his pocket. And where would that leave me? To say nothing of dear old dad.

"Maybe I'll just check with him myself," I said, bringing out my pocket com. "Tell him how conscientious you—"

All right, I really didn't want him to smile. Really not. I'd managed to forget the teeth.

"I am the mate of his-s lates-st female egg. Who do you think will be believed?"

Wonderful. Scats had sons-in-law.

I snapped my com closed again. "Then I suppose you'll be hearing from me."

"That is-ss s-sso, Ss-oft Fless-sh."

I stood there waiting for him to go. To access my corridor I'd have to turn my back on him, and I just didn't want to do it. Thankfully, a gaggle of fledgling Tolian shop clerks, each one taller than the last, came bumbling toward us, all of them arguing with plenty of limb-waving and beak-clicking. With a little fancy footwork, I managed to get them between me and the son-in-law, and contrived to spread us more, moving as they did. Temporarily defeated, the son-in-law fixed me with a meaningful glare and let me go.

I wasn't stupid enough to think this was over.

I spotted the item the first time I went into the storage room during my very next shift. I didn't touch it then, but on my third trip I moved it to a different spot in the storeroom. I wanted to know who would notice, and when.

Hey, I said I wasn't a thief, not that I didn't know how.

I admit, I have my share of curiosity. What was in the box? What made it so valuable to a restaurant in competition with *Claws & Jaws*? So the next trip into the storeroom I examined the box more closely. Suddenly, I felt like I really was in a freezer. The labels were wrong. I know labels. My work often involves the creation of false documents, idents, and labels. These were wrong for food.

Whatever was in the package was alive. Not so strange, you think? Lots of sapients preferred their cuisines living. But like I said, these weren't food labels. They were for medical stuff. *Living* medical stuff.

I have a friend whose business is transporting. He always says that the first rule is "never look in the package." Maybe he needed to amend that to "don't even look at it too closely."

Right then there was nothing I could do but go back to the floor with a smile on my face. I managed not to drop a single plate or drip any sauces on any clients.

Medical. That complicated things in a whole new way. Some sapient somewhere probably needed whatever it was pretty desperately. These Scats were using me, and I didn't like it. No matter who came out on top—Petreck or his son-in-law—they'd be left with the notion that I could be used again. I admit, I was still scared, but I was angry, too. So angry that I didn't even want to give them the package. All I needed was a way out of this that left my reputation intact, my dad free, and the bad guys empty-handed.

More or less in that order of priority.

Frat, I was looking forward to the haven of my own rooms and a nice long relax in my luxury fresher! In fact, I only got as far as the intersection of corridors eleven and nineteen. A family of Whirtles run a mail drop there, where sapients without tech of their own can buy, send, and receive image disks. The Whirtles are friends of mine. That and the few credits I slipped into their tentacles from time to time were enough for them to act as lookouts for me. A red plaque fastened to the wall meant someone had come looking for me. A blue meant someone was still there. Both together, like now, meant I knew the person, and it was safe to proceed.

Still, I opened the door quietly, and my breathing only returned to normal when I saw "someone" was my brother. I didn't even know he was onstation, since he served as cargomaster on the trade ship *Gamer's Gold.*

"A message from our mutual parent was waiting for me as soon as we docked. Thought I'd see if you needed any help, and did you know you've got nothing to eat in here?"

Fortunately for both of us, there's a food and relax center only a few corridors away. Once we were seated with a meal and beers in front of us, I filled him in. It didn't take long to bring him up to speed. It helps to be talking to someone who understood the game.

I was still pushing my sandwich around when he finished chewing. "I don't like the implications, and I don't like the threats." He took a sip of his beer. "What are you planning to do?"

"I'd like to be safe, off their hook completely, and dad along with me. And I'd like to rip them off. The first two are vital, the last one's a bonus."

I looked around, caught by movement in the corner of my eye. Two beings, one a tall Tolian, the other definitely Human, thickset and tough looking.

"Don't stare," my brother said. "Trade Pact Enforcers. Their ship's docked just down from ours."

"Are they?" I pretended to be studying my nail paint. "Have you ever noticed how one Tolian looks a lot like another?"

"Except to other Tolians, I imagine. Why?"

"I've got an idea." I stood up. "Come on, there are people I need to find."

Stealing the item turned out to be easy. As a distraction, fire is a wonderful thing. Of course, there are all kinds of safety features onstation to put fires out and prevent them from spreading. But I didn't need it to spread, I only needed the immediate chaos and panic. I needed a lot of beings running out of the place carrying things.

I'd told the son-in-law to meet me in a small bar with outside seating just inside the night zone. You could almost make out the loud sign over the double doors of the *Claws & Jaws*.

The Scat had the item in one hand, and my arm in the other, when Petreck arrived. Right on time, thanks to a com message arranged by my brother. The son-in-law had to drop me quick, and rush to explain how—and why—he'd gotten here ahead of his boss. Petreck was obviously unsatisfied by the explanation, and I had to focus really hard to look surprised, and not burst out laughing. Once again, the son-in-law was waved to a seat at the next table, the item between his feet, while the boss and I sat down. The look he was shooting me over Petreck's shoulder promised me I wouldn't live to see the start of my next day. I admit, it made the hairs on my arms stand up. My plan had better work.

"And my father? When will he be released?"

"All in good time, Fem Graine. I must examine the merchandise."

"Wait right there. You didn't say anything about having to . . ." I let my voice trail away as I saw what were unmistakably enforcers insinuating themselves around the edges of the seating area, covering obvious exits. A drop of sweat trickled down my back as the boss turned a look almost identical to his son-in-law's on me.

"Relax." I had to cough to loosen my throat. "Order something." I tapped the menu in the tabletop, relieved when the Scat started doing the same thing. "Those are Trade Pact Enforcers. That Tolian over there was pointed out to me just the other day. They can't be here for us. They don't care about a little restaurant rivalry. We're just a couple of wealthy customers having a drink and enjoying the night life." I tapped the gold tag on my cheek before I turned around to move the servo cart carrying all my packages and bags out of the Tolian constable's way.

I hoped my smile wasn't as stiff as it felt. The Tolian came through the tables, his badge displayed in his hand, nodding pleasantly at the people he passed. His Human partner, standing at the main entrance to the terrace, looked almost as surly as the Scat. The Tolian walked right past us, and my shoulders were beginning to relax, when he turned back to the son-in-law's table, right beside the end of my servo cart.

"Commander Bowman? Over here." His voice trilled like bird-song, but he wore a translator and what came out of it was perfectly understandable Comspeak.

A vigorous looking Human female appeared quickly. She indicated the box between the son-in-law's feet with the toe of her boot. "Good work, Constable 'Whix. Take this Scat in."

"That'ss-s not mine," the son-in-law's head frills were flicking from rigid to flat and back again. "It'ss-s theirs-ss." He pointed specifically at me. "It fell off her s-sservo when she moved it just now." A nice save, but his father-in-law was going to remember he'd said "theirs."

Commander Bowman turned to us. Her eyes were hard as diamonds, and there were absolutely no soft lines in her face.

"How ridiculous." I used my best rich-person tone, and let me tell you, it's good. "Imagine! Just because Hom Petreck and I happen to be sitting here."

"Indeed. I'm Commander Lydis Bowman, Trade Pact Enforcer." She flashed a badge. "May I see your idents, please?"

"Well, I really don't see—"

"Just routine, Fem."

You never saw two idents come out faster.

While the Commander looked them over—I don't know about Petreck, but mine would pass inspection by any sapient or machine—I decided I should keep playing the giddy tourist with more credits than brains. I chirped up, "Why, Chief Inspector, whatever is happening? Whatever is in that box, and however did you know where to look?" I hoped she'd give some kind of answer. I needed the boss to know it wasn't me who'd tipped them off.

"Their insider on the transport ship got cold feet and gave us the tip." The commander flashed the coldest smile I've ever seen. "Too bad thieves can't trust each other. Have a good day, Fem, Hom." She nodded at us in turn and then left, signaling to her constables to bring along the package and the son-in-law.

I leaned back in my seat and heaved a sigh of relief. I hoped my face paint—carefully applied to make me look older and richer—wasn't being wiped away by the cold sweat forming on my brow.

"I can't believe that!" I said, breathless. "How long has that guy

been working for you? I can't believe he just threw you to the enforcers like that."

"Indeed. My youngest female egg will be seeking a new mate
soon."

"Will she . . . Will she be very upset?"

"Naturally. However, she knows how the Gentek is skinned."

"Still, it's a setback." I drummed my fingers on the tabletop.
What did this do to our agreement? Then I brightened. "But then
the *Galaxy Room* still doesn't have their exotic foodstuffs, so I suppose technically your client," I tilted my head in the direction of
the *Claws & Jaws*, "will be satisfied."

The look on Petreck's face was so blank I almost had to nudge
him. For a minute there he'd forgotten what story he'd told me.
He'd make a very poor grifter.

"So," I licked my lips and tried to keep my hands from shaking.
"While I didn't actually get you the item . . ." I waited for what
seemed a *very* long time.

"Our ends have been achieved, as you say, Fem Graine."

I managed not to weep with relief.

"Your father is released as we speak." He hesitated, and I knew
the next words were hard for him. "You spoke for me to the Trade
Pact Enforcers. I am in your debt."

I bowed in acknowledgment. That was one debt I had no intention of collecting.

Once he'd gone, it took me three tries to get to my feet. Even
then, I'm sure it was only my brother's hand under my elbow that
kept me there.

"*That* was not Commander Lydis Bowman, Trade Pact Enforcer."
His voice was dry as sand, but he was laughing underneath. "I've
met her, and that was not she."

"I know that, you know that. Petreck doesn't. Not yet." I nodded
my thanks as the couple from two tables over gathered up my servo
cart and sauntered off with it.

"And the item?"

"On its way to the real Bowman, who'll take an interest in Petreck. I know someone who knows someone," I tapped the side of
my nose when my brother raised his eyebrow. "And the son-in-law's

going to be left in what looks remarkably like the brig of the enforcer's ship. It'll take him a while to get out, and in the meantime, someone will tell his ex-father-in-law where he can be found."

My brother tucked my arm in his. "And now?"

"Time to go pick up dear old dad."

... *Truffles* continues

7

* * *

REGARDLESS OF WHAT Morgan had in mind, I decided to play along—while doing my utmost to guess his plan before he chose to tell me. After all, mystery remained, despite being Chosen and Joined, something I wouldn't change. I stood with a smile, slipping my arm through the curve of his, hair curled around his neck. "Lead the way, Captain."

Regardless of why he wanted us to dance, I fully intended to enjoy myself.

A cheery attitude difficult to keep when a pair of tall reptilian figures stalked from behind a shrubbery. Sakissishee.

More commonly known as Scats.

Such beings could, I reminded myself, every muscle tensed—that *chill* rising—be reasonable. Loyal. Unfortunately, my introduction to the species had been Roraqk, the merciless pirate in league with Yihtor di Caraat. Roraqk, who'd torn a hole in this very station in order to escape with me.

The innocent had died.

"I thought they were banned from Plexis," I whispered, avoiding mental touch. Unlikely, that these could sense the deep link between Chosen, but I'd take no chances. In my experience, the creatures loathed mindcrawlers, having some rudimentary sensitivity of their own.

"Plexis couldn't make it stick," Morgan replied. "Easy, chit. Remember the Turrneds. Not all Scats are pirates. These two are merchants."

He'd killed Roraqk using his own considerable mental strength. Had saved me. We'd come so far since—

Yet I still saw that terrifying fanged snout in my dreams. Still heard that chittering laugh. Still knew what it was to be powerless.

I feared I always would.

Memory

* * *

by Sally McLennan

"IR!" FIRST MOTHER calls louder than is necessary in the confines of our home, the storeroom. Her name is Ama, she's my favorite mother, and this is how she objects to the plas crate walls I've used to form a room for my personal use.

I am Ir, and I am an aberration.

With my smaller pair of arms, I shove hair away from my eyes and, reluctantly, leave my studies. "Yes. I'm coming, Mother."

I keep my tone humble. My mothers won't endure cheek. But she needn't have summoned me. It's late night on Plexis, and my preferred time for work in our family shop, *Glamor*. I've set up a subtle alert, a mere vibration of my wrist com, to tell me it's my shift. Ama knows of the alert, though, and it distresses her. It distresses all my mothers.

Glamor, on Level 15 of the upper concourse of Plexis, is home and workplace to all twenty-seven members of my *mesh*. We're from the planet, but not the city, Auord.

Ever wondered why Auord's capital has no name that separates it from the planet on which it's found? Why its best-known inhabitants call themselves Auordians? The damp, rubbish-packed capital is the *only* land-based city of the planet Auord. Auord city is, consequently the location of the spaceport, and most of the interstellar trade on Auord, too.

Or so it was until spacers discovered the unique talents of my species. Moradhi live beyond the grime of the continent over the great oceans of Auord. There our mothers string lines between the tall rock pillars we call spires. Businesses operate in rooms hollowed out of spires. The elaborate tangles of thread between spires are homes woven by the mothers of each family, or mesh.

What separates us from other species isn't the second pair of arms with which we cling or climb—while hands not engaged in that necessary pursuit are busy with other things—nor is it the wings that grace our mothers. What makes male Moradhi special is that we remember everything but recall little beyond the fundamentals of our lives.

I understand sophisticated mathematics but don't recall being taught it. I recognize friends but don't know what we did three days ago. Individual events cannot be recalled by a male Moradhi at will. We live in the present tense. It takes our mothers to unlock our minds. Or it used to.

Hastily, I check my uniform. I step past the back entrance to the shop and join a brother wrapping purchases. On this side of the staff door, *Glamor* is all mirrors and gilt. The floor is real *orstone* from Camos. The gleaming shelves display all that a gentle being needs to improve their appearance. Schools of elegantly dressed customers eye one another as they drift through the shop. Near the comfortable chairs at reception, they are handed refreshments while their credits are taken and their costly little purchases packaged.

My hands fly, removing tags, tying ribbons in our signature burgundy and gold. Hours pass, but my mind has no time to wander. I smile at elegant persons and ensure each of my packages is superb. I'm alert to anything unusual even if I don't remember the events that established what usual is for me. I'm also ready to suggest an additional and complementary purchase, should a sister cue me to. This occupies me until my sister Aby, who is explaining the different grades of bertwee oil to a frizzy-coated Garg, peters into silence. She stares fixedly at the door.

A scraggy-haired Human stands in the door, a spacer. Only her gold airtag and proud bearing have stopped the Regillian guards on the door from ousting her.

"Bold as a sandbat!" Aby mutters. More audibly she calls, "Captain Saunders, an unexpected delight. Please, come through to the back. Issa, would you help Senator Losue with his purchase?" Only family would spot the slight stresses on unexpected and please.

A brother bustles through the staff door and taps my nearest elbow. My mothers have noticed the captain arrive on the security viswall in our storeroom, and I am being summoned. Without a word, she and Aby pass the seated customers, and I follow them into our home. The back room rises to two stories. Of the items we sell, only one or two of each are placed on the shelves. This enhances the appearance of rarity though many are indeed scarce beyond their system of origin.

So, in the storeroom, stacks of plas crates rise to the ceiling in neat towers. Each tower of crates contains the beauty products of a world. Between the worlds thus represented my mothers are at work. Two out of the three of them are weaving lengths of rope near the ceiling. A roving fertile male Moradhi visited a turn ago, and both mothers are heavily pregnant. As they work, creating hammocks and seats, they coat the threads with a complex secretion from their knuckles. Added to the fibers, the lipids and proteins are cues, detailed chemical reminders of the sensations and feelings attached to an otherwise lost moment.

Ama walks to the edge of the platform she is working on and spreads her wings. She drops in short leaps from weaving to weaving, the breeze of her descent cooling my face as she makes a final leap to the ground. "Captain Saunders," she greets our visitor with a polite smile. "Ir, Captain Saunders has been keeping an eye out for new botanicals for us."

The reminder galvanizes me. "Do you have something?" I ask the spacer eagerly.

"No, not yet, and my apologies for coming through the front, Ama! I must up fins shortly and I was nearby. I wanted to let you know that on my next run I'm hauling supplies to an outsystem planet, EF178. It's uninhabited but for a scientist surveying plant life . . ."

"Imagine being the only person on a planet!" I'm already

dreaming of going. The words "new botanicals" are an irresistible lure. I use my wrist com to query EF178. The world is far from trade routes and has no mineral resources to entice miners. But there are jungles and rolling plains.

I'm stunned into silence. Ama eyes me fondly. A world of undiscovered botanical riches is the subject of my fondest daydreams. Potential medicines! New products for *Glamor*! Both figure in my imaginings, but it is the possibility of unique cosmetic goods that excites my mothers. I barely notice Aby's offer to guide the captain back to her vessel via the service tunnels or their departure.

"Ir," Ama says softly, her tone inviting me to calm down. Hands touch my shoulders. Obligingly, I settle with my back to Ama. Her fingers touch my temples. I close my eyes and open my mind to her. She explores my memories of the day, checking any I may wish to record. For me, she works to capture in thread the essence of memories I cannot recall at will. So it is, Moradhi sleep in their memories, live in them, and often work in them, too. Mothers weave a million experiences into our homes day by day. What we smell in a moment, feel, taste, or hear, are captured by an echo of the unique balance of chemicals each experience releases in our minds.

If a being wants to record some great secret? Machines can be manipulated, their content altered or destroyed. But a Moradhi witness only recalls when his mother guides him to the appropriate thread to trigger the memory. Till then a witness won't even know that in his mind lies proof of a rite, or agreement, or decision by a court. A Moradhi male's memory is exact and unchanging, deep within his mind. This trait has been a curse and blessing to my species, the sums of money offered by temples, courts, corporations, and governmental agencies being enough to lure Moradhi from Auord and establish us in businesses across the system.

When Ama has tasted all my memories, she allows me to retreat to my plas crate cubicle, knowing that I will be too distracted to wrap packages tonight.

I search for outsystem contacts who might know the botanist on EF178. My contacts list is rich in scientists. For, inside my cubicle walls, I study botany and chemistry. I've been fascinated since my earliest days by the ingredients in our merchandise and alternative uses for each compound therein. I record my findings and keep detailed logs. Like a few other young male Moradhi, I use technological cues for my memories. This upends the Moradhi tradition of living in webs woven from our pasts, and honoring our mothers' care of us, but I want to live beyond the ropes. My mothers scramble to understand. I just hope to repay their loving patience.

A station week later I request annual leave from *Glamor* and try to allay my family's concern. My records show I've undertaken field trips before. Hom Cates, the lonely botanist, has been introduced to us by fellow scientists and has, reluctantly it seems, agreed to a single brief visit. Aby secures us a berth on the freighter for its return to EF178. We pay a substantial sum to persuade its captain to land instead of dropping supplies from orbit. Moradhi males become incoherent without a mother or sister to support them. Well on the way to seeking an established mesh to mother, or founding a new one with older sisters from other meshes, Aby is amenable to traveling with me despite the basic accommodations of our vessel.

It takes two-and-three-quarter shipdays, in tight confines between plas crates, to reach EF178. We eat our own food and sleep on fold-down bunks. Happily, there is a fresher stall and space for the significant amount of luggage I bear.

The freighter lands smoothly; as soon as the ramp opens, we hustle out, laden with gear. My feet touch earth. I ignore the crew unloading, instead trying to see everything at once, ducking past Aby to stare at the immense trees around the sealed landing area. But my traveling companion is staring in quite another direction. I whirl and stand openmouthed.

On newly cleared land beside the rudimentary launch pad is a house. A single, solitary, one-storied house. An older Human with a dusty look about him stands before it and walks toward us as soon as we have all seen him.

"Captain," he acknowledges, "Thanks to you for this. Is there a bill of lading? Good. As soon as I've checked it, the remaining credits will be in your account. I'm sorry I have no hospitality to offer you. Perhaps by next visit." He nods at the freighter captain cordially, but his words suggest both the ship and ourselves should depart now.

"Ir, please greet Hom Cates, who is the botanist you have asked to guide us," Aby whispers to me. "He's known to be reclusive."

I put myself forward, hoping Hom Cates will indeed welcome me.

"I'm Ir," I say politely. In desperation, I depart from the Moradhi norm of absolute truthfulness and forbear to mention my journey-man status. "I'm the botanist you're expecting. My sister Aby assists me." I indicate her with a tilt of my head.

His face softens when I mention botany.

"Ir, I'll guide you for a one-time visit to the jungle. I'm an ama-teur botanist, albeit a keen one."

"I've the next load waiting on Plexis. No difference to me if they stay here till I'm back." the freighter captain comments.

Our host pauses as if thinking, and my heart beats hard. But he nods to Captain Saunders in acknowledgment. Then he holds out a hand to me in the typical Human gesture of greeting.

"I'm Cates," he says, "I appreciate being able to meet people who share my interest."

I flash Cates a shy smile and wait impatiently until we are alone, gear piled beside us, and the freighter lifting into space. Cates looks uncomfortable when he faces us. His words are almost formal.

"I just need to finish getting some things together. Wait here, please, Fem, Hom."

When he returns, a light bag on his shoulders and a weapon visible on his hip, he asks: "Are you fit?"

I hesitate, hoping my life of climbing, wrapping parcels, and navigating service corridors translates into some sort of ability to keep up. Cates doubts us, eyeing Aby's slender frame.

"I'll go slow," he says, and I realize Cates is excited to show us his jungle. Stirrings of fellow feeling draw my eyes to his.

"Should we leave so near dusk?" I query. Darkness is, I recorded in my journals, the hardest thing about being away from Plexis. It is never truly dark in the great supermarket.

But Cates smiles. "Night is the best time to see the jungle." He strides toward the trees, completely ignoring the grav cart of supplies.

We walk in single file. Cates leads, and we labor under our

luggage behind him. Our voices quickly fall silent, our breath taken by the size of the trees and the energy needed to navigate around and over buttress-like roots. The air is warm, still, and fragrant. I want to stop. The scale of the trees, their solemn immensity, is balanced by the fluttering and scurrying of small lives around us. I avoid squashing a small reptile dreaming on a mossy pad and nearly obliterate an ornate fungus. Aby's folded wings collect some lichen. There's so much to explore, and we are blundering through it.

Cates looks over his shoulder.

"My first night out, I camp in a clearing up ahead. There isn't another nearby. It has drinking water, and if you want to poke around for a day or two, there's your best place to do it."

Cates is right. I step around a tree root, and my eye is drawn first to the small patch of sky above, then to the large tent at the center of the clearing. A brook feeds a pool of green water and dribbles away into the maze of roots. The tent roof is formed of solar patches, and a heat box rests inside it. Distorts ring the site; I wonder what wildlife they keep at bay. Ruefully, I set my pack on the ground, much of what I carry now unnecessary.

Cates clasps my shoulder sympathetically. "I'm so sorry. But if we repacked, we'd have never arrived before nightfall," he explained. "Plus, I want to see your setup for fieldwork, maybe use your ideas to improve my camp."

That's all it takes. Aby nods to Cates' warning to stay in camp, and heads into the tent with her gear, while Cates and I settle to rummage through my pack, right there on the moss. I hear Aby sorting through rations for dinner until she emerges to watch the forest alertly and listen to our conversation. But I don't really notice. Cates and I speak one language and it is the language of botany. When he talks about seed pods which open by a mechanism he doesn't yet understand, I am fascinated. I show him my system for collecting samples, and he makes notes. Finally, the great trees draw near as dusk springs upon us and Cates quietens. We have not got up from where we stopped to eat or drink.

"Watch," is all he says.

Eyes wide, peering into the gloom, I'm initially unsure the soft glow from the jungle is real. But, one by one, blossoms open and brighten, their petals luminescent white, like stars hung on the trees. Barely discernible beneath them, long tendrils drip viscous fluid to invite and ensnare small biters. Aby brings each of us a plate and sits beside us. She makes a low sound of wonder, and Cates smiles. Conversation dies. It's late before we retire to bed-rolls, and in the silence we've begun to be friends.

Aby waits beside my bedroll when I wake the next day. She is hold-ing two steaming cups of sombay as she smiles reassuringly.

"We're on a field trip," she reminds me. "You're looking for new botanicals, guided by Hom Cates."

While I drink the sombay, I skim my log from the day before. I can't dress fast enough, and Cates looks amused by my inclination to skip breakfast to get into the jungle. We spend a glorious day rambling near the campsite, collecting samples of interesting look-ing plants and sealing them in plas for further study. Aby hunts flora with us and we all keep watch for the sources of distant rus-tlings, barking, and whistles that sound in the jungle. Cates has warned us there is a native predator capable of killing us. We stick together, glad of his weapon, and enjoying the adventure com-pletely.

When my wrist com alerts us that it's approaching dusk, we re-treat to camp. Encouraged by Aby, Cates and I set up field desks, port lights, and scopes. We begin comparing samples.

"The *elosia*?" Cates, who has hands full sketching a botanical drawing of them, points at the white flowers with his chin, "I've synthesized something from its honeydew that has interesting properties. I knew it would be sedating, but it seems to impair telepaths, too."

My chin drops. Some believe our mothers' ability to look into their children's' memories to be telepathy. But mothers share memories as passive watchers. This limited mental sharing is an inherent part of the Moradhi mother-and-child bond. Sisters grown to near adulthood can support their mothers in caring for young males of their mesh. Outside such a relationship? Sharing thoughts and influencing others' minds is considered perverse. So, scandalized, I ask Cates "How did you find out?"

Cates face reddens. We are momentarily silent, each discomforted though for different reasons. "By accident. I'd like to run more tests, but I'm not set up yet. I was wondering . . ."

He watches my face intently as he pulls a vial of black liquid from his carrysack. He holds it out, and I barely stop all four hands from reaching at once. "I bet you have what you need on Plexis," he says, "You could com me your findings. I hope . . . when I got your first message, I hoped that you would. Maybe you can even have some more of this synthesized on Plexis and sent back for me. I'm happy to pay you." The trust in his words has gravity of its own.

Aby wanders over and hands us each a plate, cutting our conversation short. She fills the silence with questions. "How come you're alone here, Cates? I like privacy, too, but isn't this dangerous?"

Cates' chin lifts proudly. "You're right about liking privacy. Best not ask questions. It's just nice you were allowed to visit." He isn't referring to our parents' reluctant consent. A shiver moves my shoulders.

". . . As for me being alone? On the way here there was an—accident. My family died. We'd served some wealthy folk for decades, so they give me leeway to be here enjoying the jungle. It's turns since I got to be with outsiders. I confess, I tipped Saunders for bringing you. I'd asked her to look out for a botanist for me to meet. But when you arrived, well, you're so young. I wasn't sure I should talk to you." He lets us absorb this for a moment before he adds, "Let's talk plants."

With a sympathetic glance at Cates' worn expression, Aby slips away to rest beneath a portlight. Cates presses the vial into my hand and passes me his drawing of the elosia. We talk botany until exhaustion forces us to rest.

Aby's howl of outrage wakes me. Dazed with sleep, I totter to the tent door, thrusting flaps open with both sets of arms. I am neatly pinioned by large Scats waiting for someone to do just that. My arms are twisted painfully. I'm pulled onto tiptoes. Aby is on the ground, her cheek red. The Scat pointing a blaster at her has a bite wound on his forearm that drips blood. His frills pulse purple and red, and clawed fingers tighten on the weapon. I'm about to watch my sister die.

But the Scats holding me pull me around to face the tent. Hope dies as Cates, the last of us still free, stumbles into the doorway. He grapples with his holster, fogged by our late night. His eyes are bleary, his movements clumsy and slow. I cry out but before the sound escapes a blast of heat and light passes me and ignites Cates. His eyes and mouth widen. Then he combusts with a sizzling crack. Cates is seared away but for bubbling, steaming goo that singes my nostrils with an acrid stench. I open my mouth to breathe and gag.

The Scat that fired the shot addresses Aby. "Careful ss-softflesh," he tells her. "I bite back."

I thrash between my captors. Notes spill from a carrysack beside the puddle that was Cates. Pain and the dark arrive together.

I hear a discussion as if from far away.

"A Moradhi and his-ss little mother! The price they'd bring!" A com crackles. "We don't have to ss-sell them nearby!" I hear an angry voice over the distortion of the com signal. A low hiss of frustration, then, "Yes-ss ss-sir, the nuisssance Human is-ss terminated. Yes, ss-sir." The com clicks out.

Claws snick as the Scat paces toward me, and I open my eyes, terrified. I'm in a cell looking out into a gray passage. Everything is designed to be hosed clean. Bile chokes me, and I swallow hard.

"Relax, mammal," the Scat croons. "You're not in the galley yet. If you are fortunate, you will be ss-sold." He licks his snout with a long black tongue and saliva spatters to the ground, smoking. I try to register that the best possible fate for Aby and me is now slavery. I try. The com clicks on again. The voice on the other end is terse, but I don't catch her words, only the pirate's immediate acquiescence.

"Kort, bring the little mother," he says to someone beyond my cell door. "Watch her teeth. These rations-ss bite." There is malicious delight in his yellow eye.

He hits the cell release and waves at me with his blaster. "Annoy me, and I'll ss-shoot *her*," I am told. I go in the direction of the wave and pass a long row of cells. Aby follows somewhere behind me.

We are walked to a lift, and ascend several levels, before being directed into a boardroom. A female Scat, splendidly dressed in Orassian silks, sits at the head of a long table. A Human stands behind her, his expression dour. The room is so civilized, I rally.

"Captain, if you return us to Plexis our family would reimburse your costs," I say.

The Scat laughs. "Oh, ss-softflesh, we're not going to Plexis. We have business-ss elssewhere." She lets me absorb that before continuing.

"The question is, do I ss-show you our air lock, or can we wring ss-some profit from you as Roraqk ss-ssuggestss . . . ?" A flick of her eye identifies the male Scat. Her expression is disdainful.

"I've witnessed many agreements," I tell her shakily. "My sister can unlock those secrets." Aby is mute, presumably overwhelmed.

"Once we have their information, they'd make valuable merchandis-sse," Roraqk asserts from behind me. "Moradhi are rare pickingss-s."

"We'd be better off picking their bones-ss," the captain sneers immediately. "Our clientss-s diss-slike improvisssation." She waves a hand at the door, and the Human behind her interprets the gesture.

"Put them back in the brig, Roraqk."

I wake to find a Scat pacing outside my cell. His crests stand high, their color intense.

"What ship is this?" I ask. My voice shakes. He's familiar, but I don't know how I got here or who he is.

"My clan ss-ship, the great *Torquad*." Beneath the Scat's anger is pride. He eyes me and adds with a sneer, "I am Roraqk."

"You don't hold a high post on your family ship?" I gesture at his shoulders which lack crest or badge and wonder if this question will be my last.

But Roraqk's answering snarl is halfhearted. "My posssition is higher than yoursss, C-cube."

"You could take it over," I say, wondering where my mouth is leading me, improvising furiously. I can't let myself register that the Scat thinks of me as concentrated food.

"No, I couldn't, creteng. The captain iss-s my mother." Roraqk makes a strange wheezing sound at my crestfallen face. He's laughing. "Ss-she killed her mother and took the *Torquad*, meat. It'ss-ss a time-honored tradition. The problem issss, that being ss-so, ss-she has taken precautionss-s."

As he paces away, I check my pockets. The only thing in them is a torn slip of paper. On it is the drawing of a flower. The scribble alongside it says "elosia."

A memory of holding a vial, of talking to a Human named Cates, swims forward. I reach for it, waiting Roraqk out, while I frantically try to recall anything else. But without Aby's help, the memory prompted by the sketch is incomplete. Aby, however, is ominously silent. All I am sure of is, as unlikely as it seems, the vial contains something that suppresses telepathy.

Suddenly Roraqk answers my unasked question with a snarl. "Her deputy is-s a mindcrawler." His tongue scatters stinking drool as it lashes. "Filthy mammal. The feel of it in my mind." He growls, twisting as if to wring a mental touch out of his body. "At the firssst thought of mutiny, he knowss-s." His clawed hands make a slashing motion to indicate what happens after that. "My s-ssiblingss died of their attempt. Now you propos-sse *my* death?" His voice carries a threat.

"Do you have our luggage?"

Roraqk's fist bangs the plas fronting my cell and I jump. "We are piratess-s, fool. Of cours-sse, we have your luggage."

"I can fix your problem, then." I speak confidently, keeping the suspicion that I only have a sample of Cates' serum, and that untested, out of my voice. Roraqk hisses at me in disbelief.

"Ss-speak, C-cube. The cclls-s are s-sshielded in case of telepathic guestsss."

I stare. Shielding is new tech, unreliable and very expensive. It's a big investment to protect the pirates from a tiny sector of the population.

"There's a black liquid in my carrysack, a small vial. It dampens telepathy." This is where my guesswork begins. "But you have to inject it. I don't know how you'll get close enough without tipping him off."

Again, that hissing laughter. "I have a remote crawler, and her deputy'sss-s off duty now. He'll be ass-sleep." Roraqk presses a button on my wrist com, which decorates his scaly wrist. "Kort! Go into the carrysackss-s we took. I need a vial of black liquid. Mother's-ss ordersss-s." The last is a low growl that would terrify me if I wasn't already beside myself.

Roraqk watches me beadily until the com clicks again. "I've found it."

"Bring it to me," Roraqk answers calmly, "Oh, and Kort? Bring me the box from under my bunk." The Scat isn't stupid, staying in the only shielded area, and letting someone who doesn't know what is happening do his running for him. He turns to me. "You didn't bargain, ss-softflessh," he comments idly.

"I couldn't hold you to an agreement," I wave one pair of arms to indicate the cell.

"C-cube, you couldn't make me do anything out of the cell," the Scat answers, wheezing again. He moves out of sight. All is quiet until there is a scuffle and Roraqk reappears, herding Kort to a cell, a blaster aimed at his back.

When the Scat departs again, Aby comments from a cell I can't see, "Well, I guess slavery will be fun. Assuming they sell us." She sounds sleepy, but her humor is on point.

I wince and put a jovial note into my voice. "If the serum doesn't work, we'll be killed, so there is that."

"There is that," Aby agrees. "There were Tulis here while you were sleeping. They wanted me to weave for them."

Weaponsfire erupts overhead.

There is an eternity of running, bangs, and shouts. The door at the end of the hall hisses open. Will the beings approaching kill us immediately? Roraqk strides into view, a gash across his snout oozing blood. He ignores it. "C-cube!" He opens my cell door. I'm lifted off my feet, shaken, and dumped to the ground.

"It worked." Roraqk's eyes gleam, and I realize I've just been the recipient of cheerful exuberance from a Scat. Knowing he could just as easily have gutted me, I seize the moment, scrambling to my feet.

"Please take us home." I make no attempt to disguise that I am pleading.

Roraqk's crests swell. Turning his back on me, he strides into the hall, talking into my wrist com.

"Captain, Captain Roraqk," Kort calls from the next cell. Roraqk pauses but doesn't turn around. "I've always supported you. I had documents forged years ago stating your mother's mother intended to transfer ownership of the *Torquad* to you, not her daughter. They're flawless. You need them. You need me. I'm listed on them as witness. You deserve to be our captain, sir."

Roraqk turns. "Perss-ssuas-ssive, Kort, but not convincing."

"What if the document was also recorded by a Moradhi?" Aby blurts.

I hasten to add, "If you give me my wrist com, I'll make an entry that says so, and Aby can weave something into our home to confirm it. If my mesh survives, proof that you own *Torquad* would fly inside Plexis. You know our kind. I can't remember otherwise."

Again, the sibilant laughter rises. "You have a remarkable knack for making yourself usseful, C-cube. But what about your sister's memory of our arrangement? What happens if a mother checks her mind?" His tone has become sinister, and Roraqk's eyes stare hungrily down the hall in the direction Aby's voice has come from.

Aby speaks softly, persuasively. "We honor the privacy of our clients, Captain. I'll see that your legal title to *Torquad* is woven into our home. No one will reexamine Ir's memory—or mine—once a weaving exists to confirm it."

Roraqk considers this for a long moment before he pivots toward the door. "If the document iss-s good, you are free, Kort. I'll even make you my deputy."

"Sir!" Kort acknowledges enthusiastically, but Roraqk is gone.

I dig over the pile of loose items from our luggage and spread Cates' field notes across a pristine laboratory workbench. Aby stands beside me to help me remember events prior to the attack.

Roraqk, having used the full sample of suppressant on his mother's mindcrawler, has offered us our freedom only if I can replicate the drug. I try not to think about why pirates need such exquisite med facilities or the untrustworthiness of Scats. Tulis surround us, each observing me with all three eyes, as I begin to read. For the first time since the attack, I feel like myself. My wrist com waited for me on this table when I reached the laboratory.

But nothing remotely helpful springs from the pages. Doubt nips me; more to burn off restless energy than out of hope, I tip the luggage pile over again. I almost fail to see the tiny chip holder under Cates' clothes.

Seeing those is enough of a trigger, and the event traumatic and recent enough, that I recall his death. I sit on the floor and cue my recording of our meeting. I listen to my claim to be a botanist and Cates telling me he's just an amateur. Aby makes a soft, rueful sound but doesn't comment.

I return to the table with the chip and hesitate before slipping it into my wrist com. It contains cross-section sketches and chemical analyses of "a protein synthesized from elosia nectar." Finally, Cates supplies a chemical formula. I write it out and wave it at the bemused Tulis.

"Can you make this?"

My question has an electrifying effect on them. I'm left sitting at the table and musing that whomever Cates' family served didn't appreciate his abilities. I suspect the servant was better than his masters.

"The *Torquad*, captained by Roraqk, requests docking at Plexis," Kort says into the com.

"*Torquad*, welcome to Plexis. Proceed to docking ring 27 parking space 44."

I stand on the bridge listening anxiously. I'm so tired nerves are all that keep me standing. Scaled digits slide over my shoulders from behind. I startle, and hissing laughter sounds around us. So I ignore the scrape of Roraqk's claws and turn to face him. I have to look up at his bared, smoking teeth and dripping black tongue.

"Why'd you go to EF178?" I ask him.

"To remove a fool, C-cube. Our employersss dis-sslike indis-sscreet behavior."

I stare into his eyes trying to decipher that, ignoring that he is toying with me by answering my questions. We both know I won't remember asking him anything.

"Why Plexis?"

More laughter. "You will prove my ownership of *Torquad*, re-member? After that comes the ss-small matter of a freighter taking pass-ssengers where it ss-shouldn't."

"Very, very discreet passengers," I temporize.

Kort grins over his shoulder before he turns to the com again.

"*Torquad* to Plexis. We have passengers from a shop called *Glamor* refusing to pay their fare."

Roraqk is laughing.

"Your homecoming is ss-still really going to coss-st you, C-cube," he says almost crooningly.

So it does.

Aby codes into our home the story of Cates' guiding us on a re-mote jungle planet before dying in his bed of natural causes. It must've been traumatic. Details about what happened before the *Torquad* rescued us were thin, and Aby won't talk about it. My wrist com logs are similarly brief. It was an eventful trip because during our time on board, the *Torquad* was legally transferred to Roraqk by his loving mother. The transfer was witnessed by me.

I continue to work in *Glamor*, wrapping purchases. But some things are different. My mothers are more protective. They wall in a room for me and set up a laboratory with sophisticated recording devices. I'm astonished and delighted they've accepted my need to manage my own memory.

Most strangely, from this time, on my birthday, a gift arrives. It might be expensive, in good taste or bad, and it is often exotic. Enclosed in every wrapper I find an unremarkable C-cube.

. . . *Truffles* continues
Interlude

* * *

HER ARM WAS rigid where it touched his, and Morgan would have banned the Scats, innocent or not, from every public space if it spared her the memory of Roraqk. He'd his own, dark and dire. How it had felt to stop the workings of another mind. How easy to let his rage take over.

Rage that had come close to consuming him completely, when Sira had been violated on Pocular, her body cut open and used for an experiment. She'd sent him after her enemies, adding her fury to his. He'd barely made it back—

Beloved. Don't think of then. Enjoy now. "Dancing," she pleaded aloud, her tone faint, almost desperate.

In that moment, more than anything, Morgan wanted to hold her close. Kiss away the pain and promise her the past didn't matter. Help her forget. Block those memories, if that's what it took. He'd the Talent—

The mere thought made him sick inside. Sira had had most of her memories blocked once before. That it had been her decision, to remove Clan prejudice and let her come close to a Human, to him, in a desperate gamble to find a new path for her kind? Didn't matter. The scars were there. The blank spaces. She'd lost some of herself, perhaps forever.

Not again. Only one thing could ease her new fears. One thing combat the overpowering reflex to flee or fight. Didn't he know that himself?

Facing them.

"We learn from the past, chit," Morgan said, making his voice low and harsh. "Understand that Scats are who and what they are. You keep from triggering their predatory instincts, they're easy as Humans in a negotiation. Remember they're not all Roraqk," he said, stressing the name. Spotting a familiar shape, Morgan forced himself to point. "Same for them."

Her flinch when she saw the Tuli walking past was like a stab to his heart, but he refused to have pity. "Not all Tulis work for Recruiters."

"I know that," with reassuring *anger.*

Morgan made a decision. "Then there's something else you should know. You weren't the only one who fled Smegard's stronghold that night on Auord."

Home is a Planet Away

* * *

by Ika Koeck

THE TROUBLE WITH Ghika was that one could never tell how his luck would turn out. His stories of conquests in planets far beyond their home were often too fantastical to be true. Yet just as the others were beginning to think that he was nothing more than a failed embellisher, he returned a wealthy Tuli, with enough credits to purchase three burrows. And just when he had begun to gain the respect of his kind, Ghika went offplanet once more, only to crash-land near the warren two days later on his old starship, *The Moderate Flea*, with little more to boast about than patches of missing fur on his back, a singe on one of the tufts above his three eyes, and a debt large enough to force him to sell his burrows.

He spent weeks sulking in the packed communal hive, muttering to himself and ignoring the press of bodies all around him, his broad nose and whiskers twitching. Olsi, who had always observed him from a distance, thought him not a fool. Just a poor judge of what was right or simply stupid.

On his latest expedition, however, Ghika once again returned a wealthy Tuli. *The Moderate Flea* was gone, replaced by a ship twice as large and one that was anything but moderate. It had thrusters that roared so loud, it rattled the otherwise sturdy glass domes above their burrows. The portlights flickered and furniture shook as it passed overhead. It was impressive enough to draw Olsi away from her maps and vistapes. Enough to make her wonder if this was the moment she would gamble her fate and leave her crowded colony.

"I have a proposition for all you bucks and does!" Ghika announced in barks and yips as he hopped down from his ship. An entire horde of Tulis had already gathered around him by the time Olsi emerged from the burrow she shared with three dozen of her siblings. Her pale eyes widened at the size of the vessel. Its fuselage alone was half the size of her home. As the smell of fuel began to subside and the impulse to sneeze faded, she caught other smells. Offworld metal and the stink of offworld creatures. Ghika had gone much farther this time.

"We're looking for all sorts of crew. Diggers, cleaners, transport pilots, groundcar mechanics!" Ghika snuffed and sized up the crowd. He swept his short paw over the ship and moved his stubby fingers in a series of motions. A gesture for pride, certainty, assurance. "And as you can see, the offer comes with many rewards."

"Who's *we?*" someone from the crowd asked. Noses twitched, and more gestures rolled through the crowd. Here, uncertainty. There, intrigue. Olsi waved her hand in a motion of curiosity as she wended her way through the crowd for a closer look.

"An employer that surpasses all others," Ghika said, and made a gesture for pride and awe. "He pays well, as you can see. An expert negotiator of Trade Pact laws, an opportunistic entrepreneur, and one who cares deeply for his crew and ships."

"Where?" someone else asked.

"Auord," Ghika announced. "Well, Auord *first*, and then elsewhere, depending on what your assignment is. Beyond, I say. Beyond here."

Beyond. It was enough to convince Olsi to shoulder her way past the press of Tulis and back into her burrow to pack her meager belongings. After all, if a lazy old buck like Ghika could earn an honest wage, a life beyond their planet and far from the company of other Tulis could be worth exploring. Her mind made up, she lifted her paw when Ghika repeated his call for recruits.

Ghika's job offer entailed working with a decisive, determined Scat who was an expert negotiator of Trade Pact laws. What the slimy old buck failed to mention was that Roraqk was a bloodthirsty

Recruiter and the *last* alien any sane Tuli would ever wish to work for. The day Olsi realized her mistake was a month after her arrival on Auord, where she spent most of her time tuning the engines of groundcars in a dank, mold-infested hangar and trying to memorize the network of halls and corridors to avoid getting lost in a massive warehouse Roraqk shared with his Human business partner, Smegard.

Boom.

It was a faint sound. So faint that Olsi thought she had imagined it. She looked up from the vehicle's engine, her broad nose twitching as she tried to sniff for trouble. Too bad the smell of the lubricants coating the engine and the warehouse's poor circulation made it a chore to try and catch a whiff of anything other than the groundcar.

The Human working across from her, Eladia, gave a final sweep of the engine and narrowed her brows.

"Olsi?" Eladia asked in Comspeak, the common merchant and trade tongue for all beings on Auord and beyond. "Did you hear that?"

A Tuli's vocal range, mouth, and jaw structure could not form words in the common tongue as well as most humanoids, which made them valuable employees when the task required silence and efficiency. That their language was intrinsically paired with elaborate gestures meant they mostly kept to their own kind, but this slender Human learned those signs as fast as any Tuli pup. Olsi liked that about her. Liked her more for not being a Tuli.

Maybe something, the young Tuli gestured, then followed with a shrug and a fluttering of her stubby fingers. *Maybe nothing.*

Eladia frowned again, mimicking Olsi's gestures slowly. Perhaps it helped her to recall what they meant. "Maybe you're right. Could just have been me imagining—"

Another boom, louder this time. It startled the Human into cursing and caused Olsi to drop her wrench. Echoes of fast footfalls, voices shouting and screaming, came in sudden concert with the building's alarm system, which blared evacuation warnings in a monotonic tone.

Olsi huddled against the groundcar, her three eyes scanning

the vast hall of the hangar for the imminent danger. Instinct prodded at her to find a bolt-hole and hide, but where?

"Olsi, we have to get out of here!" Eladia said, her fingers tight around a tuft of fur on Olsi's arm. It took a couple of hard tugs before the Tuli found the courage to move. Olsi lumbered after the Human as fast as she could as the smaller being ducked through a door and ran down a long, empty hallway. Portlights flickered around them as another loud boom shook the building. Dust and debris rained down on them, as Olsi's nose registered the scent of other creatures.

More shouts came as they reached an intersection. Aliens of varying species, all under Smegard's or Roraqk's employ, rushed past them and turned into different corners and intersections. The sudden onslaught of smells caused her to pause, for within them came a familiar scent. She twitched her moist, spongy nose and turned her head. Another quick sniff told her it came from all the way down a corridor on the opposite side of the exit everyone else was running toward.

Ghika had passed through here. In this enclosed space, it wasn't difficult to recognize his musk. Olsi followed her nose, the softest of sounds vibrating from her throat. Another loud explosion from the levels above caused her to stumble. She moved on all fours at first, down another network of hallways, then tumbled into the first lift she could find.

It was dark when she reached the bottommost floor. Whatever remained of the portlights were dim, near useless given the urgency of her predicament. Olsi placed one hand along a wall and took several sniffs to make sure she was moving in the right direction, for once curious of the extent of their employers' questionable trade. The smell of blood, fear, and sweat was ripe in this narrow hall and opened into individual cells, empty now that everyone had found a way to flee. How many aliens had been kept in this place. And why?

Tendrils of smoke were rising from Ghika's body, or what remained of him, when Olsi entered the empty cell. She could smell his musk more than see him, but it was the old Tuli, nonetheless. The stench of blood filled every breath she inhaled, and Olsi fumbled back against the wall, the whimpers in her throat turning into something stronger, more urgent, and filled with fear. Ghika's luck had finally killed him.

She smelled the Human before she heard her. A shaft of light beamed into the cell, its brightness stinging. Between half-lidded eyes, Olsi looked up and saw her coworker. Eladia's breaths came fast as she wiped sweat from her brows. One hand was wrapped around a glowing globe, the other now grabbed the Tuli by the fur on her arm.

"Olsi, come on. Port Authority is raiding the warehouse," she said. When the Tuli hesitated, she made a clumsy gesture for *danger* and *survive*. "There's nothing we can do for him now. We have to catch the next transport out of here."

There was nothing more terrifying than that mad dash from the cell blocks, back up the lift, and down a maze of hallways and corridors the Human remembered with a precision Olsi admired. They huddled behind plas crates and kept themselves hidden whenever they heard anyone coming.

"There, look," Eladia whispered, gesturing *caution*.

A dozen or so enforcers *and* Port Authority constables marched past them, blasters drawn. Eladia was right. It was a full-scale raid.

Why is this happening? Olsi signed, her mouth agape. But the Human grabbed her hand and led her to a door disguised as a wall—one of the many escape holes their employers had thoughtfully installed around the warehouse, for this very purpose, the Tuli thought.

That Eladia found the door with such ease made Olsi wonder how long she had been under the Recruiters' employ. That she immediately found a ship for the two of them at the docks without so much as a stare and several harsh-sounding words to a recalcitrant captain made her wonder if she should start worrying. After all, did Ghika not trick her into working for Roraqk?

The sound of Olsi's stomach grumbling should have been drowned by the mill and press of the crowd and the shouts of hawkers peddling their wares. *Should* have. Several steps in front of the

Tuli, Eladia looked over her shoulder and winced. "Yeah. Me, too," she said.

If the Human could smell the embarrassment that was now intertwined with her musky scent, or saw the way the long white tufts above her eyes twitched and flicked, she gave no sign. They wove through a crowd that seemed to move in every direction but forward, to the point Olsi touched Eladia's shoulder to stop her, then planted her stocky build in front of the smaller being so that she could carve a smoother way through the mass.

Crowded. Just like home.

She had heard of Plexis' changing weather and seasonal patterns. The diversity of its inhabitants and visitors had once encouraged its founder and creator, Raj Plexis, to provide an equally diverse environment to emulate the worlds of its customers. One could never tell which planet one would visit when arriving on Plexis. To the Tuli's consternation, this part of the space station reflected the temperate, humid climate of her planet.

"Do you know where we're going?" Eladia had to raise her voice to be heard.

Olsi doubted the Human could see her answer, so she trudged forward, ducking under a servo that moved on tall metal stilts and scanned the rows of shops for signs for work. Truth was, she had no idea where to start. Plexis Supermarket was massive, almost a planet on its own. They could spend tens of drops from subspace here, hundreds even, before finding anything suitable.

Worse, all the vistapes she had studied on the planet did not prepare her for the smell. Between the sweat and stink of anything that moved and breathed here was the stench of decades' worth of alien industry. And past a row of shops with moving signs flashing outside were smells of unfamiliar spices from parts unknown. Farther down was the stench of body parts from creatures unknown. Olsi looked up to see creeping vines with spiked flowers releasing multiscented gases for reasons unknown. Made her shudder, to see the plant expand and contract like that, like it was breathing the rancid yet expensive Plexis air.

She tried not to pick at the blue waxy living patch now attached to the skin on her forehead. *Proof* of the air they paid for in advance, Eladia said, coming in with no prospects or sponsor. It had cost the Tuli almost her entire life's savings. Made her question what sort of job she would find here that could replenish what she had lost. Made her wonder if they should be charging for air back home. Maybe then the Tulis would not breed so much and overpopulate the planet.

"We'll find a better job than the last one. Don't you worry," Eladia called out behind her, as if reading her mind. "We can't keep wandering around like this. There must be someone looking to hire grunt workers somewhere on this level."

Olsi huffed, one paw clasped around her pouch where a handful of her credits remained. She turned to face the Human to make a sign for food and hunger, and paused mid-gesture, her mouth agape.

The Human was gone.

The thickness of the crowd had lessened to a trickle of aliens by the time Olsi found her way to the higher floors, where balconies offered a grand view of the levels below. She wasn't certain what her plan was. To find a vantage point high enough to try and sniff out her companion perhaps; or find a constable to help her locate the Human.

How could they help? she wondered. *I can't even speak to them.*

Her initial panic had dulled since her unexpected companion disappeared, though her urgent need to find Eladia brought the realization that she had grown close enough to the Human to care for her safety. That surprised her. Back home, she never much cared for other Tulis. There were just too many of them to care for.

Having the time to walk and think and grind her incisors calmed her, though another Tuli would be able to tell that her musk still carried a hint of fear and worry. The sudden absence of the crowd, which had reminded her so much of home, left a strange tingle to her skin. Not the bad kind. For the first time, her nose wasn't stuffed with the smell of Tuli fur or musk, apart from her own. As she entered a zone where the lights over the vast space station dimmed and changed to create an artificial night, so did the trade.

"Hey, watch where you're going!"

Olsi tumbled into a grav cart no bigger than her foot. A chatter of noise erupted from the tiny being manning the cart as the contents crashed to the floor. Plumes of smoke began to rise from the wares which fell and broke, and the stench of them caused the peddler to cough and squeal. Olsi made a gesture for *apology* and bolted as fast as she could, past a collection of furniture and onto a ramp that took her to the level above.

The two beings on that ramp jumped and hissed at her sudden appearance. Olsi froze for a moment, her nose almost touching the scaled snout of an alien with thin crests rising from nose to forehead, and a pair of thin slits staring at her from the depths of bright yellow eyes.

Despite herself, the Tuli squeaked like a pup, and cowered closer to the ramp's rails. Scats! She wondered if these two were related to Roraqk. Not that she had met the lizardlike pirate to begin with. Thoughts of explosions and Ghika's lifeless body on the cold, hard floor came to her mind just then.

"What'sss-s a Tuli doing up here alone?" said the Scat in front of her, a female judging by her scent. This one wore beads of diamonds and colorful jewels along her snout. A beautiful yellow gem dangled from the bright orange frill on one side of her head. "Where's-ss your kind?"

"Loss-st, are we?" the Scat's companion, a male smaller in size, asked. This one's crests were less prominent, and a dull green where its companion's shone bright red. He might be just as short as the Tuli was, but those jaws, plus lean, well-muscled arms with clawed hands, could no doubt cause some damage in a fight. That he wore a blaster strapped to his side told Olsi this was not a confrontation she could win.

Olsi didn't wait to see what they would do and dashed out onto the shopping concourse as soon as the ramp reached the next floor. Several Humans and two servos scattered out of her path as she blundered past, ignoring the cry of the female Scat and the shouts of alarm rising behind her.

Olsi turned into smaller lanes, then down an alleyway that was cleaner than the Tuli's best family burrow. She ran up a terrace with empty peddlers' carts lined at the sides, circled a roundabout, and wove her way through a maze of walkways. Up here, the ceilings bore the shades of deep crimson and violet, almost mirroring her planet's night sky, with the portlights flickering to a starlike luminescence.

Why must everything remind me of home? she wondered.

Her fur brushed against something cool and soft, made her pull her hand away. It wasn't until the hardened pads underneath her clawed feet touched the familiar prickled edges of grass that she stopped to catch her breath. The scent of flowers both alien and known to her enveloped Olsi's senses all at once. She emerged into a quiet intersection lined and adorned with beds of flowers, creeping vines, and the spiked flowers she'd spotted earlier in the marketplace.

This time they were dormant. No strange vapors wafted out of their buds though they let out a dim glow in the space station's artificial night. Awed by the sudden coolness in the air, and the feel of wind against her whiskers, she barreled into a small tree in a pot, then landed on her rump in between manicured hedges.

"Didn't think you could run forever, did you?" a voice came from just beyond the hedges. For the second time that night, the Tuli froze in fright.

"Forever? Oh, of course not," said a familiar voice. "Just long enough . . . till you lose interest."

A familiar voice with a familiar smell. Olsi's eyes widened in both delight and surprise, but she managed to suppress the squeak that threatened to escape her throat. As quietly as she could manage, she crawled underneath the bushes until she could see who lay beyond, her nose twitching. There was no mistaking that smell.

"The reward for finding you is too high for someone to lose interest over," the first speaker said. A Human male. He was twice the size of the Human he was now pushing down to the grass, and none too pleasant in the olfactory department. "Did you really think you could lose us in Plexis?"

"Concentration. . . . slipped," Olsi's friend said, her voice strained and her speech slurred. "Won't. . . . happen again."

Eladia's hands were bound behind her. From the relative safety of her hiding spot, Olsi spotted a bruise on the side of the Human's cheek. A low, quiet growl formed in her throat. The fur along the back of her neck stiffened as she warred with the need to stay safe or leap out of the bushes to save her only friend away from home.

Ghika died so easily, she thought. *Will I suffer the same fate? Maybe I should run to the constables now.*

No, too late for that. A second female Human emerged into the garden and added to the complexity of the situation. Reflectors on her sleek black spacer suit caught the glow of the flowers, made her seem like the pack of Human voyagers that once visited the Tuli's home planet and found it too crowded for their liking.

Whatever thoughts Olsi had to summon the authorities were smothered. She clenched her fingers and made a gesture for *frustration.*

"Smart of you, to hide under Roraqk's employ as one of his grunt workers," the female said as she surveyed the garden. There was a more relaxed air about her and she smelled pleasant, at least. "Though one wonders what your esteemed family would say if they discovered how low their beloved, gifted daughter would stoop, working with Recruiters and pirates."

"They'd say nothing, thanks to your discretion," Eladia said, her teeth bared in a smile or a snarl. The Tuli could not tell which without the hand gestures to validate that expression. "Discretion that . . . my friend . . . willing to pay . . . generously for."

"Yes, you've said that already," the female Human said with a sigh.

"So where is this *friend* of yours?" the male captor said with a growl. He, too, sported an ugly bruise, one that left one eye shut. Olsi could tell from the way he carried himself that he was in pain. She had seen bucks emerging from a territorial dispute the same way. "We can't wait all night."

He paused to turn his head toward the bushes where Olsi lay hidden, to the Tuli's alarm. For a moment, he seemed to stare straight at her, his brows furrowed and his hand clasped around a blaster strapped to his side. All at once she could smell more than the captor's sweat. Fear, anticipation, and the scent of certain lizardlike aliens the Tuli had run into but a short time ago.

"We are here," something hissed into the night. The male Scat, Olsi discovered. "Releass-se her."

"We have your payment, Manda," said the female Scat, coming to stand beside her male companion. Under the dim glow of the flowers, and the soft luminescence of the stars above, she cut an impressive figure. Her frills were fanned out, her poise straight, unfazed by the tension. "Unbind her."

"Not so fast, Jostaph," the one called Manda said, her hand raised to stop her companion from moving. "Let us see the credits first, Scat. Then we'll talk."

Something flew into the air, then landed with a clinking sound in the grass close to where Olsi's friend was being held captive.

"A bag of gems-ss, as-ss per your reques-sst," the female Scat explained.

Manda smirked, then exchanged a look with Jostaph that Olsi didn't quite trust. The grins on their faces were just as shady as the scent of their mischief. "And the credits you agreed to transfer?"

"Already in progres-ss," the female Scat motioned to her companion, who held up a small screen in his claws. Moments later a beep from the device broke the silence, and he nodded to her. "Done," she said.

"Good," Jostaph said. In the flash of a second, he whipped his weapon out and fired. Before anyone could so much as gasp, the young male Scat was on the ground, writhing in agony.

"No!" Fladia shouted. "Please, don't hurt them!"

"Move, and you're next, scum," Manda pointed at the female Scat before bending down to retrieve the bag of gems. It was enough to set the Tuli's blood boiling, and that damnable pack instinct, the one that had drawn her species so closely together, now gnawed at her to act.

Ghika had died a horrible death. She didn't like the old buck very much, but there was no sense in any more deaths involving beings she knew. Not here in this space station, so far away from her home planet. And the Human had always been kind to her. Kinder than Ghika ever was.

Decision made, she crawled forward until her upper body was

out of the hedges, hoping the glow of the buds would not give her away. With the bandits' backs to her, she had but one chance.

Jostaph hoisted the prisoner to her feet. "We're going to be rich, Manda!"

"Oh, we are going to be so much richer. Think of how much the d'Vortas will pay for her," Manda said as she tucked the bag into her suit. She flashed a grin at the female Scat. "I suggest you take your friend there to the medbay. He may very well survive this encounter."

The female Scat, however, seemed unfazed. She clasped her claws before her, her forked tongue tasting the air. If she noticed Olsi crawling forward, she gave no sign. "That is-ss but a fraction of what we can pay for her releass-se," the female Scat said. "Name uss-s your terms-ss."

"Trasi, no," Eladia said. "This isn't working . . ."

"It obviously isn't," Manda agreed. "Oh, what would her kin do to us if we fail to return her?" The Human nodded at their captive. "Have you ever crossed paths with beings more powerful? Seen how they could read minds? We got lucky with this one. I'd rather not mess with the whole lo—"

With a guttural cry, Olsi pounced on Manda before the Human could finish speaking. The Tuli sank her incisors into the Human's shoulder, ignoring her shrieks and thrashing as Olsi pressed her full weight down onto her foe.

She pushed herself off the Human just as blaster shots blackened the grass beside her. Olsi squealed and, in her panic, barreled forward on all fours to where Jostaph stood, now struggling for control over the blaster with the female Scat.

Olsi felt him fall under her weight, and on blind instinct, bit him on the neck before he could act. Determined to keep him on the ground, she kicked and scratched him with the blunt claws on her feet, over and over. Jostaph's gurgling screams turned into whimpers and cries for help, but Olsi kept kicking, until the Human grew still.

"Olsi."

In between fast breaths and the taste of blood in her mouth, she felt a hand touch her shoulder. Pale eyes wide, Olsi turned to lock eyes with her Human friend.

"It's all right. You can stop now." The Human made a gesture for *peace. Safe.*

Olsi sat up and released the limp Jostaph, her stubby fingers moving rapidly to suggest *ship,* and *flight.*

"No," the Human said. She had one hand pressed against her temple, and her gaze was on the two still and silent Humans on the grass. "Plexis . . . safe place to hide, Olsi." She shook her head, brows furrowed, and looked to the young male Scat, still groaning on the grass. "Will he be all right?"

Trasi, who now knelt beside her fallen companion and worked quickly to stanch the blood leaking from his shoulder, nodded. "He'll live. Can't s-ssay the sssame for your captorss-sss, Eladia."

Eladia sighed and sat on the grass beside Olsi. "They drugged me earlier. Couldn't tell Plexis from Auord. Couldn't read their minds."

It took a moment for Olsi to register that. Yet it surprised her more that the discovery was not troubling at all. It explained a lot of things. For a moment, she wondered if her arrival here had been coincidental.

"Coincidence," the Human muttered, and gestured *trust.* "You found me on your own. I didn't even know how I got here. Thank you, Olsi. I owe you my freedom. Ah, my head hurts." She sighed and gazed out into the garden, where the glow of the flower buds had begun to dim. "We better leave. Security . . ."

"We don't need to jus-sst yet," the Scat said, helping her companion to sit up. "No one elss-se here. Haven't you noticed? Cusstomers-s and merchantss-s avoid thiss-s place. It is-ss where beingss-s come to s-sssettle dis-ssputess, without intervention." Those cold, slit-shaped pupils now slid toward Olsi. The Tuli suddenly felt stained and dirty under the Scat's regard. She began to wipe her bloodstained mouth and groom her whiskers.

Trasi chuckled, a hissing sound that Olsi was certain would frighten the Tuli pups back home. "We are fortunate that you ss-ss-howed up. Didn't know Tulisss-s could fight like that."

"Where *did* you learn to fight like that?" Eladia asked with a weak smile.

Olsi shrugged. She was as surprised as they were. In that haze of fear and confusion and desire to protect her friend, there was little else to do but let instinct take over. Never thought of herself as much of a brawler, but two Humans lay dead at her feet. Despite herself, she quite liked that feeling of triumph.

After a brief stare with the Human, Trasi nodded and removed the yellow gem from her frill. She slipped that in Olsi's paws. "Take thiss-s. I am certain you can live comfortably on that. It will be enough for you to get a s-sship home, and more, if that iss-s your wish."

Olsi sniffed the gem. Thought for a moment about what she wanted to do, then shook her head and handed it back to the Scat. She let out a sound that was a cross between a yip and a chatter. Made a gesture for *stay*.

There was nothing back home waiting for her. The warren was overpopulated. The work left much to be desired. It felt more like home to be here, among this strange, unexpected pack, even though the circumstances of their meeting left two beings dead and one wounded. Strange, that.

"Then consider it your first payment," Eladia said. "I could use another friend out here. Trasi can't watch my back all the time, and my family won't stop looking for me." She held her hand out, then made a gesture for *gratitude*.

Olsi gave the equivalent of a Tuli smile, her lips parting to reveal her long incisors. She clasped the Human's hand, shook it once, then made a sweeping sign over her head. *Friend. Home.*

... *Truffles* continues

8

✳✳✳

HOW COULD MORGAN know about that Tuli? Had he tracked down every being involved that day? Followed trails of hapless bystanders as well as those to blame? Why?

I slammed down my barriers until only our link remained. How he knew—why he knew—wasn't important. I seethed inwardly. How dare he compare our experiences? The Tulis—I could still feel their paws groping over my flesh, the remembrance strong enough to raise bumps on my skin and speed my pulse. They'd examined me as if I'd been so much meat being shipped.

"It wasn't Olsi. Remember that, too."

Slowly, I let myself meet the gaze of those remarkable blue eyes, see the daunting patience in them. The shared anguish. The bone-deep understanding. My kind didn't believe you could read a face. Didn't bother, when Clan emotions flooded the M'hir and couldn't be hidden from the more powerful. But this face, Morgan's . . . I traced the line of his jaw with my fingertips, watched him swallow, those eyes darken . . . this I knew better than my own.

What that expression asked of me?

To admit the truth, to myself as much as to him. "I'm not who I was," I said slowly. "I don't know how to let go of what happened. Where it happened. Who did it to me." The words came out too low to be heard over the music, the voices of strangers, but Morgan gave a barely perceptible nod.

"We won. Such anxiety is irrational." I scowled. I shouldn't fear an entire species. Tulis. Scats. My own kind. The Retians—*I'M STRONGER THAN THIS!*

I'm not. With terrible *grief.*

Shaken, I answered instinct and dropped my barriers. Even as I *reached* for my Chosen, I found him already *present*. Even as our minds and hearts sought one another . . .

We were found.

Me, seeing Morgan's hunt for answers, for the complete picture of what had happened to me, to us both. Needing to know why. Needing to be ready, if we were threatened again.

Him, seeing how I'd tried to bury my horror and dismay, having no time to spare for either. Needing to be strong, for my people and myself. Needing to prepare, for we would be threatened again, and the cost? Now doubled, for we were Chosen and would die as one.

Timeless, that sharing. Over between two beats of the nearest music. We eased *away* but not apart, and I found myself at peace. Almost.

First, we both had to hurry out of the way of a Festor who stumbled toward an unsuspecting plant only to regurgitate a stream of green fluid. The being made a happy noise and headed back from where it had come, presumably in search of more. The plant sank into black goo.

There was nothing to do but laugh. "We had to come to Plexis," I complained once I caught my breath.

His lips twitched in that half-grin I loved. "Everyone does."

Will of the Neblokan Fates

* * *

by Natalie Reinelt

DANGER. THE WARNING pulsed in the awakening recesses of Soh'im's semiconsciousness. As awareness grew, an involuntary shudder tilted his hovering bulk to an off-kilter angle. When a sharp kick to his lower back set him straight again, Soh'im prayed for the dark to reclaim him. The Neblokan Fates, however, had other plans in store for him. Their first act—to pelt his forehead with rain. Normally a luxury to his kind, each drop sent pain ricocheting through his skull with the ferocity of a biodisruptor discharge.

Maybe this hadn't been such a good idea after all. Soh'im knew going in it would take everything he had to fight the knockout effects of the Recruiters' keening cone-shaped weapon. He may not have known its name, but he'd certainly seen it used enough times from his hiding place among the strewn waste; he just hadn't counted on the extent of the pain. What he did know was that it amounted to nothing compared to what he'd face if they discovered his deceit. Then . . . well, then everything he'd planned would have been for nothing. He couldn't allow that to happen. Not after the Human female had nearly ruined everything.

"I know Neblokans are useless recruits," trying to remain as limp as the grav belt encircling his ample waist warranted, Soh'im focused on the unpleasant grate of the Auordian Recruiter without giving his regained self-awareness away, "that's not why we collect them. Don't look at me like that; you know full well what that female's corpse fetched on the Plexis black market last shipment!"

"I know, I know, twice as much dead than alive."

"Yeah, that's right," the bored response of the other had no effect on the condescending tone of speaker number one, "and I for one don't care what *they* want with them. Besides," Soh'im took a hard punch to his already pounding head, "who's going to miss such an ugly offworlder? Now," that one word darkened the already sinister voice even further, "what I do care about is that we agreed to collect them for as long as we can. Got it? Good!"

The Neblokan corpse they spoke of—had they been referring to Nih'ma, his mate? No, they couldn't have. Not so close to spawning. He just had to believe they spoke of another, and he would find Nih'ma before time ran out.

The problem was Soh'im hadn't thought much past the being-captured portion of his plan. Not for lack of trying, but for lack of intel. He had no idea where they were taking him or what they would do once there. He could only hope they'd leave him unattended long enough to break free. Then where? The Auordian had mentioned Plexis, but Soh'im wouldn't be welcomed back there. Not after "the incident." *Stop!* he told himself. *There's no time for this, and dwelling on the past solves nothing.* Besides, he reasoned, others must have done far worse and still returned without consequence. He'd soon find out—or so he hoped, for Plexis was his only lead and, therefore, the only logical course of action.

A small measure of time, feeling more like an eternity, passed before Soh'im realized the rain no longer fell. Had he dozed? An anxiety-inducing thought that set his molting wattle vibrating against his will. Hopefully, the Auordians hadn't noticed. Even if they had, though, he doubted they knew much about his kind. An ignorance that would work to his advantage if true, so he could only hope they believed it nothing more than an unconscious reflex.

"Ugh! I can't wait to get away from this foul stench." Dropped onto a hard surface without warning, a winded grunt escaped Soh'im's wide leathery mouth. The belt encircling his waist caught his clothing, tearing through the rotted fabric to scrape against his flesh, as the Recruiter yanked it free. "We'll have to sanitize this, or we'll smell *him* on it for the rest of our lives. Come on, he won't be coming round any time soon, so just cover him up and shove him in there until later. No, don't bother marking it. We'll smell him easily enough; let's just hope nothing else sniffs him out in the meantime."

Soh'im, his courage mounting as their steps receded, relaxed under the stifling cover. Fools, both, if they thought they'd find him by the stench they now associated with him. They had no idea of the physiology of Neblokans.

Their world filled with dangerous night predators, Neblokans evolved into a species capable of olfactory camouflage: they could do a form of chemical mimicry by storing chemicals from their food in the flesh. Something quite useful on their homeworld, although not usually beyond it. Until now. The tarp, made of crude Human canvas, had the stale taste of mildew as Soh'im gnawed on the corner until a large section tore free, allowing him to swallow. A few more bites, and he'd be ready.

In a hurry to leave, his choking cough to dislodge a piece not quite ready to swallow echoed around the open space as he crawled from within the confines of the Auordian hiding spot into a world of pitch. Gaining an uneasy stance on stubby legs long deprived of circulation, he quickly rid himself of his rotting clothes. Draping the remains of the tarp around his naked form, he edged along the wall at his back.

Hope of discovering his whereabouts sank with every narrow aisle he traveled within the darkness. Then, while rounding yet another bend, he saw her standing in a small band of light near a conveyor belt. At least, one who looked like the brain-dead Human pest he'd encountered earlier. He couldn't be sure. Not at this distance. Nor was she his problem. The same couldn't be said of one of the others with her. A being known to him—if only by reputation—and one of his kind's greatest enemies. Roraqk. A Scat pirate who chose that instant to end the pathetic existence of one of two Auordian males conversing with him.

If Roraqk saw Soh'im, or even suspected he was someone not

belonging wandering around, he would no doubt meet the same fate as the one whose dead body now folded in upon itself. Finding a crevice among the otherwise tightly stacked plas crates, Soh'im wormed his way in. Not an easy accomplishment for most possessing a more than average girth, but a mite easier for a Neblokan capable of redistributing his bulk for just such an occasion.

Enough time passed without disturbance that Soh'im felt secure in leaving his hiding place. One problem—having remained wedged in place for so long, his swelling belly rejected the idea. In the midst of trying to coax the excess fluids rebuilding there to other parts, the platform beneath his oversized four-toed feet shuddered, shifting the crates enough for him to edge outward.

A move he wished he'd not taken, for once his wide brows cleared the crevice, he discovered himself now suspended far above the tallest stack of crates in what turned out to be an even larger warehouse than he'd first imagined. Moving back into the shadows, he waited.

The platform plummeted, unleashing a gut-wrenching knot into his nether region. An image of Nih'ma flashed before his eyes. Her wide mouth turned in a beguiling downward curve that set his pulse racing as she beckoned him to join her. No. Not "join." Find. The moment his purpose reinstated itself in his mind, his descent came to a stop with a bounce that would have sent him sprawling if not for the confines of the crevice. More jarring bounces followed before a solid thud announced he'd connected with the ground once again.

A mechanical whine followed by a hiss of compressed air announced the closure of a hatch. Unfortunately, Soh'im found his escape route barred by more plas crates. With nowhere else to go, he settled in for what he hoped would be a short journey. If not— well, he could consume his own energy stores for many cycles.

Placing his faith in the Fates, he sank into a low hibernation until the Fates saw fit to release him from his traveling prison.

Startled awake, Soh'im slid his emaciated frame from the crevice as soon as the retreating servofreighter disappeared from sight. Where was he? Mindful of his sensitive wattle, he clutched the tarp tightly around the folds of his neck when a sharp pain coursed through his pouch. Crumpling against the crate, he took several long breaths as he waited for the contraction to ebb. It couldn't possibly be the end of term already. Could it? Soh'im had lost so much time, he couldn't even remember how long ago Nih'ma had implanted her egg in his pouch or when it had hatched into 'yo. He needed to find her. Quickly.

Too many crates blocked his view. He needed to find out where he was. Then—only then—could he plan his next move. Rubbing his distended belly in a continuous circular motion he hoped would calm the 'yo, he waddled off between the crates as fast as his depleted legs could carry him. Upon reaching the outer wall of the bay, he discovered exactly where the ship had brought him. Emblazoned on the wall, along with information scripted in various languages that held no interest to Soh'im, one word stood out: Plexis.

The Fates *had* looked upon him favorably. Why else would he end up where he must be without mindful plan? Now, if only they continued their favor.

A hissing whir began in the distance and slowly grew louder. Soh'im's wattle ached with the movement of searching for a place to hide. Stumbling toward the labyrinth of crates, he stubbed his bone-thin toe and fell. His canvas, catching the air currents created by his retreat, puffed open and pulled free. As Soh'im lay there, waiting for the approaching servo to sound the alarm, it fluttered back down over his naked form. His pudgy digits stilling on the smooth surface as the hissing whir established a position directly overhead, he held his breath.

And waited . . . And waited . . .

The whirring receded. Had it decided the pile on the floor to be of no consequence? Or was it leaving to signal security? Either way, he needed to act now. In the midst of pushing himself up, he scraped his sensitive belly against a section of grated flooring. A vent, and where there were vents, there were ducts. Would they lead to the inner sections of the station, or just continue into the next storage section? As it appeared to be his only exit option, he would soon find out. Keeping the tarp over him, he worked the grate free at the painful expense of his fingers. Slipping his feet through the opening, he ran into some difficulty worming his belly beyond the unyielding metal.

A shrill beep sounded, bringing more whirring, but no running feet. It was enough to force a deep intake of breath and one final wiggle to free himself. Now squatting inside a long tunnel of duct, he maneuvered the grate back in place. A gust of cold air raced up his back and through the holes, puffing up his discarded cover. The gust subsided, but before the tarp resettled, he crawled away.

So many turns, and no way to mark his course, Soh'im began to doubt his ability to navigate the ducts. When another contraction surged through his pouch, he lay down, curled up on his side. With no point of interest within the duct to redirect the pain of the building contraction, his thoughts turned to the future of his 'yo who seemed to be in a great hurry to enter the world.

"Easy, young Tuh'yo," he cooed, stroking his prominent belly, "time enough for you to join me once we find your *matra*."

As he wondered whether his mate would approve of the name, for it had belonged to her twin who hadn't survived the transferal from the male to female at spawning, the deep roots of buried panic pushed forth. Maybe he shouldn't have chosen it. If he didn't find Nih'ma, their 'yo would meet its namesake's fate. No, best not to think that way. Focus on something else—maybe the choosing. Who would it follow? Born with no gender, all Neblokan 'yo made their choice upon maturation. Would his own 'yo choose to be an 'im like Soh'im, or a 'ma like Nih'ma?

Not that the choosing mattered, for the option to change one's sex remained open for life. Why, his own matra, long before Soh'im's spawning, had made the change. And she may have done so again before coming to the end of her corporeal existence, if undergoing the process weren't so complicated and excruciating. Unlike his matra, Soh'im, his own choice occurring without conscious thought, had never felt compelled to even try.

A cold rush of air washed over him, taking the last of the contraction with it as it passed. Time to move. But which way? Soh'im had lost all compass. However, the draft continued, and logic dictated the air flowed from the center outward, so the moment he shifted back onto his knees, he crawled headlong into the air current.

His knees bruised and bleeding, Soh'im paused beside a grate to peer from the shadowed confines of the duct out into the expanse of Plexis Supermarket. Having been here as a 'yo, and then later in life, but before mating, he knew he'd overshot the Wholesalers' Floor by the simple sight of a sign across the way. *Claws & Jaws: Complete Interspecies Cuisine.* Not a place he'd be welcomed after his last visit, no matter how badly he relished the excellent food. The sky overhead remained set to day, while the number of bodies measured too low to risk exposure. He'd have to seek a night zone before slipping from his hiding place. There, even with the higher number of patrons, no one would think twice about a naked Neblokan wandering around the entertainment district.

Another contraction struck as he settled down, rendering him senseless. When he awoke, the duct vibrated around him. His first thought: the evening "music" had begun. But no sounds, save a whooshing, reached his auditory receptors. As it drew closer, the whoosh emitted a thrum that undulated his lax flesh. Heavy brows lifted above widened eyes as realization dawned. Duct cleaning servo.

Soh'im couldn't outrun the servo unit that would shred him to pieces if he didn't vacate. Ignoring the searing pain in his skeletal shoulders, he slammed into the grate again and again. His final attack met open space, sending him sprawling onto the cold concourse floor, taking a patron's chair with him as the cleaning servo whirred past his feet. Groaning, he rolled onto his back to stare up into the wrinkled eyes of a Human. Multi-jointed fingers probed Soh'im, poking at his bony frame until they reached his swollen abdomen.

"You are with 'yo?"

"Yes," Soh'im groaned as another contraction took root. His eyes rolled up, but the Human ignored the rude gesture, possibly assuming its cause to be the pain, and nothing personal. "I'm Soh'im, and I must find my—find my mate, Nih'ma. She was taken from me, but I know she's near."

"Up with you." Those multi-jointed fingers wrapped around Soh'im's arm in an effort to arrange him into a sitting position.

But fresh pain surged through him, curling him into the fetal position. "We shall wait for it to pass."

Light fabric draped over Soh'im's aching body. Something he wouldn't have noticed if not for the soothing effect of the warmth it provided. His pudgy digits closed around the edge, drawing it up to his sagging wattle, now almost completely devoid of its natural blue color.

"Please," he begged with a small measure of strength gained from the warmth, "help me find Nih'ma."

"Fear not, Friend Soh'im, for I have already sent out word to search for her." A thin metal sheet slid beneath him followed by a quick securing of bands around his chest and legs, setting Soh'im squirming in a bid to escape. Until a soft caress crossed his brow, stilling his frenzy. "Easy, Friend Soh'im, for I am a med-tech here on Plexis, and what I need from you now is trust. Your contraction has suspended, so relax while I transfer you."

The grav stretcher left the ground behind, taking Soh'im's withered body with it. Giving way to his weariness, he closed his eyes. Until the pain struck again much too close to the last. Time was running out. Unaccustomed to exhibiting any forms of emotion to those outside of his own species other than disdain or impatience, it took him by surprise when he muttered a term explicitly used with the Fates, "Thank you," and genuinely meant it.

Doors opened to a darkened room, immediately flooded with lights when the grav stretcher crossed the threshold. The binding straps released as it settled and slid from beneath him, allowing him to sink into the softer cushion of a mattress. Hiding in the refuse, and then among the crates for so long, he'd almost forgotten the feel of a bed. Even the lesser comforts of a med unit.

The Human busied himself with the med unit's equipment.

"My name is Dalso. Your time is near, Soh'im, and I have just—" Dalso's hesitant pause set Soh'im on edge, "I am sorry, Friend Soh'im, the news is not pleasant." His withered face turned away. "Your mate, Nih'ma, I have received word she does not survive."

"How?" He dreaded the answer, but he just had to know. "What happened?"

"Her body," the med unit shook with the strike of Dalso's hip as he moved beyond sight, "was found in the lower levels during a raid. Past med data confirmed her identity." A bony hand settled on Soh'im's shoulder. "Friend Soh'im, I know you grieve, but this cannot wait. You must have a surrogate for your 'yo to survive. I have found a willing—"

"No!" Soh'im searched frantically for an alternative. When it came, he chided himself. Why hadn't he considered it earlier with his thoughts focused on this very thing? "I can go through the change—I . . ."

"Easy, Friend Soh'im. Altering your state once set is risky at the healthiest of times, but in your condition—well. I am afraid you have no other recourse but to use a surrogate." A sting pierced his neck, sending his thoughts into a foggy haze as a new set of bands encircled him. "I am sorry, *Friend*," the word, said like that, held any meaning but its intended, "but I have need of your 'yo, for it will fetch a staggering amount on the black mark—"

A blast of energy struck the doors, melting the metal into a gaping hole Soh'im had trouble bringing into focus. Three weapon-bearing Neblokans charged into the room, the first, a 'ma, felled Dalso as he scrambled toward a com panel.

"Guard the door in case the Human is not the last."

"Yes, Commodore."

"Foolish Mate," the 'ma scolded, loosening Soh'im's bonds. "What were you thinking?"

"Nih'ma?" The name escaped his lips in nothing more than a whisper, but she heard, and smiled. "I thought—that is, Dalso said you died. How?"

"It would take more than Recruiters and a black market to keep me down." Her stubby fingers stroked his leathery lips before sliding to his quivering pouch. "Later. It's time."

Extruding the sharp claw on her longer middle finger, Nih'ma sliced open the seal running across the top of her abdomen before doing the same to Soh'im's pouch. Straddling her mate, so the two

openings met, she cooed gentle words of encouragement, something uncommon at any other time in a Neblokan's life, to coax
the 'yo forth. As the 'yo passed between them, white-hot pain
seared Soh'im's innards. The world faded away.

When he came to, Nih'ma sat in a chair beside him, cradling their
newborn, whose high-set eyes and nose peeked above the safety of
his matra's pouch to stare at his *patra*. It took a long time for
Soh'im to tear his gaze away from those two wondrous blue orbs
to meet his mate's matching gaze.

"Here I came to rescue you, and, instead, you found me? Where
have you been?"

"It's a long story, and better saved for once we are away from this
place and safely home." Her hand settled over his, coaxing it toward her pouch and their newborn. "For now, thank the Fates we
are together again."

"I don't know what's the matter with me, Nih'ma," he wiped away
the moisture collecting on his sunken cheek as their 'yo took one
of his fingers into its mouth, "I can't seem to control my emotions."

"Hormones," her lips curled farther downward, sending his double heart racing. "They will pass, and you'll be your proper self
again." The grin deepened, "At least, they'd better, or I'll be finding myself a new mate."

He refrained from any verbal response. There was no need, for
as long as they both lived, they would remain bound together.

"I named our 'yo, Tuh'yo," Soh'im whispered, already feeling
the return of his normal temperament, "in honor of your twin. I
hope you approve."

"I do. And so must the Fates."

...*Truffles* continues

9

* * *

PLEXIS SET THE standard for tasteless, impossible to evade advertising. An insistent banner for the upcoming show by the *Great Bendini* had followed me into a public accommodation, bursting out in sparkles when I smacked it.

This, I decided, was low even for the night zone.

Glowing shapes swayed with the music, each sufficiently vague to convince any of the myriad species entering *Butter's Dance Ex travaganza* that they'd find a suitable partner inside. I wasn't convinced it was only for dancing. Unless, I thought, turning my head to study one as we passed, the creepy things were a warning you'd turn into something vague yourself.

The shape bent low as if studying me in return then resumed its sway, but not before tips like those of fingers pressed briefly outward in my direction. I realized belatedly we moved through a corridor lined with living dancers, any appendages or features disguised within bags of stretchy opalescent fabric.

Surely a fate worse than being stuck with a Lemmick in a lift. I did my best to hurry Morgan along, hoping the maker of the bags would move on to something less disturbing in future.

The Rainbow Collection

* * *

by Nathan Azinger

FLOWER OF PTUM was dead in space—drifting—its great, translight engines eerily quiet. Which, Shoenn Mij reflected, served one right for buying a sixth-hand freighter from a Scat.

Not that there had been a choice. The Doyenne had deemed Mij insufficiently fashionable to represent Coterie Shoenn among the Lemmick peoples, let alone offworld, and so he had been shuffled off to the cloistered village where he could work diligently for the good of the coterie and not tarnish its reputation with his appearance.

But Mij dreamed of being like the spacer legends from his books and vistapes—Rist Merrick of the *Hindmost Hero*, or the great Raj Plexis—bringing necessities and luxury goods to the fringes of Trade Pact space (for a reasonable fee). He would haul joy from shipcity to station, and bring all sapients the sort of happiness that Lemmicks found in a fine cut of cloth. To follow his dream, however, Shoenn Mij was forced to do something terribly, terribly unfashionable: run away.

Oh, he had planned it well enough, smuggling spacer study tapes into the village (an education in itself) and hoarding what he could of his allowance over the years. By the time he crept from the village and boarded the transport across the sea to Eiluj Lem,

Mij knew as much about crewing a spaceship as anyone could without actually having done it. As well, he had a stockpile of credits that he thought quite sizable. Sizable it was, too, by the standards of the village and of the Ptumep archipelago; it didn't go as far in the largest city on the continent.

Mij had stepped off the transport, his little valise clutched in his delicate hands, and made his way through the crowds. Lemmicks from every corner of the continent, the archipelago, and beyond thronged the streets; the long, supple *poruri* that projected upward from the back of their heads swayed and pulsed as they walked. Above their heads, aircars flitted from spire to spire.

The nearest information center was not far from the landing pad. Mij needed to arrange temporary lodgings, but lodgings, it turned out, were expensive in Eiluj Lem. Prohibitively so for a Lemmick of no declared coterie. He belched nervously and regurgitated some food to chew on as he made a series of quick calculations. Five days would burn through the credits he'd set aside for accommodations. Very well, then, five days would have to do.

Four days later, he had still not found a berth on an outbound freighter—twenty-three different ships had just filled their last posting, thank you very much—and he was beginning to wonder if he didn't smell. A quick sniff at the scent glands that pebbled his skin assured Mij that they were in working order. Still, he needed a way offworld. That was how Shoenn Mij found himself standing in the muddy yard of *Shako's Ship Emporium*, contemplating a big gamble.

"It is-ss a remarkable ss-ship," said the eponymous Scat. "It came into my posssesssion when the previous-ss owner died unexsspectedly."

Mij stared up at the squat ship's boxy hull. It was certainly remarkable, but for all the wrong reasons: of all the ships in the *Emporium*, it was the oldest and the smallest, and a pair of hastily-repaired scorch marks marred its skin. It was also, critically, the cheapest. He estimated that, if he could manage to talk the price down a little, he should have enough credits left over to purchase cargo and pay the requisite taxes and fees to get the little ship off the ground again. Barely.

"This ship has seen better days, Hom," said Mij as he turned to face the Scat, "but it might serve my purpose for an agreeable price."

Shako stared up at Mij, his slitted eyes framed by mottled yellow-and-purple crests, and said, "I'm ss-sure we can come to ss-some ss-ort of arrangement."

Sometime later, the haggling completed, Shoenn Mij had found himself the proud owner of a somewhat used freighter. *Thaksshouz*, Shako had called it, which he said referred to a sort of flower that had no thorns and didn't kill anything ever. The very concept seemed to disgust the Scat, but Mij found it charming. He rechristened it the *Flower of Ptum*, filled its hold with *optex*, and set a course for the Kimmcle System.

For three days—three glorious days—Mij had lived his dream. Then the translight engine failed, leaving him stranded in space.

Wiping greasy, three-fingered hands on his rough spacer coveralls, Mij made his way down the narrow corridor from engineering to the control room. It had quickly become apparent that the problem was beyond his limited ability to fix, his only option now to send out a distress call. Still, he hesitated. There were scavengers and pirates out in the deep who would feel no compunction about killing him—or worse—before taking his ship.

Mij crossed the tiny compartment and settled into his chair. He recorded a brief emergency message and set it to loop. Then he rested his elongated skull against the visplate and, pororus drooping in despair, fell asleep.

"Plexis Approach Control to *Flower of Ptum*," said a tinny-sounding voice over the comlink. "Please respond, *Flower*."

Mij snapped immediately awake. He reached for the com panel and keyed his acceptance. "*Flower of Ptum* here, this is Captain Mij. It's good to hear you, Plexis Control."

There was a short pause and then, "Your message said your translight engine malfunctioned. Do you have sublight propulsion?"

"I have maneuvering thrusters," replied Mij. Given enough time to accelerate, he could generate a significant fraction of light speed with those. Not that it did him much good; at those speeds, he would be dead long before reaching the nearest settled system—even if food and life-support held out.

"Good enough, maybe," said the controller. "You're a long way from anywhere, but our planned route will pass near you in about seventy-two hours. I'm sending coordinates for a rendezvous now. If you can't make it in time, we can commission a tow. Be aware, however, that the cheap ones aren't reliable and the reliable ones aren't cheap."

Mij fed the coordinates into the ship's comp and let it run the numbers. A moment later it spat out the results: he would make it with time to spare. Belching quietly, he confirmed the course and engaged his thrusters. *Flower* shuddered as they kicked on, and slowly began to pick up speed.

"I'll be there," said Mij. "Thank you, Plexis."

"We'll assign you a spot on the docking ring with access to the mechanics' yard," the controller responded. There was a longish pause, then, "When you get here, try not to look wounded. There are four or five ships offstation right now that have less than savory reputations. Safe journey, *Flower*."

"Safer journey, anyway," Mij said as he pushed his chair away from the console and climbed to his feet. There was much to do before he reached Plexis. He strode down the corridor, chewing cud, and began to plan.

"What do you mean my ship will have to be sterilized?!"

It was difficult for a Lemmick to look intimidating—their long, delicate limbs adapted more for flight than fight—but Mij was giving it his best shot. The passage to Plexis had been quite stressful enough, thank you. An Auordian ship had cut directly across his bow, nearly colliding with the already damaged *Flower*. To have survived that, to have made it at last to safety, and to be confronted with this . . . this *officious* Ordnex was really just too much.

"Priortoyourpurchase," droned the Ordnex, its nostril slits sealed tight, "thisshiphadaSakissisheeregistry." It made a great show of consulting its datapad. "Thereisnorecordofitbeingpurgedof*far-quae*."

Mij glowered.

"'Arquae?'" he asked.

"Anuisancespecies," the Ordnex explained, waggling its multi-jointed fingers. "BannedfromPlexis. Untilyourshipissterilizedit-mustremaininquarantine."

"How much," Mij asked, "will it cost to have the ship sterilized?"

The Ordnex named a price that made Mij stiffen in shock. It was extortion, but no less effective for it, and would leave him without enough funds to repair the ship. He would have to sell his cargo here on Plexis.

"That," he said, "is robbery."

"Nevertheless," droned the Ordnex agreeably.

Mij sighed.

"Call the exterminator."

Hours later, a much poorer Mij found himself wandering Plexis' corridors with a blue airtag on his cheek. He had expected the supermarket to be packed with sentients of every description, but everywhere he went the crowds were sparse and grew thinner as he watched. Perhaps, he thought, the air itself was to blame; it seemed cold and sterile to him. Mij couldn't blame anyone for avoiding such an uninviting atmosphere, even if it was full of in-teresting shops and restaurants—all of which, he reminded him-self, were out of his price range until he offloaded his cargo.

Optex was a programmable, color-changing rubber that had briefly been all the rage among the coteries of Eiluj Lem. Mij had found the sight of tall, willowy models striding down the runways in skin-tight clothing that changed color and pattern as they walked . . . stimulating. It was so last season, though, and Mij had gotten an especially good deal on the leftover stockpiles.

More practical uses included making and repairing visplates for industrial equipment. A mining system like Kimmcle would have paid well for *Flower*'s cargo; a commercial hub like Plexis had uses for it, too, but also a larger supply—and hence lower prices. Still, Mij stood to make a small profit.

The customs official had recommended a broker on Level 3, whom Mij assumed was another Ordnex. The exterminator had been, after all, as had the recommended mechanic. He was beginning to think they might all be related. Nevertheless, to Level 3 he went.

Up ahead, something caught Mij's attention. It was a young Human—female perhaps, though Mij found it difficult to tell in the absence of ultraviolet cranial markings—standing in front of a table and accosting passers-by with plas leaflets. A banner that read, "TACO Tuesdays," hung from the front of the table, and a tabletop display announced that TACO—the Terran Arts and Culture Outreach organization—was hosting weekly film viewings.

On a whim, Mij made his way along the concourse toward the table. What crowds there were melted out of his way. The young Human watched his approach with eyes as wide as a Turrned Missionary's. Mij stopped in front of the Human and inclined his head to look down. The Human thrust a leaflet toward him, as if extending a shield. Mij took it in one delicate hand.

"Pardon me, hmm . . . Fem?" said Mij.

"Gardiner," the Human said, "Rielly Gardiner. And yes, I'm female."

Mij breathed a sigh of relief that made the Human blanch for some reason.

"I hope that wasn't rude," Mij said. "You're the first Human I've ever met."

"Not at all," said Gardiner, shaking her head. "It happens pretty often here on Plexis. If you stay onstation long enough, you become something of an unofficial ambassador for your species. Besides," she added, with a quirky grin, "I've been here for two years and I still can't tell the gender of a Lemmick."

"Really?" said Mij. "The cranial markings are quite distinct."

Gardiner stared up at up at Mij's own immaculate skull, mouth agape. She looked for a moment as if she wanted to say something. Instead, she closed her mouth with a snap and shook her head again, the ends of her straight, brown hair brushing against her shoulders.

"My name's Mij," Mij offered, "Captain of the *Flower of Ptum*. I was wondering, if you could tell me what a film is."

"Certainly," said Gardiner, obviously back in her element. "Film was an ancient form of Human entertainment from before our species achieved interstellar travel. It involved the projection onto a screen of a series of still images to produce the illusion of movement. Most films told a story of some kind: adventure, tragedy, romance, comedy, drama. Thanks to periodic revivals of interest, we have recreations of many of the most famous films, though many more have been lost. They're tremendous fun."

"And you're showing some of these films here on Plexis?"

Gardiner nodded and said, "To foster an appreciation for Human cultures and expand the market for Human cultural artifacts. That's TACO's mandate." She gestured at the plas leaflet in Mij's hand. "We're showing one of my favorites later today."

Mij brought the leaflet up to his face and peered at it. Tapping the picture on the front with one, long finger, he asked, "What is this green-skinned creature? It's not any species I recognize."

"That," said the Human female, "is a frog. Or rather, it's a frog puppet. This film features quite a lot of puppets, actually."

Mij had numerous questions after that, and Gardiner patiently answered as best she could. As the conversation wound down, Mij felt much more knowledgeable about puppetry and terrestrial fauna and anthropomorphism among other things.

"Thank you," he said at last. "You've been extremely informative, and I'd like to watch your film. There's only one more question I have to ask."

"Go for it," said Gardiner.

"What's a Tuesday?"

When Mij met the broker, he was unsurprised to discover that his hunch had been right: it was another Ordnex. A suspiciously well-informed Ordnex, as it turned out. No sooner had the negotiations commenced, then he let slip what he knew about Mij's ship and what he suspected about his finances. He then offered to find a buyer for Mij's optex—for an exorbitant commission.

Mij walked out, of course, but not before the broker had intimated that if he didn't engage his services, he would find every buyer on the station equally well informed. If Mij couldn't turn a reasonable profit on his cargo, he couldn't afford to repair the *Flower*, and if he couldn't repair the *Flower*, he was stranded. Mij was desperate, but there'd be no hope of turning a reasonable profit if everyone on Plexis knew he was desperate.

He checked with two more brokers before making a meal of C-cubes, and another three afterward. The Ordnex had apparently made good on his threat. Mij spent the rest of the day in the main posting office, working the comlink with captains of ships bound for industrial ports. When that failed, he set up at a table with a blue placard that announced he would take on passengers. Several times it seemed as if someone was headed his way, but always they veered aside at the last moment.

By the time the lights dimmed for shipnight, Mij could not have been more discouraged. Once again, he was struck by the station's curiously anodyne air. He wondered if it was the scent of dying dreams. It certainly felt that way.

Climbing to his feet, Mij prepared to make his way back to the *Flower*. Something crinkled in the pocket of his coveralls, and Mij suddenly remembered TACO Tuesdays. He pulled the leaflet out of his pocket and examined it, then he checked his chrono. If he hurried he could just make it.

It wasn't as if he had anything else to do.

TACO had converted a vacant retail space not far from the posting office into a small, makeshift theater. An assortment of different chairs, suitable for a variety of body shapes, were arranged into rows facing a large viswall in the rear. By the time Mij slipped in, a dozen or so were already occupied, and Gardiner stood in front of them, giving a short lecture about Human art in general and today's film in particular.

Mij recognized most of it from his earlier conversation, so he turned his attention instead to a glass box sitting on a table in the near corner. The lower third of the box was filled with some . . . stuff that looked like nothing so much as a sulfurous cloud, and smelled strongly of salt and something else Mij couldn't name.

Three flat-bottomed bags of the stuff sat next to the box. A sign on the box informed Mij that this was a Human treat called pop-corn which was often eaten while watching films, that it was safe for all species currently registered as being on Plexis, and that TACO took no responsibility for ingestion by nonregistered sapi-ents. Mij grabbed one of the bags, then found a seat in the back of the hall.

As Gardiner was wrapping up her talk, Mij belched softly and tossed a kernel of popcorn into his mouth. It tasted like nothing Mij had ever eaten before, and its texture—a bizarre juxtaposition of sponginess and crunchiness—was an absolute delight. He couldn't help grabbing another handful and munching on it. Sev-eral of the other film-goers began to sniff, and a few turned to glance at Mij. He cradled his bag of popcorn protectively. They would simply have to find their own.

"Before we begin the movie," said Gardiner, "does anyone have any questions?"

One Human, seated in the middle, raised his hand. Mij guessed that it was male, being as it was larger, and significantly rounder than Fem Gardiner, but he couldn't say for sure. When Gardiner acknowledged him, he said, "I, uh, just remembered that my cap-tain needed me to do a thing somewhere else."

Gardiner sighed, then said, "You're missing a good one, Frank. Hope to see you back next time the *Keeper of Secrets* is onstation."

Frank murmured something noncommittal and slipped out of the theater. As if his exit had given them permission, others began to make their excuses as well. Before long, Mij and Gardiner were nearly alone in the theater. Only a Tolian with russet-and-gold feathers, and a broad-shouldered Human—both wearing the uni-forms of Trade Pact Enforcers—remained.

"Well," said Gardiner, "I suppose I should get this thing started before anyone else decides to leave."

"Don't worry," said the Human enforcer. "Everyone smart enough to leave has left already."

Gardiner rolled her eyes, but didn't otherwise respond.

"Lights!" she called, and on cue the lights in the makeshift the-ater winked out.

"Camera!" she shouted, and the viswall blinked to life.

And at the cry of, "Action!" the film began to play.

Mij watched in rapt attention and ate his popcorn.

When the lights came up again, Mij sat there, dumbfounded. Up front, the two enforcers climbed to their feet. The Human kept referring to his companion as "Sam," which must have annoyed the Tolian because he trilled something that his voicebox wisely chose not to translate as the pair made for the door. That just made the Human laugh.

Gardiner came over to Mij and sat in the seat directly in front of him. She draped her arms over the back of the chair, looked up at Mij, and asked, "So what did you think?"

"It was beautiful," said Mij.

"Beautiful?" asked Gardiner, raising her eyebrows. "That's not the response I was expecting. Funny? Sure. Interesting? You bet. Why beautiful?"

"Because," Mij said as he fidgeted with his empty popcorn bag, "they followed their dreams and, even though there were obstacles, they made it. They did what they set out to do. They made millions of people happy. Maybe more."

Gardiner laughed and said, "I suppose you're right at that."

"Can you answer a question for me?" Mij asked.

"It's what I'm here for," said Gardiner.

"Is it true, what the Human in the fashionable hat said? That females go gaga for balloons?"

"I suppose so," said Gardiner with a snort. "To be honest, I've never had one. That's an odd thing to fixate on, though. What makes it so interesting?"

Mij stared down at the bag in his hand, its red-and-white stripes now thoroughly mangled, and said, "I suppose it's because I identify with him. He's living my dream, bringing people happiness through the things that he sells."

Without really meaning to, Mij's entire story began to spill out of him, from his decision to leave the archipelago to his fruitless day on Plexis. Gardiner listened patiently, interrupting with only the occasional sympathetic murmur.

"I don't know what else to do," wailed Mij when he had finished his story. "Everything is falling apart. I still believe in the dream, but nobody's going to show up just in time to help me make it the rest of the way like they did in the movie."

Gardiner reached out with one hand to pat Mij on the arm. It seemed an odd gesture to Mij, but he appreciated it nonetheless. He belched to relieve his upset stomach. Gardiner wrinkled her nose, but didn't move her hand.

"I'm sorry to bother you with that," said Mij once he had calmed down.

"Don't worry about it. I wish I knew how to help."

"You could tell me where I could get a balloon," Mij said. "It wouldn't solve anything, but maybe it would put me in a better mood and help me to keep going."

Gardiner shook her head and said ruefully, "I'm afraid nobody on Plexis sells them."

Mij stiffened, a look of surprise on his face. A plan began to form.

"Perhaps," he said, "there's more than one way to travel the fringes of Trade Pact space, bringing trade goods and joy to everyone."

Mij exhaled from his methane bladder, inflating the sac beneath his jaw. Lifting a pink-and-purple balloon to his lips, he breathed into it. As his vocal sac contracted, the balloon swelled with a hiss until it was larger than a Human's head. A mass of purple dots skittered across its surface to form first one message, then another. Mij tied it off with his deft fingers and attached a small station-keeping device.

It had been a stroke of genius to keep the optex and sell his ship. Not easy at all—he had grown quite attached to the *Flower* during his short tenure as captain—but it had allowed him to rent a small manufactory and purchase the machinery he needed to turn the optex into balloons. He had even, of late, begun experimenting with his own, proprietary blend of materials.

Retail space, alas, was expensive on Plexis, and well beyond his means, but Fem Gardiner had made him an excellent deal on a slightly-used collapsible table. Most days he set up shop on Level 3, spinward ¼. It wasn't precisely legal, but then on most days security was strangely reluctant to deal with a Lemmick. Mij tittered as he remembered a very mortified Gardiner explaining *that* to him. He had been at it for several years now and regretted nothing.

Mij released the balloon. It drifted slowly upward, guided by quiet puffs of air from the station-keeping device, until it joined the brightly-colored multitude of other balloons that formed a jostling, squeaking canopy over Mij's table. The movement caught the attention of a squadron of young Regillians, whose guardians chivvied them onward, and a Human passing in the other direction.

The Human paused—a male, Mij noticed, being able to tell the difference now—and then approached the table. Aside from a set of remarkable blue eyes, there was nothing particularly noteworthy about him. He looked up at the balloons. That, Mij knew, was his cue.

"Greetings, Hom, and welcome to the *Rainbow Collection*," he said, leaning back and holding his hands out to the sides. "Can I help you find anything?"

The Human favored him with a pleasant smile and said, "I need a balloon for an occasion."

"I have balloons for every occasion of which I am aware," said Mij.

"How about a baby shower?"

Mij frowned.

"I was not aware of that one," he said.

"Oh," said the Human. "Well, then, I suppose I should decide between the green one that says, 'Felicitous Spawning,' and the— does that one say 'Condolences on your Parasite' in Carasian?"

"It can say many things," replied Mij. "Can I give you a word of advice?"

"What?" asked the Human.

Mij leaned down and, in a conspiratorial whisper, said, "Why not take both?"

A broad grin broke across the Human's face. "I've a better idea."

When he left, he was accompanied by an entire raft of balloons.

...*Truffles* continues
Interlude

* * *

T HE ELABORATE BEAUTY of *Butter's Dance Extravaganza*
wasn't what it seemed, a lesson Morgan first learned while
helping search for a pack of panic-stricken Ott. The younglings
had scattered from their pouch when their parent collided with a
servo barkeep, hiding being their innate response to attack and
less than helpful in a room full of ornate sculptures, pillars, and
annoyed dancers. When the lights went up, Butter *serselves* had fled
and the extent of *sers* fraud was exposed. None of the beautiful
"structures" could stand up to a firm push. None of it was real.

He'd come to realize Butter needed to believe sers own decep-
tion, the Atatatay refusing to relinquish it even when, as happened
often, dancers stumbled through one of sers faux waterfalls and
ripped the flimsy plas thing apart. Repairs were done in secret.

By this kinder, soft light, the *Extravaganza* was charming. Morgan led Sira through a maze of what appeared to be marble col-
umns and twinkling tiled walls—most with waterfalls, sers species
partially amphibious and serselves prone to longing—past en-
chantingly decorated ballrooms, each for a different style of dance,
all crowded with happy beings gyrating in their way to excellent
music.

Why point out to his Chosen that there were staff throughout whose sole job was, in Butter's words, "to optimize the experience" by moving the flexible walls in or out of each room to make those dancing within feel they were lucky to have any floor space? Why mention if you stayed too long without buying an overpriced drink from one of the many servo dispensers, the music quality would drop abruptly?

Details. The illusion was—

Is anything real here, other than the dancers?

—not fooling Sira in the slightest. Grinning, Morgan shook his head. *Not much.*

Silence. Then, firmly, *It's very—artistic.* Fingers squeezed his; with her free hand she pointed into the ballroom next in line. "You keep passing them all. How about that one?"

Stone spires depended from the ceiling, some meeting those rising from the floor. They glistened as if wet, and what floor he could see between the slow-moving couples, triples, and other groupings might have been water. Reflective threads with dewdrop tips dangled from hovering portlights, and all the place needed was a sharp plummet in temperature to match a cave he'd sheltered in once.

And almost lost his life, there being hungry *things* waiting inside.

"Not far now," Morgan said, tucking away that particular memory. "There's a special room. You'll see."

"Hmmm." *Been here before, then.* A lock of hair slipped around the back of his neck, then flicked his ear. *It wasn't to dance. Is it now?*

"We're here," he said hastily, ushering Sira into a longer room than those previous. There were dancers in the middle of its floor, but unlike the rest of the *Extravaganza,* these walls didn't move. Tables set within curved easi-rests lined the outskirts, except for the space reserved at one end for a smallish stage and at the other for the largish owner. The stage was occupied by a trio of Thremms whose cheek pouches bulged: freshly fed. Ready for the main act, then.

About to go around the dancers and head to where Butter squatted in all sers splendor—to get his business over first—Morgan paused. He looked down at Sira.

She looked back. While he sensed nothing but her *presence* along their link, a *warmth* forever part of him, were her eyes wistful?

Business could wait. Morgan glanced around the room, spotting a pair of Humans who moved well to the music. After an instant's study, he drew Sira into his arms, rewarded by her dazzling smile.

So far so good. Dancing. How hard could it be?

He took a step, miming the actions of the taller of the couple, and stepped firmly on Sira's toes.

They both lurched, laughed, and it wasn't hard after that.

Especially when the singer took the stage.

A Song of Plexis

* * *

by Janet Elizabeth Chase

ANSEL NEARLY COLLIDED with the chef as he came around the corner to the kitchen. It was well that it had only been a near collision as the much larger Human held a cleaver in one hand while the other held a Fowean volvox, very obviously alive.

"Chef Grainger," Ansel began, as he looked from the cleaver to the pathetic blue mass and then back to the large knife. "Is there," he paused. "A problem?"

"Problem?!" Chef growled. "That fratling pox at table 3 accused me of serving spoiled volvox!" He shook the—ingredient in Ansel's face. "You can't get fresher than alive!" The soon-to-be main dish flailed its amorphous protrusions uselessly in the chef's grip. Ansel only moved his head slightly back and out of reach. Physically, there was little Ansel could do to stop the cuisinier from charging toward the offending table if that was what he decided to do.

Ansel looked past the squirming blob to see one of the restaurant's servers standing just inside the kitchen entrance. The young Ordnex's nostril slits were opening and closing with a rapidity that was slightly troubling. She was probably the one who had delivered the unfortunate message.

Ansel's attentions went back to the very unhappy Human in

front of him. "Perhaps there was a misunderstanding," he offered calmly.

"I'll not be insulted," Chef declared, slamming the cleaver into the wall of the hallway for emphasis. Then with a wet slap, he transferred the still writhing volvox into Ansel's smaller hand.

Ansel looked down at the struggling mass and did his best not to drop it immediately onto the floor. Hom Huido, his employer and the owner of *The Claws & Jaws: Complete Interspecies Cuisine*, hated wasting food that, in all likelihood, could still be sold. And he, being in charge of accounts, hated waste of any kind. He sighed to himself, then motioned for the terrified server to come forward. He gently pried the pathetic organism from his hand and placed it into the Ordnex's. He resisted the urge to wipe his hand on Chef's nearly clean kitchen coat. Instead, he pulled loose the crisp folded napkin hanging from the server's apron tie.

"Is Hom M'Tisri available to attend table 3?" he asked as he wiped away the slimy residue. The Vilix host of *The Claws & Jaws*, with his species' natural docility, usually handled such situations.

"IbelieveHomM'TisriissettlingapartyofSkenkransHomAnsel," the Ordnex rolled out in a single breath. Then, "Anissuewiththe-placementofperches."

Ansel let out a slow breath as he deposited the soiled towel over the squirming blob. "Take it back to the kitchen," he ordered the Ordnex, then calmly turned his attention back to the still enraged chef. "I will take care of table 3, Chef Grainger. Please return to the kitchen. There are orders that no doubt require your expertise and talent."

The chef looked as if he were about to say something but kept whatever it was to a low growl before turning to follow the server into the sanctity of the kitchen. Ansel glanced up at the large cleaver still stuck in the wall and cringed not so much for the plas, which was easily repairable, but for the incredibly expensive knife that protruded from it. Hom Huido had sent all the way to Garastis 17 for that set of cutlery. Fortunately, Hom Huido was currently dining with his Human blood brother, Jason Morgan, in his private rooms. It would be best if Hom Huido didn't see the improper use of the knife.

Ansel caught the attention of another server and motioned toward the cleaver, then he headed out into the dining area. So far only Chef's pride had been insulted. Hom Huido would take the accusation of less than quality ingredients as a declaration of war.

Table 3 was occupied by two beings. One was obviously Tolian. Female, if Ansel was any expert. The telltale dark eye rings stood out among the delicate lightly colored facial plumage. The other appeared to be a Human male. Intricate tattoos that covered his neck and ran up the left side of his face implied he was Denebian. Ansel also noticed that both wore gold airtags; the Human on his cheek, the Tolian on the side of her beak just below one nostril. You paid for the air that you used while on the station. And Plexis Supermarket, being all about commerce, made sure that those with the means to buy were made obvious to those with goods to sell by way of gold airtags, as opposed to the more ordinary blue.

"Fem. Hom," Ansel said as he nodded his head toward each in turn. "I am Ansel, manager of the *Claws & Jaws*." A useful title when dealing with goldtags. "I understand you had a question regarding one of the dishes." He purposely left his inquiry nebulous.

The Human pushed his plate dismissively toward Ansel. "It's poor quality," he said bluntly in an accented Comspeak that declared quite clearly, Deneb. "Inedible," added dismissively.

The dish was the familiar pale orange color that volvox became when cooked. It looked perfectly normal to Ansel's eyes. "And yours, Fem?" he asked politely, noticing they had ordered the same dish.

The translator embedded at the base of the Tolian's throat rendered the unusually low timbre of her trilling into Comspeak. "Delicious, Hom." The words sounded thin and tinny in comparison to her natural voice.

In front of the female Ansel noticed the wide glass half full of clear liquid. With the possible dietary disasters that so many species posed, consistency was key when serving certain dishes and drinks. This style of glassware signified it held simple water. It also happened to be well-shaped to fit a Tolian beak. A thought occurred to Ansel, and he looked at the stemmed glass in front of the Denebian.

"You are drinking wine, Hom? A Denebian vintage perhaps?"

"Why would I drink anything else?" he scoffed snobbishly. "What difference does it make? There is nothing wrong with the drinks. I want something edible," he added roughly, rapping knuckles on the tabletop as he did so.

The Tolian's crest dipped slightly as she clicked her beak, a gesture showing disapproval. It was aimed, to Ansel's relief, at her companion.

"In this case, Hom," Ansel replied. "It makes a great deal of difference. Some Fowean dishes have an unfortunate reaction when mixed with certain Denebian alcohols. An error on our part." Ansel bowed his head slightly while inwardly sighing at the neophyte mistake from an experienced server. "Please, allow me to bring you something that will compliment your meal. Free of charge." He added the last in a quieter tone as though there were any possibility that his employer would overhear. Hom Huido considered gratis to be a foul word, at least when it came to the restaurant. Ansel personally believed a free drink was better than misunderstandings leading to bad publicity. The numbers added up, as the saying went.

Ansel motioned to a nearby server. "I assure you, Hom," he continued, addressing the Denebian, "Paired with the correct beverage, I'm sure it will be to your liking."

Ansel gave the order to the server who hurried toward the bar. Within a few moments the server returned with the replacement beverage and placed it in front of the Denebian. With a dubious look, the Denebian sipped the drink and tried another bite of the dish. A surprised look appeared on his face as he chewed, then pulled the plate back toward himself.

"Hom. Fem." Ansel nodded to each before leaving. Disaster avoided, he headed for the kitchen. He would have Chef schedule another training session for the servers about pairing food and drink.

Back in his small office, Ansel looked over the books for the night's receipts. It had been, by all accounts, a good one. He was interrupted by a knock on the door.

"Come," he said without looking up.

The door slid open and M'Tisri entered. "Hom Ansel. This was left for you," he said with uplifted mouth cilia, the equivalent of a smile. Offering a small folded piece of blue plas, he continued, "It is from the Fem at table 3. The Tolian."

Ansel stared at the offered item for a moment before accepting it. "Thank you."

"Hom." M'Tisri nodded and left.

Ansel unfolded the plas and found two smaller pieces of colorfully printed plas inside. On the folded piece there was a note written in Comscript in a fine hand.

Hom,

Thank you for your assistance this evening. I sincerely apologize for my manager's lack of tact. I hope you will accept these tickets in appreciation for your help.

It was signed, S'ur pri 'Sme. Ansel set the plas sheet down and picked up the tickets.

"S'ur pri 'Sme," he read aloud. "The Tolian Torch Singer."

"What do you mean you won't be working tonight?!" Huido bellowed, snapping his largest claw in the air. "What do I pay you for?!"

"Six days on, two days off," Ansel answered.

"But we have a Whirtle party of twelve tonight!"

"I know. Please push the trumquin soufflé," Ansel replied as he looked over the shipping order for the most recent delivery. "I honestly don't know why we ordered so many when only two species can eat them without dissolving their digestive tracts. And of those two the Whirtles are the only ones we see here with any regularity. Thankfully," he added.

"Where will you be?"

Ansel looked up only briefly from the plas in his hands. "Hmm? Oh, to a concert."

The last notes of the song slowly faded and Ansel clapped enthusiastically, joining the other patrons and their various forms of applause. It made for a cacophony. The solo performance had been in the Tolian's native language, her translator being disabled for the duration. She had a beautiful contralto voice; unusual for her species. And while he had not understood the words she had sung, he had been moved by them.

He was still smiling as he made his way to the exit when a rather firm grip on his arm stopped him.

"You. From the restaurant. Ansel?"

Ansel turned to find it was the unpleasant Denebian who had dined with Fem 'Sme. Her manager, the note had said.

"Hom," he returned. He had not been impressed by the individual, but manners dictated he be polite. "Thank you for the tickets."

"Fem 'Sme wanted you to have them," the Denebian said dismissively. "How did you like the show?"

"It was wonderful."

"Good, good. I don't mean to keep you from your date," he added with a glance around.

"I came alone," Ansel explained. He knew no one who would appreciate a show such as this and had planned on using the second ticket himself.

"Ah, that's fine, then," the Denebian patted him on the back. "I have a favor to ask, Hom," he continued as he maneuvered Ansel back into the now empty showroom. "Fem 'Sme is still rather upset with me about the other night. She believes I lack diplomacy. One of the few things we agree on. But it has little to do with my job," he shrugged.

Ansel thought a manager's job would have a great deal to do with diplomacy, and he mentioned this.

"Not as such," came the reply. "You, however, are quite good at it. She was rather taken with you, Hom."

"There was a need. I was happy to assist." It wasn't the first time he'd filled in for M'Tisri in that capacity.

"And I have need of you now, Hom Ansel. As I said, I am in some difficulty with the Fem. If you could go backstage and say hello, tell her how you liked the show, it would go a long way toward her forgiving me." The Denebian smiled, which made Ansel somewhat uncomfortable, but he very much wanted to see Fem 'Sme and tell her how much he enjoyed her singing.

"Certainly," he said with a small nod.

The Denebian led Ansel backstage to a door framed by two intimidating and well-tattooed Humans. One male, one female. Neither spoke. Fem 'Sme's manager knocked once on the door, then opened it.

"Get out, Pezet," came the immediate tinny response.

"There is someone to see you, Fem," the Denebian said, pushing Ansel in ahead of himself.

Fem S'ur pri 'Sme sat at a vanity table, angled in such a way that she had to turn to see the door. Her crest rose from flattened and she held out a hand, inviting Ansel into the room.

"Hom Ansel." The trilling once again rendered into Comspeak. "Welcome."

With a slight shove from the Denebian, Ansel stepped farther into the dressing room and heard the door close behind him. "Fem 'Sme," he said with a nod.

"That particular Human has no discretion." Click went the beak. "I hope he did not force you back here."

"He was kind enough to offer me the chance to compliment you on your show this evening, Fem," Ansel answered diplomatically. "I very much enjoyed it. Thank you for the tickets." As he gave another small nod, he caught a shimmer of light off her beak. During the show he had noticed how the light played off her dark eye rings as well as the curve of her beak. He could see now that she had applied glitter to those areas. "You have a striking stage presence."

She trilled, and the translator delivered, "Not as important as how I sounded." She wiggled her fingers; she was making a joke. "But still, you are kind to say so."

"You sing beautifully, Fem 'Sme," he said earnestly. "Rarely have I heard such an accomplished contralto. I found *A Night In The Trees* to be especially stirring." The theater owner had prepared programs with the set list rendered into equivalent Comscript. "All due to your talent."

Her crest rose to its full height, acknowledging the compliment. "You seem very knowledgeable, Hom."

"I have always appreciated the vocal arts, Fem 'Sme."

She gave him a curious look. "Not merely a restauranteur?" she asked with a small wiggle of fingers.

Ansel blinked, then smiled, "Merely a humble accountant, Fem."

"Oh, you are quite gracious, Hom. Something I do not often experience in the company I am forced to keep." One emerald eye swiveled toward the door of the dressing room as her crest lowered for just a moment.

"Fem?" Ansel asked curiously.

Both eyes aimed back at him. "Forced to share another's company when the only thing you have in common is business can be taxing. To both of us," she explained. "And I so rarely have time to myself," a slight click of her beak. "I hear Plexis is an experience not to be missed."

Ansel's face lit up. "That is true. I would be happy to escort you, Fem. At your convenience."

Inside his sparsely furnished apartment, Ansel relaxed in his favorite chair, an album laid open on his lap. Each page held several 2D images. He turned them slowly, occasionally pausing. On one such image his fingers ran along the outline of a treasured face. He hadn't thought of Emelia in a long time, not that he had forgotten her. Her voice had been beautiful.

He had been happy for her when she'd won admittance to the National Conservatory School. It was the best on Imesh 27, but it had been on the other side of the continent. It was what she had always wanted, and so it was what he had wanted for her. He would have followed her had she asked. She hadn't. Eventually, he had left as well.

He laid his head back and closed his eyes, remembering Emelia as she had looked. He could almost hear her voice.

Ansel tapped out the rhythm as he hummed the melody. Incapable of mimicking the Tolian language, he instead happily sang his folderol as he looked over the week's accounts.

The door to his office slid open suddenly, startling him. The enormous black bulk of his employer filled the doorframe.

"Ansel, my friend! What is that sound you are making?! Are you in pain?!" the large Carasian boomed in concern and took a step into the small office. "Has Chef been forcing his experimental dishes on you again?!"

Ansel blinked, then said, "What? No. I, I was singing, Hom Huido."

"That was singing?" Huido asked after a moment, then settled his bulk down into a more relaxed pose. "We have been friends for years, and I didn't know you could sing."

"Yes, well—" Ansel began with some embarrassment and a slight pique.

"Excuse me. Hom Ansel?" a voice called from the hall. Amber pupiled eyes peered around the Carasian's massive shape. "There is someone to see you, Hom Ansel. She's waiting at the front-of-house. A Fem S'ur pri 'Sme," the small Neblokan said.

Ansel immediately stood and made an effort to smooth his tunic. "If you'll excuse me," he said as he waited just long enough for Huido and the Neblokan to make room before he squeezed by them and disappeared down the hall.

Six of the Carasian's eye stalks followed Ansel as he disappeared around the corner. The ones remaining were fixed on the small being standing before him.

"Fem?" Huido asked the Neblokan.

She couldn't help staring up into that mass of black bulbous-tipped stalks. "Yes," she managed. Then, "A singer, I believe, Hom Huido. Performing on station," she added, nervously stroking her small pale blue wattle.

"I think he was blushing," the Carasian said, always amused by that Human biological response. "Can Humans still become smitten at his age?"

Unsure of the answer or whether the question even required one, the Neblokan performed her species' version of a shrug.

By the time Ansel had reached the host area of the restaurant, he had slowed to a more respectable walk, smoothing his tunic again.

"Fem 'Sme," he said as he gave a short bow. "It is a pleasure to see you again. I am afraid," he began, "that the restaurant doesn't open for several hours yet."

"I came to see you, Hom," she said. "You offered your services when we last spoke. I was hoping to steal you away for a short time." One slim, delicately scaled finger moved across her cheek, making to tidy already perfectly placed feathers. "The station air is so drying and I thought to purchase some bertwee oil, but I have no idea where to look. I was hoping you could accompany me."

Ansel recalled a Tolian sous chef that the restaurant had employed some time back. He seemed to have had a penchant for bertwee oil. There had been the question of a bill from *Rose Red's Tree of Life Emporium,* care of *The Claws & Jaws.* Ansel had paid it to avoid any problems with Rose herself, then deducted the amount from the minor chef's pay. Personal grooming products were not covered in employee benefits. Ansel remembered the level where the shop was, if not the exact address.

"I would be grateful," Fem 'Sme added. "I am sorry about not calling ahead. I suddenly had some free time and hoped you might be available."

"I would be honored," Ansel said happily. "If you will wait just a moment."

He made a quick trip back through the kitchen to take one of the blue employee airtags off the notice board, ignoring the odd looks the Neblokan gave him.

"I'm going out," he told her. "Please inform Hom Huido."

He was gone before she could ask when he'd be back.

Once on the correct level they did some sightseeing on the way to the *Tree of Life Emporium,* including a shop that sold what appeared to be small scaled animals, shaped like balls, enclosed in plas spheres. Fem 'Sme thought them adorable. Ansel could only wonder how the creatures were fed or otherwise taken care of. Eventually, they arrived. Once Fem 'Sme had finished with her purchases, she suggested a light snack and would Hom Ansel know of a suitable place.

One level up was a café Ansel occasionally visited when he wanted a less hectic setting than the *Claws & Jaws.* The *O Claire* was a quiet café that served only Human dishes, making it a safe choice for both of them. Ansel ordered an antipasto platter along with a fruit juice for himself. Fem 'Sme ordered water.

When the waiter had left, she said, "I find water to be the least troubling when I am touring. I have to be careful," she said gently stroking the feathers at her throat. Then she leaned forward conspiratorially and trilled softly, "I admit to being tempted by the selection of drinks at your restaurant, Hom." The translator relayed the words in the same quiet tone.

Ansel, also leaning forward, said, "I admit it as well." He was pleased the translator did not attempt to render her laughter into Comspeak. It was far too beautiful a sound. "Where are you going after Plexis?" he asked.

She drew some of the water into her beaked mouth before answering. "This is our last stop. We return to Deneb after this."

"Deneb?" The answer surprised him.

"Yes. My family does business on Deneb. I'll be able to shed my entourage," she wiggled her fingers in humor, "once back there. Pezet can be overly protective." She nibbled a cube of white cheese.

"I am grateful your manager allowed you to go shopping, then," he said, taking an olive.

"Yes," came the short tinny Comspeak though her trill was drawn out. "About that. I confess to departing while Marls and Fuyo were otherwise distracted. You no doubt saw them at the theater."

He did remember the large presence at her dressing room door.

"They are a constant presence and lack any skill in conversation. I desired more stimulating company," she continued. "And you were so gallant to offer escort," she added quickly, resting her delicate four-fingered hand briefly on his before he could offer protest.

Ansel felt himself blush. "Fem, I don't wish to get you into any trouble."

"And you won't," she insisted. "Pezet needs a good reminder of his place every so often," she added with another wiggle of fingers.

Fem 'Sme chose to return to the theater instead of her lodgings, since she was performing later on. When asked if he would attend, Ansel apologetically said he would be working but hoped to see another show before she left Plexis. He still had the extra ticket.

"As this is the last stop, the contract is open-ended. When Pezet decides he's had enough, we move on. Not the best manager I have had." She clicked her beak. "But we work with what we are given. Thank you for escorting me, Hom Ansel. I do hope to see you again before we leave."

"My pleasure, Fem 'Sme. Are you sure," he added quickly as she turned toward the theater door. "Are you sure you'll be all right?" The little hints she had let pass in conversation had concerned him.

"Gallant," she trilled. "I am sorry if I caused you worry. I assure you I will be fine."

With a nod he watched as a young Human let her into the closed theater, closing the door behind them.

Ansel let out a breath he had not been aware he was holding after the door had shut. Perhaps he could convince Hom Huido to let him have his night off a bit early.

As the door to his apartment slid shut, Ansel set his packages down. He had been able to get a few errands done himself while out with Fem 'Sme. The sound of fabric on fabric made him spin about.

"Hom." Pezet, Fem 'Sme's manager, was sitting in his reading chair. The smile on his face wasn't what Ansel would have called pleasant. "A productive shopping trip, I see."

"Hom Pezet. What, what are you doing here?"

Pezet gestured to the room. "Waiting for you."

"Me? How did you get in?"

Pezet merely shrugged in answer then continued smoothly, "I'm looking for Fem 'Sme. She left her lodgings without my permission. And since she doesn't know Plexis well enough to venture out on her own . . . ?" he indicated Ansel.

Ansel straightened as a sudden protectiveness of the Tolian came over him. "Your permission?" The pert retort escaped his mouth before he could stop it.

The tattooed Human laughed, seemingly unfazed by the question or the tone. "Yes." His stare fixed on Ansel. "It's my job after all."

"You make her out more hostage than client," Ansel retorted, the protectiveness not yet having run its course. "What kind of manager are you?"

"Oh, she isn't my client," he answered obtusely. "We have an arrangement. You might call her my charge."

That caused Ansel to pause. Among other things, Deneb was known to be the home of two notorious crime syndicates; the Blues and the Grays. Fem 'Sme had said her family did business on Deneb. She hadn't said what kind of business.

"Your charge? You mean a *plevnr c trvt*," Ansel said in his native language.

The Denebian didn't react.

"Ransom Guest," Ansel repeated in Comspeak. "Hostage."

Pezet tsked. "Hom, such hostile sounding words." He made a motion with his right hand. The pair Ansel had seen at the theater entered the room from the small hallway that led to his bedroom, making the already small room seem that much smaller. Pezet held his hand up, and the two stopped.

"Someone could get the wrong idea. Fem 'Sme is willingly under my protection as a," he gestured thoughtfully, "guarantee of promises made." His hand went to his chest. "I would be remiss if I let anything happen to her. It would be regrettable to all involved if something like this were to happen again."

It was a warning not lost on Ansel. He felt himself tense. "I won't allow you to—," he began but Pezet's cold smile stopped him.

"I can assure you," Pezet said. "She is as safe as can be. With me," he added. "Now, where is she?"

Ansel's gaze went from Pezet to the two figures across the room and back. Fem 'Sme had not seemed fearful. On the contrary, she had made light of her secret foray.

"I escorted her to the theater," he said finally. "Not an hour ago,"

The Denebian gave a slight nod. "I can see why she likes you, Ansel. Direct and, above all, honest." The last word was not said as a compliment. Pezet motioned for his two silent companions to follow as he went to the door.

As it slid open, Pezet's movement was stalled momentarily by the presence of someone else in the hall.

"We're just leaving," Pezet said to the figure in the hall as he and his guards moved past.

To Ansel's dismay, Jason Morgan stood in the hall, a concerned look on his face.

"Ansel—," Morgan began.

"Hom Morgan," he acknowledged before letting the door close, effectively cutting off any further comment.

Ansel let out a frustrated sound as he shuffled through a handful of invoices. He'd just gone over them and couldn't remember a single one. Pezet had rattled him and it made him angry, not that there was much he could have done. He'd stopped himself twice before he could call the theater. It would do nothing but provoke that rude Denebian, and he didn't want to cause more trouble for Fem 'Sme. As he placed the stack he held onto a pile reserved for Hom Huido's inspection, the door to his office opened and in came the Carasian himself.

"Ansel," he boomed, startling his longtime retainer.

"Hom Huido," Ansel began, relieved at the distraction. "I have some invoices I need to go over with—"

"Later, later! Your Tolian singer is here!" Huido boomed. "Lovely example of the species, or so M'Tisri tells me. But she seems to have a rather large *cirrip* accompanying her." A cirrip being similar to a barnacle; universally regarded as bothersome and difficult to remove. Ansel doubted the description was literal.

"Fem 'Sme? Is here?" he asked.

"Yes," Huido said as he took a step closer. "Morgan mentioned you had some," he paused, "questionable guests. Are you in any trouble, old friend?" All his eyestalks bore down on Ansel. "Something to do with this Fem?"

With a deliberate effort, Ansel stood, trying to exude calm. He should have realized Morgan would tell his "brother." "Everything is fine, Hom Huido." He truly hoped that was the truth.

The numerous eyes did not waver. Then, after a moment's consideration, "Well, then, don't keep your Fem waiting!" the Carasian ordered. He agilely moved his hard-shelled bulk behind Ansel, forcing the much smaller Human to move toward the door. A gentle prodding with a smaller claw sent him out into the hall. To Ansel's discomfort, the Carasian followed right behind.

Huido's intimidating size opened a clear path through the crowded dining room and to Ansel's surprise, to Hom Huido's own private table. Fem 'Sme was sitting at the table while her tattooed female companion stood next it. The Carasian placed himself between the Human he had described as a cirrip and Ansel.

"Fem 'Sme," Ansel said with a nod. "I am very happy to see you again. Is there something I can do for you?"

"Yes!" bellowed Huido. "You can sit!" Huido waited for him to do as directed before shifting several eyestalks to the tattooed Human.

"I wouldn't get too close, unless you want something important removed." Huido turned back to Ansel and said, "I'm sure you will be wanting your privacy," emphasis on the last word. He gave one last warning look to the tattooed female before leaving.

"Your employer is quite direct," Fem 'Sme said, one emerald eye on Ansel. The other followed the Carasian as he moved through the dining room.

Ansel sighed in agreement. "Yes, he has a way of getting his point across." Reaching under the table, he pressed a discreet button, activating the privacy screen. That particular piece of tech had always made him nervous. "I certainly hope I didn't cause you any problems, Fem. I fear I may have said some things."

The Tolian dipped her beak to each shoulder in turn, approximating a "no." "You did make Pezet quite irritated. He isn't used to anyone standing up to him, except me," she added with that wiggle of fingers. "He decidedly did not appreciate it."

"I am truly sorry—" Ansel began, terrified he had caused the Tolian problems.

"But I very much appreciated it," she finished, her crest extended. "Gallant, as I said before. And please do not concern yourself with Pezet. Our—" she paused, "—relationship goes both ways. He needs me as well. I have warned him what will happen if I hear of any hardships befalling you."

Ansel sat silent at that declaration for a moment, then said, "If you say you are well, then I accept that." He glanced at the female guard who seemed to be watching the rest of the room. With the privacy screen activated, she couldn't overhear.

Fem 'Sme touched his hand gently, returning his attention to her. "I did want to see you again before we leave tonight."

"You're leaving? So soon?"

"I am sorry you did not get to use the second ticket. My decision to play tourist did not sit well with Pezet. He closed the contract with the theater." A click of her beak. "We are booked on the *Dashing Boy*. We leave in a few hours."

"Back to Deneb?"

"Yes. It has been a long and tiring tour, but I do wish I could have stayed longer. Thank you again for our little outing. I enjoyed myself very much."

"As did I, Fem," he smiled. "I do hope you are able to return to Plexis again."

Both emerald eyes were downcast. It was the first time she had not looked at him when she spoke. "I want to say that is a possibility, Hom." Her crest flattened and she rocked her head back and forth slightly as if considering her next words. "But I cannot." Only then did she look up with both eyes directed at him. "Thank you for everything. I will not forget your kindness and friendship."

Ansel turned the small package over in his hands. The origin stamp said Deneb. It was from Fem 'Sme. Carefully he peeled back the plas closure and tipped the contents out onto his desk. There were two items. The first was a note. The second was an image disk. He unfolded the note. It was written in a fine hand he recognized.

Hom Ansel,

I wanted to send you something in appreciation of your indulgence. And, perhaps, so that you will think of me. Pezet confiscated this unauthorized recording. He is good at some things. I confiscated it from him. Thank you for being my dear friend.

S'ur pri 'Sme

Ansel's hands shook as he placed the disk into the player. The image was of an empty stage with the garish green curtains he'd seen at the theater where Fem 'Sme had performed. A moment later the image showed her walking out onto the stage. It was the theater's house recording of one of her shows. His work forgotten, he sat back in his chair as she began to sing.

The soft, low trilling coming from the other side of the apartment door stopped the large black bulk in his sponge-footed tracks. The Carasian listened, no few of his eyestalks riveted on the closed door in concentration. After a moment he let out a soft chuckle resembling the gentle clatter of saucepans.

"Smitten."

... *Truffles* continues

10

* ✳ *

THE SINGER HAD what looked like the remnants of lunch hanging from two of her three mouths, the ceiling was coated in twists of dusty plas, supposedly to resemble the flowers of some world, and my toes throbbed.

Yet her song seemed the best I'd ever heard, this place a palace, and if it was all because I held Morgan in my arms, my hair doing its best to hold him also, I wasn't about to argue. *Love* flowed between us as if we breathed it into one another and we might have danced forever—

Witchling. With charming *regret.*

—but we hadn't, after all, come here for this. *You're forgiven,* I sent, tightening my hold before letting go. And he was. *So long as we dance the rest of our lives.*

Smiling lips brushed mine. *Deal.*

A few moments dancing, if that, and Morgan had acquired the skill to not only stay away from my feet, but to whirl us with respectable flair in the direction of the large squat being whom I presumed was our business here. As we moved, my Human whispered a quick briefing in my ear.

Butter was a broker, serselves—for what I took for an individual was a permanent fusion of several entities, seniority for an Atatatay—arranging the import of beverages destined for consumption here and in many other establishments on the station. While I grasped how Butter might want to know of E'Teiso and the "new" fee, what I didn't? What my Human hoped to gain by sharing our quandary with sers.

Which wasn't new, I thought, amused. I regularly failed to predict such gains during our trading sessions. When we left the dancers, I stood by in quiet anticipation.

Just not too close. Butter resembled a rotting melon about to explode. Warty plates bulged outward over sers wide rounded form, their edges held together by what resembled protruding internal organs. They could have been, for all I could tell. There were lower thickened limbs, presently askew in all directions, and a pair of long spindly arms with extra joints sprouting from beneath what was more stalk than neck. On the neck was—

—wasn't a head. More internal-ish tubes poked upward, pink and shiny. Two ended in disturbingly humanoid mouths, complete with rouged lips. Three ended in eyes, each uniquely sized. Impolite as it was to speculate about another species' inner workings, I caught myself wondering what would happen if Butter fell down a flight of stairs. Were sers bits independent, able to sprout limbs and dash away like a fragmenting Assembler, or would a fall simply crack the being apart?

Morgan coughed, and I snapped to attention. The Atatatay was speaking, sers voice rising and falling as words alternated from the two mouths. "—you wish us to spread the word of a predicament not our own, Captain, nor of our making. For our clients to become anxious. This is bad business."

"I am sincere, Hom Butter." My Human went on a knee and put his hand over the closest wart. To my alarm, the squishy pink surrounding tissue expanded, enfolding his flesh. Almost at once, it shrank back. Morgan stood, pale pink fluid dripping from his fingers. A hovering staff member slipped him an absorbent towel, implying this was normal.

I was glad I hadn't eaten recently.

"Am I not?" Morgan asked the creature, his voice now stern.

"I believe you are," said one mouth. The other's lips remained pinched shut.

I hoped this didn't mean Morgan would have to touch more of Butter.

Apparently not, for serselves gave a disgruntled heave and shake, then settled. "We will share this news, Captain Morgan," from both mouths. From one, a qualification. "With those we find agreeable."

Morgan glared. Three eyes glared back. Both sets of lips smacked. The singer sang on, oblivious, while dancers swayed across the floor. I tried not to sneeze.

Finally, my Human shrugged and gestured enough. "I'll talk to him."

Business apparently done, we walked away, our steps timed to the music as we negotiated the shifting space between those dancing. I sensed an unexpected *satisfaction* from my Chosen. "Just who are we to talk to?" I demanded in a low voice, immediately suspicious. Someone an Atatatay considered not agreeable? It couldn't be—"Not—"

"Who else?" A chuckle. "If sers will contact everyone else, it'll be worth it."

By reputation? Nothing, I decided, could be.

Our trip through Plexis was about to take a turn for the worse.

Cinnamon Sticks

* * *

by B. Morris Allen

THE SLIME HAD been a problem.

"It's not slime. It's a podal lubricant and message deposition vehicle." With some saliva mixed in. When you ate with your feet, it was hard not to leave a bit of drool around. Even in these sterile metal corridors. Even when your heart was broken. Irredeemably broken.

The intake specialist had been unconvinced. "Looks like slime to me." She (it? Who could tell with Humans?) eyed the trail of glistening *ijva* Keevor had left behind. "Stands to reason," she said, "because—no offense—you look a lot like a slug." It gestured in apparent reference to Keevor's proudly turgid body, one foot segment high off the ground, all six tentacles bowed forward in deference to the specialist's authority. "With parasites?" It seemed to mean the *takis*, which were not parasites at all, but commensal plaquelike creatures that warned of toxic gas concentrations in the deep swamp. Would it want an explanation? "I'm not sure that's something Plexis needs. Customers slipping and falling all over the place . . ." Perhaps not.

"Not at all," he had assured it. "The ijva–the *slime*–dries to a thin, hard coat very quickly." Not technically true, but he could make it so. What was the point of being a top-class microbiologist if you couldn't alter your own biochemistry? "Think of it as art." The art of heartbreak. Though, in fact, his trail did make a very pleasing pattern, a silvery shimmer against the dull steel of the station, like the reflection of midnight clouds on a lake.

"It does have a certain quality," the specialist mused. "Reminds me of spray paint on brick."

"Your planet must be a very sad place indeed," he muttered, keeping his reverberation orifice nearly closed.

"Nonetheless," it went on as if it hadn't heard, "I can't let you in. No skills we need. This is a *supermarket*, not a research facility. Back you go."

Back where? For the first time, Keevor felt the beginnings of panic setting in, his mucal glands releasing even more ijva, preparing for a quick escape. The specialist had made it clear that if not admitted, he'd have to go right back out the air lock he'd come in. The fact that the ship which had brought him was no longer waiting didn't seem to trouble it at all, nor the fact that neither he nor his microbiome was spaceworthy.

"No, wait—" There must be something he could offer, some intersection of his skills and their needs. "I can. . . . I'm a cook! I can cook!" Cooking was a lot like chemistry, wasn't it? Mix the right ingredients in the right way, and you could synthesize what you liked.

"Sorry. Got cooks up the wazoo here, and who wants that? Can't let you in. Air supply is limited, see, and we've got none for visitors who don't shop. You have a skill, you shop, or you're out."

"Drinks! Drugs! I can make them." These aliens with their thick, impervious integuments—unable to relish the rich taste of the world through their feet, they looked for stimulants elsewhere. Or forgetfulness. Everyone had something to forget, some past they would rather not confront. Some dismal, failed romance.

The specialist arched the caterpillars on its head, which seemed to indicate thinking, but in the end it said no. "Tempting; we're always looking for something new, but everyone promises drugs, and they never are. Tempting. Sorry." It turned away, two big reptilian guards closing in to push him back to the air lock.

"Wait! Wait. I can—" What had she said? "The air situation! I can help. To . . . to keep track of visitors!" How, though? Some kind of marker in the lungs that gradually deteriorated? A simple breath test would indicate the time since application. But complex to administer. And that gray cube over there didn't seem to have lungs at all.

The specialist had turned back, waving off the reptiles. "I'm listening. What've you got?"

Think! A dye, applied to the skin, that changed color with age or exposure. That could work. But how to make it indelible? And how to renew it?

The specialist had started tapping one of two feet, which couldn't be good; its balance looked precarious to begin with. There must be *something*. Something simple, yet unique. Something that was easy to apply, hard to fake.

"Take him away," the specialist said.

"Takis!" Keevor sputtered. "Takis." They would work. Or could be made to work. "These little flat creatures you see on me. They're unique. Can't be faked. You could use them to tag visitors." It was a good solution. He could see that the specialist was interested. One more thing, then, some little twist to catalyze the decision. "Colors! They could be different colors, for visitors and residents." Probably he could make them different colors. The larval stage was already a slight blue. In the right light.

"Hmm." It was interested, all right. "Not sure I'd want one of those on me. What did you call them? Taxis? Do they hurt?"

"Takis. Not at all. It's quite pleasant. Barely noticeable." The specialist would hear what it wanted. People were like that. Certainly he had been. "And it will . . . ah . . . clean your skin." That was true enough. The specialist, with little brown spots all over its face, looked like it could use a cleaning.

They'd overlooked the ijva, in the end. And he had done some judicious localized gene-modding to his mucal glands. The ijva did dry to a hard coat now, and he made it a point not to travel in straight lines. If visitors thought the silvery tracks were art, good for them. They couldn't taste the despair and depression in the messages he'd secreted, willy-nilly, all over the station.

The takis had been a bigger success than he'd hoped for. With just a few modifications, he'd been able to preserve his life and theirs. He still looked in on the tag farm every now and then, but the Plexis administration had managed takis breeding and care better than he'd imagined. The takis were doing well; he need feel no guilt for manipulating their genetics.

He'd had to find additional work, of course. The takis-airtags had bought his entry into Plexis, but not his sustenance. The intake specialist had helped him out there. Her name was Mae, she'd told him, "You make some good drugs, and I'll find a home for them." She'd found enough homes that he'd been able to rent a little lab and retail outlet on a disregarded level. He even had his eye on permanent quarters—a long-term lease on a bar with a suitable "kitchen" area and a little living space above. He'd need to convert the stairs to a ramp, but it would work.

It had worked, so far, to keep him busy, to keep him from thinking. From remembering. But now the business largely ran itself. He had an assistant to run the easy syntheses—a lumbering, hard-shelled amphibian with clumsy grippers, but unfailing reliability and an uncanny sense of timing. And Mae to run the retail—a task she did so well that she'd given up her day job as intake specialist entirely, even preferring it to the takis-care position he could have gotten her.

"No offense, Keev, but I need excitement, you know? And feeding little slimebots just doesn't do it for me." He'd tried explaining that takis were neither slime nor bots, but Mae was impatient with science. Or maybe with facts. "Besides," she'd said with a wink, "you smell good."

"It's the ijva," he told her one day when the shop was quiet, and she'd fallen back to her favorite game of trying to describe his odor.

"It's cinnamon," she said, nose wrinkled up and sniffing. "With a touch of licorice."

It was neither; he'd tried both, and they were repulsively crude, joltingly harsh. "It's the pheromones. Not the licorice, that's just the mucus."

"And you use that to communicate, do you? Draw the little slug ladies along?"

"That's what pheromones *are*," he said for the tenth time. "Communication. Each Mocsla has a unique blend of ijva, and then, of course, we add pheromones, both voluntary and involuntary."

"Like leaving a little trail of love notes behind you everywhere you go, hmm?"

How could a creature grow to adulthood and know so little of biology? "Yes," he conceded, knowing from experience that explanation was futile. "A trail of notes." And mostly discarded.

"So nobody read your notes?" For all her ignorance, the Human was sometimes frighteningly insightful.

"I don't know what you mean." He busied himself with an orbital shaker and its cargo of cell cultures. They'd be a good source of blestomerase, which could be used to make *enska*, a drug popular with—

"No Ms. Keevor. No little Keevettes. Keevites. Keevles."

"No." No Keevles. He didn't care about that. But Lakna, now . . . Her ijva had tasted of spring days and swamp musk, of lacy clouds and moonshine, her little pheromone packets sealed with love and longing. Until . . .

"Didn't work out, hey?" How could she know? With that tiny olfactory complex in its sad little housing on her face, Mae could hardly be expected to scent the flood of sadness his ijva was leaving across the floor. "I've known you a while now, Keeve. When you think about her, your tentacles get all googly. And there's a smell of ocean."

Never judge a nose by its size. The wisdom of Plexis. "It's complicated. Go check on the dextrose delivery." There was always a delivery. Plexis ran through drugs like a swamp bat through a vine tangle.

She laughed. "I'm going. But maybe it's time to stop moping and do something, hmm? Think about it."

He'd thought about it. Not for the first time, of course. When Lakna had first turned away from his trail, he'd thought of nothing else. He'd come up with new complexities of packaging, woven pheromones into clever bouquets. He'd invented whole new classes of messenger, hijacked viruses to carry and assemble tiny factories that made their own sensory apparatus, that delivered delicate impressions of admiration, beauty, desire. And still she'd turned away.

"It's impressive, Keevor. I've never had a lover so talented, so skilled with his ijva. You do things I've never imagined, made me feel things I never dreamed of. But . . ." He'd known it was coming. How could it not? "It's all so . . . earnest." So honest. "So . . . boring. I'm sorry, but there it is. It's beautiful, what you do. But it's boring. You're an artist, Keevor. You deserve someone who appreciates you."

"'It's not you, it's me,'" agreed Mae, when he tried to explain it to her at last. "Every species has a line like that. Sucks for all of them." Her eyes took on a distant, sad look. "Us, I guess." She shook her head. "But you've got to get past it."

"With drugs?" That seemed to be her preference.

"If that works for you, yes. But you're made of tougher stuff, Keeve. You need something more creative. It's not as if there aren't plenty of Mocsla Fems coming by all the time. Whatever's in that trail of yours, they like it."

He twitched his mantle in a shrug. "They're—"

"Yeah, yeah, not Lakna. I've heard that sob story before, Keeve. Seems to me you've got two choices—love what you are, or learn to be that bad frat your lady wanted." She reached out a hand and stroked his upper foot segment, with its trace of ijva. She'd never touched him before, couldn't know what it meant. "I know what I'd choose." She took her hand back, inhaled. "Cinnamon," she said. "Maybe a touch of basil."

He embarked on a process of experimentation, with himself as the subject. Lakna had wanted . . . what was the opposite of earnest? Frivolous? Dispassionate? Exciting?

He devised whole new metabolic cycles, and inserted genes for them not just in regions of his feet, but of his mantle, cells manufacturing messengers to be spread through the air as well as his ijva. His new pheromones were dark, jolting, vibrant.

"Oh!" said Mae one morning. "That stinks." She turned her face and blinked her eyes wide. "Sorry, Keeve, but . . . wow. What did you *eat* last night? I laid out your dinner myself; same green stuff as always. Are you okay? Should I call a . . . someone?"

"I took your advice," he said. "What do you think?"

"My advice? When did I say . . . Oh." She swallowed, contorting her limited face. "So, this what a . . . um . . . Mocsla bad frat smells like? Like . . . creosote?"

"I don't know," he admitted. "The trail Lakna left me for was insipid, vapid . . . banal. It had no. . . . no subtlety."

"So you thought, 'Hey! Maybe if I smell really bad, she'll be distracted? She won't notice my uber subtlety in all the stink?' That is not what I suggested."

He shrugged. It was what he was doing.

"Look, maybe I didn't say it well. You've got Mocsla Fems down here all the time, Keeve. They like you the way you *are*. Me, too." She smiled. "And the old you smelled a whole lot better."

"Let's see," he said, and triggered one of the new pheromone diffuser pits on his mantle. The pheromones diffused out, settling onto all sorts of surfaces he hadn't even touched. He'd stolen the idea from moths. Of course, a Mocsla wouldn't pick the taste up unless she happened to walk across it, but the approach was novel, even if the diffuser pits were a little unsightly. Even his takis avoided them.

"Oh, my—!" Mae coughed. "Got to— Check something. Later." She sped out of the shop.

His new regime cut down on the visits to his shop. The proportions changed, with fewer smell-sensitive species, and more that relied on vision and sound. Even Mae, with her tiny nose, spent more time building her distribution network, and less time in the shop.

"I'm sorry, Keeve," she said. "But now you smell like something dead. Really dead. Rotting. I love you, *bebe*, but it's gross. And now it's coming out your mantle and everything. You're . . . you're *oozing*."

He missed her company, but the Mocsla who came by made up for it, in some ways. They were types he'd never have spent time with back home—artists, writers, outlaws.

"Criminals," one admitted in an unguarded moment. "I'd love to go home again, you know. Ever go to the wetlands outside Parthratin? I swear, you could spend days there deciphering old messages. All the great ones have composed there, and the shrubs incorporate it all, through their roots. Bits and pieces of old poems all stuck together, so that when you eat one of the leaves, it's like a whole course of Third Era literature all in one bite, but with a dark, menacing quality. That's what brought me here. Your trail reminded me of that."

"Thank you," he said, his tentacles stiffening with pride.

"So complicated, so . . . malevolent, I guess. But now that I'm here, it's not . . ."

Keevor sighed, a trick that he'd learned from Mae. "Not what?" he asked heavily, firing off a diffuser pit.

The other slithered around a bit, tasting the new mix. "Mmm. Different. But not . . . sincere, you know? I mean, it's complicated and unique, and I can see you put a lot of work in it. But it's . . . artificial, I guess. It *feels* like you worked at it. All it tells me is that you're talented."

"Sure it's a good thing," Mae said, when she stopped in briefly. "Not that smell. That's as foul as week-old sewage. Can't you *smell* it?" He couldn't, of course. But it tasted interesting. "Talent is good. But what do you use it for? Look, where I grew up there was a huge gallery for this guy, Unaetum, they called him. Very famous. Very talented. And what did he do? He went around making drawings that looked like a four-year-old did them. Talented, sure, but not *good*."

"Someone must have liked them, if he was famous." Mae operated more on emotion than on logic. All Humans seemed to.

"Sure, some people did. A lot, maybe. But I think they look like garbage. Just the way you smell, now. And that's a friend telling you. Ease up on the smells, Keeve. Mix in a little spice from time to time."

The business grew. They did well enough that he bought a long-term lease on a larger space, with a bar area to accommodate the customers that did come by. Well enough that he could afford to eat out on occasion. There was a nice place called the *Claws & Jaws,* run by some sort of arthropod with too many eyes. They'd encouraged him to order out, though, even waiving the delivery fee eventually.

"Not everyone loves an artist," Mae said. "I don't care for them myself." She'd grown colder over the months, as his experiments grew more extreme, and his mantle and tail grew crowded with diffuser pits, secreters, and what even he could only call oozers. His ijva was thick now, and golden, like a river of sunlight across Plexis' steel floors.

His Mocsla visitors grew ever more outre, as word spread, and Plexis ventured back into systems closer to home. Art critics came and wrote reviews both stunned and devastating. "Brilliant!" they said. "Innovative!" "Genius!" but also "Soulless." "Contrived." and "Complex to the point of falsity."

And, in the end, *she* came, as he had hoped she would.

"Hello, Keevor," she said, as if they had had just happened across each other at a garden party. "How have you been?"

They circled each other, tasting and leaving pheromone packets, messages, poems. Their ijva mixed, his golden trail layered on her silver one until they annealed into an amalgam of brass and yearning.

Missed you, his said, and *swamp grass at midnight,* and *years like centuries and seconds.*

Heard of you, hers said, *and the other guy didn't work out,* and *so impressed.*

For you, he signaled, and *love letters like grains of sand underfoot, sharp and hard and true,* and *trails that cross and cross and finally meet.* Though her trail seemed plainer and shallower than he recalled.

Sand in the trail, and *I'm a company manager now,* and *so dark.*

She left after less than an hour. *You're so talented,* she'd signaled at the end. *I always knew you'd be something big. I have trouble with just the sales reports I write. I can't imagine how you manage this. And the cost to you! I'd never be that brave. You've changed so. I just wish . . .*

They both knew what she'd wished, and he'd been hard put to

keep the anger from his ijva. He'd slithered over her trail until the words were gone, and she was back on her ship.

I wish it were more you.

"This *is* me!" he cried to the only person that would listen. "This is the me I made."

"Is it?" asked Mae from behind her mask. She wore a paper coverall now, when she came to pick up the drugs. She shrugged. "Maybe it is. Now. I . . . whatever. Got to go."

"Wait!" he cried. "Wait," for all the world just like the day of his arrival, when he'd pleaded with her to let him stay.

She turned back, eyes like steel. "Wait for what? You have some new stink you want to try on me? Sorry, Keevor. I'm no critic. I can tell you now I won't like it."

How had it gone? There had been some alcohols, some aldehydes designed to react with oxygen on exposure. He slid forward, one cautious, uncertain step, and reared up to present his front foot.

She looked him over, her eyes doing the water trick they sometimes did, and reached a tentative, paper-gloved finger toward him. She touched his foot gingerly, and drew her hand back swiftly. She held it trembling before her nose.

"Now that's some cinnamon," she said haltingly, as the eye-water dripped into her mask. "It's not good," she said. "But it's real."

... *Truffles* continues

11

✳ ✳ ✳

THE NIGHT ZONE abandoned us. Loud music and raucous enjoyment fled, along with shadow and stars as I stepped into what seemed daylight, typical of a sol-standard star. It wasn't. On Plexis, the spectrum was chosen to show the goods on display at their best. For a price. Storefronts choosing another spectrum erected canopies and offered their own lights.

While portlights hovered over each planter.

As for the impact of such unnatural lighting on the variety of beings moving in the concourses? Morgan had shown me a sign at the tag station, hard to spot and in very small print, stating Plexis wasn't responsible for the impact of any environmental condition within the station on visitors.

Shop at your own risk, in other words.

Some knew. Nrophrae huddled together under parasols—available for a fee—while spindly Trants basked. Most appeared unconcerned. Presumably, they wouldn't notice any boils or burns until safely on their way.

I squinted until I could see properly and shrugged. Everywhere I'd gone with my Human, there'd been similar revelations, Morgan delighting in the how and the why of what everyone else took for granted. There were times I could wish my Human wasn't so good at finding answers.

But didn't. Ignorance led to mistakes, potentially dangerous ones. A lesson I'd learned for myself.

We were bound, as I'd guessed, to meet with a being Huido described variously as "despicable," "a blight upon honest cooks," and, rarely, "handy to know." Keevor. The *Every Kind Friendly Eatery* was better known among spacers as Keevor's *Swill and Heave* due to the chancy quality of the food and drink. Cheapest on Plexis.

Which said it all.

Less known—my Chosen made a point to be aware—neither food nor drink formed Keevor's main product. His establishment contained a state-of-the-art laboratory which was the primary source of recreational drugs onstation, most well beyond the credits of working spacers, drugs that were species-specific and guaranteed. Customers for those, mostly gold airtags, used the discreet side door.

The rest used a gaping opening wide enough for two Carasians side by side, not that Plexis had seen such a thing. Beaded rope made a curtain I wouldn't have touched with bare flesh if it meant parts for the *Fox*.

We arrived just as the trio of spacers I'd followed earlier pushed through the beads, two holding up the third who was, yes, heaving. A dreadful smell wafted out with them, suggesting the curtain itself was some type of containment field.

And that heaving was the least of what could be caused by a visit.

Morgan touched the back of my hand. *A part of Plexis you needn't experience, my Lady Witch.* Aloud, "Wait here, chit."

"If you're going, I'm going." Instinct approved, that growing imperative to protect our link. So did common sense. The place would be packed with inebriated spacers, the majority down-on-their-luck and desperate, the rest ready to prey on the unwary. "You might need a distraction."

"But I don't," with emphasis. An unnecessary reminder of my Human's ability to blend into any crowd, should he choose. Something, admittedly, I'd yet to learn.

Staying outside made sense. That didn't mean I had to like it. I glowered my displeasure, then gave a short nod. Beneath: *Be careful.*

With a too-innocent look, Morgan put a hand over his breast. "Always."

He laughed when I "humphed" in answer.

Standing alone outside Keevor's, at a distance from either entrance, all at once I felt—different, as though I'd stepped out of a fog. While we had indeed walked and danced through any number of shared aerosols—something I preferred not to ponder deeply—that wasn't it.

For the first time since leaving the safety of the *Fox,* I felt anticipation. I was here, on Plexis Supermarket, the most famous space station in the Trade Pact. At least within the Fringe. Famous enough.

With opportunities on every level. What sort of trader would hide away on their ship? Or worse, sit on a bench—especially a bench outside the *Swill and Heave?*

As co-owner of the *Silver Fox,* I reasoned, surely it was my duty to at least look at what was being offered.

I worked my way across the steady flow of beings without being trampled or giving offense, a success in itself, reaching the row of storefronts across from Keevor's. This was the wholesaler's district, where the goods on display were samples to entice traders like me—so I did my utmost to appear disinterested, fascinating as the displays were. Salesbeings lurked, ready to trot, slither, or lunge forth at the mere hint of a paying customer.

Pay, I couldn't. Even if I could, our hold was full of truffles. Which, I thought cheerfully, narrowed my search to future trade items. If my selection impressed my captain, perhaps he'd ignore my latest misadventure with the plumbing, presently growing a tiny black puddle in the emergency air lock.

To my chagrin, the first display I encountered featured the only tech I'd no desire whatsoever to learn: servos.

On Plexis, servos were impossible to avoid. A bewildering multiplicity populated the maintenance tunnels—a machine-only world I knew better than most—while out on the concourses the more affluent used them to carry purchases, and/or themselves. Yes, they served, but that didn't mean I enjoyed their company. The notion of machines with minds and purpose of their own made my skin crawl—in that I was still very Clan—much to Morgan's amusement. My Human tried to convince me the *Fox*'s navsystem was such an enhanced device, but I'd noticed he didn't let it speak, preferring to press buttons and insert trip tapes.

As for the display? Racks of the things swung from hooks overhead like so many dismembered body parts, implying one could put bits together to suit a required function. All of it cargo I did not want in our hold. With a shudder, I walked past.

My too-quick steps landed me in the midst of the live merchandise section. The smell was no worse than the night zone, Plexis insistent on that, but the plas crates and tanks stacked to either side contained organisms destined for consumption and most appeared well aware of their pending fates, protesting in an array of squeaks and howls, or curled in sullen lumps. Also not cargo for the *Fox*. As Hindmost, I'd trouble enough keeping vermin out of the hold, thank you.

A delicate paw reached entreatingly; I hesitated an instant too long.

"Ready to eat or ready to ship, captain-good-captain." The goggles over the dealer's eyes magnified them into giant marbles. "Order now for delivery soon." The humanoid—possibly a Nertek, though no expanse of mottled skin showed for me to be sure—plunged his hands into a nearby bucket. "Free samples, captain-good-captain! Yummy-Yums!"

I backed hurriedly, trying not to bump any cages. The dealer pursued, holding out four hands loaded with slimy, unhappy purple things, as far from "Yummy-Yums" as I could imagine. I dodged around a final crate, free at last.

I heard a wail of offended dismay and hesitated, struck by guilt. This could be someone Morgan would want told about our truffles.

Or not. I glimpsed a cart tucked neatly into one of the station's irregular cavities, a holdover of its original design, and hurried closer. In hindsight, closer might not have been wise; those who plied their wares in obscure places tended to be dealers in what wasn't lawful—even here.

My determination to avoid the "Yummy-Yums" might have been an influence.

It was a curious little cart, on wheels, unusual in this place where anti-grav sleds were everywhere, its top loaded with parts I abruptly recognized.

The workings of a keffleflute.

A very old one, by the patina. I leaned over the display, unable to resist touching one of the loose keys.

"Stop that!"

I curled my fingers to stop the Clan gesture of apology—one never knew how another species would interpret unexpected motions—and quickly stepped back. "I'm—"

"Not for sale." The words sounded almost mechanical.

Which should have prepared me for who—what—stepped from the shadows.

Was it alive—or machine?

Or both?

The Locksmith's Dilemma

* * *

by Rhondi Salsitz

"AN ASSIGNMENT, PAIGEN."

She stood at attention, proud but a little curious. Since promotion, she hadn't yet secured a permanent partner and since she stood alone in front of Inspector Wallace, she didn't think she'd been paired off yet. She could be wrong in her assessment, of course, or the prospective partner could simply be late. She wouldn't be late, but she didn't like to judge others.

Paigen nibbled a bit on the bottom of her lip, schooling her cheek flaps to stay yellow in courtesy and alert neutrality, but—an assignment! Anything to avoid coding and transmit duties. She wanted to be out in Plexis, feeling the energy, deftly handling the rule of law that kept the market civilized. Her face cooled subtly. On the side of her leg, away from the inspector's keen sight and attention, she plucked at the outside seam of her uniform. Her fingers could feel impatience, but her inner core could not. She was Eima, and even though others might think her face, with its drooping cheeks, was always morose, she was not. Maybe a little today while she figured out her place in the scheme of Plexis Security, but generally not. She waited to serve.

The inspector tapped a hard copy tablet. Difficult to read from her perspective, Paigen cleared her throat in apology. "Could you shift that a bit, sir?"

The projection wavered as he did and then came back in view, much clearer, as did the entire office panel. Easier to see but not to understand.

"I'm not certain—"

"A welfare check. I'm sending you to track down this Skoranth, a runaway, and get him to phone his mother."

"Mmmm." She looked at the panel where his image reigned. "A minor, sir?"

"No. But it is worth noting that the Bhests are considered an endangered sentient species; they rarely ask for contact, and any aid we can give them will reflect credit upon us. They are a species valued for piloting and engineering. Or someone thinks they're valued. This one's been spotted on the wholesaler's level, keeps quiet, and keeps out of surveillance patterns, which is why I'm sending you in person."

"Yes, sir." She wondered what administration had leaned on Inspector Wallace to follow-through or how it had gotten down to her, but it had, and she'd carry it out. The panel went dark. Paigen thought of something and reconnected. "Oh, sir—"

The connection glitched. She knew immediately on her side of the screen that her superior had no idea she'd come back. His voice complained in mid-sentence to a second party she couldn't view at all.

"Of all the marketplaces in all the universes, he has to ship into mine."

"With respect, we don't know that the Facilitator is here, We simply have an alert that he has put out a reward for information and a second, lucrative bounty if a certain artifact is found."

"He's specifically concentrating on Plexis. I have better things to do with my time than join a legion of tale-chasers looking for anything connected with the Hoveny Concentrix. If I found anything, I'd retire promptly and move as far from Plexis as I could get."

The unseen second person laughed a bit. "At any rate, we're agreed that this will stir the locals up."

"And to that end, I want the patrols reorganized. Put 'em in threes rather than twos. If you had any odd constables out,

schedule them as you see fit, as harmlessly as you can. This is temporary but necessary."

"Will do, sir. And as for the juniors?"

"I've already given them their patrols, such as they are."

"As ordered."

The panel fluttered and went dark again, Paigen's hand still over
the screen, her fingers tingling. Out of the way? She had been put
aside?

She didn't know how she felt, exactly, and no mirrored surface
to look upon her cheek flaps to see what color she emoted. It
wouldn't matter. She had her assignment.

Sko scuttled, as was his way, from the far boundary of the infamous
night zone of this level toward its more favorable market district,
dragging his mobile kiosk behind. The concourse teemed with
life, lanes opening around him and spilling about impatiently as
he toiled with his imperfect machinery. Its lift had burned out, but
the wheels worked as well as most primitive structures of their ilk
were wont to do, and Sko held a faint hope that if he made enough
credit in the next few days, the mechanism would be replaced. He
did not allow himself to think could instead of would. Of course it
was replaceable. Of course.

Of far more worry to him was his contract. "Rent," he mumbled
to himself every few scampered steps. "Rent is due."

Ant'h rolled up behind, indeed, almost over Sko, intoning softly,
"What rent? I do not detect any contracts due." Her wheels, as the
rest of her, gleamed impeccable and incorruptible in mechanical
perfection. He saw to that. "And our airtags are current," she
added.

His, anyway. She did not need one. As for the rent . . . Ant'h must
not be told. Never, never. She could not be considered property. Sko
dusted himself off and touched Ant'h softly. "Right you are. Never
owing such. We are lucky. No, I am determining what sort of market
faces us. Who might be open to spending and who not."

"We will be fine."

"Always fine. Always. We are together, are we not?"

In answer, Ant'h halted and put out the mounting platform for

Sko to scale and then held fairly still as the two melded into one. He felt a shimmering throughout his body form, and the world about him bloomed with color and scent and noise . . . although he could do without the noise, honestly, but Ant'h delighted in enhancing the senses of the norm. He was not in the normal scale, his people never were, they had not evolved to be, their perceptions interstitial with regards to space and its universes rather than planet grounded. Still, he appreciated his partner's sensibilities. She sought only to round out his life, and she did. As *Skoranth*, the two fused, he returned to hauling the kiosk down the back pathway, avoiding the patrols and troublemakers until reaching the market's byway. He needed a busy day.

They steered up to where he'd marked an arc before, and settled into place, anchoring his kiosk and running a quick inventory of tools and instruments while Ant'h strobed advertising that barely sank into the conscious mind of their audience, because the last thing they wanted to attract was notice of the authorities. Though he hid skillfully enough within the Trade Pact, he found vigilance annoying. Skoranth kicked the kiosk into place and took his position, intoning, "Appraisals! Relic appraisals! Sales and repairs, if necessary." He would take a fair number of caustic remarks regarding the mechanical deficits of his own stall, but he could handle that. He was not an antiquities dealer, however. He was a locksmith, and a very fine one. Most of his business came from reputation, not advertising. He could take criticism.

What he could not handle, in any way, would be a default on his rental contract. His losses would be incalculable. Never. Unthinkable.

Or being picked up by the local Jellies. That, too, would be an unqualified disaster. He touched Ant'h. "Any sign of a patrol?"

"Not yet."

They would be by inevitably, and watching, inexorably. Plexis, as a system, worked only if kept within certain parameters, for air, water, and other resources. He leaned off his platform, past Ant'h who put out an appendage to hold him back.

"There was a transmission received."

"Oh?" He faked disinterest. He could not ask himself how she knew; she would have gathered up the transmit info and contents automatically.

"You did not respond. It came from home. They asked if you still lived. And they asked for you to return."

Sko made a dismissive movement. "One negates the others, does it not? If I do not live, I cannot return. Question asked and answered."

"But you do live."

"*We* live."

"You will not reply."

"I never do."

"The transmission exhibited concern. It also held a warning. Someone called the Facilitator."

Alarm poked at his sensibilities, but he shuffled it aside. "It's entrapment. Nothing more."

He was, however, disconcerted that such a message would even get through, to find him, to bother him. Sko craned his neck back as if he could scan the skies and know exactly where he was—and he could, more or less. But not by looking. No. That kind of knowledge came from deeper within him, eked out of his DNA, and he realized he would have to reset his blocks and security because Plexis had moved and the message had leaked through to find him. He wanted no more wayward transmissions to unsettle Ant'h.

On the other hand, that movement meant new opportunities. New quadrants. Good news tempering ill. He'd make adjustments, as he always did, but he would have to be cautious and temperate. Always.

As for the Facilitator. . . Unsettling, that warning. Sko handled items that, from time to time, had questionable or even unknown origin, but he had never handled anything so controversial that the famed and ill-intentioned smuggler would be interested. He wished to keep it that way. He needed business, but he would have to be discerning.

Merchants such as Skoranth drew attention from time to time from the other side of the law. He had no illusions that Plexis Security would do anything but hinder him. He wiggled his front plates nervously even as Ant'h intoned softly, "Customers."

He didn't ID them himself immediately, but Ant'h supplied that information before they'd moved even two steps closer. He knew the crew, though only by reputation, and sorted through his memory to wonder if he should even deal with them. But his curiosity held him in place as he saw the net sack one had hoisted over what passed for a shoulder, containing several objects. Sko could feel his throat quiver at the possibilities. Mysteries to be unlocked. Hidden things brought to light. His very lifeblood coursed strong at the thought and he braced himself in his shopkeeper stance to welcome the customers. His people knew, through genetic memory, where things ought to be, their spatial placement . . . but not what they were, their purpose, their cultural value, their shining mysteries. Every object he unlocked was like revealing a new star, a new sun that shone into the darkest recesses of his very being. Sko took a deep breath of desire and delight.

They emptied their bag on the kiosk table. Before even one could utter a sound, Sko put up his hand. They, like him, were vaguely what might be classified as humanoid, though Sko less when united with Ant'h, but armed and bipedal ordinarily, yes, and his hands manipulated seven quite useful digits on his greater arms, five on his two lesser. And then Ant'h had her mechanical appendages, which she normally kept relatively quiet, some customers taken aback by the abundance of arms and fingers the locksmith could bring forth. He didn't like dealing with alarmed customers.

"Provenance?"

"Unknown. All pieces are legitimate salvage." Ant'h provided the translation for the one speaking, and Sko did not frown at the fact that only one of his clients bothered to wear a com and it wasn't the one taking the lead. That might be because the com could betray inflections it didn't want revealed or because it simply didn't like the implanted unit.

There was a piece he ached to pick up first, but he ignored it. It wouldn't do to reveal his yearning, so he picked up a rather dull looking object first, a standard storage unit though he doubted that anyone had the vaguest idea on how to open it. It filled his palms, and he could detect a very minor hum within it. He hummed back, varying his pitch slightly, to see how it reacted. His audience shuffled impatiently in front of the kiosk.

"It's a tonal device," he said to quiet them, not looking up from what he held. "You know my terms? I get first look at whatever is revealed, although all the contents belong to you, and I charge by time debits. You will deposit for each item before I move onto the next."

One of them grumbled, but the one with the com unit spoke up. "Acceptable."

Sko nodded, and let Ant'h work on synthesizing the sound scales that provoked reaction from the object, its skin vibrating more and less as she worked. The lock proved to be quite simple, but they lingered over it, padding their bill, until he opened it with a triumphant twist and the shriek of a musical tone nearly out of all their hearing ranges. He spread the shell open, revealing a small crystal storage drive which Ant'h scanned and recorded immediately, and a few pieces of jewelry. He put the locker to one side and waited for his deposit. Helpfully, Sko added, "A century old, give or take a decade. That could make the jewelry of interest to collectors."

Ant'h informed him of payment and he went on to the next locked item, a helmet if he wasn't mistaken, an odd item to be locked Sko thought, which meant it was probably filled with mementos from some misjudgment or other. He needed utensils for this one, and Ant'h quickly loaded his tray with appropriate instruments with one of his lesser hands while he fiddled creatively with his greater hands. He opened it too quickly, for billing purposes, but there it was. His skill too great and the lock too simple.

Sko lowered the helmet to the table and opened it smoothly. Tools, shaped for smaller hands such as his own, nested inside and what was unmistakably a weapon. He tapped it. "You must get this registered."

He shouldn't release it to them, but then, he wasn't supposed to be unlocking sealed valuables, either. Privacy laws protected shielded items. He gave a shrug. "See that you do so. It's old enough that it is probably inoperable—"

"*Definitely inoperable*," Ant'h diagnosed for him, and he relaxed a bit. Sko didn't like unleashing mayhem on Plexis. Trouble in the marketplace had a habit of reverberating back to where it began. And bringing those in uniform with it. He brushed aside the helmet. "Next."

They fidgeted a bit, looking among themselves. His deposit registered, so he tilted his head a bit, looking from one to the other. As Skoranth, he straightened, to a more imposing height. "The third item."

"There's a fourth as well," the client with the com told him. "We have to go get it."

He waved a hand. "Whatever you wish. Now or later. If my kiosk is here, I am open for business." The back of his neck tickled a bit and he swiveled an eyestalk about, wondering if they were under surveillance. His kiosk routinely inhabited an area that would be a blind spot, but even so, he would move about. He told Ant'h to make a note to scout about a new location, and she acquiesced without dissension. That oddity brought him pause. Theirs was a partnership, but one with a certain amount of bickering and opinion exchanges, so she must have noted what he did. His location no longer felt stable. Sko added, in case they were being recorded, "Do not bring me airtags. I will not counterfeit or alter."

He reached for the third object, a drive case if he had any skill at all in his vocation, which of course he did. Navigation drives were priceless to him and even though the core would be crystal and encrypted when he exposed it, Ant'h could read and scan it before his clients even knew their information was being duplicated. He would examine it more fully later. He was Bhest, after all—-they were Bhest, his family—-and navigation rested in their blood, made up their DNA. If these fellows had come to him without booty, he could have sold them maps for contraband, jettisoned because the law was onto smuggling routes or warring domains which had blasted supply lines out of existence save for a drifting cargo net or two—he could have, if they needed, supplied them with navigational maps to the forbidden star ways, the forgotten, the abandoned.

If he wished.

He did not.

It was too great a burden to carry the secrets of a vast frontier.

As for his DNA, Sko took a little comfort in that he was the runt of the litter, as it were. He could not broadcast knowledge his life had gained, not as a Bhest should, and his family would not attain it until he died and they absorbed him and hopefully, he planned, that would not be for many, many years.

Sko's thought fell back onto his current effort, and he ran his digits over the case. "This one is difficult," he said, as if he had a rapt audience waiting on him, and fell to working it, careful because this one had locks in layers, intricate and impossible. He approached it as one might an elaborate bomb, part of his salesmanship of his skill.

Ant'h noted, *"You are perspiring."*

"Am I? Interesting," he answered, both of them subvocalizing, having gauged the hearing range of their current clientele. *"Prepared to scan?"*

"Always."

"Good. I have a feeling about this core."

One of the three muttered to his fellows, and although Sko was not an expert in their dialect, their body language suggested that they did not like the idea this item would cost them a fortune to have opened.

Without looking up, he said, almost diffidently, "This item should be quite valuable to you, once I get it unlocked. You will need to take precautions until you dispose of it." One of his picks clicked successfully and a seam opened up lengthwise. He ran his greater hand down it. "Almost done. Notice the difficulty of the securing system? A good indication of its worth."

Ant'h subvocalized again. *"Receiving alert transmissions."*

"Oh? And are our customers on it?"

"No, but it's another inquiry," and she beamed an image to him. He'd never seen anything like it and made a noise indicating his disinterest as he focused on this last locking system. Ant'h would copy the alert away, if it should ever concern them. At the moment, it did not.

At last the case opened for him. Three drive cores lay inside, their crystal construction sparkling up at him, like stars fallen from the Plexis version of sky. Sko paused for a moment, transfixed by their gemlike beauty before reaching in to lift each one and hold it up to examine for flaws or damage. And for Ant'h to read. She would not get a complete cloning of the drive, not unless it were plugged in, but they would obtain enough to make it worth their while and add to their library. His customers muttered in awe as he showed and evaluated each drive. Then he snapped the case shut and told them what they owed him for the last.

With a nod amid the grumbles, they paid and returned each item to their net bag. They pulled away, the last turning on heel to add, "We will bring our last relic back."

"I'll be here."

Or he wouldn't. Sko rubbed the back of his neck thoughtfully as they loped away, staying to the shadows of the tier although not necessarily the surveying circuits. He did, however, take a steadying breath and reached for the hydration she pushed toward him. He'd made the rent, and more, with that little transaction and now he could afford to retain Ant'h as his for a good decade longer. She did not know that he must pay for her, and it would crush her to find out; she must never know, and he could never let her go. If he returned home, his family might decide that she was not the best partner for him and force a separation. No. He knew what was best for himself. Extinction be damned. What was worth being alive if forced to be alone or unsuited? He knew his obligation, and she stood with him, joining him, making him whole and happy.

After a lull, they had a few more customers interested strictly in appraisals and insubstantial repairs, which were worth little but kept him busy and one of them intrigued Ant'h enough that she hummed happily as they examined it. Their deposit account profited slowly but steadily and that made Sko breathe a tune himself. He could feel the tension leave his shoulders and retracted his lesser arms for an internal hug of sorts. Refreshed, he returned to work.

"They're back," Ant'h interrupted mildly.

Sko turned about, for he had been fiddling with that infernal broken lift on the kiosk, thinking that if he could open any locked item in the universes, he ought to be able to repair a recalcitrant motor (and proving himself wrong) and looked at the three approaching. They looked little different from their earlier approach, if a bit more disheveled and . . . dare he say, burned about the whiskers? Were they being pursued?

He focused on the artifact in the right prehensile hold of the third one, his companions warily protecting his every step. Whatever his customer held: 1) they thought it valuable and 2) they thought it might be taken from them. Had perhaps already fought off an attempt. But he knew what the trio headed for him did not, that the artifact would be deadly to any associated with it. Ant'h had already sent him the image of it in the Plexis alert.

He bolted into action, trying to pack the kiosk and shut down his business before they could get any closer. It didn't work.

Paigen watched the appraiser work. She hadn't been there long but long enough, surveying not only the Bhest but those who frequented him. Noted, as she smoothed down the seams of her jacket, that the humanoid had cyborg qualities but definitely an internal system that radiated both interest and showmanship and nerves. It/he would be nearly as tall as she stood, though ambulated mechanically, and might be difficult to run down, if it came to that. Paigen doubted it would. She wouldn't let it. The Eima studied a reflection of herself on a nearby column and flushed with pleasure at the sight of her newly won junior security officer status. Her cheek flaps flushed faintly green to betray her slight bit of vanity. Even if it had come to caretaking, she would do her job well. She watched the customers come and go and recorded enough that she could pressure the Bhest if necessary.

Paigen had gauged it just about time to approach when, unless she were no reader of body language at all, the tradesbeing began frantically folding his kiosk in upon itself to haul ass. She couldn't blame Skoranth for his actions. The trio loping toward him looked like trouble in anyone's report, and Plexis had broad standards. She positioned her 'scope on the object one of them carried, a battered bit of debris if she ever saw one.

The lopers cleared holsters, closing in on the hapless Skoranth who plowed to a reluctant stop. He threw up his arms in negation.

"Stop there! I'll have nothing to do with it. I am closed for business."

The local portlight went out. Figures grew indistinct except that of the Bhest, barely chest-high to his salvager clients but who shone with a brilliance of his own, one which quickly got damped when it was obvious he'd become an easy target. Paigen drew a bit closer for a better view and reaction position.

She saw a tall and confident figure stride out of a darker shadow, armed and moving with purpose, in a body language that stilled the others. To Paigen, new as she was, he exuded menace.

"Don't anyone move. Especially you three." Even in the dim light, the barrel of his weapon gleamed, and his voice, gravelly and rough, vibrated with intent. "I'll take that."

Hearts thumping, Paigen guessed the object was the "certain artifact" of interest to both the inspector and the mysterious Facilitator. If so, she and the Bhest were in deep trouble.

The newcomer spit to one side in disgust even as he threatened the lopers. The poor Bhest swung about fluidly, arms moving as if he could signal for aid.

Paigen knew that she was all the help available for Skoranth. She signaled for backup and readied herself to step out. She kept her 'scope on the menacing new arrival. From here, at best she had a flank shot; at worst, no shot at all.

"The bounty can be divided, or I can take it all."

"How much?" said one of the three.

"I take half and you three split the rest. We all gain reputation as well as credit, and I hear the Facilitator has a good memory for those who benefit'm."

The three jostled one another before one blurted out, "We found it! It's ours!"

The newcomer peeled his lips back from his teeth and raised his weapon.

"You can't accept a commission on our salvage. We claim client privilege! The Facilitator can deal with us." The loper carrying the object tossed it at Skoranth who scampered forward to catch it before it could fall, then carried it back with a cry of dismay.

An emotion Paigen shared. In the eyes of Plexis Authority, his now became the legal responsibility to protect and guard the object against all misfortune, and his duty to do the job for which he'd taken a retainer. Skoranth froze.

It was a ploy, she realized in the next instant. Barrels came up, the lopers aiming their own heat, and Paigen swiftly freed her tangler. The newcomer laid down fire, scouring the walkway and flashing up at the lopers' boots to drive them back.

His attention turned to the Bhest, holder of the object. Counting her options, Paigen tensed for desperate measures.

"Incoming!" Ant'h warned and activated all her cladding and shields. She wrapped herself tightly about Sko, as he put all his focus on the artifact. He could not resist it. Out of instinct, he reached out to protect the relic, the ancient bit of luggage shielded against the vagaries of space and time, its dull metal sides pocked and ravaged by solar winds and shrapnel. It sang to him even as Ant'h did, hers of warning and the artifact's one a herald of glory. He gathered it in, this relic of deep space, even as the lopers snarled and surrounded him in defensive fury. As he reeled it in, hugging it close in protection because he had no choice, a violent force hit him.

It knocked him across the byway and against a wall, the fabrication sounding as he landed. Bits and pieces of Ant'h went flying. His own brain seemed to scramble inside the nesting she'd provided and his greater and lesser arms tightened about his precious bundle.

Even the violence as the villain shot again, clipping him and swinging him about, couldn't muddy the attraction of it, the glorious song it sang to him. He had to unlock it and set it free. It had waited for . . . centuries? Gripping the piece closely, his lesser hands ran over it and locked their grips on it, freeing his greater hands to examine the locks and safeguards and pry them open. Like petals of a flower, he thought to himself, waiting to bloom— and they, he and Ant'h, the sun to ripen them.

A seam opened with a slight but rewarding whine as his head pounded, and Sko could barely see as he laid the object open. He implored Ant'h to scan what he'd revealed. She did not answer. He felt about himself and realized that her shielding, her cladding, even her mechanical arms had been ripped from her shell.

She'd given all she could to protect him.

Sko began to weep even as he activated his own poor cameras to record what he'd just unlocked, seconds of exposure before it snapped shut in his arms. Then he felt Ant'h activate, weakly, as their mysterious assailant laid the hot barrel of his weapon alongside Sko's head. It whined as it gathered a charge. "A mechanical symbiote. No one will miss it. No recording, no evidence." He put a hand on the artifact and prepared to yank it free.

A voice, feminine but firm, snapped: "Cease fire and hold!"

A uniformed figure appeared in his peripheral view.

Ant'h let go.

The relic exploded.

A blinding flash set her on her heels, and the air rained bloody for a moment, spattering her. It took her a moment to realize that the object had detonated. Paigen started for the broken being and his shattered bundle, her hearts pounding in her chest, her cheeks flaring with heat. She discharged the tangler, sending the lopers to the ground, arms and legs waving but their weapons on hold. As for the newcomer . . . little remained of him.

As the lopers kicked and cursed in their net, the Bhest keened in distress. She reached him and put a hand out, surprised to find it shaking. He dodged away from her and, fractured, Skoranth rolled back and forth unevenly, retrieving wreckage, armor that had given him protection beyond measure. Bit by shattered bit, he gathered all he could, no piece too unimportant. The only shards he threw away Paigen could see had possibly come from the instigator.

She disengaged the net. The lopers climbed to their feet and glared at her. "Our salvage, little Jelly—"

"Gone. Be glad it didn't take you out as well."

Grumbling among themselves, they backed away and then disappeared among the planters.

The constable found a mechanical appendage underfoot and held it out as she slowly approached. Perhaps part mechanical, but the sorrow on the Bhest's face undoubtedly came from within. He took it and managed a weak smile.

"Will you be all right?"

"Always. Our core is solid. We will rebuild. Inside, we are intact. It must be." He hugged the appendage to himself.

"You're certain."

Sko nodded, his face still wet. "We are reassured. We live still."

"I . . . I am directed to have you contact home."

He looked at her, big, dark eyes brimming with his tragedy. "When there is time. I have work to do. This is home, here and now. It must be again."

She watched him roll off to his battered kiosk, patting and talking to the small pile of debris arranged there even as he began to reattach minute bits. His four arms moved surely and quickly.

Backup answered her call with typical Plexis tardiness. Paigen answered crisply, "No need, the situation is concluded. I'll handle the report and notify maintenance of a cleanup."

"A demolition has been recorded."

"Yes. An attempted robbery set off a relic. Contained explosion. No fault of the tradesbeing involved, and he has no accountability for it. It'll be in my report." Paigen found no sympathy for the would-be robber. She watched Skoranth continue to scuttle back and forth, putting himself back together.

"The Bhest?"

"Yes. Please inform the inspector the welfare check has been made." She terminated the transmission and took a step forward, finding another gleaming bit and took it to Skoranth who crooned when he saw it and promptly reattached it.

He patted himself and then Paigen's wrist. "I have seen the stars," he said. "And they have looked back. All will be well. She must be."

... *Truffles* continues
Interlude

* * *

BOWMAN. THE FACE. Now Keevor's, preferred meeting place for those on Plexis who felt free to commit violence. Morgan was mildly surprised his inner warning hadn't sounded yet.

Didn't mean safety. Only that any threat wasn't imminent. Until it was, they both knew Sira mustn't use her Power to get them clear.

Not even then, he thought grimly. They'd made the Clan known to those who could help them survive as a species and efforts were underway to do just that but . . .

. . . Sira knew as well as he how fragile that relationship was. A mistake—such as a too-public display of the Clan's incredible Power—could end it. There were those with reason to want the Clan extinct.

And if any place in the universe held secrets, most for sale, it was Plexis.

If there was any place on Plexis to find those trading secrets, it was in Keevor's. The stench made Morgan almost nostalgic. How many deals had he made in this cesspool—and how many had he walked away from—

Another life now, with another life in it. He *reached* along their link, reassured to find Sira preoccupied. She was the most curious person he'd ever met. Doubtless, she'd have a story for him.

Morgan slipped through the crowd along the left wall where the lights were marginally brighter. He'd warn Keevor about Plexis' new Consumables fee. The being served the worst liquor on the station, granted, but in such quantities he was a major importer. There were those who dismissed Keevor as an odorous slug with the disposition of a mad Brexk. Few knew—or would credit—that the alien was a gifted biochemist. Fewer that Keevor had created the airtags everyone wore—including the fakes. A story there, he'd always suspected, but one the grim little alien wasn't sharing.

And he hadn't come to talk to him.

If he wanted to free the *Silver Fox*—and Huido, damn his eyeballs for the situation but they were, in the end, brothers, and who'd have guessed it'd be the *truffles*—

It was time to reach into the dark.

A Traitor's Heart

* * *

by Karina Sumner-Smith

AFTER MORE THAN two years of snow, rotten ice, and bitter, hardscrabble fights over a find barely worth the marker used to claim it, Triad Third Maja Anders had more than earned her vacation.

Her plan was simple: a few days on Plexis to shop and gather supplies, then a blessed tenday on Areill, a small moon close to Plexis' planned path that happily catered to Humans. The brochure had shown everything she wanted. There were more swimming pools than she had fingers, filters on the resort domes to make the sunlight appear yellow, and—most importantly—no ice that wasn't part of some fruity drink.

It had been, she reflected sourly, a good plan. But her transport ship was almost due to undock, and here she was some ten levels below, secreted in the corner of a less-than-reputable spacer bar and hoping to remain unnoticed.

Maja leaned back, using the flickering menu projection as cover as she scanned the room.

The bar was set to station night, the light pillars set between tables doing more to accentuate the shadows than illuminate the patrons and their drinks. It was a blessing. What little Maja could see over hunched shoulders and bowed heads—or, in one case, the

shielding bulk of chitin plates—told her that the less she knew of
the business negotiated across those scarred tables, the better.

The establishment's reputation had nothing to do with the
drinks or questionable selection of food on the menu; a reputation
that should have been enough to make any respectable Triad member steer well clear, even on their free time. Yet here she was—and
there, across the room, was 'Flix.

Triad Second 'Flix Pt'r X'ai sat with his back to her, crest low
and feathers ruffled. The chair across from him was empty—
conspicuously so. As she watched, the Tolian looked from that
empty seat to the door and back again. Every few moments he'd
whistle, a soft noise of distress that the device implanted in his
neck didn't need to translate.

'Flix didn't want to be here. *That makes two of us*, Maja thought,
and willed the Tolian to rise. Oblivious, the foolish pile of feathers
remained, his hand straying to check the small package concealed
in the satchel by his side.

He hadn't done anything wrong—yet. Yes, 'Flix was meeting
someone in a bar frequented by smugglers and pirates, and yes, he
had brought something with him, but that didn't mean anything.
While Maja had her suspicions, those didn't mean anything either.
Not anything, at least, that she could bring before the First.

Of everyone Maja worked with, 'Flix would have been the last
she'd peg to illegally sell Hoveny artifacts—if the broken shards
and scraps they'd scraped from their site even deserved the name.
But if he'd brought an artifact with him, however questionable—if
he was waiting to meet one of the many dealers Maja was all too
aware frequented this establishment—

Well. That would be something else entirely.

Maja glanced up as the server approached her table.

"Ready to order?" The being's tone indicated that her response
had better not be "no"—not unless she wanted to be unceremoniously removed from the premises.

It was her airtag, she knew, its golden shine a sharp contrast to
the grubby coveralls she'd donned atop her vacationer's clothes. A
grandie's airtag. A few days before, it had seemed a welcome luxury.

"I'd like to order, um—that." She pointed randomly at the Human-safe section of the menu.

The server snorted, dismissed the flickering menu projection, and stomped away without another word. She probably wouldn't be thrown out, not if she stayed quiet and spent her credits. But it was a near thing. *If only they knew,* she thought with a snort of her own. Missing the shielding protection of the menu, Maja turned back to 'Flix.

The Tolian was no longer alone.

Maja sucked in a shocked breath. Across the table from 'Flix sat a large Human male with more muscle than sense, his coveralls rolled down around his generous waist to reveal a stained shirt and forearms crisscrossed with scars. And his face—

Maja knew that face. His hair was grayer than she remembered, his cheeks broader, his expression more lined. But she would have recognized him anywhere—and run.

There was no running now; 'Flix and his companion sat squarely between Maja and the door. Even rising would draw attention. Instead, she bowed her head, letting shadow shield her expression and airtag alike.

The Human went by the name of Verrick, and he was identified in his warrants as a smuggler. Smugglers were generally offended by the comparison. In truth, Verrick was a pirate, and the strong arm of a captain even more callous than he was. From abduction to drug-running, there was little they would not do for the right price. Even murder and large-scale destruction could be bought.

As she knew all too well.

Maja had expected 'Flix to meet with some small-scale trader, perhaps an antique shop owner who didn't mind dealing in black market items. There were enough of those to be found on Plexis. But pirates? If 'Flix had come to sell artifacts, or set up contacts for a future sale, he couldn't have picked a worse one. Maja only had to scan the room to spot at least three beings who would have not only given him a better price, but were infinitely less likely to leave him with a sucking gut wound for his trouble.

"Get up, 'Flix," Maja whispered. "You know this is a mistake."

If he left now, he'd probably be robbed regardless—but that was nothing more than he deserved. At least he'd get out alive.

A drink slammed onto Maja's table, its contents splashing across the tabletop, her coveralls, and folded hands with equal enthusiasm. Suppressing a gasp, Maja looked to the server. The being silently dared her to protest her treatment—or perhaps ask for a cloth to mop up the liquid. She did neither.

"Thank you," she said instead, keeping her tone light. "I'm parched."

The server closed one set of transparent eyelids as it glared; then, more slowly, a second. The air holes on its thick neck flared in apparent irritation.

"I expect a tip," it said at last, before leaving her alone to drip on the table.

Maja shook the sticky beverage from her fingers. At least, she *thought* it was a beverage.

Thick, bile-yellow liquid pooled in the bottom of the glass, topped with a frothy green-brown layer that looked like dying algae. It smelled like pickles gone to rot—as, now, did she.

"Delightful," she muttered and looked back to 'Flix's table.

The conversation did not appear to be going well. Verrick's expression had grown dark, and he had one callused hand outstretched in clear demand. 'Flix's feathered bulk was increasing in agitation, while his shoulders heaved; he'd started to pant. Maja could hear the high whistles of his speech, but not the words of the translation. To her, he sounded as he always did: imperious and aloof, no matter his distress. Even negotiating an illegal sale with a known criminal, he sounded disapproving.

Briefly, hope flared as 'Flix stood and held his satchel to his chest as if it were an egg. But when Verrick heaved himself to his feet, tossed a credit chit on the table, and started for the door, 'Flix followed.

Maja swore—then nearly choked as she inhaled the fumes of her noxious beverage.

Now what?

She still had nothing that she could bring before the First—no true evidence, only suspicions and the strange coded messages on the coms that had brought her here in the first place. She hadn't even managed to see what 'Flix had hidden in his satchel.

She could report that 'Flix had met with pirates on Plexis, but Triad Third Maja Anders had no reason to know criminals' identities. She had no cause to suspect that she knew where 'Flix was being taken, nor the identity of the person with whom he would shortly meet. Maja Anders didn't know the back routes that would get her there first, before any such meeting could begin, nor how to position a recorder to capture every spoken word.

But she had not always been Maja Anders.

Maja looked down at her hands. *Just forget it*, she told herself. *There's still time to catch the ship.*

A tenday of sunshine and warmth, a landscape that wasn't carved from frozen rock—not to mention drinks that weren't noxious pickle sludge. Nothing to stir up old pain and frustration, all the sharp edges of a life she no longer lived. All she had to do was keep her head down and go.

Even if 'Flix was dealing artifacts from their find—

Even if there was little more waiting for him at that meeting than a blade to the back—

Even if she never saw 'Flix again—

Maja closed her eyes. She couldn't even finish the thoughts.

"Damn it, 'Flix," she muttered. She tossed payment for the drink onto her wet table and followed in the pair's wake, a silent shadow that slipped into the crowd with the ease of long practice.

She didn't even *like* the stupid bird.

Maja's first time on Plexis Supermarket, she'd been six years old. Old enough, she'd thought, to know everything, to have seen everything. She'd been a jaded creature in pigtails—until she'd come to Plexis.

"There," a crew member had told her. She couldn't, now, remember which one; they'd been a rotating family for her, caring and fun and often interchangeable. Her only constant had been Manny; her guardian, she supposed, though he'd always felt like her father. He was the one who'd taken her in after she'd been found as a squalling infant, the only survivor of a pirate attack on the trader ship *Dalton*.

That's what they'd called her, too, her birth name lost to cold space and ash. It was as good a name as any.

Dalton had shaken her head at the crew member. She didn't care what was out the viewport window. It was all the same to her.

But they'd taken her hand and lifted her up, letting her see Plexis on their approach. Dalton had gasped, then plastered her face and hands to the window. She'd refused to leave, barely willing to blink. They'd had to bring her a chair so she could stand and watch when first one crew member's arms, then a second, got weary from her weight.

She'd seen ships before; she'd seen stations. But never before had she seen something so massive, like a whole jigsaw world made by sentients' hands. Even Plexis' bright sign caught her eye, the glittering words turning in her vision as their ship moved toward the yawning maw, bristling with ship connections.

"It's so beautiful," she'd whispered.

"Hah! You have a strange eye for beauty, little one," Manny had told her, chuckling, but he hadn't disagreed.

If the outside had awed her, the interior of Plexis Supermarket had shocked Dalton silent. She'd walked with wide eyes and one hand pressed to the waxy tag on her cheek, trying to see everything at once. The shopping corridor arced in either direction, stores and restaurants vanishing into the distance. She'd seen glittering jewelry with beads like small worlds and a pet store with furry lumps that purred and chittered. There were stores with long scarves in gold and green, shoes and silver claw-caps, herbs and strange spices that made her sneeze, furniture for bodies large and small.

There'd been so many *people*: Gentek and Ordnex, Turrned and Carasians, Humans and creatures for which she knew no name, with tentacles or feathers, scales or knobbled hides or skin so slick with slime it shone mirror-bright in the station's lights. She'd been all but lost in that crowd, clinging tightly to Manny's ivory-tipped hand—and loving every moment.

At last, Manny had knelt before her, the Brill's leathery bulk splitting the stream of shoppers like a stone in a stream. Though he'd worn only the lightest clothes, already he'd begun to sweat, rivulets running down his face and arms.

"Are you ready to see the next level?"

"There's another level?" Dalton had asked, her voice small, as she looked toward the automated ramp. "Are there stores there, too?"

Manny had laughed so hard he'd near shook the floor. "Oh, little one, just you wait."

Crowds, Maja had long ago learned, were like living creatures: each had its moods and had to be handled with care. The crowds in Plexis? Even now, she knew them as well as any beloved friend.

A friend, but an ill-tempered one. The crowd in the hall beyond the bar was far from jovial, but that was only to be expected on such a low level of the station. She spotted a few disagreements in the corridors, the usual posturing between members of rival shipping clans, even the parting of the crowd as off-duty members of a mercenary ship strolled by, but nothing that required her attention.

Good. It would make her job that much easier.

She trailed the pirate and her coworker for about a quarter turn, tracking the spire of 'Flix's feathered crest. Just long enough for her to confirm their destination: the lower docking rings, where Verrick's ship had always parked. Then she cut down a side corridor, sidestepped a servo, and made her way toward Plexis' back halls.

Maja stuck out in the service corridors like a sore thumb, but she still knew the codes and signals. A hand gesture here, a quickly passed chit there, and those that traveled these ways looked aside as if she were no more than a passing shadow. Some things never changed.

As she made her way toward the docking ring, she tried to predict who 'Flix would meet. If this was a new deal, or there were concerns with the item 'Flix provided, Verrick might have orders for another crew member to validate the piece. On the other hand, if there was another issue—'Flix hadn't brought the right number

of items, say, or there was a debate over a previously agreed price—
Verrick might escalate the issue directly to his captain.

If only she knew what 'Flix had taken from their find. There
hadn't been any artifacts worth selling—at least, not that she had
seen. A scrap of worked metal. Three short links of shimmering
chain. A narrow tube that could have been a machine rod, or a
part of a stylo, or nothing at all.

Or had there been more discoveries—better ones, secret ones—
that had been hidden from her entirely?

In the two years that she'd worked with her Triad, Maja had
never felt that she'd made a deeper connection to either 'Flix or
Arendenonail, despite her efforts. Their First was quiet and imposing, a titled scholar who thought he deserved to be in the mountains of Aeande XII, battling the glacier, rather than scratching
through rock and permafrost on the backwater world of Rylan III
for decayed Hoveny scraps. He'd argued loudly against Maja's in-
clusion in the Triad—a fact he hadn't tried to conceal—and sent
a request every few months for her replacement, all denied.

There had been a thousand possible reasons for his dislike. She
was new and unproven, and their find bore little fruit. Worse, she
was Human. Perhaps, she'd thought no few times, he wanted her
to bond with a dog to amplify her weak senses. No matter: she'd
kept her head down, worked the coms, and kept digging, so to
speak.

'Flix had been another matter. No disapproving silences from
him: if anything, he had a comment for her every action, none of
them good. There were times that he'd all but bodily pushed her
aside from her console to complete some scan himself, his low
whistles translating to a string of abuse made both harsher and
more amusing by the monotone of his translating device.

Perhaps the Tolian had only been covering his tracks, hiding
evidence of his dealings the only way he could. If only she had
remote access to their site's systems, perhaps she could have discovered more.

Maja shook her head; soon it wouldn't matter. She had a recorder with her—months of hardscrabble work on the find meant
she never left it behind, not even on vacation. So long as she

reached the ship's air lock in time, she could get the proof she needed to implicate 'Flix and then wash her hands of the whole situation.

If she could rid herself of one of the two members of her Triad, maybe daily life would get a little easier. *Small mercies*, she thought, and broke into a run.

"When you play a role," Manny told her once, "*be* the role. You become that person, understand? But always keep a little part of yourself separate. That's the part that watches."

Dalton had nodded, wide-eyed, and committed the words to memory. She'd repeat them before she went to sleep, murmuring softly into her covers: "Be the person, have a part that watches."

It was part of a game called Surveillance. When Manny or his crew went to meet a supplier or dealer, she'd be there. Rarely at Manny's side—a Brill with a small Human child as a companion was memorable—but *somewhere*. She was the little Fem weeping and wailing that she couldn't buy crystal cakes. She was the happy Hom pressed to the pet store window, his indulgent parents looking on. She was the sleepy little one held in her weary nanny's arms, waiting at the docking gate.

Through it all, she watched. When they'd head back to the ship, Manny would quiz her. Where were the security guards stationed? Where were the cameras? Was anyone following? Was anyone watching?

Some were tests; Manny would pay people to watch or follow, give her someone to find. Others were trial runs, her answers corroborated by Manny's crew, her mistakes and missed observations pointed out so that next time she could do better.

And sometimes, sometimes, it was real.

One afternoon on a small supermarket out on the fringe, Manny had been called to a meeting with a new ship trying to earn its place in one of the Facilitator's smuggling rings. Conversations with Manny's underlings had gone poorly; the captain would only believe the word of Manouya, the Facilitator himself.

"Can't fault their vigilance," Manny had said with a chuckle, despite the inconvenience, and made preparations.

Dalton had been playing the role of the studious child, her nose in a book, while her "mother"—Manny's third-in-command, Alexis—scurried about, trying to find passage to take her little scholar to boarding school. Alexis drew the eye; Dalton watched quietly from her shadow.

Which perhaps is why she was the first to see a face pass by not once, but twice in the crowd, both times headed spinward. He'd doubled back unseen—how? Why?

She'd tugged on Alexis' arm. "Mom, I need to go to the accommodation," she'd said. Code for a problem. Dalton had whispered what she'd seen; and, as the Human bought himself a snack, Alexis got eyes on Dalton's suspect.

"Enforcers," she'd said into her hidden microphone. "All teams, abort."

The meeting had been a trap. Thanks to Dalton, Manouya and his crew were gone from the supermarket within moments, vanished like breath into air. The enforcers had tried to follow, but there was little in the Trade Pact that could outsmart the Facilitator when he knew to run.

Much later, Dalton had learned that even as Manny trained her, there had been plans to send her away. Life aboard a smuggler's ship, some Humans said, was no life for a child. She could go to a city or colony; somewhere that she could have a real family, real parents, and a life other than this one. But this was the only life she'd ever known.

There were very many ways to be a smuggler, and as the years slowly passed, Dalton learned them all. On the books, she had been a shop owner, a trader, an antiques dealer, a tour guide, an accountant, and a drug dealer—all legal, of course. She'd dealt in offworld artifacts and outlawed literature, restricted foodstuffs and rare alcohol, bottled oxygen, and even a particular highly regulated scent that smelled like turpentine to Humans and was irresistibly erotic to Nrophrae.

Off the books, she was Manouya's favorite, his brightest pupil; some said even his heir. Not, she'd thought, that he was in any hurry to vacate the position. The Facilitator's rule was uncontested—and why would any complain when all grew so profitable under his guidance?

Profitable enough that few of the Humans within the Facilitator's sprawling organization thought to question why they rarely saw the elusive Manouya himself, if ever. Profitable enough that those few who'd heard rumors that Manouya wasn't Human discounted such tales—or kept their thoughts behind closed lips. The rare souls who knew the truth? They were the top of Manouya's many-faceted organization, keepers of the Facilitator's most closely guarded secrets, and—as Dalton came to learn—the time always came when those secrets were best kept through a quiet, final end.

As the years rolled on, more days than not, Dalton sat at Manny's right hand and learned. It was one thing to know the tricks and techniques of smuggling—the forgeries and hidden compartments, the methods of bribery and brute force and sleight of hand. It was another to know the strategy behind it all, the shifts in markets and governments and interstellar trade that would make interest in one item rise and another fall, affect regulations and profit margins, or create demand where none had existed before.

If asked if she were happy in this life, Dalton would have only been confused. What other life was there? She lived the whole of her ambition—what else was there to want?

But all it took was a single red-toothed sentence to make everything fall apart.

Smugglers had a hundred uses for a small Human child, from message runner to spy, but none quite so memorable as the ability to fit into small spaces.

Maja had grown considerably since the last time she'd tried to access the station-behind-the-station, the narrow maintenance walkways, service corridors, and ventilation shafts that made Plexis run. It was a tighter fit than she remembered. Even so, she squeezed in though a maintenance access port, adding a coating of grime to her pickle-smelling coveralls. She was going to burn this outfit when she was finished, and gladly.

Maja made her way through the maintenance tunnel on hands and knees, slithering to make it through some of the tighter turns. She didn't want to think about how she'd get out again.

At last she found what she wanted: a ventilation duct in the corridor leading from air lock designation 405-B. A lock in an area with a cheaper docking fee, a permissive airtag check, and guards who were enthusiastic about payments to look the other way. An area, in other words, favored by pirates.

Verrick's captain might have moved to another docking ring or bribed a different set of guards, but Maja didn't think so. Still, her stomach fluttered with nerves she hadn't felt in years as she set up her recorder and pointed it toward the air lock.

A moment passed.

Two.

Five.

Maja was about to back away, cursing, wondering where onstation the pirate could have taken her stupid coworker, when the pair entered the corridor below. She went still, listening.

'Flix was squawking about some perceived slight, much to Verrick's obvious irritation—but even he fell silent as the air lock doors irised open.

A Human came through the air lock, two guards at her back. She was tall and thin like a rod of pure iron, her ash-gray hair shorn close to her skull. She dressed simply: spacer's coveralls accented with thin red lines, heavy boots, and the concealed shape of a weapon on her right hip.

Captain Bennefeld of the pirate ship *Dashing Boy*.

Maja couldn't count the nights that she'd lain awake these past years, considering what she'd do if she ever saw Bennefeld in the flesh. She'd imagined destroying the *Dashing Boy* and the business that rested upon its scarred hull; she'd imagined all manner of violence, little though her skills trended to the martial. She'd even tried to envision scenarios in which she stood tall, spoke a few cutting words, and walked away—though, even in dreams, she'd failed to imagine words that could carry the weight of everything she had to say.

Never had she thought she'd lie quiet and do nothing at all.

Bennefeld came forward, her steady walk that of a predator. She looked 'Flix up and down, clearly unimpressed.

"You're not Arendenonail," Bennefeld said softly, naming the First in Maja and 'Flix's Triad.

Maja would have sworn if she could. As it was, she exhaled long and slow, pushing out her frustration with that breath.

She was the only one in their Triad that was clean? The irony of that was sharp enough to cut.

The Tolian stood up straighter, his feathers puffing in a dominance display as he whistled a shrill response. "No," came the translation. "I've come in his stead."

"I've had a long wait to speak to an underling."

'Flix bristled. "I'm no underling, but a partner. And our find hit snags—the delay was unavoidable." If a Tolian could sniff in disdain, 'Flix would have.

The captain's lips raised in the bare curve of a smile. "Of course, Hom. But now you've come to keep your side of the bargain."

A nod.

'Flix drew a lumpy bundle from his satchel, holding it to his chest before reluctantly drawing back the coverings. Maja expected artifacts; instead, she saw the glitter of a small fortune in currency gems. More, she calculated, than 'Flix and Arendenonail together could have earned in a year.

The captain gestured for one of her guards to take and count the currency. When the guard nodded at the total, Bennefeld brought forth a small package which she handed to 'Flix. Maja caught a glimpse of fine metal links woven into delicate mesh. A hat, perhaps?

Maja blinked in incredulity. 'Flix wasn't selling, but buying.

More: he was clearly buying artifacts from a trove of so-called finds that had flooded the market some years earlier, each marked with a Triad's seal—and condemned by Manouya as fakes. "Everyone wants to discover history," he'd told her with a sigh after turning down yet another lot of the ridiculous so-called artifacts. "If they can't discover it, they'll invent it."

Inventing history was exactly what her Triad was aiming for, Maja realized. A single great find could rewrite their futures. More to the point, if he played his cards right, it could transform Arendenonail from a backworld Triad Analyst to a top interstellar scholar.

'Flix seemed relieved as he rewrapped the artifact and stashed it in his satchel. He nodded to the captain, then turned to go. Verrick's hulking shape blocked his departure.

Captain Bennefeld raised an eyebrow. "You will be back, right, Hom? For the next delivery."

"Yes, of course," intoned 'Flix's translator. But one only needed to glance at his body language to know that he was lying.

Oh, Arendenonail, Maja thought as she briefly closed her eyes. *You never should have let 'Flix speak for you.* They were going to skip out on the deal—and the pirates knew it.

One find; that's all Arendenonail wanted. Enough to give him status, funding—and the limelight that came with it. No need to continue dealing with pirates, no matter the terms of their agreement.

"That's what I thought." Captain Bennefeld spoke with the finality of a closing door. "It's been pleasant doing business with you, Hom. Verrick, if you would?"

The pirate's lackey nodded as the captain returned to the *Dashing Boy,* bringing her guards with her. 'Flix watched her go before turning to Verrick.

"Right this way," Verrick said with a broad smile and a gesture toward the hall. "I'll show you a faster way back to your transport."

'Flix hesitated—as well he should—perhaps only just realizing what a dreadful situation he'd managed to get himself into, alone with a pirate in the rough backside of the station.

No witnesses but Maja, unseen.

If you value your life, 'Flix, she thought, *do* not *go with him.*

'Flix glanced around, whistling softly. There were at least two other ways out of this corridor—three, if one counted blasting through the wall into the storage rooms beyond—but 'Flix could see no escape. He nodded reluctantly and went in the direction Verrick pointed.

Verrick grinned wider behind the Tolian's back. Anticipation, Maja thought, of what was to come. Even so, she could only wait, silent and unmoving in her hiding spot, as the pair disappeared from sight.

In her mind, she lived that day over and over again.

Dalton had been sent at Manouya's express request to oversee the end of an interrogation of a Human male named Bax. A young Human, they'd found, who'd been selling information on one of the Facilitator's most profitable rings to the Auord Port Authority, directly resulting in the seizure of three ships, the death of two crew, the loss of untold millions in goods, and the destruction of relationships that had taken decades to build.

The Jellies counted it as a significant victory. They'd tried to hide Bax, their informant; they'd failed. Bax had run from the Facilitator's justice; he hadn't run far enough.

Dalton remembered standing at the door to the ship's starboard hold, which served as a crude interrogation room, and staring at the doors' scratched metal. She took a deep breath. She'd never enjoyed this part of the job.

She pressed a button; the door slid open. Inside, a Human male hung in the center of the hold by his wrists, his bare feet dangling a hand's span from the ground. Two of Manouya's crew were with him; they had, she hoped, already gained some of the answers they sought.

Bax looked up as Dalton entered. There was fear in his swollen expression, yes—all knew what it meant to come before Manouya's right hand—but something else, too.

Bax gathered the scraps of his courage. "Look at that," he said, voice trembling despite himself. "Dalton herself here to punish my little *rebellion*. That's a laugh."

"Really?" Dalton let the door swish shut behind her. "And why's that funny, Bax?"

"Don't you know?" Bax looked to the beings on either side of him, Emerson standing guard, Aelian carefully cleaning the congealing blood from her hands. For a moment he looked as if they three shared some dark secret to which Dalton was not privy; then, as Aelian put down her rag, Bax flinched and looked away, shivering.

Don't get distracted, Dalton told herself.

"I assume you've had a good conversation with our friends here?" She gestured to Emerson and Aelian. "Manouya has one last question for you, Bax: who else betrayed us to the Jellies?"

Bax shook his head. "I told you. It was just me."

Dalton stepped forward, careful to avoid the splatters on the ground. She leaned closer until she could smell his breath, the tang of his blood and sweat.

"Bax," she whispered. "I know you're lying. You gave them information to which you have no access. We know *everyone* who had that information." She pulled back. "Think of it this way. You're not betraying a coconspirator. You're saving anyone who's actually innocent."

He just shook his head, whispering something that might have been, "No, no, no."

Dalton sighed and stepped back, then nodded to Emerson. She looked to her hands, waiting. She'd never liked this part, but could not deny that harsh methods of justice were sometimes necessary. Order must be kept, even here.

A few moments later the sounds of fist on flesh ceased. There was only the creak of the chains as Bax swung back and forth, and the rough, aching cough of his breathing.

"Last chance, Bax," Dalton said quietly. "Come clean, and you'll earn an easier end. Manouya is not without mercy."

"Mercy." Bax laughed a terrible, choking laugh; it was all but inaudible. "I think you're the only one who's ever known Manouya's questionable mercy." His sides heaved as he struggled to gain control, despite the pain. His head lolled, blood and sweat dripping as he spat on the cold metal floor. Something in the gesture seemed to give him strength—the splat of the bloody saliva, that moment of stark defiance.

Bax looked up. Met her eyes. Grinned with teeth stained dark.

"He never told you, did he?" He laughed again, then coughed on his own blood. Still he spoke through the red and salt. "He never told you what your name means. *Dalton.*"

There was more; his end was neither swift nor merciful, and knowing what he had done, Dalton thought it no less than he deserved. Yet to her, or of her name, Bax said nothing more—and no matter who she asked, or how, Dalton could find no one who'd explain.

Maja was stuck—in more ways than one.

Getting into the maintenance shaft had been one thing; getting out was another. The corners that she'd managed to wriggle around on her way in were all but impossible to navigate in reverse, and now she found herself well and truly wedged. Given the accumulated dust, it'd be years before some servo discovered her decaying body.

Even as she struggled to free herself, her mind spun: *What're you going to do with the recording, fool?* If it weren't for the tight quarters, she would have shaken her head at her own stupidity.

Bring the transgression before the First—that had been her first reaction, the whole of her plan. A Maja Anders plan, a habitual behavior engrained through years of careful practice. Now she had the recording in hand, she knew the last thing she could do was turn it over to the authorities.

Any Triad member dealing Hoveny artifacts was sure to meet swift justice, and Maja had evidence that implicated not one but two members of her Triad. That she herself was innocent didn't matter, nor would the fact that she'd reported the transgression. Not in the end.

Any authority would have to confirm her innocence. Her identity would come under scrutiny, every detail poked and prodded for evidence of falsehood. It didn't matter how carefully she'd constructed her past; under such examination, her lies would be discovered. And if they uncovered her true identity? She'd never see sunlight again.

No, if 'Flix and Arendenonail's dealings came to light, she'd lose everything, one way or another. But if 'Flix came to harm, killed by pirates—or even if the ridiculous plan were successful, their claim on Rylan III exalted for its single, glorious find—the truth would be uncovered regardless. It was only a matter of when.

Her days as Maja Anders were numbered. The countdown sounded like her hammering heartbeat, the huff of her breath in the stale, dusty air.

Her only way out was to run. Run fast enough, far enough, that her trail would be cold before any investigation sought to follow. New job, new name, new home—certainly wouldn't be the first for any of those. She could start again.

Abandoning 'Flix to his own foolish end.

She knew she should go, just leave it all behind. But if that were her path, she never would have followed 'Flix from the bar.

Her only leverage was the recording. Her thoughts spun. Maybe if she—

With a gasp, a rip of her grimy, pickle-scented coveralls, and the loss of no little bit of skin, Maja was free. She wriggled down the rest of the maintenance shaft and popped back into the service corridor beyond the range of the *Dashing Boy*'s scans. Without even shaking the dust from her hair, Maja ran.

Down the hall, into a back service room, and—

She skidded to a stop.

Too late.

Before her, Verrick had 'Flix in a hold, a knife to the Tolian's already-bleeding torso. 'Flix flailed, a panicked writhing that neither freed him from that grasp nor helped him evade further damage from the blade.

Maja winced at the sight, even as some part of her heaved an irritated sigh. Verrick had always been too fond of knives. Yet, despite his "fun," he'd at least done his job; Maja saw the edges of the wrapped artifact protruding from his back pocket. Payment and artifact both in the pirates' possession. She could have told her Triad that it was the best outcome they could expect, especially if they were reneging on a deal.

"Hey." Maja's voice echoed in the corridor's narrow confines. "Let him go."

"You're in the wrong hall, Fem," Verrick said, sparing her a bare glance. "I think you'd better turn around and go, don't you?"

'Flix shrilled in pain as the knife dug deeper. "Ow," said the flat monotone of his translator.

But Maja hadn't moved. "You're making a mess, Verrick." She hid a grin as the pirate twitched at her use of his name. She'd surprised him. Good. She'd surprised 'Flix, too, from the incredulous look on the being's face—a look that was quickly erased by another jab of the knife.

Given the blood already staining his clothing and patterning the floor? She had to move quickly.

"Your deal's gone wrong."

"My deal's gone exactly as planned. You're just increasing the body count."

"Nah," she said, letting her carefully cultivated accent slip. "It's all tits-up. You just didn't know it until now."

"That so?"

He thrust the knife in deeper. Then, as 'Flix shrieked, he tossed the Tolian onto the floor between them. 'Flix curled into a ball on the cold metal, shivering and panting, while Verrick calmly cleaned the blade.

"Look at me, Verrick."

Nonchalantly, the pirate glanced toward her—then squinted, looking harder. "Wait. Don't I know you?"

Maja shrugged, wishing she could calm her pounding heart. "You tell me."

The pirate tilted his head, considering. He had always preferred force to negotiation, believing in physical power—whether in body, weapon, or ship—over cleverness, but he was still smart. And, unfortunately, good at his brutal job.

"No," Verrick said slowly. "No, I recognize that face."

As the pirate watched her, Maja knelt beside 'Flix. She ripped off part of his coveralls and pressed the fabric to the wound.

"What are you . . . how can you . . . ?" Even the translator had no words for the sound that followed.

"Just press down on the wound," she murmured. "You have to stanch the bleeding."

Verrick watched, a stream of cold calculations running behind his eyes. "What was your name again? You're Manouya's wonder child, aren't you? The poor little orphan, all grown up." He laughed an ugly laugh.

"What's he saying?" 'Flix panted.

"Doesn't matter. Just keep quiet."

"But he said—"

"'Flix," she snapped. "Keep your stupid beak *shut*."

The Tolian's eyes went wide. Never in all the time they'd worked together had Maja so much as raised her voice to him.

Long overdue.

Still he made to speak—to argue, to complain, she didn't know. Didn't, at that point, care. Instead, she pressed harder on the wadded fabric, increasing the pressure on his wound; there was already so much blood. 'Flix's eyes rolled back and he whistled, his hand scrabbling weakly at her arms.

Ignoring her one-time coworker, Maja looked back to the pirate. "The deal's a bust," she repeated. "The First suspected these two all along—and you know how they feel about messing with anything pertaining to the Hoveny Concentrix. Everything was tracked, monitored, and recorded. The vid's already on its way to the authorities—including Plexis Security."

'Flix's low whistle from beneath her hands spoke as much of despair as it did of pain. *Hang in there*, she thought to him. *It'll all work out.*

"Then why," Verrick asked slowly, "are you talking to me? One scrawny Human alone in a Plexis back hall." He lifted his cleaned knife, turning it to catch the light. "You don't look much like security. Not much like an enforcer, either."

"I have a copy of the recording with me, if you don't believe." She lifted her recorder in one bloody hand. "But I intercepted the feed. Put it on a time delay to give us a little moment to talk."

"About what?"

"I think we could make a deal, you and I. Consider this: if you—"

Suddenly, 'Flix deflated under her hands. His muscles went slack as unconsciousness claimed him.

"'Flix?" Maja made to pat his face, only to realize how heavy the wadded fabric had become, saturated with blood. Verrick must have nicked an artery; 'Flix was bleeding out.

She swore. "Get me a spray bandage. We need to get him to a med unit—"

Verrick guffawed, incredulous. She took a breath, then another, trying to stem her rush of anger and disgust.

She'd been away from this work too long. Her request had been a Maja reaction, nothing more.

She looked back to the Tolian. Saw the color of his skin, the seeming thinness of his closed eyelids, the erratic twitch of the muscle movements beneath her hands. He had moments to live, if that, and there was nothing that she could do to save him. Even so, she pressed down, harder and harder, as if she could stop that end with hands and will alone.

Too late, she thought. Too thin a plan, too long getting here, too distant from her days as a smuggler. She could only watch as 'Flix died under her hands.

Verrick paid no attention as the Tolian breathed his last, that thin whistle of air somehow loud in the empty space. Instead, the pirate said, "What was this about a deal?"

Time to bluff her way out of this situation. But she could not look away from 'Flix's body. Could not, in that moment, find the strength to rise.

"What, nothing else to say to me? Come on, I want to hear about this plan of yours."

"Verrick," she said slowly. "I need you to get Captain Bennefeld now."

The pirate laughed and crossed his arms across his chest. "You want me to do your laundry, too? Fetch you some slippers?" He swore—using a particularly creative combination of names for her.

Her hands had become stone; her blood, ice. She felt each breath as it entered her, filled her; felt the metronome beat of her heart. She ran her hand down the side of 'Flix's feathered head once, slowly—a gesture of affection she would not have wanted, nor felt, had the Tolian still lived.

She had not liked 'Flix. He'd been a smart being in some ways, as stupid as rocks in others, and he had not deserved to die. Certainly not like this.

One breath. Another.

"Verrick. If you know who I am, then you know my presence here is a threat." Each word was a cold stone cast between them; and her eyes, when she looked up from 'Flix's body to stare down the pirate, were colder still.

"Get your captain," she said again. "Bring her here."

This time, Verrick complied.

Nearly thirty hours after Bax's interrogation, Dalton stumbled into Manny's office. He was alone, bent over his work, humming a low prayer.

"They were yours," she said in accusation.

Exhaustion should have slurred the words, but anger made

everything clearer. Her voice. Her past. The look in Manny's eyes as he lifted his head from the displays arrayed on the low tabletops that served as his desk. Manny's office was frigid; it always was, by Human standards. But it was not the cold that made Dalton shiver, or tightened her jaw, or made her restless hands tremble by her sides.

She had not slept or showered since the interrogation; she'd barely paused in her research long enough to visit the accommodation and eat a package of crackers she'd found in a drawer. There had only been the work—the truth that she'd managed to dig out, sliver by sliver, from where it had been so carefully hidden.

Hidden, she knew now, only from her.

Manny shifted his bulk, leaning back on his ample haunches as he gave her his full attention.

"Yes," he said. He did not need to ask who she meant.

Even so, she said their names: "Andreas and Lila, Mikael and Sanders—"

Manny lifted a hand to stop the flow of the names of her parents and brother, her aunts and uncles, and the many people they had hired. With that gesture of ivory-tipped fingers he asked for silence, but that—here, now—she could not give.

"There were forty people aboard the trader ship *Dalton*, and they all worked for you."

There came a moment of silence as he looked at her. Dalton knew the real Manny: smiling, jovial, ever the optimist. In almost all of her memories, he was laughing. She'd seen this face before— his blank face, stripped of emotion—but never before had it been turned toward her.

The rare times she saw this expression, someone usually died. Even that thought was not enough to deter her.

"Yes," Manouya said again.

"There really was a pirate attack. The *Dashing Boy* attacked and destroyed the *Dalton*—but not for anything in their holds. Not for information, or hostages, or anything else that they carried. They were attacked because *you ordered it*. You hired the *'Boy* to kill them."

"You've been doing your research, I see."

"Surprised I've discovered your dirty secret?" Dalton all but spat the words.

Manny's thick lips twisted, a gesture akin to a Human's lift of an eyebrow. "Surprised, only, that it took you this long to look."

"I trusted you!"

Manny laughed then, the rumbling sound full of genuine humor. "Grasis' Glory, child. Why would you ever do that?"

She'd thought, she'd believed—

But no, that couldn't matter now.

"In your research, did you find records of what the *Dalton* did? I don't believe I left many intact."

Despite her anger, the words came swift and smooth, just as he'd trained her: "It was a trader, clean record. Double holds, concealed compartments along the engine bay, dummy hold alongside the engine. It followed Plexis for six years, then worked the Deneb run for four."

"And what did they do for their other employers?"

"Their other . . . ?" Dalton swallowed.

"They were freelancing," Manny said. "Did you not find that part? Up to a third of the goods they transported were off the books they shared with me. They were stockpiling money. Establishing their own network of contacts."

"For what?"

Manny smiled. "To overthrow me."

As if that were possible. There had never been any question why Manouya was the mastermind behind every major smuggling ring in Human space—at least, in his opinion. "Smarter than the lot of you," he often said with an emphatic fist to his own chest. Having watched his operation for as long as she could remember, Dalton couldn't help but agree.

It was not just his leadership or techniques, his ability to see barriers not for their strengths but for the holes one might slip through. It was that he had a mind for patterns, one that was exemplary even for a Brill. He saw patterns in people and behavior as much as in money; he understood the tangled relationships between businesses and governments, information and power, in a blink of an eye.

She understood, then, what he was not saying. One trading vessel—a mere forty people, no matter how terrible that tally—was no threat to his shadow empire or his place at its head. Still she spoke the words: "One ship?"

"No. The captain and crew of the *Dalton* were but the ringleaders. They spread dissent like slow poison, drip by drip into an open vein. Into my networks, my contacts, my clients. Into my captains and ships."

"And you let them?"

A low chuckle. "For a time. What better way to diagnose weakness in the flesh, while honing the knife to cut it out?"

"And the fate of the rest?"

"Of the whole of the *Dalton* rebellion," Manny said with a twist of his thick lips, "there was only a single survivor. You."

He had killed them, every one. Yet all she could think . . .

"Manny, *why*?" Dalton whispered. "Why didn't you tell me?"

Why keep this from her for so long? Hadn't she proven herself to him, time and again? Or did he think that she was like her parents and older brother, her aunts and uncles? Did he think that in her chest beat a traitor's heart?

For a span of a breath she ached with that thought, before she at last understood the import of his last words: that she was the only survivor. What was it Bax had said? That she didn't know what her own name meant. That she was the only one who had ever known Manouya's questionable mercy.

Realization felt like a blow to her chest. "My name," Dalton said. Her words came slow, each one a painful birth. "I wasn't named for the ship, was I? I was named for the rebellion."

Manny chuckled; he always liked when she proved herself clever. "The rebellion, and its failure."

"My name is a warning. A reminder of what happens to those who dare cross you."

Her parents' rebellion hadn't just been stopped. She knew Manny; she knew what he would have done. From root tip to unfurling leaf, he had destroyed them: every ship, every business, every record, every life. Every single drop of traitor's blood was no more than dust and ruin scattered unceremoniously among the stars.

Every drop, but one. The sole survivor of the *Dalton* rebellion had been brought back into the fold and raised at the Facilitator's knee, taught to cleave to him as a plant reaches for the sun.

The words were ash and blood in her mouth: "That's all I am, isn't it? I'm proof of your revenge—and the whole of your mercy."

Deny it, Dalton dared him silently. *Tell me I'm wrong.*

Then, as the silence grew between them: *Please.*

Because perhaps revenge was why he'd kept and raised her—but as the years passed, hadn't she become something more to him? If not his daughter or heir, then at least—*something*. She'd always thought that in his strange, alien way, Manny loved her. After all she'd done, after all she'd *become*, surely now she was more than a reminder to those who'd consider betrayal.

But Manouya, the Facilitator, the mastermind and uncontested ruler of every criminal smuggling ring in Human space, and the only father she'd ever known, simply looked at her, icy, impassive. A moment passed. A second.

"Was there anything else?" he asked. A quiet, final dismissal.

No denial. No excuse. No explanation. No apology.

He wasn't going to say anything else, Dalton realized. Not now, not ever. She stared at him, heart thundering, throat thick with unshed tears. She wanted—

She *needed*—

She didn't even know. But it was not this.

At last she took a breath, squared her shoulders, and met Manouya's eyes. Nodded once. Then she turned and walked away without looking back.

She kept walking, leaving everything behind. Her training. Her friends. Her father. Her name.

She walked out of the ship. Out of this life. Forever.

Or so she had thought.

Because as she knelt with 'Flix's blood soaking into her filthy coveralls, she did not feel like Maja Anders anymore. All she felt was a deep, aching silence that roared through her like a scream.

It had been a hard thing, starting again from nothing—but she had done it. She'd known how to navigate the complexities of worlds throughout the Trade Pact, the ins and outs of life on a starship, the immigration laws and legal complexities of some dozen potential homes. She'd crafted Maja Anders piece by careful piece, creating an alternate self so believable that no one would have cause to dig deeper.

She could have made a life for herself in any number of ways. She could have been a trader, an antiques dealer, an evaluator. But no, she'd wanted to do something *real*. If she dealt in history, let her carve it from rock and soil; if she paid in sweat and blood, let it be her own. She had no deep love of Hoveny artifacts or the secrets they might tell, but she knew enough from her years with the Facilitator to eventually earn a place for herself in a Triad.

And now . . . *this*. One way or another, she'd known she'd have to start again. But not like this.

Three pairs of footsteps approached. Two sets stayed back; she listened as that single set of sharp, precise steps drew closer. Stopped.

Maja would have been afraid; she knew it. She'd constructed this identity so carefully, and everything about Maja—from her sheltered, onworld upbringing to her years of scholarly study—should have made her crouch and cringe. Maja would have run, terrified.

No, more: Maja wouldn't have been here in the first place.

Had she ever truly been Maja Anders?

"You seem to have wandered off the beaten path," said a quiet voice.

She looked up to meet Captain Bennefeld's eyes. Nodded once in acknowledgment.

"So it seems." She turned back to 'Flix, limp and unmoving before her. The air smelled of blood and dust. "This has all gone terribly wrong."

"Verrick told me of the recordings. That you proposed a deal."

She shook her head. "That doesn't matter now."

She'd never imagined seeing Bennefeld for the first time through a ventilation grate; she'd never truly believed that she'd speak to Bennefeld at all. Yet here she was.

"Tell me," she asked, speaking words she'd never imagined. "Do you know who I am?"

Unspoken beneath: do you know what you did to me?

This person had killed her family in cold blood. Bennefeld had probably never had second thoughts about that job, never wondered about the lives she'd taken—or the life, singular, that had been left behind. The destruction of the *Dalton* had been just one unsavory task among the many that were Bennefeld's bread and salt.

She should be angry, she knew. Angry for the deaths of her blood-kin and all that worked for them; angry for the loss of her true name and the life she could have had. And she *was* angry— but not, she realized, for those deaths. Not anymore. She had no memories to affix to those losses, only a few bare scraps of information that she'd been able to recover after the Facilitator's purge. Now that the shock of discovery was years past, she could not maintain her blaze of righteous anger.

No, if she felt anger toward Bennefeld and her crew, it was only for what those long-ago actions had meant for Dalton at the very end. The loss of everything she'd ever wanted, the life she'd loved. The loss of Manny and his place in her heart.

And now, Bennefeld had ended Maja Anders.

This pirate had destroyed her life not once or twice, but three times over, all unknowing.

"Yes," Bennefeld confirmed. "I know who you are."

Do you? She looked down at her bloody hands and laughed, the sound a pale echo of Manouya's deep chuckle. *That makes one of us.*

Because it was all falling apart now, everything she had built for herself, everything she had strived to achieve on her own. The last of Maja Anders was crumbling, patterns of thought and habit flaking like old paint—and as that sense of self fell away, piece by painful piece, she felt so very relieved.

Never had she lived a constructed identity for so long. Never had something she thought she wanted, something she thought she deserved, felt so false or constraining.

Which left . . . what?

Because if she no longer felt rage toward Bennefeld—was that what forgiveness was, a weary end to hate?—she could not say the same for Manouya. She understood why he had destroyed her family and the rebellion they'd nurtured; had something similar happened when she'd worked at Manny's side, she would have had a hand in the distribution of such justice, too. What she could not comprehend was what he had made her become.

Why had he raised her, trained her, created her to be his small, Human-shaped shadow? She'd called herself the proof of his revenge, the whole of his mercy—and he had not denied it. Yet now, she realized, there had to be something more, something deeper. Not love, as she'd once believed; nothing like a Human heart beat within the Brill's chest. Not kindness. But something.

She knew so many of his secrets—and he had let her walk away.

It was then that she realized: she was the only Human that Manouya had ever trusted. His right hand, they had called her; his daughter, his heir. Did it matter that none of those titles had been true? She alone had the power to speak in his name.

She breathed deep, smelling blood and dust, as something within her woke. The part of herself that she had kept separate, secret even from herself through all her years as Maja. The part of herself that had watched.

Since she was a child at Manny's knee, she'd tracked the movements of the Trade Pact—the legal and illegal alike. Pirates and governments, stock markets and insurgencies, traders and royalty and refugees. All the crisscrossing webs of hope and greed, love and revenge, that reached across the known worlds.

Patterns, that watcher within her whispered. *Patterns within patterns*—just as Manouya had taught her.

What had he wanted her to see? What was it that Manouya feared?

Betrayal, that voice said. But no, it was deeper than that: a traitor in his midst. A threat in Human form that for all his cleverness, all his threats, all his power and cruelty, Manouya could not uncover or burn away.

Or was it bigger than just his smuggling empire? She let her mind range farther, wider, thinking about traitors in the Triads, the fears of the First; thinking about the chatter on the coms that she'd listened to long into the night. There was, she thought, something there—a pattern she could only begin to glimpse, unfurling in her head petal by slow petal.

One that spoke of a great power moving in secret within the Trade Pact.

Manouya had been waiting for her to see it, she realized. He had been testing her, the way he'd tested her with their game of Surveillance; the way he'd tested her with the burden of her name. It was a test she'd spent years failing. But not now. Not anymore.

Manouya had made Dalton because he needed her, one Human he could trust among the untold billions. One Human who would never betray him; a Human who, because of her own foolish heart, never could.

For one long moment, she stared at 'Flix's cooling body, the patterns of his blood. Then Dalton stood, met the eyes of the one who had destroyed her life three times over, and smiled.

"I think it's time we came to an agreement, you and I."

Captain Bennefeld inclined her head. Dalton knew that Bennefeld's ever-present bodyguards had their weapons trained on her, waiting for a false move—or a nod from their captain. They didn't matter. There was only Bennefeld, and the path Dalton could already see waiting before her.

"The recordings, I presume?"

Dalton waved a bloody hand. "Irrelevant. Consider them destroyed. No, I'm carrying information of great value to the Facilitator. In return for your cooperation, he will reward you handsomely. In his name, I promise you that."

Bennefeld raised a slow eyebrow, considering. At last she asked, "In exchange for what?"

Dalton smiled; it was a sad smile, one that spoke of loss and regret and all the possible lives she would not live. Then she said, "I need you to take me home."

In the end, she was her father's daughter.

...*Truffles* continues
Interlude

* * *

KEEVOR'S HAD THE traditional back corner booth with a privacy shield and a hidden but effective exit in case of trouble. The righthand bench was presently occupied by a solitary figure, appropriately cloaked and hooded. Morgan approached, aware of the subtle stir from those seated at the booths nearest, the shift to move hands or whatever toward hidden weapons. Aware, but unconcerned.

If they'd orders to stop him, it would have happened already. A needle in the crowd. A puff of gas. The guards made themselves known, that was all.

He paused outside the light spilling over the table. "I'd like a word, Dalton."

"Captain Morgan." The hood tilted back, revealing the face of a Human female, his age or thereabouts, with features unforthcoming on useful details such as world of origin or past. No one asked. A pleasant face, until you noticed the chill analysis of those brown eyes. She nodded at the opposing bench. "I didn't think you'd reconsider our offer."

Morgan took the step to enter the light. "I haven't." Until today, he'd stayed as far as possible from the shadowy ring of smugglers

Dalton represented, well aware they crossed boundaries he'd set himself long ago.

Knowing once you were in—there was no coming out.

The hint of a smile. "Sit anyway, Captain. That answer just won me a good number of credits. Least I can do is buy you a drink."

He didn't move. "I won't waste your time. I'm here as a professional courtesy. Many of your clients import consumables—"

An eyebrow lifted. "Duties and Tariffs?" Dalton's fingers made a throwaway motion. "They can tie up your little *Fox*. They don't concern us."

Having, no doubt, ample bribes—or threats—in place. "I assumed as much," he countered smoothly.

"Then what?" Almost lazy, if you didn't know her. "If you want us to intercede, well—the offer still stands. Work for us. Everyone knows you've a—let's call it, a nose for trouble, Morgan. Now that's currency in any market. Deal's good for you both."

She knew he'd taken a partner. A mate. He should have expected it; Dalton collected information the way others hoarded gems and would automatically add anyone so close to him into the bargain. To be used—

NEVER. Somehow Morgan kept the *violence* of his reaction from Sira. Easier on the outside; no expression beyond courteous attention touched his face or voice, "I'm getting my ship back." And more, but he'd keep it to what she'd understand. "All I want is your word you'll stay clear of my play."

A startled pause, then Dalton laughed. "You've backbone, Morgan. Shame you aren't ours." Amusement wiped from her face, she leaned forward to stare at him. "Tell me. Why should I do that?"

So he did.

Leaving Keevor's tended to make a fresher—and on one occasion burning his clothes—a matter of some urgency.

The encounter with Dalton left him feeling filthier on the inside, but what choice had he? Through her, he'd keep at bay— hopefully long enough—those who influenced what happened at the docks. Reduce the situation to the Department of Duties and

Tariffs versus those they proposed to gouge. Officer Esaliz E'Teiso versus a hold full of truffles.

In return? He'd given her a suggestion, nothing more. That it was time she sought employment elsewhere. If Dalton assumed it was his famed "nose for trouble," if she'd gone still and cold, her eyes anything but?

If even as he'd walked away, she'd slipped through the back exit?

It wasn't a lie: Bowman was coming for the Facilitator. Anyone close would go down, too.

Dalton should be one of them. If she wasn't, it was on him. So much for keeping his distance. So much for steering wide of their business. He'd invited them into his, now. Into Butter's and Rose's and Sedley's and—into Huido's—Morgan winced. There'd be shouting. Probably breakage.

The huge Carasian did his share of rule bending. Morgan's lips quirked. Maybe he'd bring up the small matter of the stew and the priests first.

He lowered his inner barriers, sharing *warmth*, his *resolve*.

There was no stopping now.

Sira. Meet me at the tearoom.

The Restaurant Trade

* * *

by Chris Butler

THE HUMAN HAD eaten his meal alone, with a minimum of fuss and mostly unnoticed by the other patrons of *Claws & Jaws*. Which was remarkable given his huge frame was only partially concealed by an oversized, slightly shabby business suit. He made his table look small. His ragged hair had been dyed, but not recently, because it was showing gray at the roots.

He called his waiter over and, with a sly voice, said, "Might I speak with the chef? I would like to thank him personally for such a fine meal."

Huido had kept a watchful eye on the being as the night waned and his restaurant emptied. He'd had more than a few run-ins with a similarly large Human called Terk, a Trade Pact Enforcer. The resemblance, however slight, did not sit well with Huido. Now there were only a couple of Retian priests remaining in the far corner of the restaurant, and this formerly quiet diner was suddenly asking to speak to his chef.

"I'd be happy to convey your message," the waiter was saying, "but our proprietor does not allow the kitchen staff into the dining area."

"Then might I . . ."

"Nor can I allow you into the kitchen."

Huido had been resisting the urge to come out of the semi-shadow toward the back of the room. He'd been wallowing in a somber mood, thinking of absent friends and an absent brother. And of too many bills to pay. At last he shifted his bulk into motion and padded toward the Human's table.

"I'm pleased you enjoyed your meal," Huido boomed. "It is the best in the quadrant, is it not?"

The Human looked up at Huido's imposing figure. "A bold claim, but I won't disagree. If I'm not mistaken, am I addressing Huido himself, the owner of this establishment?"

"You are."

"Well, this is quite perfect because, in all honesty, it is to you I wished to speak."

"Not the chef?"

The Human made a small throaty sound, which Huido could not readily interpret. It could have been amusement, but it could have been anything.

"I had thought of approaching the chef as an . . . intermediary, but in truth it is you I wish to negotiate with."

Huido trained each of his eyestalks upon the Human, affording him his undivided attention and causing the seated diner to shrink back slightly under the intense scrutiny.

"Let me introduce myself," he said, finding his voice again. "I am Theodore G. Brody. I recently read an article in which you, Huido Maarmatoo'kk, said that you would, and I quote, 'give your right claw for the recipe for Pashwali's Ocean Stinger stew.'"

Huido roared with laughter, rattling the presently empty rings affixed to his carapace. "The finest stew I ever tasted, and no mistake."

Brody removed a small data card from an inner pocket and wafted it left, then right. "This is the recipe," he said. "The data is heavily encrypted, of course. I can give you the card or the encryption key for free, but if you want both, we will have to negotiate. I am wondering, How much is your right claw worth?"

"I'll take the encryption key," Huido said. "If it's free."

Brody made a sound that was somewhere between a gasp and a squeal, definitely amusement this time. "Very good, Maarmatoo'kk, very good. Plexis being known for its pickpockets and the like, for how long would I retain possession of the card if you had the key?"

Huido was thinking that it was the Human, not he, who had spoken carelessly, but he supposed it was never going to be that simple.

"I'll leave you my contact details," Brody said. He pocketed the data card and withdrew an ident decorated with extravagant font and logo. "You have a day to consider. Make me an offer."

Huido reached out with his lower right handling claw to take the ident. "Are you planning to leave Plexis, or do you intend to stay?"

Brody pulled on a thick overcoat and pressed a wide hat into place. "It would be nice to have enough money to consider either."

"Passage out is more affordable," Huido advised him.

Brody paused on his way to the door. "I was thinking more of . . . buying my own ship," he said. "If I was leaving."

Huido snapped a claw in irritation as the Human went out into the night, and the door swung shut behind him. He recalled the exquisite flavor of Ocean Stinger stew, Pashwali's heavenly dish. He could almost taste it. Was it really as divine as he remembered, or had the intervening years played tricks with him and enhanced the flavor in his memory?

He allowed himself one more shake and rattle, and then tried to push the entire notion from his mind. He already had bills to pay. He definitely could not afford to buy Theodore G. Brody a ship.

A loud banging brought Huido to the restaurant main entrance early the next station day.

"All right, all right," Huido muttered as he unlocked the door.

Two from Plexis Security stared up at him, both Human males. One constable looked quite senior, the other young and muscular. Huido peered at the idents they were holding up and concluded they were genuine. "You'd better come in," he said, and he led them toward the bar.

"An accusation has been made against you," the elder Human said. He had introduced himself as Officer O'Connell.

"Oh?" Huido's mind raced over recent events, but a likely cause for complaint did not immediately occur to him.

"Do you know a Human named Theodore G. Brody?"

Huido shifted his eyes. All of them. He had a feeling resembling the moment when you've found a musty old jar at the back of the cupboard, and you've unwisely taken the lid off.

"Hom Brody dined here last night," the Carasian admitted. "He was very complimentary about the meal."

"It wasn't a business meeting, then?"

"Certainly not."

"Well, Hom Huido, Brody claims he offered you some data—a valuable recipe, he said—but you refused to pay him. Subsequently, not far from here, he was attacked and a set of data cards was stolen. He claims *you* are responsible."

It had been said that Huido's head resembled two shiny black saucepans mounted one above the other. If so, they might well have been clattering together in that moment, so affronted by this accusation was the Carasian. "I did no such thing!"

The officers cast nervous glances at each other while Huido went on, at great length, to deny any involvement, most vociferously.

"Brody admits he didn't actually see you," O'Connell said when the Carasian paused.

"I'm glad to hear it," Huido said, calming a little.

"And yet he is adamant you were the assailant," said the younger constable.

His elder glared at him, then returned his focus to Huido. "Was there anyone else in the restaurant while Brody was here?"

"Hardly anyone. Brody came in late, and it was a quiet night. My waiting staff were here, of course, the chef, and a couple of Retian priests—I'm afraid I can't identify them for you. They don't give names."

"Well, then it seems we're done here for the moment. Let us handle this, Hom Huido. We'll look into who else could have been responsible."

They thanked Huido for talking to them and retreated toward the door. For the moment, at least, they seemed satisfied with

Huido's denials. But the younger one said, "We might need to speak to you again," before Huido closed the door.

The Carasian paced back to the bar area, poured a beer into his claw, and lifted the claw to his mouth. Beer was Human food. He pondered why he'd chosen it at that particular moment. Partly it was because he liked it, and partly because this was exactly the kind of muddle Humans were forever getting themselves into.

He knew he should leave the whole thing alone. The accusation made by Brody had no grounds whatsoever, but it grated on Huido that his good Carasian name should be impugned in this manner. He considered the Retians, the only other customers in the restaurant while Brody was waving the data card around, quietly eating their meal, drawing no attention to themselves. Had they concealed their ident because they were up to no good?

Perhaps he might make a few inquiries.

It would not be inaccurate to say there was a great deal of corruption in the grunt-level workings of Plexis. Small payments eased one's way through any number of onstation processes, from climate controls to vermin inspections.

Karen Tanaka was an inconsequential Human in the lowest levels of air administration. All air usage while on the legendary Plexis Supermarket had to be bought and paid for, which meant Tanaka knew more about arrivals and departures on Plexis than anyone. Or at least had access to the data.

She smiled broadly as Huido approached. "My friend—what brings you to my lowly station?"

"I was just passing," he said loudly, and more quietly added, "I'm looking for some Retian priests."

She raised an eyebrow, settled down at her station, and keyed in his request. "Hmm, that's odd. We get a few Retians on Plexis now and then, but there are dozens of them here right now."

"Why would that be?"

She regarded him shrewdly. "To answer that would mean accessing data that is not strictly within my remit."

"I tell you what, my lovely Tanaka. Do this for me, and I will send you a large selection of Huido's finest dishes, sufficient to restock your freezer. How's that?"

She nodded. Her eyes shone, lit by hidden depths and distant stars. "Okay, but none of that Ormagal chowder, it's disgusting."

"Understood," he said, but he understood only that she did not have the palate to appreciate it.

She typed some more. "So it seems there is a wealthy artisan on Plexis, recently arrived, who has promised a substantial reward to anyone of any species who can cure him of his illness."

"And this relates to the Retians how?"

"They're here to . . . pray for him."

Huido knew a scam when he heard one. And an opportunity. "This 'artisan.' I need his name, species, symptoms, and where I can find him."

Before following up on the artisan and the Retians, Huido attended to another matter. He returned to the restaurant and called the chef into his office. The diminutive Whirtle had only worked at *Claws & Jaws* for a few station stops. It slumped down, blinking its three eyes repeatedly. Which could have meant any one of a number of things, but distressed agitation was a distinct possibility.

"A Human was here last night," Huido said. "He asked to speak to you."

One of the chef's tentacles floated up, and it scratched behind an ear opening. "He asked for me by name?"

"No, he just asked to speak to the chef. When I intervened, he claimed it was me he came to see. Hard to be sure with Humans, but I think he was improvising, and not very convincingly."

The chef continued scratching.

"So my question is, was the Human really looking for *you*? And I suggest you tell me the truth without any of the tiresome resistance I occasionally encounter from people sitting where you're sitting now."

"Was the Human's name Theo Brody?"

"Indeed, it was."

"Well, see, the thing is, Hom Huido, well, at one time I worked for him. But I came here to start over, to turn my life around. And I'm very grateful for your—"

"What was it you did for him, in your previous . . . situation?"

"Honestly?"

"Please."

"I stole things for him. But I don't do that now, nothing like that now, those days are behind me."

Huido considered for a moment, giving thought to all he knew of the chef, and all he might not. "Are you *good* at stealing things?"

"In those days?"

"We can start with that."

"Yeah, I was good at it, but I don't—"

"Oh, I'm sure you still could. To, just as an example, keep working in my kitchen."

The Whirtle's nostrils flared dramatically. "What is it you want from me, Hom Huido?"

The Carasian tipped forward. "First, I want someone less conspicuous than myself to follow some Retian priests."

With the beginnings of a plan forming in his mind, Huido made his way through Plexis' massive structure of concourses and levels to arrive at the pay-as-you-go on Level Five that currently served as accommodation for wealthy artisan Hypol Parr.

Parr's personal assistant, a demure humanoid female dressed in a white full-length hooded garment, greeted him, making only brief eye contact and saying no more than was necessary. "Do you have something to offer, Hom?" she inquired.

"I believe I might be able to help, Fem, if I could examine Hom Parr," Huido announced.

She gave a small nod and consulted an appointment diary, which shimmered in midair beside her. "There is a slot available shortly, if you are prepared to wait."

"Your client has other appointments?"

"Indeed, so. Hom Parr is currently being visited by a Tuli spiritual healer, and later there's a prayer session scheduled with Retian priests."

Huido spread his great claws. "With so many cures being offered, how will you know which succeeds and who should receive the reward?"

"We will make a determination based on the evidence," she replied firmly. "Our judgment will be final and binding."

Huido agreed to the terms. While he waited, he sent a message to his Whirtle chef advising him of the Retians' schedule, and after a short wait was brought into the presence of Hom Parr. The artisan turned out to be an Atatatay, a species that matured by fusing individuals. By Parr's small, uncomplicated stature, sers had a long way to grow.

Beyond that observation, Huido had little understanding of sers or any alien's physiology, but made a good show of pressing down on things, listening to other things, and inspecting various lumps.

In truth, Huido had no idea how to help. Parr's symptoms amounted to severe unending fatigue. He suspected the Retians believed a placebo cure was as likely to work as any more tangible remedy, and were opportunistically attempting to take credit for any recovery sers might happen to enjoy. Well, it was worth a shot.

After the examination, he spoke again to the assistant. "I'm convinced an ingested remedy is required. *Strevet*. It is generally administered as a broth or chowder but is very rare." He paused meaningfully. "I happen to have a supply. I will have some sent over later today."

"Very well. Good day to you, Hom Huido."

"You've got some kind of nerve inviting me back here," Brody said. Nevertheless, he was sitting opposite Huido in the *Claws & Jaws*.

A waiter delivered a small dish of Stonerim olives to the table, and withdrew from earshot.

"The thing is, Hom Brody, I believe I know where your stolen data is. For a price, I can recover it."

"What kind of swindle is this? You're telling me you didn't steal my data, but miraculously you know where it is? I've heard it all now!"

"Regardless of the likelihood, it is the truth. And I'm guessing you had more than the recipe for stew for sale. In fact, the officers who came here said something about 'a set' of data cards that were stolen. Plural. So I'm thinking an entrepreneur such as yourself doubtless had numerous offers to make to various individuals."

Huido sat patiently while the Human appeared flustered. Eventually he calmed, giving the Carasian a sour look. "How much?"

Huido pushed a slip of plas across the table. "My price is not negotiable."

Brody turned the plas over, made a choking sound, but then nodded his agreement. They sat in uncomfortable silence for a few moments. Brody stabbed an olive with a pick but didn't eat it.

"I'll contact you when I've recovered the data," Huido said.

Brody stood up abruptly, scowled at a table of shocked diners as he passed them, and careered toward the exit doors.

"You were right to leave Brody out of this part, Hom Huido. He's no good in a fight."

"I thought as much," Huido said, looking down at the Whirtle who, despite its compactness—and the retiring nature of its kind, "run first" being a Whirtle axiom—looked like it might stand up for itself if necessary. It'd already proven surprisingly adept at following Retians. Right back here, to their base of operations, a storefront with an "opening soon" sign tilted forlornly beside the door. The windows were covered in opaque plas. Someone hadn't paid their taxes.

The chef stowed a small set of trinoculars back in a satchel slung around its wide neck. "As far as I can tell, they only use the main entrance. If we go via the service access, we might not encounter any resistance, at least to begin with. I don't think they're armed, but couldn't we bring more with us?" Caution was a Whirtle virtue.

"I'm not a team player," Huido said, giving a little shake to rattle the weaponry now attached by hooks to his carapace. He added thoughtfully, "Unless it's a team of one."

"So where do I fit in, Hom Huido? If the Retians do put up a fight . . ."

"They won't, and you've already been helpful. Finding this place was our first step. I know Retians. A group of unarmed priests

won't give me any trouble. Just follow me and don't get in my way."
Eyestalks bent. "I might need you to open a safe or something."

The Whirtle flexed its tentacles in anticipation. "Ready, Hom."

This wasn't a high-end level; the service corridor behind the store-fronts was narrow. The Carasian had to go sideways in order not to cause weaponsfire he'd have to explain later. Servos clicked and clanked, as usual, but the corridor itself seemed to twist and turn in unnatural ways, and soon they were disoriented.

"What is this?" Huido complained, unsure where they were. How far had they gone?

"Old trick," his chef said. "Maze-ware. There's tech here, messing with our perceptions. It's a cheap way to secure a perimeter if you don't have enough guards." The Whirtle regarded Huido. "Or the right kind of guards."

"Can you turn it off?"

The chef was already reaching into its satchel. It took out something resembling a mechanical spider and set the device loose. It scuttled off. "Give it a few minutes, Hom."

"How did you even get that onto Plexis?" Huido asked, feeling a mix of admiration and disquiet.

"I never expected to use it," the Whirtle said, not really answering the question.

After a few minutes, whatever had been scrambling their sense of direction was disabled and the spider came scurrying back. The chef gathered it up, and they continued to the access door.

It wasn't locked. Huido opened the door a fraction and saw a single Retian, in priest robes, pacing forward and back through the open space he needed to cross. He waited until the being had his back to him, then burst through the door. The priest turned and, almost in slow motion, the loose skin of his Retian face twisted into an expression of terror, a reasonable response to seeing an oncoming Carasian, claws snapping in the air.

Huido grabbed him by the collar, while the Retian's webbed hands flailed uselessly. "Don't make a sound," he commanded. "We're going after the rest. Nod your head if you understand me."

The Retian nodded silently.

The priests barely knew what hit them as Huido stormed into the empty store. The few who tried to confront him were easily cowed by his thunderous presence, and soon they all had their hands raised in surrender. They stood helplessly as he circled the room, observing countertops covered in the stolen loot.

"Looks like they've been very busy collecting this lot," Huido said.

He stood over one of the priests and demanded, "Is this everything?" The Retian looked anxiously over his shoulder and pointed to a backroom. The chef soon had that door unlocked, revealing hundreds more data cards and circuit boards in their possession.

Huido instructed the Whirtle to collect any data cards that looked like the one Brody had shown him. The rest he left with the Retians. The Carasian then melted the lock on the entrance, trapping them all inside.

Once safely away from the scene, an anonymous call to Plexis Security led—in a while, it being breaktime—to the priests' mass arrest.

The same two officers from Plexis Security arrived at Huido's door the next morning.

"This is purely a courtesy call, Hom Huido," Officer O'Connell said, "to inform you that we no longer consider you a suspect in the matter of Theodore Brody's stolen data cards. Arrests have been made."

"Oh? Can I offer you a drink, officers? And might I ask who was responsible?"

They declined the drinks. The younger one looked regretful in doing so.

"Retian priests," O'Connell said. "They came to Plexis on the pretense of helping an artisan by the name of Hypol Parr. Once onstation, they appear to have embarked on an extensive crime spree. We've recovered a great many stolen data cards and other tech."

"What did they want the data for?"

"Oh, they weren't after the data; they just wanted the tech."

Ret 7 being, at best, soggy, and no fit place for technology or Carasians. Huido shuddered noisily. "Ah, I see. Well, I am glad Hom Brody got his data back."

O'Connell grinned, but without any warmth. "Not the case, I'm afraid. If Brody's data is in among the haul somewhere, I doubt it'll be found before the tech is resold to cover costs. The Retians neglected to pay rent." Plexis had priorities.

The Carasian snapped a claw in summons. His assistant, Ansel, came hurrying forward, a bottle of Brillian brandy in his hands. Huido gestured for him to give it to O'Connell. "A parting gift, Constable. To show there are no hard feelings."

O'Connell hesitated, then took the bottle. "I'll enjoy it when I'm off-duty."

Huido showed them to the door. "You must dine here sometime," he called after them. "And tell your friends about us."

Huido rumbled into the kitchen to visit with his chef later that day. "A fine outcome," he announced cheerfully.

The Whirtle blinked. "If I may ask, Hom Huido? What did Brody have to pay for his data?"

Huido recalled, with a great deal of satisfaction, handing the bag of data cards to Brody and telling him that his key would undoubtedly decrypt one of them. It had taken the Human several hours to find it, all spent under the Carasian's staring eyestalks. Amazing how much a Human could sweat.

"It was a fair trade," Huido said. "I asked for three things. A significant sum of money, the recipe for Pashwali's Ocean Stinger stew, and a promise that he would never again try to contact my chef."

The Whirtle's trio of eyes widened in surprise. "You'd do that for me?"

"It seems I have."

The chef stood quietly for a long moment. Then at last he said, "Thank you, Hom Huido."

Huido passed a large sheet of plas to his chef. "Let's see if this recipe is worth all the trouble."

"Coming right up, boss . . ." The Whirtle studied the recipe. "In a few days."

The Retians were in a great hurry to leave Plexis, and permitted to do so. Naturally, without the recovered tech, which had been confiscated by station authority. Plexis would deal with the haul as it saw fit, and no one could or would dispute it.

According to Karen Tanaka, just before leaving, the Retians incurred a further penalty. Their bill for air shared while onstation had mysteriously tripled. They were advised that while their representatives were welcome to challenge this, it would require someone to remain on Plexis, which would inevitably increase their total consumption, with the certain outcome that their bill would increase further.

They were wailing with anguish as they departed. Huido occasionally thought of this, and invariably startled those around him with a booming laugh.

The Atatatay artisan, Hypol Parr, enjoyed a remarkable recovery, fleeting fame, then relocated to Ormagal 17. Huido speculated that he might have been in league with the Retians all along. But this was never proved.

The substantial payment from Theodore G. Brody cleared Huido's debts at a stroke, though Ansel took great care to ensure the transaction was untraceable. Better safe than sorry.

As for Pashwali's Ocean Stinger stew, it was as delicious as Huido remembered, and became a permanent fixture on the à la carte menu. And for many years to come, a great many patrons who stumbled across his restaurant on Plexis were heard to agree with its proprietor, that *Claws & Jaws* served the finest food in the quadrant.

... *Truffles* continues

12

* * *

*T*HE EXALTED GODDESS *Tearoom* was, despite its name, a claustrophobic shop snugged close to the side of the *Claws & Jaws*. Bins of dried wisps of plant material lined the walls, each labeled not in Comspeak, but a script I didn't recognize. The lettering was exotic, not least because it appeared hand done, and I wondered if customers bought what was in the bins more for the art than the contents.

Not a question to ask at the moment. I did my best not to elbow the shelves, squeezed beside Morgan in front of the counter. Behind it, an aged humanoid of indeterminate species—alien wrinkles continued to baffle me—waved hands in dismissal. "Bu-sy time. No soc-ials."

I resisted the temptation to look over my shoulder at the empty space behind us.

My Human bent his fingers, using them to hook his hands together as he bowed. "We need to speak, Ruggio."

"If not buy-ing tea, Ja-son, don't clog my floor." A dry spit to the side.

Rather than be offended, Morgan chuckled and bowed again, lower. "A joy to see you, too, old friend."

"Bah." The wrinkles reformed into what I took for a smile. "This the Si-ra?"

"Hello." Copying Morgan's gesture, I bowed.

Wrinkles collided. "You stu-pid? He bow. You too old. You jig-gy." The little being vigorously bobbed its head up and down, then moved its shoulders, revealing extra joints beneath the frilly shawl. "Jig-gy!"

"I couldn't possibly," I said truthfully.

Ruggio stopped its performance to give me a long suspicious look. Suddenly, another wrinkly smile. "Smart Si-ra! So what's this need to speak, Ja-son?"

Morgan leaned on the counter and told our tale of truffles.

It was after we were once more outside, a package of overpriced tea now tucked under my arm, that I stood firm and looked at my Chosen with my own suspicion. "What's the point of all this?"

"Folks need to know."

"Then why not use coms? Why—" I held out the package, with its lettering that looked disturbingly like the "Yummy-Yums" of my previous encounter.

Morgan's lips quirked. "Coms don't get it done, Witchling."

"Get what done?" I kept my voice down with an effort. We weren't alone here—a steady line of beings were heading for where we should be, the *Claws & Jaws,* so temptingly close.

"One last stop, I promise."

You could tell me, I sent impatiently.

Instead of the teasing grin I expected, his face turned serious, the blue of his eyes darkening with intensity. "This is how Plexis works. The real Plexis. You put out the word. If others think it matters, they do the same. What happens after that?" An expressive shrug. "I've no idea."

I'd learned about gambling, this past year. I'd also learned about him. "You're betting it's something to help us." In disbelief, I waved the package of tea at the bustling multi-species horde of shoppers around us. "You believe in them."

Something vulnerable touched his face, quickly controlled. "I believe we'd better make our last stop before a certain Carasian gets wind of what we're up to from someone else." *Are you with me?*

Always, I replied, whatever I thought of his plan. A lock of hair brushed the back of his hand. Aloud. "Where next, Captain?"

"Captain Morgan."

His face assumed that pleasant, yet unreadable expression as we both turned. "Constable."

Plexis Security, when we didn't need help or a delay. I found myself facing an older Human. The constable wore authority like someone else would wear a comfortable coat. Her keen gaze recorded everything about me before locking on Morgan. "Word's out you've an issue with your cargo."

I tensed.

"Officer E'Teiso has an issue," he corrected. "Thought you'd be taking it easy today."

She scowled. "And let scum like you walk around loose?"

Morgan grinned. "Glad to know you still care, Hutton."

"Huh."

Humans. Sorely perplexed, I looked from one to the other as Morgan held out his hand and the constable took it in a firm, brief grip.

"Say hi to the big guy for me." She walked away into the crowd.

"What was that about?"

"That," Morgan said, as if it were all the explanation necessary, "was Plexis, too."

The End of Days

✷ ✶ ✷

by Tanya Huff

ELAINE HUTTON RAN both hands back through her short, graying hair and squared her shoulders. Two station days, she told herself as she entered the Plexis Security offices. Two station days and you're out. You can handle anything for two station . . .

"Hutton! Got a going away present for you!"

. . . days. She narrowed her eyes as Marion Burr, the C-shift supervisor crossed the room toward her. She didn't trust the smile on the other's pale face. Hardly surprising. As a whole, she trusted Burr as far as she could spit a Retian. By the other wall, Jurz, Burr's shift second, hooted softly, his crest rising. Elaine braced herself. If the Tolian was amused, it wouldn't be good.

"It's something you've always wanted." Dimples dug deep into both cheeks, Burr waved at the kid sitting behind one of the shared desks, frowning at the screen, the long, slim fingers of one hand buried in thick dark hair.

At first glance, Elaine thought he could be one of the kids she kept an eye on. Unaffiliated to any of the gangs, they scratched out a mostly legal living, and she helped when she could to keep it that way. Then she realized this kid wore a Plexis Security uniform just like hers. Well, just like hers had been a long time ago—shiny and new and unstained with cynicism.

"We got you a rookie!"

"Did you keep the receipt?"

"I've always loved your sense of humor."

Elaine returned the edge in Burr's smile with a flat, unfriendly stare. "I'm in this uniform for two days. Heading back to Imesh 27 in three."

"For reasons which remain unclear to me."

"I was born on dirt, I'll die on dirt. Put him with someone who cares."

The edge of Burr's smile sharpened. "You care, Hutton. That's your thing, isn't it? Chambal!"

The kid stood, all long limbs and youthful grace, and hurried toward them. Older than Elaine had assumed, but not by much.

"Constable Elaine Hutton, this is Constable Geoffrey Chambal. His mother . . ."

"Is Navreet Chambal. She owns *Adornment* on Upper Retail Level 104, spinward ¾." *Adornment* sold the kind of jewelry Elaine would never be able to afford. Or want, for that matter. In her experience, that kind of wealth was a target—although she realized that after a lifetime in security, her experience might not be the norm. The kid looked apprehensive—no surprise—and Burr looked far too pleased with herself for Elaine to attempt to change her mind.

"What did you do, kid?" she asked as they made their way down to sublevel 384.

"Do?"

"To get put with me."

Chambal waited until three Whirtles passed on a rising ramp, each turning so their airtags were visible to the two security officers, then said, "I asked to be put with you."

"Were you high?"

He rolled dark eyes. "Three years ago, one of my fathers brought some undeclared gemstones onto the station for my mother's shop. He got past the Port Authority, but you caught him on the concourse. You told him no one looks that innocent unless they have something to hide. When he tried to bribe you with one of the gems, you refused."

"It was one of the smaller gems," Elaine pointed out.

The rookie gave her a look of such intense sincerity, she barely managed to keep from smacking the back of his head. He'd lose his idealism soon enough, no point helping it out the air lock. "I checked," he said. "You've never taken a bribe. Not so much as a free coffee."

"And that's why I'm still a constable, two station days from retirement."

"You have integrity."

She snorted. "I'm a joke."

"I don't think so."

It might have started as integrity, but it was habit at this point. Elaine Hutton was the constable who didn't take bribes—it gave her an identity among the masses of shoppers and staff seething through Plexis. It also kept her from the upper levels. Not because those on the lower levels were less likely to offer a bribe, but because, with few exceptions, their bribes were of the sort station security didn't mind missing. The occasional case of brandy from The *Claws & Jaws* couldn't really be counted as an exception given that Inspector Wallace took personal advantage of the Carasian's reluctant generosity.

"Your parents approve of your job choice?" she wondered, scanning the approaching level for familiar faces.

Chambal shrugged. "My parents are part of a line marriage. I have three blood siblings and seventeen line siblings."

"They're happy you're out of the house?"

"Something like that." He smiled, his teeth very white and very straight and very indicative of a comfortable childhood. "I didn't want to be StaSec, I wanted to be an enforcer."

Elaine nodded a greeting at a passing merchant before asking, "We're second best?"

"Third. The Trade Pact wouldn't take me either."

When she laughed, he blushed. "I wanted to be an enforcer, too," she told him. "Failed the psych."

"Too ethical?"

"I can't remember." She shrugged and stepped off the ramp onto the crowded concourse. It had been devastating when it happened, but . . . "Time passed."

"They said I was too soft." Chambal's resentment remained evident. "Said I should try again after a little seasoning."

"Not bad advice." And she bet his mother was happy he'd remained on Plexis where she could intervene in that seasoning if necessary.

"Why would dispatch call us to deal with a stopped cart?" Chambal followed her into the service corridor.

"We're not dealing with the stopped cart, we're dealing with what stopped it." Elaine squinted down the corridor snaking off into station distance and pointed at the line of stationary carts, quivering with the need to fulfill their programming. "There. Don't touch the waste canisters," she added, jogging forward. "A few of them are overly enthusiastic about protein recycling."

"You're kidding."

"I could be." She spotted two carts approaching from the other direction, about to add to the jam, and sped up. The carts were muttering to themselves when she stopped beside them, knelt, and checked for a pulse even though it was obvious he was dead and had been for a while. "You might have mentioned the body," she snarled into her wrist com, then broke the signal before dispatch could answer.

The young Human male in worn spacer overalls and equally worn boots had the pale, almost translucent skin of those who seldom saw light from an actual sun.

Chambal swallowed audibly. "What killed him?"

"No idea." No blood. No burns. No breaks in his physical integrity. No visible damage of any kind except the pale pink mark on his cheek where his airtag had been. Which raised the question: Where was his airtag now? Elaine ran her hand over the area, a couple of millimeters off the floor, fairly certain the tag would find her if she couldn't find it. Nothing. She reached into the dark, narrow space under a waste canister. Her fingertips touched fur.

"What is it?" Chambal asked as she pulled the small animal free.

He wouldn't know; he'd lived his entire life on Plexis. "It's a cat. A revenant—a biological rebuild from history, in this case ours. Like the dragons on some inner systems." Very few species had accompanied Humanity from its long-lost home. Dogs. Chickens. Head lice. At least what now passed for those species. Who knew for sure—or cared?

A small, but full-grown tortoiseshell, the cat snuggled up against Elaine's tunic and began to purr after a short protest over the boorish handling. "A pet. Dead kid must've smuggled her on."

"Must have?"

"We have a dead body and an illegal animal. Nine times out of ten, one and one makes two."

"Okay. But he's not a kid, he's got to be my age at least."

"Your point?"

She could almost hear Chambal's eyeroll. "How did he smuggle in a live animal?"

"Possibly as food. Or he brought her in for someone with enough pull to blind the Port Authority."

Chambal reached down tentatively and stroked between the cat's ears. "How do you know it's a her?"

"Coloring." They were too close to the *Claws & Jaws* receiving area. Legalities concerning the introduction of new life-forms to Plexis aside, Elaine couldn't leave the cat here, she'd end up as an entrée. To her surprise, as she stood, the cat clawed up her uniform and perched on her shoulders. When she stepped away from the body, the soft, warm weight across the back of her neck shifted, easily adjusting to the movement.

The closest cart bumped against her hip, one, two, three times.

"Do that again," she snapped, "and I'll pull your delivery license."

It gave a high-pitched whir and reversed so quickly it cracked against the next cart in line.

"Record the scene," she told Chambal, ignoring the escalating mechanical argument. "When you think you have enough details, double it. I'll call in a servo and, when you're done, we'll take the body to the morgue."

Chambal paused, right hand on his wrist com, dark brows rising. "There's a morgue?"

"There is. Gets used less often than you'd think." Elaine reached up and stroked the cat. "It's not actually that hard to get rid of a body on Plexis."

"It isn't?"

"What did I tell you about touching the waste canisters?"

Expression carefully neutral, Elaine watched Inspector Wallace circle the body on the table. While able to admit the head of security was both stubborn and shrewd—character traits she usually appreciated—she neither liked nor respected the official. He was pompous, self-serving, and secretive, and she couldn't help but compare him to his predecessor, Inspector Duran. Wallace's opposite in almost every way that mattered, the Auordian had been cleaning house when an unfortunate accident in a temporarily unmonitored section of the waste stream had cut her career short. They hadn't retrieved enough of the body to determine cause of death.

"One more dead spacer down on his luck," Wallace sneered, paused at the end of the table, and stared up the length of the body. "Probably thought he was here to make his fortune. Seen one, seen them all. Right, Constable Hutton?"

"Sir."

"He reminds you of those delinquents you persist in making excuses for, doesn't it? They'll end up the same way, mark my words. As for this one . . . if no one claims the body in two station days, recycle it."

Chambal took a step forward. "We're not going to find out who killed him?"

"No, we're not going to find out *who* killed him, Constable Chambal. We don't know *what* killed him." The inspector waved a hand. "No blaster holes, no knife holes, no blunt force trauma. Eyes are clear, no burst capillaries, so he wasn't smothered. No swollen membranes . . ."

"It could still be poison," Chambal interrupted. "Or drugs."

Wallace nodded. "It could be drugs. But why would we care about self-inflicted wounds? Are we even certain he was killed?" the inspector continued without waiting for a response. "He could've just dropped dead. People do that." Thin lips curled into a disingenuous smile. "His death hasn't disrupted the smooth running of the station or the lives of the shoppers. There's nothing on the security recordings . . ."

"And you don't find that suspicious?"

Elaine hid a sigh as the inspector raised a brow at the accusatory tone. Upper level entitlement was going to get the kid's ass kicked.

It seemed Chambal had realized that as well. He took a step back and added a conciliatory, "Sir."

Wallace flicked his gaze over to Elaine, then back to Chambal. "I find that leaves us with no suspects. And nothing to open an investigation with."

"Except a dead body," Elaine reminded him.

A muscle jumped in his jaw. "Except that."

"Should we find out who he is, sir?" Chambal laid the obsequious on a little thick. All or nothing at his age.

"We'll find out if he's reported missing or if someone comes to claim the body," Wallace said dismissively. "Get back to 384. Try not to get the rookie killed, Hutton." He pivoted on a heel and left.

"Is he always so . . . cold?" Chambal asked the moment the door closed.

"No." The inspector had always put self-interest first and, sad to say, dead spacers weren't rare, but that was overly disinterested in process even for the inspector. And why had he come to the morgue if all they had was another dead spacer down on his luck?

It was either unimportant enough to ignore.

Or important enough to bring Inspector Wallace to the morgue.

It couldn't be both.

He'd wanted to get a look at the body. He'd wanted to identify the body?

"You didn't tell him about the cat."

That cat was asleep in a duffle bag tucked into a shadowed corner. She'd eaten an astonishing amount of shrimp paste and shown no interest in the body on the table. Nothing suggested she was the corpse's cat. Or he was her Human. But she'd been there in the maintenance corridor beside the body, and Elaine didn't believe in coincidence.

"Constable Hutton? Are we going to find out who killed him?"

The dead kid's hands were soft. He had a pleasant, unassuming face. Straight, short brown hair, neither dark, nor light. No distinguishing features at all.

Except . . .

He had dirt under his fingernails.

She took a deep breath and let it out slowly. "Yes. We're going to find out who killed him."

"Even though the inspector . . ."

"Inspector Wallace expressed his opinion on the body. He ordered us back to 384. He did not, at any point, instruct us to not investigate the death."

Chambal smiled wide and white.

"That said, it might be better if you walked away." Something or someone powerful enough to bring the inspector to the morgue would be powerful enough to put Geoffrey Chambal on a table of his own. Just another cocky kid in a uniform not smart enough to back down. Elaine could take care of herself, but she wouldn't be around to hold Chambal's hand for much longer.

He drew himself up to his full height and glared down at her. "I'm not going anywhere."

"Let's hope." He was an adult—however young an adult—armed and in uniform. She had to either assume he could take care of himself or have the body on the table remain nothing more than meat with a face. "You see anything strange about this?"

"Besides no visible cause of death? No. Nothing. He's eminently forgettable."

"Isn't he just." Elaine bent to get a closer look at his single tattoo. The oval design on his left forearm was a familiar pattern; she'd seen hundreds over the last few years, inked into every age, gender, and species. At his age, a total absence of ink would have been notable, but attention slid past a design so popular.

"At least we know he's not Denebian."

Walking over to the bench that held the deceased's personal belongings, she made a noncommittal noise. Denebians covered themselves in tattoos, the ink a history, a warning, a celebration. "Watch the door. I don't want the attendants back in here until I'm done."

Another question. Why had Inspector Wallace dismissed the attendants as he walked into the morgue? Because two constables were witnesses he could control?

The overalls were worn but clean. She sniffed and frowned at the almost familiar scent.

His boots were a style five years old at least. Not that it was unusual for broke kids to wear secondhand clothing.

Even without an official investigation, the body would be scanned before recycling; Plexis preferred to know what went into the waste stream. Elaine lowered the diagnostic scanner and positioned it over the body. If it was going to happen anyway, she'd be breaking no rules and, more importantly, setting off no alerts.

Technically, security personnel didn't play with the tech in the morgue, but what were they going to do? Fire her? "No poison. No drugs. Not even recreational." The insides were as aggressively unremarkable as the outsides. Except . . . "Trace amounts of rodamine, but not even close to what would have killed . . ."

"Mmmrup?"

Elaine turned to see a black-and-orange head poke out of the duffle bag. "Come on, then."

Oozing out onto the floor, moving more like a liquid than a solid, the cat stretched both rear legs, crossed the room, jumped up onto the end of the table, and landed back onto Elaine's shoulder.

"Does she understand what you're saying?" Chambal asked, dark eyes wide.

"Not unless someone's messed with her intelligence levels." The variegated fur was soft and plush under Elaine's fingers. "And it wouldn't matter if they had. Cats do what they wa . . ."

"Is that . . . ?"

The tag had attached itself to the back of Elaine's hand. If asked, she'd have scoffed at the thought of a cluster of microorganisms looking disgruntled, but that was the best description of the waxy blue patch at the base of her knuckle.

"DoyouacceptresponsbilityfortheairyoushareonPlexis?" Barely waiting for an affirmative response, the Ordnex applied a tag to the Denebian's right cheek, obscuring most of her starburst tattoo. As she hurried to catch up to the rest of her crew, the Ordnex began to turn to the next in line.

Elaine cleared her throat. "Andohbay."

The Ordnex sighed and closed her station. "HowcanIhelpConstableHutton?" she droned, ignoring complaints from those waiting to be processed.

"Sorry to slow things down, Ando. I need the data off this tag."

"Thereareproceedures." Andohbay paused. Took a long look at Elaine's face. And sighed again. "Ihonorthememoryofmymaternal unit . . ."

"Thisisnotthemomentofdeath." One long, multi-jointed finger tapped the screen. "Thetagwasdisplaced."

"How? Best guess," Elaine added quickly.

"Electricshock. Bigonethough."

"HEY! I have places to be!"

Elaine turned slowly to face the big Human at the front of the line and locked her gaze on the florid face. "Please excuse the delay, Fem. This booth will reopen when we conclude a security investigation." Her tone made it clear what security would be investigating next should there be any further shouting. When she was certain the other understood—few of those who parked in the less than prime spaces on Plexis' belly wanted to attract security's interest—Elaine turned her attention back to Andohbay. "Electric shock strong enough to stop a Human heart?"

"Mybestguess—absolutely. Broadenoughbeamwouldthrowoff-electronicsintheareatoo."

"Thanks, Ando. *Haglen-durnon.*"

"Sure.Whatever." Andohbay waved it off. "Enjoyyourdirt. Andyourpronounciationstillsucks."

"Maternal unit?" Chambal asked as they walked away and the line began moving again.

"Old friend. Made the best *hurglon* you've ever tasted."

"I've never tasted hurglon."

"Your loss."

Sorge Nolan. The body had a name. Elaine studied the information they'd pulled from the tag point's database, while Constable Chambal gave directions to a lost shopper. He knew his way around, she'd give the kid that. "Ident card's a fake," she said as Chambal joined her. "A good one, but a fake."

He peered over her shoulder at the image on her wrist com. "How can you tell?"

"Experience."

"That's not . . ."

"Do you have any idea how many fake ident cards I've seen?"

"No, but . . ."

"Neither do I. This is fake." She slid her hand into the duffle and stroked the cat. The quality of the forgery didn't match the quality of the dead kid's clothing. Or lack of quality. "Looks like we're checking used clothing stores."

"All of them?"

A little too slow to avoid a playful claw, she pulled her hand out of the bag and rubbed the blood off her finger with her thumb. "If we have to."

Chambal tripped over a loose pile of shoes, righted himself, and twitched his tunic back into place, trying to look as though he'd meant to do that all along. "What are you doing?"

"Ever notice how used clothing has a particular scent?"

"No."

Of course he hadn't. Up on level 104 they didn't wear used clothing. "The cleaning chemicals linger." Pulling a heavy sweater from the overflowing bin, Elaine held the fabric under her nose and breathed in. Cleansers weren't necessarily unique to each establishment, but she'd recognize the almost familiar scent of the overalls should she smell it again.

"No, it wasn't him." Kir Whol, the proprietor of *Why Wear Worn*, commonly known among its more frequent customers as *W3*, waved a tentacle over the image on Elaine's wrist com. "Is he dead? He looks dead."

Elaine sighed. "Kir Whol, I'm out of here in less than two days. I don't have time to gossip."

"Fine. Was another Hom bought the overalls. Taller. Like him." He pointed past her at Chambal. "But older. More colorful."

More colorful could mean any number of things. Comspeak took interesting turns species to species. Following the old StaSec truism that the simplest answer was usually the right answer, Elaine asked, "Multiple tattoos?"

"Yes. Many."

Which raised the odds the Human they looked for was Denebian.

"Did you get a name?" Chambal asked.

Elaine and the Whirtle exchanged a look as identical as differing physiognomies allowed. "Can you remember anything unique about him?" she asked, both of them ignoring the kid's question.

Tentacle drumming on the counter, the Whirtle narrowed two of three eyes. "His scent was . . ."

Another tentacle touched the respirator he'd removed to hang around his neck as they talked. ". . . sweet. And sharp. Sweet-sharp."

"Pickles!" Chambal exclaimed, then flushed as he realized he may have been a bit overly emphatic.

Kir Whol nodded. "Yes. Like pickles, but sweet like fruit."

"Shouldn't we have searched the shop for the original clothing?"

"No."

"But . . ."

"The killer couldn't possibly have been stupid enough to sell the clothing he stripped off the body to the same shop where he bought the overalls and boots." Elaine sidestepped a hurrying shopper, set the duffle bag on the edge of a waist high planter and leaned back against it, feeling the warmth of the cat and the vibration of her purr even through layers of fabric. "Daniel!"

Chambal turned a confused expression her way. "What?"

"Who," she corrected, nodding across the concourse at a young Human male hurrying toward them, his heavy boots clumping against the floor.

"You bellowed, StaSec?" he asked sulkily as he arrived.

"Hey!"

Elaine cut Chambal's protest off. "Any chance you or yours were in the maintenance passages in behind *Claws & Jaws* last spin or so?"

His green eyes narrowed. "We had nothing to do with it."

"I know what caused the power outage, Daniel, I want to know if you saw anything unusual."

"Like?"

She raised her brows. Daniel used the maintenance passages as his personal shortcuts around the station and knew exactly what she meant by unusual.

A lock of shaggy dark hair fell into his face, but his hands remained in his pockets. "We haven't taken the backway for forty-eight. Rose got inventory in, so we've been burning."

"You're going to take his word for it?" Chambal loaded the pronoun with disdain.

"Daniel doesn't lie to me." She noted the flash of pleasure under the sullen exterior and added, "Keep your eyes and ears open."

"Why?" he muttered. "You'll be hitting dirt in another two."

"We talked about that."

"Whatever."

"I'm leaving you the contents of my quarters."

"What?" There were two spots of color high on his cheeks as he finally raised his head to meet her gaze.

"Everything that doesn't belong to the station, everything I can't fit into a carryall, is yours. You can keep it. You can sell it. Your choice."

Eyes wide, arms waving, he had to close his mouth before he could speak. "That's . . . nebular! That's totally stardust!" Then he frowned, remembered, and slumped back into his sullen posture. "You're still leaving."

"I'm still leaving. So will you someday."

"Yeah. Right." He spun on a heel, took two steps, paused, sighed, straightened, and turned again. "Hey, Hutt-hutt? Thanks. And, you know, have a life."

"You, too. Actually, wait, I need you to do something for me." She picked up the bag just as the cat climbed out of the planter and back into it, shaking dirt off one back foot. "Take this to my quarters."

Holding a handle in each hand, he stared down into amber eyes then up at her. "Can Jack visit? I mean, he'll fusion!"

"Sure." Jack was crazy about animals. The cat would be safer with him and Daniel than anywhere else on Plexis. "Make sure she has water. She likes shrimp paste. Don't let her out, and don't spread the word. This is important, Daniel. Don't tell Rose. Don't tell Warren. The cat witnessed a crime, and no one can know where she is."

He rolled his eyes. "Please."

"We have history," she explained to Chambal as Daniel left cradling the bag.

"I got that," he muttered, sounding remarkably like the younger Human. He perked up halfway across the concourse. "Are we going to *Claws & Jaws*? I've never been. My mother has a . . . thing."

"Sympathies to your mother, and no. We're going next door."

Chambal glanced at the hostel, then at the arched entryway to the Skenkran-operated cafeteria on the other side, then at Elaine. "You're joking."

"I don't have a sense of humor. The cafe's the only place on the station that sells pickled nicnic which . . ." She held up a hand to forestall an interruption. ". . . smells both sharp and sweet and tastes disgusting to everyone but a Skenkran."

"But we're looking for a Denebian."

"And there can't be more than one Denebian who eats enough pickled nicnic that the smell clings to him. We're lucky they're open. Must've paid their taxes this quarter." She led the way past the nearly empty tables to the service counter.

"There's no one here," Chambal pointed out, using his height to peer over the top of the displays.

"It's self-serve." Diners tapped their ident cards against the containers and took their chances.

He squinted up at the two flickering lamps above the counter. "These lights don't do the food any favors."

"It's not the lights. There." She pointed. "Pickled nicnic."

"That's edible?"

"That's what I've been told. Come on." She tapped her ident against a reader set into the surface of the counter. A piece about half a meter wide folded up out of the way. "There's an *office* in the back."

"Should I be worried about the way you said office?"

"Not if your shots are up to date."

The two Skenkrans working desultorily in the prep room barely glanced up as they passed. Security personnel were there often enough they could be ignored.

She'd seen the office in worse shape. Fresh "mud" had been packed against the walls, leaving the center of the room clear. "Flir."

"Constable Hutton." Flir raised both arms, the fold of gliding skin flapping. "My old friend. You've made a trip to our *wesong* for nothing. Our taxes have been paid."

"I'm not here to close you down. I need to know where I can find a male Denebian who eats pickled nicnic."

Translucent membranes slid across Flir's eyes. "That's . . . unusual."

Elaine shrugged, the motion aggressively nonaggressive. "Easier to remember him, then."

"Unlike people who desire an audience while they eat . . ." Flir tossed their head in the general direction of the *Claws & Jaws.* ". . . . *my* customers are here for privacy."

"Your customers are here for cheap food and a near-death adrenaline rush. I'd rather not check your stasis chambers, but I will if I have to."

"I've heard you have a ship to catch."

"Won't take long to get a StaSec team down here." She raised her wristcom.

"Keevor's . . ." Chambal stared wide-eyed at the entrance to the *Every Kind Friendly Eatery.* "I've heard about this place."

"As StaSec, you'll hear about it a lot more. And learn to call it the *Swill and Heave.* Try to not to look so . . . young," Elaine added, pulling open the door.

The smell hit her first. As her eyes adjusted to the dim light, she spotted three Lemmicks in one of the booths, the prevailing odor of Keevor's masking their scent.

"I always thought Lemmicks were kind of pleasant and inoffensive. You know, except for . . ." He rubbed his nose.

"There's a top and a bottom to every species, kid. This is where most of them hit bottom." She made her way toward the bar, ignoring the resentful silence.

"What do you think you're doing, Jelly?"

She turned in time to pull Chambal to her side as the big Human rose to his feet and swayed belligerently in place. Fingers wrapped around Chambal's wrist, she kept the rookie's hand away from his weapon. "Do you have any idea of the paperwork you have to fill out if you fire that thing? Even in here?"

"Your baby Jelly bumped into me, Hutton."

"Don't care, Murray. Sit down."

Mouth open, bellowing inarticulately, Murray dove forward.

Elaine shoved Chambal out of the line of attack with one hand and punched Murray in the throat with the other. When he went down, she kicked him in the stomach. Twice. As half a dozen others surged to their feet yelling abuse, she snarled, "Are you stupid? You want to fight, you wait until I'm gone."

Multiple forms of respiration sounded loud in the sudden, reclaimed silence.

Chairs and other seating arrangements scraped against the floor as the fighters sat and picked up their drinks.

"You okay, Murray?" When he grunted an affirmative, she continued to the bar, Chambal hurrying to keep up. "Sal."

The bartender polished a glass. "Constable Hutton."

"I'm looking for muscle going by Dillon Bryant."

Sal nodded her fluorescent pink head toward the door. "That's Bryant trying to run."

Bryant turned at the sound of his name and pulled a weapon, although Elaine couldn't identify the type. Before he could pull the trigger, Chambal picked up an empty beer stein and threw it, hitting Bryant's forehead with a meaty thud. Bryant's shot went wild and half the lights in the back of the bar went out.

"That's going on StaSec's tab," Sal said, cleaning another glass.

"Take it up with the inspector. Good arm, kid."

He blushed. "Cricket. Top bowler of the Retail League. I expected the mug to shatter."

"Keevor knows better than to stock the bar with breakables,"

Elaine told him as she slapped Bryant in restraints. "He'd never cover his overhead."

"Has he talked?"

"Good morning, Constable Hutton." Burr flashed dimples. "Excited that it's your last day before your dirty retirement?"

Maybe she'd drop by before leaving and punch that smarmy smile off Burr's face. "Has Bryant talked?"

"About what?"

"About the body."

Burr spread both hands in the universal gesture for *I have no idea what you're talking about, and I'm lying when I say that.* "He's in on a restricted weapons charge."

"He's wearing expensive clothing that doesn't quite fit him and, if we check, has probably been made to measure for the body in the morgue. A body likely killed with that restricted weapon he's carrying."

"I didn't know you cared so much about fashion."

Punching Burr was looking better and better. "I want to talk to Bryant."

"No one talks to him. Inspector Wallace's orders."

Punching Wallace had begun looking pretty good, too. What, or who, was powerful enough to keep Bryant from talking? She knew the type; he'd spill at the first opportunity to cut a deal. More importantly, what or who was powerful enough to to bring Inspector Wallace in on it?

It was a short list.

A very short list.

"One last day with your usual miscreants, then. Was there anything else, Constable Hutton? I'm sure I don't have to tell you how to spend your last day on the job."

Elaine headed for the door, caught Chambal's arm as he entered, and pulled him out with her. "You're still with me, kid."

"So we'll never know why he was killed?"

"At least we know who killed him." Elaine leaned back on the planter and watched a servo, packages swinging, maneuver delicately around a group of Turrned.

"Good thing the cat isn't with you."

"Why?"

Chambal grinned and looked even younger than usual. "You didn't know? She . . . uh . . . relieved herself in that planter yesterday. Dug a hole, buried it."

The body in the morgue had dirt under the nails.

"There's security drones on the concourses all the time," Chambal pointed out hurrying to keep up. "Why are the planters under fixed surveillance?"

"Because this is Plexis," Elaine told him. "Half the people here will steal live vegetation, half will eat it, and half will try to have sex with it."

"That's three halves."

"I can do the math, kid."

The security footage was available to anyone with enough clearance, and Elaine's code was still in the system—although she wouldn't have put it past Burr have removed it early just to be an ass.

"That's a lot of data," Chambal muttered, pulling the screen closer.

"Yes, it is." At least they had a rough time frame. And Bryant wouldn't have traveled far from 384.

"There's a lot of planters," Chambal sighed a couple of hours later.

"Yes, there are."

He searched in silence for a while, then sighed again. "This is boring."

"Not everyone finds a body their first day on the job." As far as Elaine was concerned, combing images beat being pleasant to shoppers. "There. That's the kid in the morgue." If they hadn't been concentrating on the planters, she'd have never noticed him. No one was that nondescript by accident.

"Right, then!" Chambal was already at the door when Elaine called him back. "What?"

"I think we should check recent arrivals before we head out," she told him, entering the codes for the first class lounge.

It was late when they arrived at the luxury hotel on Upper Level 22 spinward ¾. She'd considered leaving Chambal behind, but he'd been there from the beginning, so he needed to be there at the end. The hotel had its own security, but even out of uniform, her ident card got her as far as the door of the suite where a large, Denebian fem dressed in a suit tailored to minimize impressive musculature, blocked the way. The suit a virtual sign saying bodyguard.

Elaine opened the duffle bag. "Please inform Raymon Clear that we have something of his."

The bodyguard looked down at the cat, then held out her hands. "I'll see that she's delivered."

As she'd anticipated this, Elaine released the bag and, ignoring Chambal shifting in place, said, "I'd like to deliver the other piece in person. It's too small and delicate to go by way of a third person."

The tattoo of birds in flight replacing the bodyguard's left eyebrow rose.

Now *that* is a flat, unfriendly stare, Elaine thought as the other examined her face.

"I'll let him know," she snarled at last and disappeared into the suite.

The floor absorbed the sound of Chambal tapping the toe of his boot. "Now what?"

"Now we wait."

"We wait?"

"Get used to it, kid. It comes with the uniform."

"We're not in uniform. And stop calling me kid. Could you have taken her?" he asked after a moment.

"Who?"

"You know." He nodded toward the door.

"She's twice my size and likely knows more dirty tricks than I've ever heard of."

"So no?"

"Maybe."

The door of the suite opened into a large reception room with lush carpeting, low, plush furniture, and, to the left, a wall of windows overlooking an unfamiliar city. A bird, or possibly a lizard, flew past.

Plexis had no viewports, ensuring privacy for those coming and going from her docks, but even knowing it was fake, the view was magnificent and Elaine had to stop herself from stepping toward it.

Raymon Clear stood by an inner door, cradling the cat against a tunic that had probably cost more than Elaine's entire wardrobe. He looked younger than Elaine knew he was.

"You have something of mine, Constable Hutton?"

Elaine held out her hand, the data disk on her palm.

He nodded at the bodyguard who took the disk and slid it into her wrist comp. "First level access only," she announced after a moment. "There's been no attempt to breach the firewalls."

"We went only far enough to identify the owner," Elaine added.

Clear raised a brow. "Why didn't you turn the disk in to the authorities, Constable?"

"Does it contain criminal data, Hom?"

"Of course not."

"Then why would I? Particularly when I already had something of yours to return."

He stroked the cat. "Ah, yes. And you found the . . ."

Elaine didn't know the word. It sounded nasty, and as though it had a short shelf life.

". . . who killed my messenger."

Not only a messenger. Not from the grief in his voice. "I regret to inform you, the body is no longer in the morgue."

Clear nodded. "I'm aware." He stepped away and the door behind him opened. Dressed in rich Denebian clothing, exposed skin as tattooed as any of his people, the dead kid lay on a bier draped in glistening silks. Elaine glanced up at the fixtures and the UV lights they now contained. Offered enough credits, hotels were willing to redecorate.

"Why . . ." Chambal began.

Elaine cut him off with an applied elbow. Sometimes those with enough credits, like a high ranking member of the Blues—one of the two ruling Denebian syndicates—needed their messengers to be unrecognizable. Everyone knew Denebians had multiple tattoos.

Clear's smile was enigmatic as he waved the door closed. "Our organization is in your debt, Constable Hutton, both for your actions regarding our messenger and the return of our property. We dislike debt, it complicates things. So . . ." He stroked the cat again. Her tail smacked against his side. ". . . how can we discharge it?"

She'd never taken a bribe. Not a case of brandy, not a free wrist com, not a large enough payout from the Grays—the Blues competition—to make the dead messenger disappear. Not so much as a cup of coffee. "I'd like the cat."

Chambal sucked in a disbelieving breath. By the time he finished coughing, the cat was back in Elaine's duffle bag.

Clear's second smile was triumphant. "So, it seems we've found the price of the incorruptible Constable Hutton."

"No. You've found the price of Elaine Hutton." She nodded toward the chrono on the wall. "I haven't been a constable for seventeen minutes."

"Are you sure about this dirt thing?" Chambal asked at the boarding gate.

"Born on it, will die on it," Elaine told him, shifting her grip on the duffle bag. "Besides, cats don't belong on a station."

"I guess." He shifted in place, looked like he might be going in for a hug, until Elaine glared that thought off, and finally said, "So, any last words of advice?"

She'd told him who to keep an eye on—both those who might need his help and those most likely to be up to no good. She'd given him a list of her most useful contacts. She'd left him with information on Inspector Wallace to use as he saw fit. She'd brought him to the attention of someone high in a criminal syndicate although, as yet, there was no way of knowing if that was a good thing. Not bad for just under two station days. As he seemed to be waiting for words of wisdom, she said, "Not doing a thing can be as powerful as doing a thing."

"That's not . . ."

"Also, don't eat at the Skenkran café."

"I know that." He rolled his eyes. "*Everyone* knows that."

Everyone didn't. She smiled. "You'll do, Constable Chambal. You'll do."

...*Truffles* continues

13

✳✳✳

THERE WERE THINGS about my new life I doubted I'd ever be able to explain to my sister, Rael, let alone Pella, whose conception of alien was an unfamiliar Human delivering an order to her estate. At least Rael had met the Drapsk. In fact, she and our cousin Barac were on Drapskii now—a wholly implausible circumstance.

Before Jason Morgan.

As was this. I watched a giant shelled being grasp my Human around the waist with a single claw, to raise him ceilingward in order to align dripping pointed fangs just so, and smiled indulgently at the pair. Not that I'd volunteer for a Carasian's intimate greeting, but through Morgan, I'd learned what it signified: trust and love, beyond any physical differences.

Though there'd be the usual bruises on my poor Human's ribs.

"Enough!" Morgan hammered on Huido's head carapace. "Put me down, you big oaf."

"Your grist is excellent," the creature observed as he complied. Several eyestalks bent to aim their shiny black orbs at me. "As always, yours is peerless, Sira."

I'd yet to gain a clear idea what grist was to Huido, other than being related somehow to our Power and, in some peculiar manner, state of mind. Still, the compliment was sincere, and I smiled. "Thank you."

Coyly. "I take it your shell-mate has proven worthy in the pool?" Huido roared with laughter at my blush.

"Could we take this elsewhere?" Morgan asked mildly. We stood inside the entrance of the *Claws & Jaws,* those at nearby tables trying a little too hard not to pay attention.

Our final stop had been the Skenkran café, also a neighbor. To my surprise, it was open; the last time, it had been closed for violations of the Plexis food service safety code—a code lax enough to let Keevor's remain open, also related to the "shoppers beware" signage. The place appeared overripe for another closure, so I'd been mutely grateful Morgan simply gave his message to the first Skenkran we encountered.

Freeing us, at last, to come here. Home, even to me. Tension I hadn't noticed eased from my shoulders as Huido led us through his immaculate kitchen, with its wonderful blend of mostly appetizing aromas, to the corridor giving access to the living quarters.

Before he could take us to his private apartment, Morgan rapped a knuckle on the nearest claw. "Let's not bother your wives."

I heartily agreed. Giving Huido bad news wasn't something I'd want to do within snatching distance of the predatory side of the family.

Eyestalks bent to stare at Morgan.

"We haven't eaten yet," I volunteered helpfully. On cue, my stomach rumbled.

"Of course you haven't! Come." Huido turned in place, raising a smaller handling claw to urge us toward the smaller dining area, framed by privacy field and plants. "I've a new menu."

I hoped it didn't include truffles.

"Forget Esaliz." Clawtips met with a dismissive *chink*. "Enjoy your meal."

They were on a first name basis? For a change, Morgan looked as confused as I felt. I lowered the glass I'd raised out of harm's way, having been ready to leap from the table as my Human broached the news of the truffles. "You know the officer?" he ventured cautiously.

Huido poured beer into a handling claw. "That gluttonous crust of a *crasnig* shows up any time I've truffles on the menu. Appalling manners." Smug. "One of my best customers. You wouldn't believe how many it can tuck into that maw—when not complaining about the price. Which, I keep telling it, will only go up as word spreads."

Morgan grimaced. "Explains why our cargo was the first hit with this new fee."

"Doesn't matter." Eyestalks parted to allow the claw, and beverage, access to a hidden mouth. The ensuing *slurp* was loud and satisfied. "As I said, brother, forget about Esaliz."

"I don't see how." Morgan put down his glass. "Unless you can pay—" he let his voice trail.

"E'Teiso will take the *Fox*!" I blurted.

Unperturbed, Huido paused to regard us both. "Only if we offload the truffles."

Morgan's frown deepened. "What are you up to?"

A jaunty wave; the hovering portlight lifted out of range, sending prisms across the cutlery. "Ansel!"

At the bellow, Huido's personal assistant hurried forward. "Yes, Hom Huido?" he asked faintly.

"Explain the truffle situation to my blood brother."

The older Human paled, but put aside his tray. "Yes, Hom Huido." Competent—Morgan had assured me there was no question who was responsible for keeping the *Claws & Jaws* solvent all these years—but Ansel always seemed frail to me.

I supposed any of us looked that way next to the Carasian.

"When the station opened to the public," Ansel began hesitantly, then warming to his topic, "Raj Plexis defined her authority as applicable to everything and everyone within, as well as to that exterior of the hull vital to operations within, as well as to those contracted directly by Plexis to perform tasks related to—"

"The point," Huido rumbled.

Ansel coughed once. "Yes, Hom Huido. A starship parked

against Plexis is legally neither within the station nor part of its vital exterior hull. Until a cargo leaves that ship and enters Plexis, it, too, is effectively outside station authority and—"

A claw snapped again. "And that truffle-sucking F'Feego can't levy fines on it."

This seemed a bit—optimistic. "But the previous cargoes—" I pointed out. "—the other truffles—"

"What truffles? Relished and digested. By Esaliz itself, among others." Huido laughed so hard I feared for the table. "Waste recycling has the final products for sale. Stop worrying."

Morgan's eyes narrowed. "You've a buyer elsewhere."

The Carasian poured more beer into his handling claw, then into his mouth with a satisfied slurp. "I do."

Well, that was promising.

Or maybe not. A muscle jumped in my Human's jaw as he leaned forward, and there was nothing cheerful in his expression. "Where."

"Word of my delectable recipe has traveled." Somehow Huido managed to look humble—a feat for a mass of black shiny plates studded with rings for weapons. "It was inevitable."

Morgan turned to Ansel. That worthy answered in a very small voice, "The owner of *The Salty Appendage* has made a very generous—"

"No."

Eyestalks gathered to stare at Morgan, but Huido's response was mild. "They're my truffles and my recipe—"

"No."

The Carasian grew in size, swelling up and out, claws raised.

Unimpressed, my Human leaned back, fingertips together.

Neither budged. The ensuing silence was thunderous.

Someone, I decided, had to be reasonable. "Where's *The Salty Appendage*?" I asked brightly.

My Human's "Doesn't matter—" almost drowned out Ansel's "Auord."

Pocular. Plexis. Now Auord. I supposed Ret 7 should be next, to fill out the list of places—truths—left to confront. I reached for my glass, then changed my mind and picked up my spoon.

"It's not about the truffles. We can't let E'Teiso win this," Morgan said, low and hard. "We can't cut and run. If we do, what's to stop Plexis from imposing fees on every consumable import? How many will go out of business? How long could you last?"

Huido rattled, the unsettled sound all there was for a moment, then reluctantly, one eyestalk bent to Ansel. "Do the numbers."

Instead of going to a comp system, as I would, Ansel's eyes half closed and his lips worked without sound.

What was he— I looked at Morgan.

Who nodded, clearly pleased. *Ansel's good at that.*

Good With Numbers

* * *

by Heather LaVonne Jensen

ANSEL WIPED A trickle of sweat from his forehead with his sleeve. Hands on hips, he arched his back, stiff from pouring molten lanthanum into setting molds. *Nine pours,* he thought, *six crucibles per pour, 14 molds per crucible, six ingots per mold, each ingot priced at 25 credits—that's 113,400 credits' worth we've earned for the mine today.* From the angle of the triple suns in the lavender sky, he had about seven hours of daylight left. Ansel frowned, and glanced at the row of seething crucibles. The days seemed to grow longer as he grew older. He absently brushed the ubiquitous yellow dust off of his trousers.

The younger miners slogging from the open pit to the refining sheds on Ansel's right were slathered in yellow mud from crown to toe. The soaked, messy bags of rare earths they carried on bowed backs dripped slippery mustard trails behind them, rendering the path increasingly hazardous as the day wore on. They trudged along in silence. The heat and the hard labor, as Ansel knew from experience, tended to put workers in a trancelike state, until all they could do was put one foot in front of the other until quitting time. One step at a time, Ansel, only 145 units himself, had once carried 100-unit bags of packed mud up and down that same hill for twelve hours a day. *Maybe no one knows what they are capable of,* he thought, *until life forces them to find out.*

Lost in thought, Ansel started in response to a booming voice close behind him.

"This dust gets everywhere, Kraden. Takes forever to slough off."

"Always with the complaints! You'll see, Hom Huido, this new sideline's worth investing in."

Ansel turned around, and his eyes widened. The mine's burly foreman, Kraden, stood beside what looked like the offspring of a servo tank and a monstrous crustacean. The shiny black creature stood a head taller than the foreman, and its massive bulk would dwarf a personal transport. Independently mobile eyestalks sprouted through the gap between the two bowl-shaped armored plates that protected its head. Its lower asymmetrical claws were like siege weapons; the upper pair of claws on its carapace served as arms. In Ansel's opinion, the formidable being was the stuff of nightmares.

The Carasian shook itself with a sound like falling shale. "So where is this amazing product of yours?" it asked. A few of its eyestalks bent to study Ansel, who shivered.

"It's in the glazing shed, Hom. We've perfected the erbium-promethium stabilizing agent, the luminescence is remarkable . . ." The foreman hurried off, and the living black servo trundled in his wake.

Time to get back to work, Ansel thought. He pulled his elbow-length leather gloves back on, picked up a long-handled ladle, and scooped out some of the gently-roiling lanthanum. With the focus and eye for detail that had earned him this job, he decanted it into a mold.

"Pink!" bellowed a voice from the direction of the glazing shed. "What's remarkable about pink?" The huge armored being burst from the shed and stormed across the yard.

Running after Huido, a ceramic tile in his hand, the foreman shouted, "Hom Huido, wait! Let me show you!"

The creature halted with a clatter. Its eyestalks swiveled in Ansel's direction, and it demanded, "Do YOU find the color pink remarkable?"

"It . . . it's calming, Hom," Ansel stuttered.

The winded Kraden pushed Ansel aside and held out his tile. "Please, Hom, look. It changes colors based on light levels. Out here, it's greenish-blue. See?"

With surprising delicacy, the smaller of the handling claws dipped to take the tile. "Interesting. What causes the effect? Radioactive decay?"

"Oh, no! This mine contains the safest mix of rare earth isotopes in the quadrant," said Kraden. "The stabilization process both preserves promethium's luminescence and eliminates harmful radiation."

"It's a novel use for surplus erbium," the creature conceded, "and waste reduction is a smart move in any business, but at .013 credits per tile, can you imagine how many tiles you'll have to ship to scrape a lousy 20% profit?"

"12,165.79," Ansel said automatically, then blushed when both beings turned to stare at him.

Eyestalks clustered, bending his way. "And a load that size would weigh?"

The talking assault vehicle obviously expected Ansel to answer. "About 1,459.89 units."

"Transportation costs will eliminate your profit margin, Kraden."

The foreman's voice became a persuasive wheedle. "But I've found a buyer, Hom. He'll take all we produce at 0.0237 credits each."

Armored plates slid over one another with a sibilant hiss. The being asked Ansel, "How many tiles will we need to clear a 20% profit on that?"

"1,668.37, Hom," answered Ansel.

"Now that's remarkable," the Carasian said. To Ansel's horror, the giant strode closer, until its shiny black bulk blotted out the suns. Ansel held his shoulders back and pushed out his thin chest, but the bravado of his pose was betrayed by the shudder that wracked his body.

The creature spoke. "This one is wasted on lanthanum."

Kraden frowned. "You're right. He'd be of more use tracking inventory. The clerk I have now can barely add."

Ansel listened with growing wonder. Could this be real? Might he really be assigned to work the warehouse? He flashed a tentative smile at the Carasian, and could have sworn one of the shiny black eyes dipped, like a wink.

Ansel scanned his company-issued ID badge, and the loading dock door whisked to the side. Carston, ostensibly Ansel's co-manager but Kraden's crony in truth, shoved a grav sled over the threshold. "'bout time," he grunted. "It's hot out here."

"What was the trouble delivering Hom Huido's tiles to *The Fortunae*?" Ansel asked. As usual, a delivery that should have taken fifteen minutes had lasted several hours; from Carston's breath, Ansel figured he'd had a few fortifying beers along the way before heading back to "work" at the warehouse.

"Ain't so easy. Shipcity's a maze. Out in the sun all day, probably got heatstroke . . ."

The insectile drone of Carston's complaints seldom ceased. After a while, the sound faded to white noise. Ansel grinned. He'd probably miss it if it stopped.

Ansel grabbed a rag to wipe down the dusty sled, and saw something that made his heart skip a beat. "Carston, there are still tiles in here!"

Carston blinked bleary eyes. "Those broke ones was in a box what fell off the sled. I shut the box up again after—he'll never notice."

Ansel, knowing Hom Huido's perfectionist temperament, had his doubts. Huido had ordered a shipment of Kraden's tiles for his newest venture, an interspecies' restaurant named the *Claws & Jaws*, located in the legendary Plexis Supermarket. Ansel didn't understand the appeal, but demand for the color-shifting tiles remained steady. Lord Lianjie, Kraden's wholesaler on Camos, put in a new order every six months.

Ansel made a mental note to issue a partial refund, and gathered up the pieces. Along the tiles' broken edges, he noticed something odd; a strata of tiny brown crystals. He put a chunk in his pocket to show Kraden, and tossed the rest into the recycler.

"Excuse me, Hom," said a cheerful voice. Ansel stepped aside as a towheaded youngster pushed a second grav sled into the loading dock. "It's the lanthanum order for Captain Ivali."

"Excellent, Tom," Ansel told the young apprentice. "It's getting late, why don't you head home? I'll deliver it."

The ramp to Captain Ariva Ivali's ship was packed with merchandise. Blue-suited figures crawled around and over the boxes, bags, and crates, wielding hand-held scanners. At the bottom of the ramp, arms crossed and foot tapping an impatient rhythm, stood the trader, a slender Human female with gray-streaked blonde hair. When she caught sight of Ansel, she called out, "Hello, my friend! You've arrived just in time to watch Port Authority search my shipment for contraband. They seem to be under the impression *Ryan's Venture* is a smuggler's scow."

The constable looked up from the box he was riffling through and grimaced. "Captain Ivali, Port Authority is making no accusations. It's a random security check."

"You held a lottery, and I'm the lucky winner?" Captain Ivali frowned. "You do realize the launchpad is about to close for the night? If I miss my docking tug, the creteng in that tank will die before they reach Plexis."

The officer sighed. "No one wants to inconvenience you, Captain. The tug is scheduled for you and will be available following our inspection."

Ansel cleared his throat. "Sorry to intrude. May I load these boxes on the ramp?"

"The ramp is full; I'm afraid it's not possible . . ."

"Of course it's possible," Ivali cut in. "Have your people unload the creteng tank, and put it in the shade under the ramp, like I asked you to do in the first place. Then there'll be plenty of room."

The constables glanced at one another, their dismay obvious, but complied, switching on the anti-grav device under an enormous cylindrical container and easing it down the ramp. Ansel would have bet a cycle's pay that *Ryan's Venture* would never again be singled out by Imesh 27's Port Authority.

The boxes of lanthanum were soon stacked in the tank's place.

"Great to see you again, Ivali," said Ansel.

"Likewise. This provincial backwater does have its bright spots." Captain Ivali scowled at the security officers. "Well, it has one, anyway."

Ansel could hear the shouting from outside the warehouse. He quickly tapped the entry code into the keypad and shoved the sled inside. A prolonged tinkling crash echoed through the building. Ansel hurried toward the sound, face pinched with worry. *So much for an early night.*

The voices grew intelligible as he approached. "I can't believe you gave him the wrong tiles!"

Ansel peeked around the storage room's steel door and saw Kraden strike a cringing Carston, who tried and failed to block the blow with his forearm rather than his face. The two were surrounded by smashed tiles and shredded boxes, the ruins of the second tile shipment.

"It's not my fault. They all look the same!"

Carston's whiny protest seemed to incense Kraden. He grabbed a tile and shoved it in Carston's face. "The tiles for Hom Huido are marked, you idiot! Lord Lianjie will have our heads for this!"

Kraden punctuated his speech with a punch; Carston took it on the chin and toppled like a felled tree.

Ansel winced. The doorknob in his hand rattled.

Swift as a striking snake, Kraden's head whipped around. "You! Where were you while this was happening? This is your fault, too!"

Ansel slammed the door, shoved home the nighttime lockbolt, and sprinted toward the service exit like a scalded rezt. He didn't deserve to be beaten for Carston's mistake.

It wouldn't take Kraden long to kick down the door. Ansel raced through the shipcity, eyes wild. The warehouses were closed, the main walkways almost empty. *Where to hide, where to hide?* His gaze lit upon the creteng tank still under the *Venture*'s ramp. *Perfect!*

Ansel ducked under the ramp and slid into the narrow space between tank and starship. Before he could talk himself out of it, he unfastened the tank's lid, lifted the hatch, and hopped inside. If he lay submerged on his back, face tilted toward the opening and fingers gripping the lock bar inside the hatch for dear life, he had enough space to breathe. The life signs of the creteng would camouflage his own if Kraden attempted to scan for him.

The tank was surprisingly loud. Clangs and thumps from the tethered ships nearby shuddered through the water. A bubbling sound came from the air hose beside him that kept the water oxygenated for the fish. His rasping breaths were amplified.

Footsteps vibrated through the water. This was it. Ansel held tight to the lock bar and prayed for Kraden to walk on by. A distorted voice reached him instead. "Get that tank into the hold. Cap'n's going nova."

Before Ansel could react, the lock bar slid sideways, pinching his fingers, and the click of the anti-grav switch echoed through the tank. The suddenly unruly water billowed over him, clung to his face and smothered his shout. He groped for the air hose—who would have thought anti-gravity would make movement so difficult—and after a heartbeat's-worth of panic, found it.

He held tight to the pressurized hose and took deep breaths, in through the mouth, out through the nose. He didn't dare make a mistake; he'd choke and drown. It felt strange to concentrate so hard on an activity he'd always taken for granted.

Ansel banged on the side of the tank with his free hand. They had to hear him, didn't they?

The sound was deafening inside his little water-filled world, but the thumps must have sounded much softer on the other side. A wave of disorientation and dizziness eventually announced the absence of the anti-grav, but the footsteps grew distant and faded away.

Again panic rose in Ansel's throat, along with bile from his stomach. He swallowed it down. He wouldn't give in to fear. Breathe in, breathe out. The moments became hours as his world narrowed to fit a hosepipe the thickness of his tongue. Ansel drifted into the same trance he'd perfected while working in the mines.

He scarcely heard the running footsteps, didn't notice the

change in light levels when the tank lid was lifted away, and fought the hands that wanted to separate him from the tank's air hose. When a sharp pinch on his arm made him gasp, he finally realized he'd breached the surface and his ordeal was over.

"Stupidest thing I've ever seen! What were you thinking?" Captain Ivali's acerbic voice was at odds with the concern in her eyes. She toweled Ansel down herself and snugged a blanket around his shoulders. "You could've been killed."

Ansel couldn't breathe deeply enough. The metallic recycled air was the most delicious thing he'd ever tasted.

It wasn't until he was sitting in the medbay, swathed within a nest of blankets and cradling a hot cup of sombay, that he was able to explain himself to the captain's satisfaction.

Ivali shook her head. "Either you're the luckiest being I've ever met, or Providence has a fondness for fools," she said. "If we hadn't reviewed the security cameras when we did, I doubt you'd have lasted the night."

"Probably not," Ansel agreed, "but nobody knows what they're capable of until life forces them to find out."

Captain Ivali snorted. "Lovely. Remind me to stitch that into a sampler. Pithy remarks aside, what am I going to do with you?"

A good question, since *Ryan's Venture* was already in subspace. "You're going to Plexis, Captain. Could you take me to the *Claws & Jaws*? I need to talk to Hom Huido."

Ivali nodded. "Plexis I can do, but we're on a tight schedule. I've a promise to keep for the *Silver Fox*. We'll point you in the right direction."

Ansel sighed with relief, and his shoulders sagged. The med-tech lifted the cup from his hand as he crumpled like a paper doll onto the narrow cot. He was never sure later whether he'd said "thank you" out loud, or only thought it.

"You want the wholesaler's level. Up that ramp. From there, turn right at the first—not the second—servo parts dealer. Keep walking till you're through the first night zone. Can't miss the *Claws & Jaws*. You'll be fine. Got it?"

Ansel nodded, and explored the waxy airtag on his stinging cheek with a fingertip, anxious but unwilling to admit it. The *Venture's* first officer slapped him on the back. "Good luck," he called over his shoulder as he hurried back into his ship.

When the crowded ramp spilled into the vast reaches of Plexis Supermarket, Ansel's jaw dropped. It was huge! The mine on Imesh 27, the nearby shipcity, and the countryside between them could fit inside this shopping area, with room to spare. He'd thought his tiny shipcity was loud! Here, a thousand voices fought to be heard. He'd thought the walkways at home were crowded! Creatures he'd never imagined, wearing clothing he'd never seen before, choked the vast reaches of the concourse. Ansel's knees wobbled, and he swayed.

A tap on the shoulder startled Ansel out of his near-swoon. A friendly-looking creature in a reassuring security uniform asked, "Can I help you, Hom?"

"It's . . . so big. Everything."

The guard lifted the ID badge Ansel still wore around his neck with a jointed appendage and gave it a quick glance. "First time on Plexis, Hom Ansel? It can be overwhelming. Where are you headed?"

"I need to find the *Claws & Jaws* restaurant."

The security guard swiped its single digit across a hand-held screen. "Here it is, ¼ spinward." When Ansel still looked confused, it took him by the shoulders. "That way," it said, and gave him a little push.

Ansel waded through what felt like a lunatic's obstacle course. He was groped by eager storekeepers, spun around by fast-moving streams of shoppers, and tripped up by more merchandise than he'd thought existed in the quadrant.

Thanks to a slow-moving group of foul-smelling Lemmicks, he almost passed by the colorful *Claws & Jaws: Complete Interspecies Cuisine* sign that hung over a pair of Huido-sized double doors. With a dizzying surge of relief, Ansel slipped inside the darkened restaurant and shut the chaos out.

"Well? What did you do with my saucepans?" an angry voice demanded. Hom Huido approached the door at full steam, his largest claw snapping in threat.

"I don't—I mean, I never had—your what?" Ansel pressed his back against the door.

"Saucepans! I've been waiting all morning!"

"I'm not—I don't know where they are. I'm Ansel, Hom Huido? From Imesh 27? I work in the warehouse?"

"You don't sound very sure about it." A small claw lifted Ansel's chin, and Huido's eyestalks bent to examine him. "You are him. What are you doing here?"

Ansel shivered. "It's a long story."

"Then let's hear it over breakfast." Huido bustled off toward the kitchen. "Any preferences? Choose something that doesn't require a saucepan."

Ansel polished off his second helping with a satisfied sigh. "So that's all I know, Hom. Kraden assaulted Carston because he sent you the wrong tiles."

Hom Huido shifted in his seat. "Doesn't make sense. Tiles are tiles. I've already put them up." He indicated a faintly-glowing blue line on the wall at chair-rail height.

"I just remembered." Ansel dug in his pocket. "I have a piece of one of them; it's a little odd."

"Let's see it." Huido scraped a clawtip along the broken edge of the tile. The tiny brown crystals twinkled in the dim light. "Strange. Encased in the clay, whatever it is. Follow me."

Ansel followed Huido through the kitchen into a hallway; at the end waited a coded security door. Huido blocked Ansel's view of the keypad, but Ansel recognized the keys he pressed by the standardized tones. The warehouse door used the same equipment. He kept this information to himself, however, since Huido probably wouldn't be happy to know he'd given Ansel acccss by accident.

The room inside was huge but bare, except for a long semicircle of rocks, a deep empty depression that filled most of the available space, and a bench littered with tools. Ansel spotted a portable com system, empty beer cans, and a half-assembled tape reader amid the mess.

Huido swept a section of the bench clear and directed the powerful beam of a work lamp on the half-buried crystals. He turned them this way and that, tapped them with a hammer, and used them to scratch various substances. "It's no good," he said, "I can't identify these. We need an expert."

Ansel stood nervously at Huido's side in the tiny jeweler's shop as the shopkeeper examined the tile again, this time under higher magnification. Huido clicked an impatient claw like a castanet.

The shopkeeper rubbed her ocular spread. "If I hadn't seen it, I wouldn't've believed it," she said. "That's painite, that is."

"Painite? What's that?" Ansel asked.

"Only the rarest gem in the quadrant."

"Don't they use it to focus matter-conversion lasers?" asked Huido.

"You're a fella knows his gems," the shopkeeper acknowledged. She handed the broken tile back to Huido.

"What's it worth?" Ansel asked.

"Whatcha got there'll buy you a new aircar." The shopkeeper cocked her head to one side, a motion made easier by a Neblokan's lack of shoulders. "Wouldn't be looking for a buyer, would you?"

"Not today," rumbled Huido, steering Ansel toward the exit.

The two hurried down the concourse to the restaurant. Neither spoke. Ansel was quiet because he didn't know what to say, but he suspected Huido was too upset to speak; the huge being's armor rattled like dried seed pods in a gale-force wind. When the doors of the restaurant closed behind them once more, Huido bellowed with fury.

"Liar! Cheat! Thief! I'll boil him in tar; I'll split his sternum and fill him full of lead! How dare he steal from me!"

"Hom?" Ansel's voice trembled. "I don't understand."

"That slimy bottom-feeder! He found painite in the mine. That's why he invented his pretty tiles, so he could smuggle it out and sell it to the highest bidder without cutting me in. I'll rip his head off and stuff his corpse with entrails!"

Ansel couldn't smother a smile. "Won't his own entrails get in the way? Sorry, Hom Huido, sorry," he said, when every one of Huido's eyestalks swiveled in his direction. "You're right to be angry, but what do we do?"

Huido's larger claws lowered to the floor. "No point contacting Plexis Security. The inspector will charge us with smuggling, and I don't have enough credits to protest my innocence."

A crash from the main entrance! Between Huido and Ansel's feet rolled a fizzing, spinning metal cylinder. A strong citrus scent filled the air.

"Get back!" Huido leaped forward, amazingly agile for his size, and swept Ansel aside with a claw, knocking him sprawling into a booth. He grabbed the smoking grenade with the other claw, and tossed it back. Then, like a punctured air bladder, Huido sank slowly to the ground. "Get rum," he whispered. His eyestalks retracted into the gap in his armored head, and the giant lay still. The heap that was left looked more like a scrap heap than the vibrant being Ansel knew.

He'd said rum. Maybe it would help, maybe it was an antidote? But how could he get it into the prostrate Huido? Ansel had seen him drink before, a complicated procedure that required pouring liquid into a hollow claw, then stuffing it in the gap in his face where his mouth was located.

Ansel grabbed a bottle from the drinks cabinet, and hurried back to the Carasian. To his dismay, even up close he couldn't figure out where the rum should go or how to get it there. He settled for splashing a thin stream of the amber liquid inside the gap between the two halves of Huido's head, and hoped some of it would get into whatever he used for a mouth.

A metallic squeal from the kitchen pierced the silence, and Ansel jumped. The bottle fell from his hand and sloshed its contents in an arc across the floor. Ansel knew that sound. Someone was using a high-speed steel drill, probably boring through the lock in the access door leading to the service corridor behind the restaurant.

The drinks cabinet stood open; the right side, large enough to store industrial-sized casks of fermented beverage, was empty. Transparent tinted plas formed three tiers of windows on the cabinet doors, so it wasn't an optimal hiding place. A clatter from the kitchen told him the lock had given way. The cabinet would have to do. Ansel squeezed inside, and eased the door closed behind him.

The heavy tread of booted feet approached. "You should set the charge," someone whined. "I'm no good with explosives."

With a jolt, Ansel recognized Carston's voice.

"You don't have to be. Why do you think we use optical detonators at the mine? Even an idiot can work them."

Ansel shuddered. And that was Kraden.

Through the tinted window, Ansel watched both of his former coworkers scramble over Huido's bulk into the dining area. "It stinks in here. You sure this stuff only hurts Carasians?" Carston asked.

"Yes! Shut up and give me that prybar." A scraping sound, then a familiar tinkling crash, echoed through the tiny cabinet. Kraden was taking down the tiles.

He'd come armed with a drug that would take Huido out of the picture, so why did he need explosives from the mine? The tiles were valuable, but why bother to blow the place up? Wouldn't that draw unnecessary attention, give Plexis Security a reason to scour its surveillance records? Kraden was a thinker; he wouldn't take a stupid risk.

Peering through the tiny window, Ansel watched Kraden crack off and bag tiles as he worked his way down the wall, while a surly Carston, his face swollen and decorated in blue-and-purple hues, dumped a pile of equipment on the floor in the center of the room.

If Kraden wasn't afraid of Plexis Security, maybe he was afraid of something else. Ansel closed his eyes and focused on the latest shipping manifest for Kraden's special client. When it came together in his mind, Ansel "read" the figures off the sheet. One by one, he recalled the tile manifests, all the numbers clear and distinct in his memory.

Since the first shipment, the number of tiles shipped had been steadily decreasing at a rate of about 23%. It wasn't abnormal for production to go down as a seam drifted farther into the earth and mining became more difficult, but it could put Kraden in a precarious position if his client had a quota to fill. Maybe Kraden had no choice but to deliver this batch of tiles. Maybe the consequences would be dire if he did not. And maybe, just maybe, Kraden's client could be Ansel's friend.

All Ansel had to do was sneak out of the drinks cabinet, scramble over Huido, and get to the com system in the Carasian's apartment without being seen. Simple. Ansel hoped Ivali was right, and her "Providence" had a fondness for fools.

"The cable's loose on this cap," complained Carsten.

"What? Let me see that." Kraden bent over the explosives alongside Carston, their backs to Ansel. This was his chance.

Carefully, he opened the cabinet and unfolded his slender frame, a bottle of wine in each hand. Carston's head lifted.

"Ansel?! How the—?"

Ansel threw the bottles in Kraden's direction and bolted. He clambered over his immobile Carasian friend on all fours and slid down the other side. Reaching the keypad, he jabbed in the code as Kraden vaulted over Huido and gave chase. The door swung wide. Ansel darted through and slammed it shut. It shook on impact with Kraden's body, but didn't give way.

Kraden's fist thumped against the door. "Fine! Stay in there! We'll blow this place to bits with you in it!"

Ansel waited until Kraden stomped away, then plucked a food wrapper off the com and typed in the calling code he'd seen at the top of every tile order. "Is this Lord Lianjie?"

"Yes?" said an impatient voice. "What is it?"

"Your pardon, Lord, but I'm calling with bad news. This is Ansel, from the rare earths mine on Imesh 27. I regret to inform you that your shipment has been stolen."

"You must be mistaken. I spoke to Mr. Kraden this morning. The shipment will be on a freighter in the morning, headed my way."

"Sir, I wish that were true. If you'll examine your call logs, you'll see that Mr. Kraden contacted you from an offworld location. Painite deposits are running low. I must inform you, it appears Mr. Kraden opted to keep the last shipment for himself. Your tiles were rerouted to an unsuspecting restaurant owner on Plexis, for safekeeping. I'm sorry to say Mr. Kraden is there now, retrieving the tiles."

"What's the name of this restaurant?" growled Lord Lianjie.

"The *Claws & Jaws*."

"I have associates on Plexis. I'll send them to check out your story."

"Please advise them to move quickly and exercise caution, sir. Kraden has already incapacitated the restaurant owner, and I believe he plans to blow up the restaurant to conceal his crime."

"If Kraden has double-crossed me, my associates aren't the ones who'll need to worry. Your story had better be true."

"I wish it weren't, sir," Ansel said.

The com clicked off, and Ansel closed his eyes. He'd done all he could. The rest was up to someone else.

"Hom Huido, it was a good thing the med-tech had the antidote to that gas." Ansel looked shyly up at the massive being. "I couldn't find your mouth."

"That explains why I smelled like a distillery when I woke up. What were you thinking?"

Ansel blinked. "Before you passed out, you said, 'Get rum.' I thought it might help."

"I was trying to tell you to get in the *room*. Waste of good rum. How did you—no matter." Eyestalks bent. "You saved both us and the restaurant, and I have it on good authority that Kraden and Carston will be spending the rest of their lives as indentured asteroid miners in a lonely colony on the Fringe. How did you know the client's com number, anyway?"

"I guess you never know what you're capable of until life backs you into a corner and forces you to find out."

"Hmm. Speaking of corners, my little corner of Plexis could use an assistant manager; someone who could double-check the books, keep track of shipments, watch over the help. What do you say?"

Ansel stared, a lump rising in his throat. After all this, Hom Huido was offering him a job?

The Carasian rumbled. "Tell you what; I'll build you a separate apartment. We'll put it at the end of the staff wing. What do you say? Will you stay here with me? I need someone I can trust, someone who has my back when things don't add up."

Ansel smiled. "I've always been good with numbers."

. . . *Truffles* continues
Interlude

* * *

HUIDO'S EYESTALKS TENDED to drift, pairs straying toward where Sira sat, her face obscured by a waterfall of red-gold hair. Morgan doubted she noticed, her outward attention for the lines her spoon drew through the remaining sauce on her plate.

While inward? She didn't shield herself against him, but there was an air of *preoccupation* he wouldn't disturb. Huido's doing, something unlikely to sink between those gently pulsing head plates.

It'd take more than a hammer to knock tact into them. Ansel's numbers were convincing. A fee on their imported goods could ruin most, if not all, of the smaller restaurants. Huido?

"I don't like it." Sullen.

Morgan made himself lean back. "Which part?"

"You telling everyone." Eyestalks milled. "Involving others in our business. Maybe Rose," the Carasian conceded, then shook his bulk with an ominous rattle. "But Keevor? Smuggler scum? That ORDNEX!" A daunting focus—on him.

"They needed to know." He turned over a palm. "You're on the same station. Maybe together—"

"We go with my plan. You'll take the cargo away from here."

About to argue, the Human hesitated. There was something false in Huido's bluster. Taking the truffles elsewhere helped only themselves, only this once. Why? It wasn't as if the Carasian lacked empathy for the others. His hearts were in the right place—ask Ansel to calculate how much of the restaurant's product went out the side door, into the appendages of those who'd otherwise have gone hungry.

Huido's afraid and doesn't want to admit it, even to himself. I recognize the signs, Sira added ruefully.

His wise Chosen. It had to be. "You've gone all in, haven't you?" If the restaurant failed, Huido's wives would leave him. "You can't risk losing this cargo."

The Carasian might have turned to stone.

Ansel twitched.

Morgan blew out an exasperated breath. "Fine. We'll do it your way. Just—tell me you've another market."

A claw able to snap the table in two waved jauntily in the air, barely missing the glassware. "I will in abundance, once palates are educated. Until such glorious times, my brother—" a sigh like rain on plas, "—I'm at the mercy of those willing to risk a novelty."

Meaning *The Salty Appendage.*

Meaning Auord.

He shouldn't have pushed Sira so hard. Shouldn't have brought up Roraqk or Recruiters or the Tulis. Shouldn't have come to Plexis.

Most of all, he should never, Morgan thought darkly, have agreed to truffles.

Huido needs our help. Somber gray eyes regarded him; Morgan suspected his thoughts hadn't been private. "We'll do it," Sira said out loud.

"That's the spirit!" Huido boomed. "More beer!"

"Not so fast," Morgan countered.

He loses his family. We lose the Fox.

Trust me. "We've started something." He hoped. Had to believe. Bad as Butter, that. "If nothing comes of it, we'll do your way, Huido." *You could stay here—*

An annoyed *flick* of Power made him wince.

Lips quirked, Morgan gestured apology to his Chosen before turning to his dearest friend. "Give my plan a chance first. There's more to Plexis than a truffle-obsessed bureaucrat."

Kindness? Sira's eyebrow rose.

Or self-interest. Or both. Morgan shrugged and half smiled. "Stranger things have happened here—"

He was interrupted by a commotion at the entrance. Huido surged to his feet. "What's going on?"

A staffer approached the table. "Hom Huido. Plexis Security is here. I've made them wait, but they want Captain Morgan—"

Sira rose, the ends of her hair whipping back and forth. "They can't have him."

Peace, Witchling. My Human stood, heart starting to pound. "I've the feeling this isn't about me at all."

Morgan revised his thinking when he saw who waited in the lobby of the restaurant: the head of Plexis Security, Inspector Wallace, no less, flanked by a burly Human constable and a flustered-looking Whirtle with tentacles clutching a noteplas. Wallace had indeed, on a few occasions, been after him in particular.

Perhaps for better reasons than Terk.

The moment Wallace set eyes on him, he snapped, "Morgan! This is your fault. I want you to stop this nonsense. At once!"

"And if you aren't paying customers, I want you out of my restaurant!" Huido heaved himself forward, claws raised, and the officials stumbled back to give him room. Those at the front of the line to enter the restaurant attempted to do the same. Those behind weren't cooperating, resulting in a few collisions and an unfortunate odor.

Morgan settled the big Carasian with a look, then addressed Wallace, keeping it calm. "Inspector. Exactly what 'nonsense' would you like me to stop?"

Sira came to stand at his side. Silent. Watchful. Wallace glanced at her then away, dismissing the most formidable presence on the station.

But then he'd always been a fool.

14

* * *

THE INSPECTOR AND the others were tense, their motives and purpose as yet unclear, but Morgan's calmness sent a signal. The hint of *hope* I sensed reinforced it. I made myself smaller, holding in my Power, damping down emotion. We'd faced far worse than this presumably honest, demonstrably ineffectual official.

On the other hand, we could hardly keep blocking the entrance to the *Claws & Jaws*. I turned to Huido. "Perhaps a table?"

An eyestalk bent my way. The rest glared at Wallace, doubtless why beads of sweat glistened on the Human's forehead. A grudging, "If you wish."

The Human constable perked up, but Wallace's bushy brows met in a scowl. "There's no time to waste. Captain Morgan must come with us immediately."

"I trust this isn't a problem with our ship," my Human said, his face set in polite interest.

The Whirtle consulted its noteplas, muttering to itself. The other constable gave it an irritated glance and snapped back, "The only thing wrong is your scow's still attached to our station."

If he believed this would get a reaction from Morgan, I thought with contempt, he was stupider than he looked.

Those waiting to be seated had had enough. "We've reserva-
tions!" This from a Skenkran wearing an unusually shiny gold
airtag. A chorus of similar protests followed, with a few suggesting
on how to cook the Port Jellies, it being Plexis.

Ansel eased around his employer. "I'll see to our customers."

The inspector drew himself up. "Let's go—"

"Where?" Huido asked with deceptive mildness.

"Warehousing. But only Morgan—"

"Bah!" The Carasian heaved forward, scattering constables and
customers as he lumbered through his own door to the concourse
beyond. Wallace turned an unfortunate color and muttered to
himself, but was helpless to do other than follow behind.

This could be interesting, chit, Morgan sent, a promising gleam in
his eye. Before the remaining constables could blink, he swept me
with him in Huido's wake.

For the wonderful thing about a giant, motivated Carasian?

No one got in our way.

15

***

THE WAREHOUSE LEVEL was novel territory for me and probably most on Plexis, being the zone between pending and paid in full. Neither the curious nor lost were welcome.

Spacers didn't belong here either, yet my Human, it turned out, did. The occasional worker paused to raise a limb in greeting. When an aircar swooped overhead, it being large enough here for their use, and his name rang out, I echoed it. "Jason?"

"Didn't start out in a ship, chit," came the intriguing reply. Then, *tell you later*

I did know something of this level, it being part of my education as Hindmost to learn where our cargoes went. A maze of service tunnels connected docked ships, including the *Silver Fox,* to the vastness of this receiving area, curving the length of the station; others, less obvious, connected individual warehouses to the wholesale level and above. The air over our heads buzzed with servos as well as aircars, some carrying small urgent packages, all equipped with vids and sensors.

Theft—from inside or out—was an ever-present concern.

As was tripping, I quickly discovered. Plexis had installed enormous sealable doors at intervals, their rims coming to the midpoint of my shins. While I applauded any precaution aimed at

containing explosions, escaping whatevers, or leaks, the need to
continually step over such barriers—or trip—was a nuisance. For
the staff here as well, since makeshift ramps cluttered every possible path, the majority suited only to a specific species—not all
humanoid—and, to make it worse, all were painted dirty gray to
match the floor.

Morgan moved through the cluttered open space as easily as on
the deck of the *Fox*. Huido, on the other hand, appeared to delight
in crushing ramps under his ponderous spongy feet. Wallace and
his constables negotiated their way with the same irregular steps
that I used, though the unfortunate Whirtle, having to hump over
the rims, had begun to wheeze.

Ahead and behind, to either side, the floor curled inward like a
drying leaf—a leaf larger than some cities, perspective playing its
tricks. Looking so far made me dizzy—and risked tripping—so
after that first glance, I kept my eyes down.

Until I heard Morgan's soft, "Ah."

I slowed and lifted my head, understanding at once.

The rest of Plexis was already here.

Interlude

* * *

THERE'D BEEN HINTS. He'd summed them in quick glances. Closed doors. Lights off or dimmed. Signs in windows. Could have been ordinary—plumbing issues; a rumored food inspection—but Morgan dared hope. After all, when was the last time the night zone had gone silent, its benches full of bemused half-drunk spacers?

Now, he believed. They were a considerable distance from the physical office of Duties & Tariffs but, even with Huido, getting through the crowd blocking the rest of the way wouldn't be easy.

They halted in unison. Inspector Wallace turned. "Captain Morgan, disperse these—these individuals! At once! Commerce is being obstructed!" He pointed to the growing lines of stopped freight cars beyond. Warehouse staff perched on the nearest. Some looked to be eating lunch.

Some, Morgan knew, were Dalton's, in charge of particular cargoes. If they kept quiet, didn't push back or take advantage of the commotion, she'd listened.

Wallace concluded with a desperate, "What are you waiting for—stop them!"

Sira carefully didn't laugh; she did share her *amusement*.

"What makes you think I can?" Morgan asked, honestly curious.

"Don't you hear what they're chanting?!"

The Human politely cocked his head. True, there were raised voices ahead, but the result—given the diverse vocal organs in use—was more cacophony than chant.

"Do you, Inspector?" Sira asked, all innocence.

Wallace's mouth worked, but nothing came out. He gestured impatiently at his constable. The sound levels rose and fell, echoing through the expanse of the receiving area, making the Whirtle raise its own voice to be heard: "A common phrase is 'Eat Your Fee!'" It flipped a page on its noteplas. "With variations, some improbable. There's been an abundance of 'Free the Truffles' and 'First Truffles, Then Beer!'—a dozen or so explicit suggestions regarding F'Feego reproduction—"

"Yes, yes, but the most used word is 'truffles.' Your cargo, Captain Morgan. They've come for you. Stop them!"

They'd listened.

For the first time he could remember, Jason Morgan found himself speechless.

16

A CLUSTER OF Nrophrae pushed by. They wore aprons, stained with the same amber liquid as sloshed in the globes they carried.

Suddenly, there were more such, everywhere I looked. A grav sled passed us, loaded with—if that wasn't Butter serselves, I didn't know my Atatatay. I did recognize the begoggled "Yummy-Yum" dealer. If I'd thought Plexis drew customers from a wide variety of species, it was nothing compared to the vast—and occasionally unlikely—biological spectrum of those involved in station food services.

None paid attention to Plexis Security. I wasn't sure Inspector Wallace noticed he'd moved to stand shoulder-to-shoulder with his Human constable, or that the smaller Whirtle had managed to squeeze itself between them.

All acknowledged Morgan. My Human frozen in place, Huido returned waves and clicked his claws merrily. They were, after all, his truffles.

I joined in after a moment, and it all might have been some mad spontaneous celebration, except for the seriousness of expressions, color changes, and in several cases, odors. These weren't happy beings.

They were determined.

To do what became clear as Morgan finally stirred, his hand finding mine. *Witchling*—his mindvoice full of emotion.

Items arched gracefully through the air, aimed at the personnel door fronted by the thickest part of the crowd. That most either missed or landed in the crowd didn't seem to matter, which made more sense when a globe smashed on the floor near me, releasing a blue goo that smelled deliciously familiar. Nicnic jam.

They were throwing food. Consumables, I corrected, since beer was definitely soaring, too.

The dexterous caught and rethrew misdirected offerings. Others were quickly drenched by whatever struck. A few, this being Plexis, consumed what came their way—in the spirit of a common cause I sincerely hoped there weren't any consuming one another. Tasty beings knew to keep a polite distance from their predators; not as easy in what was becoming a mob.

The door rapidly disappearing behind a spectrum of sticky goo and smashed containers remained closed. If there'd been security guarding it, I assumed they'd taken one look at the oncoming mass of irate cooks, wait staff, and bar owners, and realized they weren't being paid nearly enough to stay.

More importantly, you did not want to anger those responsible for your food and drink. Something I hoped was sinking in to a certain F'Feego's consciousness.

Interlude

***

MORGAN SHOOK OFF the paralysis that had gripped him. He'd asked Sira to trust him. Claimed Plexis would answer—

No one could have seen this coming. He didn't need the acrid taste of *CHANGE* to see how it could end. The station's tolerance had limits, especially here at the beating heart of its economy. At any moment, the great section doors would close, trapping them all between. At any moment—suffice it to say accidents happened in space and all it would take would be some panicked fool in operations venting the "air they shared."

Or under orders. *This has to stop,* he sent to his Chosen.

I'm open to suggestions, she replied.

We need a distraction—spotting a familiar slug, Morgan rapped on the nearest bit of black shell, gaining Huido's attention. "Pick up Keevor."

Eyestalks went rigid. "What?! Touch that—"

"Catch him!" For a slug, Keevor could move, leaving a glistening silver trail others were avoiding. "Hurry!"

With an aggrieved rattle, the Carasian obeyed, lunging forward to snatch the small alien in one great claw. "Now wh—"

The question vanished behind a loud keening WAIL louder than any previous shout. Keevor, rightly concerned about being squeezed in two, was squirting a thick brown mucus that *hissed* on contact with Huido's carapace. In reaction, the Carasian flung his small purple attacker, still oozing mucus, as far away as possible.

As those beneath ducked and howled, Morgan turned to Sira, putting his palm against her forehead. *Now!*

17

***

ACCEPTING THE LOCATE from Morgan, I concentrated and *pushed* . . .

. . . to find myself, and my Chosen, standing in a service tunnel, one narrower than any I'd seen before but still lined with the ubiquitous waste canisters, chewing their contents. I blinked in the dimmer light.

"This way." He was on the move, heading for a nearby door.

A figure formed from what I'd thought a shadow—was shadow itself, wreathed in black, the squat twisted shape confusing, if not the needler's glint.

Morgan stopped, a finger's flick keeping me still. "Morrab." He stretched his hands out, open and empty. "Raj didn't need to send you. We can resolve this."

The needler's tip drifted my way. "Dangerous."

"Not to you," my Chosen asserted, though well aware I was ready to drop this being into the M'hir. His voice turned grim, "Plexis will break unless we act, now. There'll be no fixing it."

"How can you know?" Morrab's voice was raspy, as if hardly used.

"I *taste* it." A pause during which I tried not to shiver—needlers were banned for good reason—then Morgan said, "So do you."

After another too-long moment, the needler swung aside. "Go." The other faded into the shadow of a canister.

Giving us a chance—before taking action of his own. *Who's this Morrab?*

Also Plexis. Morgan busied himself with the palm lock on the door. It slid to the side, and we went through.

He didn't close it behind us, a neglect I accepted, though it gave me another *chill.*

I refused to look over my shoulder to see who might follow.

I'd expected the station's Department of Consumables Duties & Tariffs to be a typical busy office setting: comps lining the walls and an elaborate com system. Humans weren't the only species prone to them.

Instead, we stepped gingerly between shoulder-high stacks of plas, most of it discarded food packaging, but I spotted noteplas tucked in here and there, as well as insulation panels. The air was bitingly dry, masking the smell that would otherwise permeate every corner. The ceiling was hidden behind swathes of purple cargo net, the net sagging alarmingly under the weight of black round bags. Bags I fervently hoped stayed where they were while we were underneath.

If there'd been portlights, they were buried in plas or lost inside the netting. Illumination came from utility glo-sticks shoved with no apparent order into the plas stacks.

After three turns, one dead-ending on a wall, we found ourselves at the official entrance, a door as plain as the one from the service tunnel. By the thuds and moist *smacks* coming from the other side, the crowd hadn't run out of food to throw.

"Now what?" I asked my captain.

Morgan looked around, a speculative gleam in his eye. *We aren't alone, chit.* "Officer Esaliz E'Teiso," he said. "I'm Captain Jason Morgan of the *Silver Fox.* We spoke earlier on coms about our cargo. The truffles. The person with me is Sira Morgan. Please come out so we can continue our conversation and resolve this."

"If you've come—-*shurr*—to pay the fee, you can't do that in person."

We looked up. All I could see were black bags.

"You must pay—*shurr*—Plexis com."

"Please come down," Morgan replied. *Up and left, chit.*

There. What I'd thought another bulge in the net was a being about my size wearing it—or tangled in it. Possibly both. *Is it stuck?*

I doubt it. "You've made a serious error, Officer E'Teiso, but it's not irreversible. Credit may still be yours. Please come down."

The bulge wiggled. "I'm not—*shurr*—finished my *wrosk*." With a tinge of embarrassment.

Don't ask, Morgan sent, before I could. "I suggest you do so promptly, Officer." The door shuddered under a louder *THUD* than any before. "Those outside your door are not inclined to patience."

A chubby arm appeared, the digits at the end holding a black bag in triumph. "I'm done." The bag joined the others in the net.

Many biologies weren't this tidy, I reminded myself.

The F'Feego detached and lowered itself by unrolling from a long strip of cargo net, the ends tied with little bows at intervals to prevent fraying. Impressive. I knew from experience the stuff wasn't easy to handle.

Once on the floor, I could see the F'Feego was humanoid, if having paired limbs and a head over a torso qualified. Those limbs were fleshy and rounded, as though built from beads, and the head was similar, round and with features sunken within soft pits of pink freckled skin. There were two large red eyes, three narrow openings I assumed were nostrils but could, I suppose, have been ears, and a mouth presently pinched shut. The top of E'Teiso's bald freckled head came up to my chin. Its torso was rounded, too, straining the fastenings of what was, indeed, a Plexis Port Authority uniform.

Part of one, none too clean, held together with string.

This humble being was the source of our troubles?

"I am down—*shurr*." The sound explained by a flutter of the nostril openings. "What is your purpose—*shurr*—here, Captain? Payments go to Plexis com." Said wearily, as if repeated to everyone.

I could see the change in Morgan's face; felt it myself. "We're here to help, Officer E'Teiso," my Human said gently. "Are you aware what's happening outside?"

"A practice mass evacuation—*shurr*—perhaps there has been false advertising of a sale—"

"They've come after you. You've made everyone angry by trying to tax incoming food."

Shoulders like round balls hunched. "It is not I—*shurr*—*shurrrrr*—not I! I do what comes." The F'Feego rushed away, nails on its long toes clicking, but it wasn't flight. It stopped at a stack and fussed at the top, then moved to the next, digging with frantic haste through layers of packaging and insulation. "This!" it exclaimed in triumph, whirling to shove a scrap in Morgan's direction.

The stacks were its filing system? I couldn't argue—there were Clan who'd approve.

Morgan took the scrap, scanned its contents, then looked up, blue eyes ice-cold. "This isn't an official policy change—this is an unexplained, unsigned directive to charge a new fee. Whomever sent it is a thief, using you and your office to skim honest importers. Why didn't you question it?"

"I—*shurr*—implement." E'Teiso's digit flicked a piece of plas sticking out from the multitude, then another and another. "I don't—*shurr*—question." A long—*SHURRRRRRRR*—then, in that weary tone, "I answer questions."

Doubtless with "payment goes to Plexis com." Having been on the asking side, I found myself less than sympathetic.

Morgan crumpled the directive in his fist. "A name, E'Teiso."

The F'Feego, proving it had some understanding of Humans, backed away until it collided with a stack, then crouched, digits out in defense. "Not that—-*shurr*—question! Not my job! Make payment, unload—*shurr*—your cargo, and go!"

Punctuated by another *THUD* on the door.

Jason, I sent quickly. *The truffles.*

A wave of *approval* answered. "Oh, we're not unloading," Morgan said casually. "We've another market."

E'Teiso's red eyes bulged until I feared they'd pop loose. "You can't—"

A shrug. "Can't afford to unload here, so it's only good business. This is Plexis. You understand how it works."

The F'Feego came closer, digits curled to its chest. "Captain—*shurr*—Hom Huido needs more truffles!"

"He says he's done with them. This cargo's for *The Salty Appendage*. That's on Auord," Morgan added helpfully.

"'Auord?'" weak and followed by–*SHURRRRRRRRR*—"But I need—my wrosk—truffles—*SHURRRRR*—" With a pathetic flexing reach of its digits, "—keep me regular."

I really hoped the cargo net overhead didn't break.

Interlude

**

IN MANY WAYS, Morgan thought, E'Teiso was Plexis, too. A simple being, part of a system it didn't control, doing its job and not a bit more.

From the sounds outside, the cost could be its life. Not something the F'Feego understood . . . yet.

There was a listener, close by and deadly, who did. Whether Raj Plexis had ordered him to assassinate the F'Feego and placate the crowd with its corpse, or to signal a larger, more terrible response, Morrab would act to end this. The question was how. An outsider, Morrab, with discretion.

Morgan counted on it. "We'll unload the truffles on Plexis, Officer E'Teiso, after you have written down the name—or names—of those behind all this." He held up a hand before the F'Feego could utter a word. "That's not our business." It was Morrab's and, for an instant, he pitied those named—but only for an instant. Plexis survived because enlightened self-interest—call it common sense—set limits on greed. "After you do, you'll go outside to announce the fee on our cargo was a clerical error and apologize for causing concern."

"They'll—*shurr*—kill me."

Not so unaware, then. "We'll be with you," he promised.

We will? with some *alarm.*

We started it, he told her. Spreading the word, drawing in friend and foe alike, starting ripples flowing outward that had—oh, yes—finally caught the full attention of Raj Plexis.

Up to them to finish.

18

* ✳ *

IN THE INTERESTS of not being assaulted with food and drink—and worse, their containers—Morgan instructed Officer E'Teiso to request a truce before we opened the door. Having been in the night zone during a food fight, I'd have requested full body armor. At least one of the bags Butter used for his dancers.

But no. A truce it was. Having come this far, I thought resignedly, it was either trust my Human knew this place and people, or 'port us away. The latter wasn't an option. Besides, I knew that look.

Morgan was making his move.

Predictably, the F'Feego's voice broadcast into the receiving area outside only increased the *THUDS* and *SMACKS*. Undeterred, my Human grinned and gave the now-trembling being a friendly clap on the shoulder. "My turn."

He leaned into the crevice between stacks, home to a reasonably up-to-date com panel, and pressed the control. "Morgan here. Stand down and clear the entrance." Straightening, he pulled out the portable com and gestured to the door. "Shall we?"

The abrupt silence wasn't as reassuring as he might think, but I matched his smile. "Lead on, Captain."

"First things first." Morgan went around the nearest filing stack and shoved. Hard.

Plas tumbled down, E'Teiso crying out in protest, but my Human was only getting started. Seeing his plan—to make a barrier in front of the door—I helped, tossing E'Teiso's files, and meal remains, on top. In short order we had a waist-high heap.

"Back here," Morgan ordered. We stood behind the barrier, the unhappy F'Feego between us, facing the door. "Open it."

With a stretch, E'Teiso was able to place its digits over the palm lock.

The door slid halfway open and stuck, something I noticed later, having ducked behind our flimsy shield to avoid the flood of consumables pouring through.

A move not entirely successful.

When the flow stopped, I stood, brushing futilely at goo, salad, bits of cooked bone, and not so cooked flesh. The beer made a sort of glue; the sombay, more a stain. Morgan and E'Teiso were coated, too, though somehow my Human had managed not to get any on his face or hair.

Mine shuddered itself clean, adding a shower of—yes, those were prawlies, not all dead—to my coveralls.

E'Teiso used its digits to dig out its eyes and mouth, spat, then blinked accusingly at me.

I shrugged. "Could have been worse."

Interlude

✳ ✳ ✳

WORSE IT MIGHT become, and quickly, but there wasn't time for doubt. Morgan climbed over the barrier and sloshed through the mess, leading the way outside.

They'd listened, for a wonder. Enough to leave a semicircle of littered flooring open. Beyond was a ring of ominously quiet beings. Some he knew.

Most he didn't—

"Let me THROUGH!" Serving staff or restaurant owner, they scattered as the giant Carasian, food bits hanging from his carapace and claws, lumbered forward at full speed.

"Maybe we should wait inside—" Sira said.

"It's all right," Morgan said, hoping it was. Sure enough, all at once, his friend started to slow.

Only to skid.

With the awe-inspiring inevitability of a star collapsing, Huido lost his footing and a significant mass of armored flesh—with weapons clipped to their rings—lifted into the air.

Only to twist, contort, and come down, nimble as an Anisoptera, on two balloon-feet.

A smattering of applause came from those who'd expected the

outcome to be mashed Humans and F'Feego, plus a serious dent in the station bulkhead.

"BROTHER!" Huido bellowed, surging forward—with more care—great claws snapping with vicious intent. "You've brought my enemy!"

E'Teiso hid behind Sira.

Morgan held up his hand. "Peace, you big oaf. This fine official has come out to assure you it was all a mistake. Haven't you, Officer E'Teiso?"

When the F'Feego didn't move, Sira stepped to the side and pulled it forward, keeping her hands on its shoulders. "Go ahead," she urged. "No one's going to hurt you."

A few growls from the crowd promised otherwise, but they'd wait on Huido. Something the wily Carasian knew full well. No accident, Morgan thought fondly, that almost crash. If there was anything Huido did exceptionally well, it was make an entrance.

"Here." Morgan handed the F'Feego the portable comlink, willing it not to faint. To cooperate. "Please, officer. Answer their question. What about the truffles?"

Nothing could have looked less imposing than the food-covered F'Feego, but most in the crowd couldn't see it anyway.

The voice, when it came, rang out sure and strong and likely familiar.

"I am   *shurr*—Officer Esaliz E'Teiso, of the Department of Duties & Tariffs. A clerical error—" the "—*shurr*—" drowned out by a multi-organed roar, and several *yipyips*, of approval "—imposed a fee on this good captain's cargo—"

A spontaneous chant of "Free the Truffles!" forced a pause.

Morgan raised his arm. Huido a claw. Silence spread from the front row back. When satisfied, the Human nodded at E'Teiso to continue.

"There is no—*SHURRR*—legal fee on imports to be consumed—*SHURR*—on this station." The F'Feego raised its voice. "On my watch—*SHURRR*—there will NEVER BE!"

The receiving area exploded, this time with cheers.

Did you expect that? Sira sent.

From Officer Esaliz E'Teiso? *I've learned never to be surprised.*

Cautious, yes. Those named as behind the grab would be dealt with—possibly demoted to sanitation—possibly spaced. Not their problem. This newly bold F'Feego could be the innocent in all this, freed to say whatever it wished and taste popularity, however briefly.

Or it was nothing of the kind, Morgan thought darkly, using them—the truffles—to remove its superiors and advance itself.

Officer Esaliz E'Teiso would bear watching. But that was normal on Plexis.

Having achieved their goal—and aware they weren't making any credits in the warehouse level—the crowd melted away. E'Teiso, after insisting on a reservation at the *Claws & Jaws* for truffles as soon as possible, retired to the shambles of its office.

"Well, that turned out—"

"Don't say 'well,' brother, until we know what he's upset about now," rumbled Huido, eyestalks aimed at the approaching Inspector Wallace.

"We did what he wanted," Sira protested.

The Human did appear agitated, walking so quickly the Whirtle constable somersaulted over a rim trying to keep up.

Morgan laughed. "I'd say it's this," with a sweep of his arm to indicate the sea of wasted food and litter. In the distance, vermin were sniffing the edges.

Huido rattled in outrage. "He can't blame us for the excesses of others! We did not throw consumables."

"He can't think we'll—" Sira's face as she surveyed the mess was a mix of dread and calculation. She'd developed a knack with the *Fox*'s sweeper, beyond doubt.

"Not our job," the Human assured her. He'd worked sanitation. Plexis could pretend it relied on servos for its dirty, dangerous jobs, but there was an army of "invisible" beings in the tunnels and back corridors. Offer them overtime, out here in relatively open air?

According to his friend Minnic, they'd draw lots for the chance.

"C'mon, chit. We've perishable cargo to unload. My guess is, Wallace has heard more than enough about 'truffles.'"

I do believe you're right.

The Materials At Hand

***

by Jessica McAdams

MINNIC LOOKED UP and down the service corridor before he stuck his finger into the joint between the doorframe and the wall. He was allowed to be here, and as far as he knew, taste-testing the algae the cleaning servos were supposed to eliminate wasn't illegal, but he had just finally earned enough to pay for his wife to join him, and he didn't want to mess that up. Plexis was about to enter the Powti System, and that made tickets from the Powti's refugee center cheap enough that Raphic could make the flight, and Minnic could pay the entrance fees when she arrived.

Risking any kind of trouble just wasn't worth it, and you never knew what one sapient or another would find offensive.

Maybe this algae creeping around the doorframe was sacred to the people who were rich enough to own the establishment on the other side of the wall. They certainly spent enough money on keeping their rooms dripping with water vapor and oxygen: their doorframes grew enough algae and mold to have the servos overwhelmed and breaking down in the corridor practically every week. Minnic didn't know if they used the service doors often enough that the stuff got out that way, or if the delicious-looking algae had actually defeated the structural integrity of the supposedly air-tight seals around the doors. If it was the latter, it was a safety hazard, but safety was not his assignment.

Cleanliness was, and fixing the cleaning servos was all he ever wanted anyone to catch him doing.

But no one was there to catch him right now. The only thing moving was the servo he'd come to fix, and it only buzzed in its patient holding pattern, so Minnic ran his first finger down the joint and scooped up a lovely pile of the green goo. He popped it into his mouth and rolled it over his tongue. *Mmm.* Good enough to serve at the chief's table, back when the Dineaps had a chief.

Looking around once more to make sure he was unobserved, Minnic scooped up a bit more of the algae, wiped it on the kerchief he kept in his uniform pocket, and folded the kerchief neatly around it. Popping it back into his pocket, he turned to the servo. Now that he had a sample he could cultivate in the little table-greenhouse back in his small rented room down in the sublevels, he was happy to repair the servo that would eliminate the rest of the algae from all the joints and corners and crevices in the corridor.

Well, eliminate it for another few days, anyway.

Minnic linked his fingers together, and gave himself a good, joint-crackling stretch, looping his joined hands over his head, all the way behind his back, and then bringing them to the front again. Ah, that felt good. He missed having trees to swing through. He bent over the servo, and began to pry out the excessive algae that had gummed up the works and mixed with the servo's lubricant to make a kind of stiff paste. He'd probably also have to replace the filter or recalibrate the sensors, but even though he was on the pay scale as a janitorial *technician*, Minnic had found that most of his work was a matter of muscle, and not of mind.

"Here now, what's this?" Minnic sat back on his heels, and stroked the fur on his cheek thoughtfully. There was more than algae and lubricant stuck in the servo. Something stiff was wedged in there, too, and that shouldn't be, given that the cleaning servo was programmed to follow close on the heels of the waste canister. Someone had to have dropped it fairly recently.

Minnic tried pulling at it with his fingers, but it wouldn't budge, so he took a pair of pliers out of his belt. The other members of the cleaning crew had laughed at him the first day he'd walked onto the job with his dad's old hand tools clanking around his waist, but Minnic didn't mind. Sometimes the best tools were the simplest ones. Back in the bad days on Dineaps, electric pulse attacks had knocked out all the power tools and motors, leaving many families stranded up in their eyries. But Minnic's dad had been able to jury-rig a block and tackle system with the stuff on his tool belt—got their whole family out before the troops who'd been following the pulse attack had reached their part of the forest.

Got Raphic's family out, too. Now, if only Minnic could do his dad one better, and get their families out of the refugee center. This job was a start.

Minnic grasped the stiff edge of whatever-it-was with the tips of the pliers and pulled, hard. It came out without ripping, which surprised him. Awfully tough stuff, this . . . well, *whatever-it-was* was still the best name Minnic had for it.

It was a small rectangle, dark blue and so matte that it seemed to swallow the light. Minnic turned it one way and then another, but could make nothing more of it, so he slipped it into one of his many pockets and went back to cleaning the algae out of the servo.

He was so intent on his work that he jumped when a voice behind him said, "All right, scum-sucker, give me that brick back, or you'll regret it."

Minnic swiveled on his knees and found himself looking down the wrong end of a blaster. He skittered back onto his heels and stood up, pressing himself against the wall.

The blaster was being held by a short female humanoid of a species Minnic didn't recognize. She was also holding some kind of scanner, and it was beeping insistently at his right inside jacket pocket.

The humanoid scowled, hooked the scanner onto her belt, and stepped closer. "C'mon now, I haven't got all day. Give it back, and I'll let you go."

Minnic could hear his heartbeat in his ears and feel it in his neck. Oddly, he could also feel it in the set of molars he'd been slowly filing down, in hopes that when Raphic rejoined him, he could soon have them decoratively capped to show that he had become a father. The current racing of his pulse made those teeth ache.

Minnic pulled out the dark blue rectangle—the "brick"?—and handed it to his attacker, who pocketed it herself.

"Okay," said Minnic. "Didn't know it was yours. Sorry about that."

But the blaster stayed leveled at his head. "Sorry about this, too," she said.

"Wait!" shrieked Minnic. "I did what you wanted. I'm not going to say anything to Security. I'm just a janitor. I don't care what you're smuggling."

"'Smuggling'?"

"Sure." Minnic shrugged, and tried to make himself look non-threatening. It was hard, given how he towered over the little human-oid. "I go everywhere on this station. I know stuff happens. I don't care. I just want to do my job. You don't need to worry about me."

His attacker squinted up at him, her finger slightly relaxing away from the trigger. "Huh," she said. "I'd never thought about that." Her free hand rubbed the blue airtag on her cheek. "I guess that's true, though . . . you *can* go anywhere on this station."

The last time Minnic had worked the service corridors in the upper levels of Plexis, he had enjoyed it. The smells coming from the restaurants here were better, the things patrons discarded were more interesting, and there were so many decorative plants that no one noticed if someone like him occasionally snuck a leaf or two for a midday snack. In fact, last time he'd worked in the upper service corridors, not only had he found a new and helpful tool for his belt, he'd also found a bottle of Omacron wine that was only half drunk. After his shift, he'd traded the bottle to a co-worker in exchange for a beautifully-made and barely-used dress he knew Raphic would love.

On Plexis, the barter economy among the janitors who worked the corridors was second only to the barter economy among the grunts who worked at the recycling plant.

But now he walked the upper service corridors with a feeling of dread in his belly. Not only was his gut heavy with guilt, but his trousers were hanging heavy on his hips, weighed down as they were with more than a dozen of the smuggler's "bricks."

She'd explained that this was the actual price of his life: not merely giving her back her property after he'd found it stuck in the servo, no. No, that wasn't enough. She insisted that he had to go to a trade mission on the upper level, pretend to work on the cleaning servo there, and at the same time drop a small mechanical bug behind a certain desk.

"I'll get in trouble," said Minnic. He could almost smell the musk of his wife's neck fur. If he were arrested, who would be there to welcome her at the air lock? Who would help her and the rest of his family find jobs?

Plexis had seemed like such a safe haven, so full of possibilities, so full of nooks to hide in and vantage points to look out of.

Now it felt like just as much of a trap as the eyries back home under the eyes of the invading army. He was not going to do that again. He was not going to be trapped again. Not again . . .

"You won't get in trouble. My friend just left us a message on the comp there, and I have to access it directly. No one's going to care."

"Then why don't you do it?"

She shoved the blaster into his belly, all pretense at being reasonable gone. "Do it, or I shoot you."

And then, as if afraid that threat wasn't enough, she had loaded him down with both the brick he'd been carrying, and more like it. She zapped them all with her scanner, and sweetly informed him that he was now programmed to explode if he didn't do exactly as she said.

That had been too much. Minnic told her she was welcome to kill him, but he wasn't helping any saboteurs.

"I'm not a saboteur," she said. "I'm a smuggler. You said so yourself. Those bricks are what I'm smuggling, but they're not going to do me any good here on the station. I need the info my friend left me, and I need it now, so I can get out of here." She paused. "You do *want* me to get out of here, don't you?"

Minnic had agreed that he did, and so he went. He took the service corridors as far as he could, not eager to walk through the crowds out in the public part of the station—especially not in the upper levels, where his coveralls would stand in stark contrast to the elegant clothing of the wealthy customers who frequented that part of the massive mobile supermarket.

In fact, he *was* noticed when he exited the service corridors—by a security officer who was standing, hands folded and yet alert, near one of the ramps. One of the officer's five eyes flicked first to Minnic's airtag—blue and the wrong color for this level—but then blinked away once it also took in his maintenance uniform.

I can go anywhere on this station, Minnic thought miserably. *She's right.* So could the security guard, he supposed.

But the security guard had training and a weapon. His freedom was real, and not an illusion. All Minnic's freedom of movement was buying him right now was guilt—that, and a growing fear that somehow this would all go wrong, and he'd never get to see his wife again.

Everyone noticed him at the trade mission, too, but again, no one stopped him. Minnic knelt beside the servo the trade mission had contracted out from the station to clean its floors, and changed its filter, even though it clearly didn't need it. With a gulp, he also brushed against the comp console in question, opening his hand to release the tiny mechanical bug as he did. It skittered away into a crack, and was lost to his view.

He trudged back down the service corridors, feeling both hot and staticky. The fur under his coveralls seemed to twitch and writhe against the bricks strapped next to his legs. He went down to the air lock where he'd been instructed to go.

He paused a moment before pressing his palm to the lock. This was so close to the transfer point where Raphic's ship was scheduled to arrive in just a few hours. It was the same side of the station, and only two levels up. He leaned his forehead against the cool metal wall of the corridor, just for a moment. What kind of place was he bringing his family into? What kind of father-to-be was he to think of nesting a litter of babies in such a hive of crime?

He'd thought he was bringing his family to freedom—to the chance at a better life, the kind of life they'd thought had died back in the fires on Dineaps.

Instead, he was just bringing them back into another conflagration, into a different kind of war zone, and one where he had no weapons, no training . . . and no route of escape.

He was not a father like his father. He never would be.

Minnic pressed his palm to the lock. It did not open automatically, but the vid above it glowed briefly red, and Minnic wearily turned his face toward it so that his tormenter could see that he had obediently come as he had been told.

The door slid open, and Minnic was greeted with the now-familiar sight of the wrong end of the smuggler's blaster barrel. He stepped in through the door, and found himself in a giant shipping container that was attached, limpet-like, to the side of the station.

The smuggler was not alone this time. A male of her species stood just behind her. His blaster was also drawn, but he was staring at a handheld screen. "He did it," the male confirmed. "I'm getting the itinerary now."

Itinerary of what? Minnic wondered. The ship that was going to pick up their stolen goods?

"Can I go now?" Minnic asked. He shook one leg irritably. "Would you take these things off? I just want to go and get some dinner." He thought longingly of his little tabletop greenhouse, and the beautiful plate of colorful algae appetizers he'd planned for Raphic's arrival.

"I don't think so," said the female. "We can't let you run off and tell on us."

"He's coming in two levels up," said the male. "Less than an hour from now."

"I'm not *going* to tell on you," insisted Minnic. How could he get these people to understand that all he wanted was to never think of any of them ever again?

The female looked at her companion. "We can't risk it," she said.

The male flicked his gaze toward her, then gave a short nod.

"Sorry about this," said the female. "Your bad luck, I guess. We've been looking for a way to take out the Curian commissioner for months, and this is the closest we've been able to get."

"You're not smugglers," Minnic said, the realization coming all too late.

The female shook her head. "I'm sorry. But you have to understand: he's a war criminal. He deserves it."

I don't! thought Minnic, but he couldn't bring himself to say the words aloud. What difference would it make?

The male raised his blaster at him.

Now Minnic did shout. "Wait!" he cried.

"Why?"

Minnic licked his lips, then pressed the tip of his tongue against one of his shaved molars. *Just a chance, just give me a chance . . .* "I haven't had time to make peace with the goddess," he said.

Would they even know what that meant? The two smugglers looked at each other. Then the female said, "We can't afford the time to wait for you to make your prayers. We have to get out of here."

Minnic looked at the pile of "bricks"—the pile of explosives. "I can't die unshriven," he pleaded. "I can die—I don't want to, but I can. But you can't let me die damned. You have to give me time."

"Just leave him," said the male. "This place is going to be gone in an hour."

Please, please, please . . . thought Minnic. *Please . . .*

Minnic was elated that they'd listened. He was even more elated when they tied his hands behind his back, securing him to one of the container's giant shelves. They pulled off his tool belt and threw it on the other side of the bricks, but that was all they did before they left out the air lock door, securing it behind them.

As he rolled his shoulders in a preparatory stretch, Minnic chuckled in disbelief. Some sapients! Thinking everyone was just like them! He squatted down and easily looped his tied hands to the front of his body, where he could easily reach the hard plastic tie with his teeth. *Just because your species doesn't have level-three brachiating ability . . .*

His smugness lasted long enough for him to chew through the ties around his wrists, and for him to reclaim his tool belt, cinching it back tight around his waist, but it disappeared as he reached the door.

Then he stopped, standing stock still and staring. *No.* And he thought he'd been so clever! But they'd not just secured the lock, they'd destroyed it—and the com panel above it.

I can't get out. And he couldn't call for help, either. Minnic's hand reached automatically for the tools at his belt, but not with much hope. Plexis might allow algae to grow around internal doors, but the air locks that ships and shipping containers latched onto were serious hardware. He'd have to hack at the door frame for days to make any headway.

Minnic glanced back at the pile of explosive bricks, which the terrorist pair had activated before they left.

He was pretty sure he didn't have days.

No com, no way out. Minnic tapped his fingers in a frantic rhythm against his belt. No com, no way out, no time. What *did* he have? He ran his hands up and down his coveralls, patting all of his many pockets.

He stopped over the pocket that held his kerchief.

He had part of the mess he'd cleaned up earlier in the day.

He had algae.

Minnic glanced away from the air lock door and down to the— much smaller—service port beside it. Too small to crawl through, even with his flexible shoulders. Just big enough for a cleaning servo to get through.

Had the bombers, in their haste, signed the boilerplate contract for full service from Plexis?

Minnic knew there was only one way to find out.

He had to make a mess.

The first servo came in quick response when Minnic wiped his collection of algae across one of the sensor points at the corner of the nearest floor plate. Usually the sensors called for the servos when a large enough layer of dust and grime built up over them, but they weren't foolproof, and a big enough spill at the right point would trigger a servo call.

Minnic temporarily disabled the servo's locomotive ability and levered it open. He filled the inside fluid reservoir with almost half of the explosive bricks and was about to send it on its way when he realized that if he did that, he'd be dooming all the workers in or near the recycling center to the same fate he himself was trying to escape. He quickly pulled the bricks all out again, and then smoothed down the fur on his face, which was standing up in horror at the fact that he'd almost become a mass murderer.

Mass murder . . . that was still what was going to happen, if he couldn't come up with a better solution. It was just that he would be the one dying—along with everyone on this level, and on the next couple of levels above and below him.

Raphic. She was supposed to arrive within the hour, and only two levels up. The person the criminals were trying to kill must be coming through the same transfer point where she was scheduled to arrive. She would die if he couldn't figure out a way to stop this explosion . . . Minnic almost put all the bricks back. Let the recycling workers die—they weren't Raphic!

But no, no. He couldn't. He just couldn't. He'd be as bad as the couple who'd set this all up, as bad as the soldiers who'd burned his people in their nests back on Dineaps.

Minnic tapped the servo, the frantic rhythm of his fingers slower now.

These were tough little machines, these cleaning servos.

Tough little machines. Little machines. Small machines. Small . . .

How small could he make his problem?

Minnic began to hum as he sealed up just one brick in the little servo, and left it tipped over on its side at the far end of the container, locomotion still disabled. He knew more about the servos than he knew about the explosives, but . . . but if they needed this many bricks to make a big enough explosion to blow up the concourse two levels above . . . Minnic calculated. Maybe. Just maybe. The servos really were tough little machines: well-built, and made to stand up to a lot of abuse, and even built to handle the fairly serious chemical reactions that could happen when they were sent to clean up the kind of messes that a station swarming with every kind of life saw with some regularity.

Minnic carefully wiped up his algae from the first sensor, walked to the next one, and covered it up, too. How many servos could he prompt to come to him . . . how many were even on the station?

He counted the bricks, and compared it to the number of

levels on Plexis. Enough, he thought. There were probably enough servos.

He just wasn't sure if there was enough time.

The last brick was in the last servo. His algae hadn't held up to being wiped and rewiped over and over, and he didn't like to think about the various bodily fluids he'd had to produce to trigger sensor after sensor in the floor plates. Undignified. Dirty.

But it had worked. He looked at the collection of disabled servos now lining the far end of the container, piled like firewood, ridiculously spinning their cleaning pads in vain.

Minnic sank down next to the ruined air lock, chewing absently on the edge of his lip. Would it be enough? Would a hundred tiny explosions, each contained in its own little case of fluid, plastics, and tough metal, be better than the giant uncontained one the terrorists had planned? Or was he wrong? Maybe he had just added more shrapnel to an already unstoppable disaster.

As he eyed his work with misgiving from the far side of the container, another thought occurred, less horrible than imminent death, but still daunting: *They're never going to let us stay.*

That pile of repurposed servos, levered open and resealed: they weren't just a desperate solution to danger, they were *property damage.*

In trying to survive, he had been forced to become a vandal. Anger flooded Minnic. He hadn't asked for this, he hadn't asked to make this choice!

All he had wanted was a home for his family. All he had wanted was the freedom to live in a good place and make a nest that would see his beautiful Raphic a pleased and preening mistress over a brood of promising littermates.

He'd thought he'd found that. And now—one way or another— he was going to lose it all.

Minnic closed his eyes. He'd been bluffing when he'd talked about needing to make confession before he died, but now that it was coming to it . . .

He startled at a banging noise beside him, and clambered to his feet as a line started to glow in the air lock door, next to the ruined lock. Less than a minute later, the lock popped out on his side, as if pushed, and the door was jimmied open.

Minnic's boss, a Whirtle, humped through, and waved its tentacles in dismay at the sight of him. Behind, a uniformed security guard peered past them both and frowned at the ruined pile of servos at the far end of the container.

"So this is where they were all going!" his boss said. "Minnic, what did you do to them?"

Apology, fear, and accusation all poised themselves at the end of Minnic's tongue, but what came out was a truncated, "Get out! They're going to—"

Behind them, in unison, all of the servos blew up.

Training for his new job had taken almost a year. But the Curian Trade Pact Commissioner, in gratitude for saving *nis* life, sponsored Minnic through the schooling.

Minnic's old boss, in janitorial, had had some things to say about the property damage. When the servos blew up, tough little machines that they were, it looked more like a series of giant water bottles burping than a hundred little bombs wreaking havoc.

But the servos were still completely ruined.

However, the security officer who'd arrived with Minnic's boss, and who'd examined the wreckage, and raised his eyebrows at the estimated weight and makeup of the explosives, had taken down Minnic's account of the event with an increasing attitude of respect, and assured Minnic that he would put in a good word for him.

"Trust me," he'd said, "we'd rather clean up this mess than the one we would have had if you hadn't been so quick on your feet."

Plexis Security caught the two responsible before they could leave the station.

Then Plexis Security offered Minnic a new job.

Minnic stood every day at his new post: a lovely little level just up past where the underbelly of Plexis ended and the expensive shops began.

Minnic wasn't trapped and he wasn't hunted. He looked at the shoppers passing him with genial good will. Some of them had blue airtags on their cheeks and some had gold. It didn't matter: this was Plexis, and there was always a chance to move up.

He settled his hands more firmly around his belt, which still, with permission, hung heavy with a few of his father's old hand tools—as well as his newly-issued service blaster.

This was a good place, and people like him were going to keep it good.

He ran his teeth over his newly-capped molars. Raphic was settled and happy in her nest, and their babies were thriving. Plexis was no trap, as he'd feared. No, it was a forest of metal and plas, fit for tourists and families, smugglers and shop owners, but not terror, not wars. Not while he lived here and kept it safe.

I am free, he thought. *I'm going to stay that way.*

He smoothed down the front of his new uniform in satisfaction.

And I can still go anywhere *on the station.*

. . . *Truffles* concludes
19

✳ ✳ ✳

MORGAN LEANED ON the railing, looking down. "So, Witchling. What do you think of Plexis now?"

I joined him, gazing at the complex massed confusion below. "I don't know how," I admitted, "but it works."

"Given a chance," he agreed.

It'd be a long time, if ever, before I thought of this place as home, the way my Chosen did. Still, there was something special here. I'd seen it for myself. Not kindness, I thought, searching for another word to describe what I saw—and what had happened—

Community.

Chosen did that, finish thoughts. Complete one another. I smiled to myself. "I'd like to come back and see more. Just not right away," I added quickly.

He chuckled. "What, no more dancing?"

My hair slid down his arm to loop, warm and confident, around his wrist.

Oh, there'll be dancing, I promised. And before anyone could notice, or anyone care . . . I concentrated . . .

. . . and put us back where we belonged, in our starship.

Without any truffles at all.

The Writers of *Tales from Plexis* (in Alphabetical Order)

B. Morris Allen, "Cinnamon Sticks"

B. Morris Allen is a biochemist turned activist turned lawyer turned foreign aid consultant, and frequently wonders whether it's time for a new career. He's been traveling since birth, and has lived on five of seven continents. When he can, he makes his home on the Oregon coast. In between journeys, he edits *Metaphorosis* magazine, and works on his own speculative stories of love and disaster. His dark fantasy novel *Susurrus* came out in 2017. Find more at www.bmorrisallen.com and @BMorrisAllen.

Morris was immediately enticed by Keevor, the mysterious, odoriferous gourmand. There had to be more story there. Allen is from the Pacific Northwest, so slugs quickly found their way into the story. They don't really smell, but there's all that slime to work with . . .

Nathan Azinger, "Rainbow Connection"

Nathan lives in the Pacific Northwest with his beautiful wife and spastic cat. He practices martial arts (a hobby he shares with his wife), watches birds (a hobby he shares with his cat), and writes science fiction and fantasy (a hobby he'd like to make into a career). He is of the opinion that the quintessential Czerneda story contains three elements: a plot that is driven by legitimate conflicts of interest, interesting (and often messy) biology, and characters named after hockey players. That's the sort of story he set out to write.

Paul Baughman, "Jilly"

Paul Baughman has been a lifelong reader. He was introduced to SF by his best friend, who had pointed out Heinlein's *Have Spacesuit, Will Travel* on the school library's shelf in fourth grade, but he fell in love with the genre when he read Andre Norton's *Catseye* in seventh.

Paul has a BS degree in Computer Science and has worked in the field in various positions including documentation, tech support, programming, and systems and network administration. With his wife and daughter, he shares quarters with a varying number of varying species of pets. He writes from the realm of Hostigos (AKA the center of Pennsylvania). The universe of the Clan Chronicles has such a rich and detailed background that it reminded Paul of the space adventures of Andre Norton. He is honored to add to that background, in the form of a youthful Thel Masim. "Jilly" is Paul's first sale.

Marie Bilodeau, "An Elaborate Scheme"

Marie Bilodeau is an Ottawa-based author and storyteller, with eight published books to her name. Her speculative fiction has won several awards and has been translated into French (*Les Éditions Alire*) and Chinese (*SF World*). Her short stories have appeared in various anthologies. Marie is also a storyteller and has told stories across Canada in theaters, tea shops, at festivals, and under disco balls. She's won story slams with personal stories, has participated in epic tellings at the National Arts Center, and has adapted classical material.

Marie fell in love with Julie's words from scene one of *A Thousand Words for Stranger*, when her love for 'Whix and Terk was forged. That love only deepened by writing this story (so much love! And I love you, too, Bowman! <3). When not gushing about books she loves, Marie is cohost of the Archivos Podcast Network with Dave Robison, cochair of Ottawa's speculative fiction literary convention CAN-CON with Derek Künsken, cochair of Ottawa ChiSeries with Nicole Lavigne and Matt Moore, and is a casual blogger at *Black Gate Magazine*. More at www.mariebilodeau.com.

Chris Butler, "The Restaurant Trade"

Chris Butler's published fiction includes the novel *Any Time Now*, and the novella *The Flight of the Ravens*, which was shortlisted for the BSFA Award for short fiction. His short stories have been published in *Asimov's Science Fiction*, *Interzone*, and *The Best British Fantasy 2014*. He is currently working on a new novel, as well as more short fiction. Chris lives in Brighton & Hove in the UK. You can find further information at www.chris-butler.co.uk and on twitter at @cbutlerwrites.

With so many vivid alien species to be found within the pages of the Clan Chronicles, Chris wasted no more than a few nanoseconds before choosing Huido Maarmatoo'kk to feature at the heart of his story. Huido is the strangest of alien life-forms, and yet easy to relate to, dynamic and fun.

Wayne Carey, "Enigmatic Little Monster"

Two decades ago, *A Thousand Words for Stranger* caught Wayne's eye with its wonderful cover art, and then his heart and mind when he read it. Julie's wonderful universe of the Clan and the Trade Pact, so reminiscent of Andre Norton's work, excited his imagination and brought a sense of nostalgia . . . that Sense of Wonder. When the opportunity arose to contribute to Julie's Clan Chronicles in *Tales from Plexis*, he leaped at it at warp speed. Among all the fantastic characters, both alien and Human, he found Bowman one of the most fascinating, changing in the reader's eyes throughout the series, but always remaining her own steadfast self. How interesting would it be to see her in her capacity as an enforcer investing other aspects of the Trade Pact . . .

Another draw to Julie's work as a whole is a mutual background in biology. Because of a love of science fiction, Wayne turned to a career in science with degrees in biology and education, and always had the desire to write from an early age. His stories have appeared in a variety of anthologies such as *Legends of New Pulp Fiction*. His novels include *The Nanon Factor*, a young adult contemporary science fiction thriller that blends a murder mystery with cutting edge technology, and *Allan Quartermain and the Beast Men*, a sequel to H. Rider Haggard's *King Solomon's Mines*.

Janet Elizabeth Chase, "A Song for Plexis"

Janet Elizabeth Chase lives in rural northern Nevada along with her family and numerous freeloading animals. Janet found her way to writing speculative fiction due to well-placed nudges from a good friend. She has stories in two previous anthologies edited by Julie; *Misspelled*, and *Fantastic Companions*. When she was asked to write for an anthology set in Julie's Trade Pact universe, she was beyond excited since this was the setting that initially introduced Janet to Julie's incredible stories and wonderful characters. This story is about one of those characters that we could have done with just a little bit more of. Isn't that always the way?

Julie E. Czerneda, "A Hold Full of Truffles"

What started as a series of small introductions per story blossomed into a new story of Sira and Morgan. Julie blames her fellow authors for being so inspiring she couldn't help but join the fun. www.czerneda.com

Elizabeth A. Farley-Dawson, "Chicken"

Elizabeth A. Farley-Dawson grew up on the west coast of Florida, watched space shuttle launches from her driveway, and wanted to be an astronaut. Or maybe an artist or a writer. But she also loved nature and discovering new things (thanks to family camping trips, *National Geographic*, and documentaries), and thought maybe she should be a scientist, and sketch and write on the side. So she became an avian ecologist, married a fellow wildlife biologist, and moved where jobs and graduate school took her and her husband, spending an extended time in Texas. She recently earned her PhD in Biology and currently lives in North Carolina with partner-in-exploration Dan, their two cats Sage and Merlin, and soon, a small human. Just when Elizabeth needed her "fun" creativity rekindled after completing the dissertation, the *Tales from Plexis* contest presented the longtime fan of the Clan Chronicles a rare opportunity to write for a favorite author. Being fond enough of feathered beings and obscure ecological trivia to make it her career, it was inevitable she write about the Tolian P'tr wit 'Whix. She is elated to have sold her first work of fiction and unexpectedly realize her dream of becoming an author.

Doranna Durgin, "Finding Parker"

Doranna Durgin is an award-winning author (the Compton Crook for Best First SF/F/H novel) whose quirky spirit has led to an extensive publishing journey across genres, publishers, and publishing lines. Beyond that, she hangs around outside her Southwest mountain home with her highly accomplished competition dogs. Aside from being a long-time super fan of Julie's work (*A Thousand Words for Stranger* being a particular favorite!), Doranna could hardly resist the chance to work with a Hoveny-sniffing bio'face dog, as she does indeed track with her Beagles—a Champion Tracker, an up-and-coming youngster, and a middle dog who is so excited about it all that he might just do with a bio'face of his own. Look closely and you'll see glimpses of him in Cory!

Doranna's most recent releases encompass the three books of the Reckoners trilogy—a powerful ghostbuster raised by a spirit, her brilliantly eccentric backup team, a cat who isn't a cat, and a fiercely driven bounty hunter from a different dimension who brings them together when worlds collide. More at www.chang espell.com.

Tanya Huff, "The End of Days"

Born in Halifax, NS, raised in Ontario, educated at Ryerson Polytechnic (it's a university now, but polytechnic sounds cooler) Tanya

Huff is the author of thirty-three books, roughly a hundred short stories, the occasional magazine/newspaper piece, and one television episode (S1E9, Stone Cold, Blood Ties, based on her Vicki Nelson contemporary fantasy/vampire series). Her story for Plexis touches on two themes she returns to again and again in both her fictional and her nonfictional life, self-awareness and competence. Interestingly enough, competence is one of the many things she admires about our Plexis host, Julie Czerneda.

Heather LaVonne Jensen, "Good With Numbers"

Heather LaVonne Jensen's daily conundrum is whether to read science fiction or write it. She found *The Martian Chronicles* at age seven and has been hooked ever since. Tuesday, a calico cat who dabbles in theoretical physics (www.catsgrokspacetime.com) condescends to live with her, and she has three grown children. She's married to the world's funniest, kindest, most supportive man, although he'd prefer her to stop saying that and instead call him by his nickname, 'D*** It Jim, You Evil B******,' because he wants to be an Evil Overlord someday.

Heather couldn't help but wonder why a humble, introverted person like Ansel would choose to hitch his star to the outgoing, outspoken Huido; how did such an unlikely pair of beings become lifelong friends?

Heather's Twitter handle is @Heather_Listens, and her nonfiction writing website can be found at www.heatherlavonnejensen.com.

Ika Koeck, "Home is a Planet Away"

After spending fifteen years learning and honing her writing skills, the last thing Ika Koeck thought she would be was a butler for two very active, very needy cats. Humanitarian by day, fiction writer by night, Ika writes fantasy, science-fiction and the occasional horror story. Ika's work has been published in several pro and semi-pro rated markets, including DAW Books, Cast of Wonders and Apex Publication. When she isn't writing or working, Ika can be found slamming down heavy barbells at a crossfit gym, rescuing and re-homing cats, training for a running race somewhere, and sampling the best *teh tarik* in town as a tea connoisseur.

Mark Ladouceur, "The Sacrifice of Pawns"

When he was young Mark Ladouceur dreamed of being Captain Kirk, but is more likely to have been the red-shirt who dies before the intro to demonstrate how serious things are. He is a part-time writer and full-time father and husband. When not living in his daydreams, he resides in Southern Ontario with his excellent wife, two awesome daughters, and a prince of a dog. His story "Windigo" appeared the anthology *Mythspring*, and "The Company Car" appeared in *Storyteller* magazine. He feels privileged to have staked a small claim in Julie's Trade Pact Universe and to have come to know a mostly unknown character.

Violette Malan, "A Thief By Any Other Name"

Violette Malan is published by DAW Books. She is the author of the Dhulyn and Parno sword-and-sorcery series (now available in omnibus editions) and *The Mirror Lands* series of primary world fantasies. As V.M. Escalada, she's the author of the Faraman Prophecy series: Book One, *Halls of Law*, and Book Two, *Gift of Griffins*. Like her on Facebook, follow her on Twitter, and website-wise check either www.violettemalan.com or www.vmescalada.com.

She strongly urges you to remember that no one expects the Spanish Inquisition.

When asked why she wanted to write a story set on Plexis Station she said: "I like to write about con artists, and they flourish in a place where there's people, and money—things that Plexis has in spades."

Jessica McAdams, "The Materials at Hand"

Jessica McAdams lives in Los Angeles with her husband and their four children. (Also part of the household are an adoring dog and a disdainful cat.) After years of handing Julie Czerneda's books to friends and saying, "Read this; she writes the best, most *alien* aliens ever," Jessica is incredibly honored to get to write a story set in Plexis. (Jessica also thinks her fellow fans should read Julie's *Species Imperative* trilogy, because anyone who loves Huido really needs to meet Brymn and Fourteen.) When Jessica's not writing or editing, she enjoys knitting, hiking the local trails, and traveling up to the mountains whenever she can. You can find her online at jessicamcadams.com or follow her on Twitter at @JessMcAuthor, where she tweets about books, short stories, and the constant struggle to get more words on the page.

Sally McLennan, "Memory"

"Memory" is Sally McLennan's first foray into science fiction. This is fitting because in 2009, when Julie was Guest of Honor at New Zealand's Natcon, Sally exclusively read fantasy. To acquaint herself with Julie's writing she read *Beholder's Eye*. Worlds opened up, Sally fell in love with a blue blob, and inspiration followed. Sally joined classes run by Julie who became a dear friend and mentor. It has been a magical journey from New Zealand to Plexis. Julie Czerneda has been a role model, and the Clan Chronicles an example of what to aim for, throughout.

Sally McLennan has been steadily published since her first book, *Deputy Dan and the Mysterious Midnight Marauder*, in 2008. This children's title won a Sir Julius Vogel award in 2009. Her short stories have been published in magazines and anthologies in New Zealand, America, England, and Australia. Sally has a young adult series of dark fantasy novels in development. She lives in an old church in rural New Zealand. On the land around it she breeds Clydesdales and milk goats. Sally enjoys sitting in local cafes and hugging a cup of tea, while stringing words into a story.

Donald R. Montgomery, "A Traded Secret"

Donald R. Montgomery is a new author and *A Traded Secret* is his first professionally published story. A public servant by day, he spends most of his evenings and weekends (and sometimes lunches) writing science fiction. His debut novel is currently on submission.

Discovering *Tales From Plexis* was a happy accident, borne of a fan-type email and a question. It's a rare opportunity to write for either a great author or an industry veteran, and Julie is both. Seriously, if you've finished *The Clan Chronicles* and haven't yet read *In the Company of Others*, you must, must, must pick up a copy.

As for *A Traded Secret,* the idea tumbled out of one half-remembered description in *A Thousand Words for Stranger* and a lot of frantic rereading. Or at least a draft of it did—Don rewrote it three times (or was it four?) before finally gritting his teeth and letting Julie take a look. And he's glad he did—who knew the chance for feedback would turn into jumping for joy?

And lastly, he'd like to thank you for reading his work. Travelers hungry for more can find it at donrmontgomery.com

Fiona Patton, "Anisoptera With a Side Order of Soft Blast"

Fiona Patton was born in Calgary, Alberta, and now lives in rural Ontario with her wife, Tanya Huff, two (*perfect*) little dogs, and a large collection of cats. She is the author of seven novels published by DAW Books and nearly forty short stories. She has always loved space stations, although, to be honest, her first experience in *2001: A Space Odyssey* was more confusing than anything. (*hey, I was six!*) Especially when the station's AI is trying to kill everyone. (*As they are all clearly prone to do.*) And there was never enough of the station in *Star Trek: Deep Space 9* to suit her. (*It should have been the main character. I'll bet it would never have tried to throw Captain Sisko out an air lock.*) So it was with (*great*) pleasure that she embarked (*launched herself*) on an exciting exploration of Plexis Supermarket; researching (*combing though Julie's books for even the tiniest detail and leaping down the Wikipedia rabbit hole for more*), writing (*rewriting*), reading (*and rereading*), discussing (*babbling incessantly*), and wandering (*running*) with Daniel, Jack, and Warren through its ins, outs, corridors and concourses, restaurants, shops and public venues. She is (*very much*) looking forward to reading (*diving into*) the full anthology to see what other elements of this latest (*favorite*) space station may be revealed.

Natalie Reinelt, "Will of the Neblokan Fates"

Natalie Reinelt is a Canadian writer from Brantford, Ontario, with a deep-rooted love of storytelling. The production of her one-act children's musical *Lilian's Dream* recently performed at the Left of Center Kids' Festival under her direction. Natalie makes her fiction writing debut with the story of a harsh Neblokan, briefly introduced in a garbage-strewn alleyway in Julie Czerneda's *A Thousand Words for Stranger*, who goaded Natalie into sharing his tale. Building on her recent success, her hopes and aspirations are that the Young Adult fantasy novels she writes, and will continue to write for as long as The Fates allow, will someday be available to you in a galaxy—er, um—bookstore not too far away . . .

Rhondi Salsitz, "The Locksmith's Dilemma"

Rhondi Salsitz rarely writes under her own name, claiming it's too difficult to pronounce, spell, or remember, but this time is an exception. A long-time DAW author, she's used a number of pen names in several genres such as suspense thriller, fantasy, science fiction, and romance, for audiences from ten to ninety. She writes regardless of various cat antics and family, travels whenever she can, and reads from dawn to midnight. Nothing is better than a good book. She is thrilled to be working in Julie Czerneda's universe and hopes her tale of a humble locksmith pleases readers. Visit her at www.rhondiann.com.

Karina Sumner-Smith, "A Traitor's Heart"

Karina Sumner-Smith never thought she'd get to play in one of Julie E. Czerneda's rich, detailed universes—but here we are! When it came time to create a story, it was Manouya who stood out, though at the time he'd appeared in Julie's books only briefly. A jovial-seeming Brill in charge of nearly every major smuggling ring in Human space? Surely, there was more to the story . . .

Karina is also the author of the Towers Trilogy from Talos Press: *Radiant, Defiant,* and *Towers Fall.* In addition to novel-length work, Karina has published a range of science fiction, fantasy, and horror short stories that have been nominated for the Nebula Award and WSFA Small Press Award, reprinted in several Year's Best anthologies, and translated into Spanish and Czech. Visit her online at karinasumnersmith.com.

Amanda Sun, "The Stars Do Not Dream"

Amanda Sun is the author of the acclaimed Paper Gods series, *Ink, Rain,* and *Storm,* set in Japan and published by Harlequin Teen. She also wrote *Heir to the Sky,* about floating continents and monster hunters, and has contributed to several anthologies. Many of her novels and short fiction have been Aurora Award nominees and Junior Library Guild selections, as well as Indigo Top Teen Picks and *USA Today* features. When not reading or writing, Sun is an avid cosplayer, gamer, and devoted Turrned fan. Should Plexis orbit this close to Earth, she'll be first in line for that mushroom stew at *Claws & Jaws.* Get free Paper Gods novellas and other goodies at AmandaSunBooks.com.

The Editor and Artist

Julie E. Czerneda

For over twenty years, Canadian author/former biologist Julie E. Czerneda has shared her curiosity about living things through her science fiction, published by DAW Books, NY. Julie's written fantasy too, the first installments of her Night's Edge series (DAW) *A Turn of Light* and *A Play of Shadow,* winning consecutive Aurora Awards (Canada's Hugo) for Best English Novel. Having completed her Clan Chronicles series with *To Guard Against the Dark,* Julie's latest SF novel is *Search Image,* Book #1 of her new SF series, The Web Shifter's Library, bringing back her beloved character Esen the Dear Little Blob. Julie's edited/co-edited numerous award-winning anthologies of SF/F, including SFWA's *2017 Nebula Award Showcase,* but nothing prepared her for the sheer joy of opening her Clan Chronicles to fans of the series to produce *Tales from Plexis.* In 2019, Julie will be GOH at ConStellation. Meanwhile, Julie is hard at work on a new fantasy standalone, *The Gossamer Mage.* Visit www.czerneda.com for more.

Roger H. Czerneda

Roger Czerneda's love of photography began when he worked at his uncle's camera store. After obtaining a Bachelor of Science degree from the University of Waterloo, Roger worked as an environmental chemist and computer programmer, all the while continuing to develop his photographic and graphic design skills. By 1986, Roger grabbed his camera and computer and began life as a professional, first in film and now totally digital. He's made the leap from commercial and industrial photography to also express himself as a visual artist. Roger is drawn to subjects in the real world that inspire the imagination or that tell a story. www.photo.czerneda.com